BOOKS BY GEORGE ALEC EFFINGER

GEORGE ALEC EFFINGER

A FIRE IN THE SUN

BANTAM BOOKS
NEW YORK • TORONTO • LONDON • SYDNEY • AUCKLAND

A FIRE IN THE SUN

A Bantam Spectra Book / April 1990

ISBN 0-553-27407-4

Published simultaneously in the United States and Canada

Bantam Books are published by Bantam Books, a division of
Bantam Doubleday Dell Publishing Group, Inc. Its trademark,
consisting of the words "Bantam Books" and the portrayal of a
rooster, is Registered in U.S. Patent and Trademark Office and in
other countries. Marca Registrada. Bantam Books, 666 Fifth
Avenue, New York, New York 10103

PRINTED IN THE UNITED STATES OF AMERICA
OPM   0 9 8 7 6 5 4 3 2

My grandfather, George Conrad Effinger, whom I never knew, was a police officer in the city of Cleveland during the Depression. He was killed in the line of duty. This book is dedicated to his memory, growing fainter now each year in the minds of those people who did know him, except for his policeman's shield, Badge #374, hung with pride in a station house in Cleveland.

Children begin by loving their parents; after a time they judge them; rarely, if ever, do they forgive them.

—OSCAR WILDE
The Picture of Dorian Gray

We'd ridden for many days out the coast highway toward Mauretania, the part of Algeria where I'd been born. In that time, even at its lethargic pace, the broken-down old bus had carried us from the city to some town forsaken by Allah before it even learned what its name was. Centuries come, centuries go: In the Arab world they arrive and depart loaded on the roofs of shuddering, rattling buses that are more trouble to keep in service than the long parades of camels used to be. I remembered what those bus rides were like from when I was a kid, sitting or standing in the aisle with fifty other boys and men and maybe another two dozen clinging up on the roof. The buses passed by my home then. I saw turbaned heads, heads wearing fezes or knit caps, heads in white or checked *keffiyas*. All men. That was something I planned to ask my father about, if I ever met him. "O my father," I would say, "tell me why everyone on the bus is a man. Where are their women?"

And I always imagined that my father—I pictured him tall and lean with a fierce dark beard, a hawk or an eagle of a man; he was, in my vision, Arab, although I had my mother's word that he had been a Frenchman—I saw my father gazing thoughtfully into the bright sunlight, framing a careful reply to his young son. "O Marîd, my sweet one," he would say—and his voice would be deep and husky, issuing from the back of his throat as if he never used his lips to speak, although my mother said he wasn't like that at all—"Marîd, the women will come later. The men will send for them later."

"Ah," I would say. My father could pierce *all* riddles. I could not pose a question that he did not have a proper answer for. He was wiser than our village shaykh more

1

knowledgeable than the man whose face filled the posters pasted on the wall we were pissing on. "Father," I would ask him, "why are we pissing on this man's face?"

"Because it is idolatrous to put his face on such a poster, and it is fit only for a filthy alley like this, and therefore the Prophet, may the blessing of Allah be on him and peace, tells us that what we are doing to these images is just and right."

"And Father?" I would always have one more question, and he'd always be blissfully patient. He would smile down at me, put one hand fondly behind my head. "Father? I have always wanted to ask you, what do you do when you are pissing and your bladder is so full it feels like it will explode before you can relieve it and while you are pissing, *just then,* the muezzin—"

Saied hit me hard in the left temple with the palm of his hand. "You sleeping out here?"

I looked up at him. There was glare everywhere. I couldn't remember where the hell we were. "Where the hell are we?" I asked him.

He snorted. *"You're* the one from the Maghreb, the great, wild west. You tell me."

"Have we got to Algeria yet?" I didn't think so.

"No, stupid. I've been sitting in that goddamn little coffeehouse for three hours charming the warts off this fat fool. His name is Hisham."

"Where are we?"

"Just crossed through Carthage. We're on the outskirts of Old Tunis now. So listen to me. What's the old guy's name?"

"Huh? I don't remember."

He hit me hard in the right temple with the palm of his other hand. I hadn't slept in two nights. I was a little confused. Anyway, he got the easy part of the job: Sitting around the bus stops, drinking mint tea with the local ringleaders and gossiping about the marauding Christians and the marauding Jews and the marauding heathen niggers and just in general being goddamn smooth; and I got the piss-soaked alleys and the flies. I couldn't remember why we divided this business up like that. After all, I was supposed to be in charge—it was my idea to find this woman, it was my trip, we were using my money. But

Saied took the mint tea and the gossip, and I got—well, I don't have to go into that again.

We waited the appropriate amount of time. The sun was disappearing behind a western wall; it was almost time for the sunset call to prayer. I stared at Saied, who was now dozing. Good, I thought, now I get to hit *him* in the head. I had just gotten up and taken one little step, when he looked up at me. "It's time, I guess," he said, yawning. I nodded, didn't have anything to add. So I sat back down, and Saied the Half-Hajj went into his act.

Saied is a natural-born liar, and it's a pleasure to watch him hustle. He had the personality module he liked best plugged into his brain—his heavy-duty, steel-belted, mean mother of a tough-guy moddy. Nobody messed with the Half-Hajj when he was chipping that one in.

Back home in the city, Saied thought it was beneath him to earn money. He liked to sit in the cafés with me and Mahmoud and Jacques, all day and all evening. His little chicken, the American boy everybody called Abdul-Hassan, went out with older men and brought home the rent money. Saied liked to sneer a lot and wear his *gallebeya* cinched with a wide black leather belt, which was decorated with shiny chrome-steel strips and studs. The Half-Hajj was always careful of his appearance.

What he was doing in this vermin-infested roadside slum was what he called fun. I waited a few minutes and followed him around the corner and into the coffeehouse. I shuffled in, unkempt, filthy, and took a chair in a shadowy corner. The proprietor glanced at me, frowned, and turned back to Saied. Nobody ever paid any attention to me. Saied was finishing the tail end of a joke I'd heard him tell a dozen times since we'd left the city. When he came to the payoff, the shopkeeper and the four other men at the long counter burst into laughter. They liked Saied. He could make people like him whenever he wanted. That talent was programmed into an add-on chip snapped into his bad-ass moddy. With the right moddy and the right daddy chips, it didn't matter where you'd been born or how you'd been raised. You could fit in with any sort of people, you could speak any language, you could handle yourself in any situation. The information was fed directly into your short-term memory. You could literally become another person, Ramses II or Buck Rogers in the 25th century, until you popped the moddy and daddies out.

Saied was being rough and dangerous, but he was also being charming, if you can imagine that combination. I watched the shop owner reach and grab the teapot. He poured some into the Half-Hajj's glass, slopping some more on the wooden counter. Nobody moved to mop it up. Saied raised the glass to drink, then slammed it down again. *"Yaa salaam!"* he roared. He leaped up.

"What is it, O my friend?" asked Hisham, the proprietor. —

"My ring!" Saied shouted. He was wearing a large gold ring, and he'd been waving it under the old man's nose for two solid hours. It had had a big, round diamond in its center.

"What's the matter with your ring?"

"Look for yourself! The stone—my diamond—it's gone!"

Hisham caught Saied's flapping arm and saw that, indeed, the diamond was now missing. "Must have fallen out," the old man said, with the sort of folk wisdom you find only in these petrified provincial villages.

"Yes, fallen out," said Saied, not calmed in the least. "But where?"

"Do you see it?"

Saied made a great show of searching the floor around his stool. "No, I'm sure it's not here," he said at last.

"Then it must be out in the alley. You must've lost it the last time you went out to piss."

Saied slammed the bar with his heavy fist. "And now it's getting dark, and I must catch the bus."

"You still have time to search," said Hisham. He didn't sound very confident.

The Half-Hajj laughed without humor. "A stone like that, worth four thousand Tunisian dinars, looks like a tiny pebble among a million others. In the twilight I'd never find it. What am I to do?"

The old man chewed his lip and thought for a moment. "You're determined to leave on the bus, when it passes through?" he asked.

"I must, O my brother. I have urgent business."

"I'll help you if I can. Perhaps I can find the stone for

you. You must leave your name and address with me; then if I find the diamond, I'll send it to you."

"May the blessings of Allah be on you and on your family!" said Saied. "I have little hope that you'll succeed, but it comforts me to know you will do your best for me. I'm in your debt. We must determine a suitable reward for you."

Hisham looked at Saied with narrowed eyes. "I ask no reward," he said slowly.

"No, of course not, but I insist on offering you one."

"No reward is necessary. I consider it my duty to help you, as a Muslim brother."

"Still," Saied went on, "should you find the wretched stone, I'll give you a thousand Tunisian dinars for the sustenance of your children and the ease of your aged parents."

"Let it be as you wish," said Hisham with a small bow.

"Here," said my friend, "let me write my address for you." While Saied was scribbling his name on a scrap of paper, I heard the rumbling of the bus as it lurched to a stop outside the building.

"May Allah grant you a good journey," said the old man.

"And may He grant you prosperity and peace," said Saied, as he hurried out to the bus.

I waited about three minutes. Now it was my turn. I stood up and staggered a couple of steps. I had a lot of trouble walking in a straight line. I could see the shopkeeper glaring at me in disgust. "The hell do you want, you filthy beggar?" he said.

"Some water," I said.

"Water! Buy something or get out!"

"Once a man asked the Messenger of God, may Allah's blessings be on him, what was the noblest thing a man may do. The reply was 'To give water to he who thirsts.' I ask this of you."

"Ask the Prophet. I'm busy."

I nodded. I didn't expect to get anything free to drink out of this crud. I leaned against his counter and stared at a wall. I couldn't seem to make the place stand still.

"*Now* what do you want? I told you to go away."

"Trying to remember," I said peevishly. "I had something to tell you. Ah, yes, I know." I reached into a pocket of my jeans and brought out a glittering round stone. "Is this what that man was looking for? I found this out there. Is this—?"

The old man tried to snatch it out of my hand. "Where'd you get that? The alley, right? *My* alley. Then it's mine."

"No, I found it. It's—"

"He said he wanted me to look for it." The shop-keeper was already gazing into the distance, spending the reward money.

"He said he'd pay you money for it."

"That's right. Listen, I've got his address. Stone's no good to you without the address."

I thought about that for a second or two. "Yes, O Shaykh."

"And the address is no good to me without the stone. So here's my offer: I'll give you two hundred dinars for it."

"Two hundred? But he said—"

"He said he'd give me a thousand. *Me*, you drunken fool. It's worthless to you. Take the two hundred. When was the last time you had two hundred dinars to spend?"

"A long time."

"I'll bet. So?"

"Let me have the money first."

"Let me have the stone."

"The money."

The old man growled something and turned away. He brought a rusty coffee can up from under the counter. There was a thick wad of money in it, and he fished out two hundred dinars in old, worn bills. "Here you are, and damn your mother for a whore."

I took the money and stuffed it into my pocket. Then I gave the stone to Hisham. "If you hurry," I said, slurring my words despite the fact that I hadn't had a drink or any drugs all day, "you'll catch up with him. The bus hasn't left yet."

The man grinned at me. "Let me give you a lesson in shrewd business. The esteemed gentleman offered me a thousand dinars for a four-thousand dinar stone. Should I take the reward, or sell the stone for its full value?"

"Selling the stone will bring trouble," I said.

"Let me worry about that. Now you go to hell. I don't ever want to see you around here again."

He needn't worry about that. As I left the decrepit coffeehouse, I popped out the moddy I was wearing. I don't know where the Half-Hajj had gotten it; it had a Malaccan label on it, but I didn't think it was an over-the-counter piece of hardware. It was a dumbing-down moddy; when I chipped it in, it ate about half of my intellect and left me shambling, stupid, and just barely able to carry out my half of the plan. With it out, the world suddenly poured back into my consciousness, and it was like waking from a bleary, drugged sleep. I was always angry for half an hour after I popped that moddy. I hated myself for agreeing to wear it, I hated Saied for conning me into doing it. *He* wouldn't wear it, not the Half-Hajj and his precious self-image. So I wore it, even though I'm gifted with twice the intracranial modifications of anybody else around, enough daddy capacity to make me the most talented son of a bitch in creation. And still Saied persuaded me to damp myself out to the point of near vegetability.

On the bus, I sat next to him, but I didn't want to talk to him or listen to him gloat.

"What'd we get for that chunk of glass?" he wanted to know. He'd already replaced the real diamond in his ring.

I just handed the money to him. It was his game, it was his score. I couldn't have cared less. I don't even know why I went along with him, except that he'd said he wouldn't come to Algeria with me unless I did.

He counted the bills. "Two hundred? That's all? We got more the last two times. Oh well, what the hell—that's two hundred dinars more we can blow in Algiers. 'Come with me to the Kasbah.' Little do those gazelle-eyed boys know what's stealing toward them even now, through the lemon-scented night."

"This stinking bus, that's what, Saied."

He looked at me with wide eyes, then laughed. "You got no romance in you, Marîd," he said. "Ever since you had your brain wired, you been no fun at all."

"How about that." I didn't want to talk anymore. I pretended that I was going to sleep. I just closed my eyes and listened to the bus thumping and thudding over the broken pavement, with the unending arguments and laughter of the other passengers all around me. It was crowded and hot on that reeking bus, but it was carrying me hour by hour nearer to the solution of my own mystery. I had come to a point in my life where I needed to find out who I really was.

The bus stopped in the Barbary town of Annaba, and an old man with a grizzled gray beard came aboard selling apricot nectar. I got some for myself and some for the Half-Hajj. Apricots are the pride of Mauretania, and the juice was the first real sign that I was getting close to home. I closed my eyes and inhaled that delicate apricot aroma, then swallowed a mouthful of juice and savored the thick sweetness. Saied just gulped his down with a grunt and gave me a blunt "Thanks." The guy's got all the refinement of a dead bat.

The road angled south, away from the dark, invisible coast toward the city of Constantine. Although it was getting late, almost midnight, I told Saied that I wanted to get off the bus and grab some supper. I hadn't eaten anything since noon. Constantine is built on a high limestone bluff, the only ancient town in eastern Algeria to survive through centuries of foreign invasions. The only thing I cared about, though, was food. There is a local dish in Constantine called *chorba beïda bel kefta,* a meatball soup made with onions, pepper, chick-peas, almonds, and cinnamon. I hadn't tasted it in at least fifteen years, and I didn't care if it meant missing the bus and having to wait until tomorrow for another, I was going to have some. Saied thought I was crazy.

I had my soup, and it was wonderful. Saied just watched me wordlessly and sipped a glass of tea. We got back on the bus in time. I felt good now, comfortably full and warmed by a nostalgic glow. I took the window seat, hoping that I'd be able to see some familiar landscape as we passed through Jijel and Mansouria. Of course, it was as black as the inside of my pocket beyond the glass, and I saw nothing but the moon and the fiercely twinkling stars. Still, I pretended to myself that I could make out landmarks that meant I was drawing closer to Algiers, the city where I had spent a lot of my childhood.

When at last we pulled into Algiers sometime after sunrise, the Half-Hajj shook me awake. I didn't remember falling asleep. I felt terrible. My head felt like it had been crammed full of sharp-edged broken glass, and I had a pinched nerve in my neck, too. I took out my pillcase and stared into it for a while. Did I prefer to make my entrance into Algiers hallucinating, narcotized, or somnambulant? It was a difficult decision. I went for pain-free but conscious, so I fished out eight tabs of Sonneine. The sunnies obliterated my headache—and every other mildly unpleasant sensation—and I more or less floated from the bus station in Mustapha to a cab.

"You're stoned," said Saied when we got to the back of the taxi. I told the driver to take us to a public data library.

"Me? Stoned? When have you ever known me to be stoned so early in the morning?"

"Yesterday. The day before yesterday. The day before that."

"I mean *except* for then. I function better with a ton of opiates in me than most people do straight."

"Sure you do."

I stared out the taxi's window. "Anyway," I said, "I've got a rack of daddies that can compensate." There isn't another blazebrain in the Arab world with the custommade equipment I've got. My special daddies control my hypothalamic functions, so I can tune out fatigue and fear, hunger and thirst and pain. They can boost my sensory input too.

"Marîd Audran, Silicon Superman."

"Look," I said, annoyed by Saied's attitude, "for a long time I was terrified of getting wired, but now I don't know how I ever got along without it."

"Then why the hell are you still decimating your brain cells with drugs?" asked the Half-Hajj.

"Call me old-fashioned. Besides, when I pop the daddies out, I feel terrible. All that suppressed fatigue and pain hit me at once."

"And you don't get paybacks with your sunnies and beauties, right? That what you're saying?"

"Shut up, Saied. Why the hell are you so concerned all of a sudden?"

He looked at me sideways and smiled. "The religion has this ban on liquor and hard drugs, you know." And this coming from the Half-Hajj who, if he'd ever been inside a mosque in his life, was there only to check out the boys' school.

So in ten or fifteen minutes the cab driver let us out at

the library. I felt a peculiar nervous excitement, although I didn't understand why. All I was doing was climbing the granite steps of a public building; why should I be so wound up? I tried to occupy my mind with more pleasant thoughts.

Inside, there were a number of terminals vacant. I sat down at the gray screen of a battered Bab el-Marifi. It asked me what sort of search I wanted to conduct. The machine's voice synthesizer had been designed in one of the North American republics, and it was having a lot of trouble pronouncing Arabic. I said, "Name," then "Enter." When the cursor appeared again, I said, "Monroe comma Angel." The data deck thought about that for a while, then white letters began flicking across its bright face:

> Angel Monroe
> 16, Rue du Sahara
> (Upper) Kasbah
> Algiers
> Mauretania
> 04-B-28

I had the machine print out the address. The Half-Hajj raised his eyebrows at me and I nodded. "Looks like I'm gonna get some answers."

"Inshallah," murmured Saied. If God wills.

We went back out into the hot, steamy morning to find another taxi. It didn't take long to get from the library to the Kasbah. There wasn't as much traffic as I remembered from my childhood—not vehicular traffic, anyway; but there was still the slow, unavoidable battalions of heavily laden donkeys being cajoled through the narrow streets.

The Rue du Sahara is a mistake. I remember someone telling me long ago that the true name of the street was actually the Rue N'sara, or Street of the Christians. I don't know how it got corrupted. Very little of Algiers has any real connection to the Sahara. After all, it's a hell of a long hike from the Mediterranean port to the desert. It doesn't make any difference these days, though; the new name is the only one anyone ever uses. It's even found its way onto all the official maps, so that closes the matter.

Number 16 was an exhausted, crumbling brick pile

with two bulging upper stories that hung out over the cobbled street. The apartment house across the way did the same, and the two buildings almost kissed above my head, like two dowdy old matrons leaning across a back fence. There was a jumble of mail slots, and I found Angel Monroe's name scrawled on a card in fading ink. I jammed my thumb on her buzzer. There was no lock on the front door, so I went in and climbed the first flight of stairs. Saied was right behind me.

Her apartment turned out to be on the third floor, in the rear. The hallway was carpeted, if that's the right word, with a dull, gritty fabric that had at one time been maroon. The traffic of uncountable feet had completely worn through the material in many places, so that the dry gray wood of the floor was visible through the holes. The walls were covered with a filthy tan wallpaper, hanging down here and there in forlorn strips. The air had an odd, sour tang to it, as if the building were occupied by people who had come there to die, or who were certainly sick enough to die but instead hung on in lonely misery. From behind one door I could hear a family battle, complete with bellowed threats and crashing crockery, while from another apartment came insane, high-pitched laughter and the sound of flesh loudly smacking flesh. I didn't want to know about it.

I stood outside the shabby door to Angel Monroe's flat and took a deep breath. I glanced at the Half-Hajj, but he just gave me a shrug and pointedly looked away. Some friend. I was on my own. I told myself that nothing weird was going to happen—a lie just to get myself to take the next step—and then I knocked on the door. There was no response. I waited a few seconds and knocked again, louder. This time I heard the rattle and squeak of bedsprings and the sound of someone coming slowly to the door. The door swung open. Angel Monroe stared out, trying very hard to focus her eyes.

She was a full head shorter than me, with bleached blond hair curled tightly into an arrangement I would call "ratty." Her black roots looked as if no one had given them much attention since the Prophet's birthday. Her eyes were banded with dark blue and black makeup, in a manner that brought to mind the more colorful Mediterranean saltwater fish. The rouge she wore was applied

liberally, but not quite in the right places, so she didn't
look so much wantonly sexy as she did feverishly ill. Her
lipstick, for reasons best known to Allah and Angel
Monroe, was a kind of pulpy purple color; her lips looked
like she'd bought them first and forgot to put them in the
refrigerator while she shopped for the rest of her face.

Her body led me to believe that she was too old to be
dressed in anything but the long white Algerian *haïk*,
with a veil conservatively and firmly in place. The problem was that this body had never seen the inside of a *haïk*.
She was clad now in shorts so small that her well-rounded
belly was bending the waistband over. Her sagging
breasts were not quite clothed in a kind of gauzy vest. I
knew for certain that if she sat in a chair, you could safely
hide the world's most valuable gem in her navel and it
would be completely invisible. Her legs were patterned
with broken veins like the dry *chebka* valleys of the Mzab.
On her broad, flat feet she wore tattered slippers with the
remains of pink fuzzy bows dangling loose.

To tell the truth, I felt a certain disgust. "Angel
Monroe?" I asked. Of course that wasn't her real name.
She was at least half Berber, as I am. Her skin was darker
than mine, her eyes as black and dull as eroded asphalt.

"Uh huh," she said. "Kind of early, ain't it?" Her voice
was sharp and shrill. She was already very drunk. "Who
sent you? Did Khalid send you? I told that goddamn bastard I was sick. I ain't supposed to be working today, I told
him last night. He said it was all right. And then he sends
you. *Two* of you, yet. Who the hell does he think I am? And
it ain't like he don't have no other girls, either. He could
have sent you to Efra, that whore, with her plug-in talent.
If I ain't feeling good, it don't bother me if he sends you to
her. Hell, I don't care. How much you give him, anyway?"

I stood there, looking at her. Saied gave me a jab in
the side. "Well, uh, Miss Monroe," I said, but then she
started chattering again.

"The hell with it. Come on in. I guess I can use the
money. But you tell that son of a bitch Khalid that—" She
paused to take a long gulp from the tall glass of whiskey
she was holding. "You tell him if he don't care enough
about my health, I mean, making me work when I already
told him I was sick, then hell, you tell him there are plenty

of others I can go work for. Anytime I want to, you can believe that."

I tried twice to interrupt her, but I didn't have any success. I waited until she stopped to take another drink. While she had her mouth full of the cheap liquor, I said, "Mother?"

She just stared at me for a moment, her filmy eyes wide. "No," she said at last, in a small voice. She looked closer. Then she dropped her whiskey glass to the floor.

ater, after the return trip from Algiers and Mauretania, when I got back home to the city the first place I
headed was the Budayeen. I used to live right in the
heart of the walled quarter, but events and fate and Friedlander Bey had made that impossible now. I used to have a
lot of friends in the Budayeen too, and I was welcome
anywhere; but now there were really only two people
who were generally glad to see me: Saied the Half-Hajj,
and Chiriga, who ran a club on the Street halfway between the big stone arch and the cemetery. Chiri's place
had always been my home-away-from-home, where I
could sit and have a few drinks in peace, hear the gossip,
and not get threatened or hustled by the working girls.

Once upon a time I'd had to kill a few people, mostly
in self-defense. More than one club owner had told me
never to set foot in his bar again. After that, a lot of my
friends decided that they could do without my company,
but Chiri had more sense.

She's a hard-working woman, a tall black African with
ritual facial scars and sharply filed cannibal teeth. To be
honest, I don't really know if those canines of hers are
mere decoration, like the patterns on her forehead and
cheeks, or a sign that dinner at her house was composed of
delicacies implicitly and explicitly forbidden by the noble
Qur'ân. Chiri's a moddy, but she thinks of herself as a
smart moddy. At work, she's always herself. She chips in
her fantasies at home, where she won't bother anyone
else. I respect that.

When I came through the club's door, I was struck
first by a welcome wave of cool air. Her air conditioning,
as undependable as all old Russian-made hardware is, was
working for a change. I felt better already. Chiri was deep

in conversation with a customer, some bald guy with a bare chest. He was wearing black vinyl pants with the look of real leather, and his left hand was handcuffed behind him to his belt. He had a corymbic implant on the crest of his skull, and a pale green plastic moddy was feeding him somebody else's personality. If Chiri was giving him the time of day, then he couldn't have been dangerous, and probably he wasn't even all that obnoxious.

Chiri doesn't have much patience with the crowd she caters to. Her philosophy is that *somebody* has to sell them liquor and drugs, but that doesn't mean she has to socialize with them.

I was her old pal, and I knew most of the girls who worked for her. Of course, there were always new faces—and I mean *new*, carved out of dull, plain faces with surgical skill, turning ordinary looks into enthralling artificial beauty. The old-time employees got fired or quit in a huff on a regular basis; but after working for Frenchy Benoit or Jo-Mama for a while, they circulated back to their former jobs. They left me pretty much alone, because I'd rarely buy them cocktails and I didn't have any use for their professional charms. The new girls could try hustling me, but Chiri usually told them to lay off.

In their unforgiving eyes I'd become the Creature Without A Soul. People like Blanca and Fanya and Yasmin looked the other way if I caught their eye. Some of the girls didn't know what I'd done or didn't care, and they kept me from feeling like a total outcast. Still, it was a lot quieter and lonelier for me in the Budayeen than it used to be. I tried not to care.

"*Jambo*, Bwana Marîd!" Chiriga called to me when she noticed that I was sitting nearby. She left the handcuffed moddy and drifted slowly down her bar, plopping a cork coaster in front of me. "You come to share your wealth with this poor savage. In my native land, my people have nothing to eat and wander many miles in search of water. Here I have found peace and plenty. I have learned what friendship is. I have found disgusting men who would touch the hidden parts of my body. You will buy me drinks and leave me a huge tip. You will tell all your new friends about my place, and they will come in and want to touch the hidden parts of my body. I will own many shiny, cheap things. It is all as God wills."

I stared at her for a few seconds. Sometimes it's hard to figure what kind of mood Chiri's in. "Big nigger girl talk dumb," I said at last.

She grinned and dropped her ignorant Dinka act. "Yeah, you right," she said. "What is it today?"

"Gin," I said. I usually have a shot of gin and a shot of bingara over ice, with a little Rose's lime juice. The drink is my own invention, but I've never gotten around to naming it. Other times I have vodka gimlets, because that's what Philip Marlowe drinks in *The Long Goodbye.* Then on those occasions when I just really want to get loaded fast, I drink from Chiri's private stock of *tende,* a truly loathsome African liquor from the Sudan or the Congo or someplace, made, I think, from fermented yams and spadefoot toads. If you are ever offered *tende,* DO NOT TASTE IT. You *will* be sorry. Allah knows that I am.

The dancer just finishing her last number was an Egyptian girl named Indihar. I'd known her for years. She used to work for Frenchy Benoit, but now she was wiggling her ass in Chiri's club. She came up to me when she got offstage, wrapped now in a pale peach-colored shawl that had little success in concealing her voluptuous body. "Want to tip me for my dancing?" she asked.

"It would give me untold pleasure," I said. I took a kiam bill from my change and stuffed it into her cleavage. If she was going to treat me like a mark, I was going to act like one. "Now," I said, "I won't feel guilty about going home and fantasizing about you all night."

"That'll cost you extra," she said, moving down the bar toward the bare-chested guy in the vinyl pedal pushers.

I watched her walk away. "I like that girl," I said to Chiriga.

"That's our Indihar, one fine package of suntanned fun," said Chiri.

Indihar was a real girl with a real personality, a rarity in that club. Chiri seemed to prefer in her employees the high-velocity prettiness of a sexchange. Chiri told me once that changes take better care of their appearance. Their prefab beauty is their whole life. Allah forbid that a single hair of their eyebrows should be out of place.

By her own standards, Indihar was a good Muslim woman too. She didn't have the head wiring that most

dancers had. The more conservative imams taught that
the implants fell under the same prohibition as intoxicants, because some people got their pleasure centers
wired and spent the remainder of their short lives amp-
addicted. Even if, as in my case, the pleasure center is left
alone, the use of a moddy submerges your own personality, and that is interpreted as insobriety. Needless to say,
while I have nothing but the warmest affection for Allah
and His Messenger, I stop short of being a fanatic about it.
I'm with that twentieth-century King Saud who demanded that the Islamic leaders of his country stop drag-
ging their feet when it came to technological progress. I
don't see any essential conflict between modern science
and a thoughtful approach to religion.

Chiri looked down the bar. "All right," she called out
loudly, "which one of you motherfuckers' turn is it? Janelle? I don't want to have to tell you to get up and dance
again. If I got to remind you to play your goddamn music
one more time, I'm gonna fine you fifty kiam. Now move
your fat ass." She looked at me and sighed.

"Life is tough," I said.

Indihar came back up the bar after collecting whatever she could pry out of the few glum customers. She sat
on the stool beside me. Like Chiri, she didn't seem to get
nightmares from talking with me. "So what's it like," she
asked, "working for Friedlander Bey?"

"You tell me." One way or another, everybody in the
Budayeen works for Papa.

She shrugged. "I wouldn't take his money if I was
starving, in prison, and had cancer."

This, I guessed, was a dig, a not-very-veiled reference
to the fact that I had sold out to get my implants. I just
swallowed some more gin and bingara.

Maybe one of the reasons I went to Chiri's whenever
I needed a little cheering up is that I grew up in places just
like it. My mother had been a dancer when I was a baby,
after my father ran off. When the situation got real bad,
she started turning tricks. Some girls in the clubs do that,
some don't. My mother had to. When things got even
harder, she sold my little brother. That's something she
won't talk about. I won't talk about it, either.

My mother did the best she knew how. The Arab
world has never put much value on education for women.

Everybody knows how the more traditional—that is to say, more backward and unregenerate—Arab men treat their wives and daughters. Their *camels* get more respect. Now, in the big cities like Damascus and Cairo, you can see modern women wearing Western-style clothing, holding down jobs outside the home, sometimes even smoking cigarettes on the street.

In Mauretania, I'd seen that the attitudes there were still rigid. Women wore long white robes and veils, with hoods or kerchiefs covering their hair. Twenty-five years ago, my mother had no place in the legitimate job market. But there is always a small population of lost souls, of course—people who scoff at the dictates of the holy Qur'ân, men and women who drink alcohol and gamble and indulge in sex for pleasure. There is always a place for a young woman whose morals have been ground away by hunger and despair.

When I saw her again in Algiers, my mother's appearance had shocked me. In my imagination, I'd pictured her as a respectable, moderately well-to-do matron living in a comfortable neighborhood. I hadn't seen or spoken to her in years, but I just figured she'd managed to lift herself out of the poverty and degradation. Now I thought maybe she was happy as she was, a haggard, strident old whore. I spent an hour with her, hoping to hear what I'd come to learn, trying to decide how to behave toward her, and being embarrassed by her in front of the Half-Hajj. She didn't want to be troubled by her children. I got the impression that she was sorry she hadn't sold me too, when she'd sold Hussain Abdul-Qahhar, my brother. She didn't like me dropping back into her life after all those years.

"Believe me," I told her, "I didn't like hunting you up, either. I only did it because I have to."

"Why do you have to?" she wanted to know. She reclined on a musty-smelling, torn old sofa that was covered with cat hair. She'd made herself another drink, but had neglected to offer me or Saied anything.

"It's important to me," I said. I told her about my life in the faraway city, how I'd lived as a subsonic hustler until Friedlander Bey had chosen me as the instrument of his will.

"You live in the city now?" She said that with a nostalgic longing. I never knew she'd been to the city.

"I lived in the Budayeen," I said, "but Friedlander Bey moved me into his palace."

"You work for him?"

"I had no choice." I shrugged. She nodded. It surprised me that she knew who Papa was too.

"So what did you come for?"

That was going to be hard to explain. "I wanted to find out everything I could about my father."

She looked at me over the rim of her whiskey glass. "You already heard everything," she said.

"I don't think so. How sure are you that this French sailor was my dad?"

She took a deep breath and let it out slowly. "His name was Bernard Audran. We met in a coffee shop. I was living in Sidi-bel-Abbès then. He took me to dinner, we liked each other. I moved in with him. We came to live in Algiers after that, and we were together for a year and a half. Then after you was born, one day he just left. I never heard from him again. I don't know where he went."

"*I* do. Into the ground, that's where. Took me a long time, but I traced Algerian computer records back far enough. There was a Bernard Audran in the navy of Provence, and he was in Mauretania when the French Confederate Union tried to regain control over us. The problem is that his brains were bashed out by some unidentified *noraf* more than a year before I was born. Maybe you could think back and see if you can get a clearer picture of those events."

That made her furious. She jumped up and flung her half-full glass of liquor at me. It smashed into the already stained and streaked wall to my right. I could smell the pungent, undiluted sharpness of the Irish whiskey. I heard Saied murmuring something beside me, maybe a prayer. My mother took a couple of steps toward me, her face ugly with rage. "You calling me a *liar?*" she shrieked.

Well, I was. "I'm just telling you that the official records say something different."

"Fuck the official records!"

"The records also say that you were married seven times in two years. No mention of any divorces."

My mother's anger faltered a bit. "How did that get in the computers? I never got officially married, not with no license or nothing."

"I think you underestimate the government's talent for keeping track of people. It's all there for anybody to see."

Now she looked frightened. "What else'd you find out?"

I let her off her own hook. "Nothing else. There wasn't anything more. You want something else to stay buried, you don't have to worry." That was a lie; I had learned plenty more about my mom.

"Good," she said, relieved. "I don't like you prying into what I done. It don't show respect."

I had an answer to that, but I didn't use it. "What started all this nostalgic research," I said in a quiet voice, "was some business I was taking care of for Papa." Everybody in the Budayeen calls Friedlander Bey "Papa." It's an affectionate token of terror. "This police lieutenant who handled matters in the Budayeen died, so Papa decided that we needed a kind of public affairs officer, somebody to keep communications open between him and the police department. He asked me to take the job."

Her mouth twisted. "Oh yeah? You got a gun now? You got a badge?" It was from my mother that I learned my dislike for cops.

"Yeah," I said, "I got a gun *and* a badge."

"Your badge ain't any good in Algiers, *salaud.*"

"They give me professional courtesy wherever I go." I didn't even know if that was true here. "The point is, while I was deep in the cop comp, I took the opportunity to read my own file and a few others. The funny thing was, my name and Friedlander Bey's kept popping up together. And not just in the records of the last few years. I counted at least eight entries—hints, you understand, but nothing definite—that suggested the two of us were blood kin." That got a loud reaction from the Half-Hajj; maybe I should have told him about all this before.

"So?" said my mother.

"The hell kind of answer is that? So what does it mean? You ever jam Friedlander Bey, back in your golden youth?"

She looked raving mad again. "Hell, I jammed *lots* of guys. You expect me to remember all of them? I didn't even remember what they looked like while I was jamming them."

"You didn't want to get involved, right? You just wanted to be good friends. Were you ever friends enough to give credit? Or did you always ask for the cash up front?"

"Maghrebi," cried Saied, "this is your *mother!*" I didn't think it was possible to shock him.

"Yeah, it's my mother. Look at her."

She crossed the room in three steps, reached back, and gave me a hard slap across the face. It made me fall back a step. "Get the fuck *out* of here!" she yelled.

I put my hand to my cheek and glared at her. "You answer one thing first: Could Friedlander Bey be my real father?"

Her hand was poised to deliver another clout. "Yeah, he could be, the way practically *any* man could be. Go back to the city and climb up on his knee, sonny boy. I don't ever want to see you around here again."

She could rest easy on that score. I turned my back on her and left that repulsive hole in the wall. I didn't bother to shut the door on the way out. The Half-Hajj did, and then he hurried to catch up with me. I was storming down the stairs. "Listen, Marîd," he said. Until he spoke, I didn't realize how wild I was. "I guess all this is a big surprise to you—"

"You do? You're very perceptive today, Saied."

"—but you can't act that way toward your mother. Remember what it says—"

"In the Qur'ân? Yeah, I know. Well, what does the Straight Path have to say about prostitution? What does it have to say about the kind of degenerate my holy mother has turned into?"

"You've got a lot of room to talk. If there was a cheaper hustler in the Budayeen, I never met him."

I smiled coldly. "Thanks a lot, Saied, but I don't live in the Budayeen anymore. You forget? And I don't hustle anybody or anything. I got a steady job."

He spat at my feet. "You used to do nearly anything to make a few kiam."

"Anyway, just because I used to be the scum of the earth, it doesn't make it all right for my mother to be scum too."

"Why don't you just shut up about her? I don't want to hear about it."

"Your empathy just grows and grows, Saied," I said. "You don't know everything I know. My alma mater back there was into renting herself to strangers long before she had to support my brother and me. She wasn't the forlorn heroine she always said she was. She glossed over a lot of the truth."

The Half-Hajj looked me hard in the eye for a few seconds. "Yeah?" he said. "Half the girls, changes, and debs we know do the same thing, and you don't have any problem treating *them* like human beings."

I was about to say, "Sure, but none of them is my mother." I stopped myself. He would have jumped on that sentiment too, and besides, it was starting to sound foolish even to me. The edge of my anger had vanished. I think I was just greatly annoyed to have to learn these things after so many years. It was hard for me to accept. I mean, now I had to forget almost everything I thought I knew about myself. For one thing, I'd always been proud of the fact that I was half-Berber and half-French. I dressed in European style most of the time—boots and jeans and work shirts. I suppose I'd always felt a little superior to the Arabs I lived among. Now I had to get used to the thought that I could very well be half-Berber and half-Arab.

The raucous, thumping sound of mid-twenty-first-century hispo roc broke into my daydream. Some forgotten band was growling an ugly chant about some damn thing or other. I've never gotten around to learning any Spanish dialects, and I don't own a Spanish-language daddy. If I ever run into any Columbian industrialists, they can just damn well speak Arabic. I have a soft spot in my liver for them because of their production of narcotics, but outside of that I don't see what South America is for. The world doesn't need an overpopulated, starving, Spanish-speaking India in the Western Hemisphere. Spain, their mother country, tried Islam and said a polite no-thank-you, and their national character sublimed right off into nothingness. That's Allah punishing them.

"I hate that song," said Indihar. Chiri had given her a glass of Sharâb, the soft drink the clubs keep for girls who don't drink alcohol, like Indihar. It's exactly the same color as champagne. Chiri always fills a cocktail glass with ice and pours in a few ounces of soda—which should be a tip-off to the mark: you don't get ice in your champagne in the real world. But the ice takes up a lot of space where the more expensive stuff would go. That'll cost a sucker eight kiam and a tip for Chiri. The club kicks three bills back to the girl who got the drink. That motivates the employees to go through their cocktails at supersonic speed. The usual excuse is that it's thirsty work whirling like a derwish to the cheers of the crowd.

Chiri turned to watch Janelle, who was on her last song. Janelle doesn't really dance, she flounces. She takes five or six steps to one end of the stage, waits for the next heavy-footed bass drum beat, then does a kind of shrugging, quivering thing with her upper body that she must think is torridly sexy. She's wrong. Then she flounces back the other way to the opposite end of the stage and does her spasm number again. The whole time she's lip-synching, not to the lyrics, but to the wailing lead keypad line. Janelle the Human Synthesizer. Janelle the Synthetic Human is closer to the truth. She wears a moddy every day, but you have to talk to her to find out which one. One day she's soft and erotic (Honey Pílar), the next day she's cold and foulmouthed (Brigitte Stahlhelm). Whichever personality she's chipped in, though, is still housed in the same unmodified Nigerian refugee body, which she also thinks is sexy and about which she is also mistaken. The other girls don't associate with her very much. They're sure she lifts bills out of their bags in the dressing room, and they don't like the way she cuts in on their customers when they have to go up to dance. Someday the cops are going to find Janelle in a dark doorway with her face pulped and half the bones in her body broken. In the meantime, she flounces in time to the ragged screams of keypads and guitar synths.

I was bored as hell. I knocked back the rest of my drink. Chiri looked at me and raised her eyebrows. "No thanks, Chiri," I said. "I got to go."

Indihar leaned over and kissed me on the cheek. "Well, don't be a stranger now that you're a fascist swine cop."

"Right," I said. I got up from my stool.

"Say hello to Papa for me," said Chiri.

"What makes you think I'm going there?"

She gave me her filed-tooth grin. "Time for good boys and girls to check in at the old *kibanda.*"

"Yeah, well," I said. I left the rest of my change for her hungry register and went back outside.

I walked down the Street to the arched eastern gate. Beyond the Budayeen, along the broad Boulevard il-Jameel, a few taxis waited for fares. I saw my old friend, Bill, and climbed into the backseat of his cab. "Take me to Papa's, Bill," I said.

"Yeah? You talk like you know me. I know you from somewhere?"

Bill didn't recognize me because he's permanently fried. Instead of skull wiring or cosmetic bodmods, he's got a large sac where one of his lungs used to be, dripping out constant, measured doses of light-speed hallucinogen into his bloodstream. Bill has occasional moments of lucidity, but he's learned to ignore them, or at least to keep functioning until they go away and he's seeing purple lizards again. I've tried the drug he's got pumping through him day and night; it's called RPM, and even though I'm pretty experienced with drugs of all nations, I never want to take that stuff again. Bill, on the other hand, swears that it has opened his eyes to the hidden nature of the real world. I guess so; he can see fire demons and I can't. The only problem with the drug—and Bill will be the first to admit this—is that he can't remember a goddamn thing from one minute to the next.

So it wasn't surprising that he didn't recognize me. I've had to go through the same conversation with him a hundred times. "It's me, Bill. Marîd. I want you to take me to Friedlander Bey's."

He squinted back at me. "Can't say I ever seen you before, buddy."

"Well, you have. Lots of times."

"That's easy for *you* to say," he muttered. He jabbed the ignition and pulled away from the curb. We were headed in the wrong direction. "Where did you say you wanted to go?" he asked.

"Papa's."

"Yeah, you right. I got this *afrit* sitting up here with me today, and he's been tossing hot coals in my lap all afternoon. It's a big distraction. I can't do nothing about it, though. You can't punch out an *afrit*. They like to mess with your head like that. I'm thinking of getting some holy water from Lourdes. Maybe that would spook 'em. Where the hell *is* Lourdes, anyway?"

"The Caliphate of Gascony," I said.

"Hell of a long drive. They do mail orders?"

I told him I didn't have the slightest idea, and sat back against the upholstery. I watched the landscape slash by— Bill's driving is as crazy as he is—and I thought about what I was going to say to Friedlander Bey. I wondered how I should approach him about what I'd found out, what my mother had told me, and what I suspected. I decided to wait. There was a good chance that the information in the computers linking me to Papa had been planted there, a devious means of winning my cooperation. In the past, I'd carefully avoided any direct transactions with Papa, because taking his coin for any reason meant that he owned you forever. But when he paid for my cranial implants, he made an investment that I'd be paying back for the rest of my life. I didn't *want* to be working for him, but there was no escape. Not yet. I maintained the hope that I'd find a way to buy my way out, or coerce him into giving me my freedom. In the meantime, it pleased him to pile responsibility on my unwilling shoulders, and gift me with ever-larger rewards.

Bill pulled through the gate in the high white wall around Friedlander Bey's estate and drove up the long, curved driveway. He came to a stop at the foot of the wide marble stairs. Papa's butler opened the polished front door and stood waiting for me. I paid the fare and slipped Bill an extra ten kiam. His lunatic eyes narrowed and he glanced from the money to me. "What's this?" he asked suspiciously.

"It's a tip. You're supposed to keep that."

"What's it for?"

"For your excellent driving."

"You ain't trying to buy me off, are you?"

I sighed. "No. I admire the way you steer with all those red-hot charcoals in your drawers. I know I couldn't do it."

He shrugged. "It's a gift," he said simply.

"So's the ten kiam."

His eyes widened again. "Oh," he said, smiling, *"now* I get it!"

"Sure you do. See you around, Bill."

"See ya, buddy." He gunned the cab and the tires spat gravel. I turned and went up the stairs.

"Good afternoon, *yaa Sidi,*" said the butler.

"Hello, Youssef. I'd like to see Friedlander Bey."

"Yes, of course. It's good to have you home, sir."

"Yeah, thanks." We walked along a thickly carpeted corridor toward Papa's offices. The air was cool and dry, and I felt the gentle kiss of many fans. There was the fragrance of incense on the air, subtle and inviting. The light was muted through screens made of narrow strips of wood. From somewhere I heard the liquid trickle of falling water, a fountain splashing in one of the courtyards.

Before we got to the waiting room, a tall, well-dressed woman crossed the hall and went up a flight of stairs. She gave me a brief, modest smile and then turned her head away. She had hair as black and glossy as obsidian, gathered tightly into a chignon. Her hands were very pale, her fingers long and tapered and graceful. I got just a quick impression, yet I knew this woman had style and intelligence; but I felt also that she could be menacing and hard, if she needed.

"Who was that, Youssef?" I asked.

He turned to me and frowned. "That is Umm Saad." I knew immediately that he disapproved of her. I trusted Youssef's judgment, so my first intuition about her was most likely correct.

I took a seat in the outer office and killed time by finding faces in the pattern of cracks in the ceiling. After a while, one of Papa's two huge bodyguards opened the communicating door. I call the big men the Stones That Speak. Believe me, I know what I'm talking about. "Come in," said the Stone. Those guys don't waste breath.

I went into Friedlander Bey's office. The man was about two hundred years old, but he'd had a lot of body modifications and transplants. He was reclining on cushions and drinking strong coffee from a golden cup. He smiled when I came in. "My eyes live again, seeing you O my nephew," he said. I could tell that he was genuinely pleased.

"My days apart from you have been filled with regret, O Shaykh," I said. He motioned, and I seated myself beside him. He reached forward to tip coffee from the golden pot into my cup. I took a sip and said, "May your table always be prosperous."

"May Allah grant you health," he said.

"I pray that you are feeling well, O Shaykh."

He reached out and grasped my hand. "I am as fit and strong as a sixty-year-old, but there is a weariness that I cannot overcome, my nephew."

"Then perhaps your physician—"

"It is a weariness of the soul," he said. "It is my appetite and ambition that are dying. I keep going now only because the idea of suicide is abhorrent."

"Perhaps in the future, science will restore you."

"How, my son? By grafting a new zest for living onto my exhausted spirit?"

"The technique already exists," I told him. "You could have a moddy and daddy implant like mine."

He shook his head ruefully. "Allah would send me to Hell if I did that." He didn't seem to mind if *I* went to Hell. He waved aside further speculation. "Tell me of your journey."

Here it was, but I wasn't ready. I still didn't know how to ask him if he figured in my family tree, so I stalled. "First I must hear all that happened while I was gone, O Shaykh. I saw a woman in the corridor. I've never seen a woman in your house before. May I ask you who she is?"

Papa's face darkened. He paused a moment, framing his reply. "She is a fraud and an impostor, and she is beginning to cause me great distress."

"Then you must send her away," I said.

"Yes," he said. His expression turned stonelike. I saw now not a ruler of a great business empire, not the controller of all vice and illicit activity in the city, but something more terrible. Friedlander Bey might truly have been the son of many kings, because he wore the cloak of power and command as if he'd been born to it. "I must ask you this question, O my nephew: Do you honor me enough to fill your lungs again with fire?"

I blinked. I thought I knew what he was talking about. "Did I not prove myself just a few months ago, O Shaykh?"

He waved a hand, just that easily making nothing of the pain and horror I'd suffered. "You were defending yourself from danger then," he said. He turned and put one old, clawlike hand on my knee. "I need you now to defend *me* from danger. I wish you to learn everything you can about this woman, and then I want you to destroy her. And her child also. I must know if I have your absolute loyalty."

His eyes were burning. I had seen this side of him before. I sat beside a man who was gripped more and more by madness. I took my coffee cup with a trembling hand and drank deeply. Until I finished swallowing, I wouldn't have to give him an answer.

3

efore I had my skull amped, I used to have an alarm clock. In the morning when it went off, I liked to stay in bed a little while longer, bleary and yawning. Maybe I'd get up and maybe I wouldn't. Now, though, I don't have a choice. I chip in an add-on the night before, and when that daddy decides it's time, my eyes snap open and I'm *awake*. It's an abrupt transition and it always leaves me startled. And there's no way in hell that chip will let me fall back asleep. I hate it a lot.

On Sunday morning I woke up promptly at eight o'clock. There was a black man I'd never seen before standing beside my bed. I thought about that for a moment. He was big, much taller than me and well built without going overboard about it. A lot of the blacks you see in the city are like Janelle, refugees from some famine-stricken, arid African wasteland. This guy, though, looked like he'd never missed a sensible, well-balanced meal in his life. His face was long and serious, and his expression seemed to be set in a permanent glower. His stern brown eyes and shaven head added to his grim demeanor. "Who are you?" I asked. I didn't get out from under the covers yet.

"Good morning, *yaa Sidi,*" he said. He had a soft, low-pitched voice with a touch of huskiness. "My name is Kmuzu."

"That's a start," I said. "Now what in the name of Allah are you doing here?"

"I am your slave."

"The hell you are." I like to think of myself as the defender of the downtrodden and all that. I get prickly at the idea of slavery, an attitude that runs counter to the popular opinion among my friends and neighbors.

29

"The master of the house ordered me to see to your needs. He thought I'd be the perfect servant for you, *yaa Sidi,* because my name means 'medicine' in Ngoni."

In Arabic, my own name means "sickness." Friedlander Bey knew, of course, that my mother had named me Marîd in the superstitious hope that my life would be free of illness. "I don't mind having a valet," I said, "but I'm not gonna keep a slave." Kmuzu shrugged. Whether or not I wanted to use the word, he knew he was still *somebody's* slave, mine or Papa's.

"The master of the house briefed me in great detail about your needs," he said. His eyes narrowed. "He promised me emancipation if I will embrace Islam, but I cannot abandon the faith of my father. I think you should know that I'm a devout Christian." I took that to mean that my new servant wholeheartedly disapproved of almost everything I might say or do.

"We'll try to be friends anyway," I said. I sat up and swung my legs out of the bed. I popped out the sleep control and put it in the rack of daddies I keep on the nightstand. In the old days, I spent a lot of time in the morning scratching and yawning and rubbing my scalp; but now when I wake up, I'm denied even those small pleasures.

"Do you truly need that device?" asked Kmuzu.

"My body has sort of gotten out of the habit of sleeping and waking up on its own."

He shook his head. "It is a simple enough problem to solve, *yaa Sidi.* If you just stay awake long enough, you will fall asleep."

I saw that if I expected to have any peace, I was going to have to murder this man, and soon. "You don't understand. The problem is that after three days and nights without sleep, when I do doze off at last I have bizarre dreams, really gruesome ones. Why should I put myself through all that, when I can just reach for pills or software instead?"

"The master of the house instructed me to limit your drug use."

I was starting to get aggravated. "Fine," I said, "you can just fucking *try.*" The drug situation was probably behind Friedlander Bey's "gift" of this slave. I'd made a bad mistake on my very first morning *chez* Papa: I showed up late for breakfast with a butaqualide hangover. I was moderately dysfunctional for a couple of hours, and that earned me his disapproval. So that first afternoon I passed by Laila's modshop on Fourth Street in the Budayeen and invested in the sleep control.

My preference is still a half-dozen beauties, but these days I'm always looking over my shoulder for Papa's spies. He's got a million of 'em. Let me make it clear: You *don't* want his disapproval. He never forgets these things. If he needs to, he hires other people to carry his grudges for him.

The advantages of the situation, however, are many. Take the bed, for instance. I've never had a bed before, just a mattress thrown on the floor in the corner of a room. Now I can kick dirty socks and underwear under something, and if something falls on the floor and gets lost I know just where it'll be, although I won't be able to reach it. I still fall out of the damn bed a couple of times a week, but because of the sleep control, I don't wake up. I just lie there in a heap on the floor until morning.

So I got out of bed on this Sunday morning, took a hot shower, washed my hair, trimmed my beard, and brushed my teeth. I'm supposed to be at my desk in the police station by nine o'clock, but one of the ways I assert my independence is by ignoring the time. I didn't hurry getting dressed. I chose a pair of khaki trousers, a pale blue shirt, a dark blue tie, and a white linen jacket. All the civilian employees in the copshop dress like that, and I'm glad. Arab dress reminds me too much of the life I left behind when I came to the city.

"So you've been planted here to snoop on me," I said while I tried to get the ends of my necktie to come out even.

"I am here to be your friend, *yaa Sidi,*" said Kmuzu.

I smiled at that. Before I came to live in Friedlander Bey's palace, I was lonely a lot. I lived in a bare one-room flat with nothing but my pillcase for company. I had some friends, of course, but not the kind who dropped over all the time because they missed me so much. There was Yasmin, whom I suppose I loved a little. She spent the night with me occasionally, but now she looked the other way when we bumped into each other. I think she held it against me that I've killed a few people.

"What if I beat you?" I asked Kmuzu. "Would you still be my friend?"

I was trying to be sarcastic, but it was definitely the wrong thing to say. "I would make you stop," said Kmuzu, and his voice was as cold as any I've ever heard.

I think my jaw dropped. "I didn't mean that, you know," I said. Kmuzu gave a slight nod of his head, and the tension passed. "Help me with this, will you? I think the necktie is winning."

Kmuzu's expression softened a little, and he seemed glad to perform this little service for me. "It is fine now," he said when he finished. "I will get your breakfast."

"I don't eat breakfast."

"*Yaa Sidi*, the master of the house directed me to make sure that you eat breakfast from now on. He believes that breakfast is the most important meal of the day."

Allah save me from nutrition fascists! "If I eat in the morning, I feel like a lump of lead for hours."

It didn't make any difference to Kmuzu what I thought. "I will get your breakfast," he said.

"Don't you have to go to church or something?"

He looked at me calmly. "I have already been to worship," he said. "Now I will get your breakfast." I'm sure he'd note every calorie I took in and file a report with Friedlander Bey. It was just another example of how much influence Papa exerted.

I may have felt a little like a prisoner, but I'd certainly been given compensations. I had a spacious suite in the west wing of Friedlander Bey's great house, on the second floor near Papa's own private quarters. My closet was filled with many suits of clothes in different styles and fashions—Western, Arab, casual, formal. Papa gave me a lot of sophisticated high-tech hardware, from a new Chhindwara constrained-AI data deck to an Esmeraldas holo system with Libertad screens and a Ruy Challenger argon solipsizer. I never worried about money. Once a week, one of the Stones That Speak left a fat envelope stuffed with cash on my desk.

All in all, my life had changed so much that my days of poverty and insecurity seemed like a thirty-year nightmare. Today I'm well fed, well dressed, and well liked by the right people, and all it's cost me is what you'd expect: my self-respect and the approval of most of my friends.

Kmuzu let me know that breakfast was ready. *"Bismillah,"* I murmured as I sat down: in the name of God. I ate some eggs and bread fried in butter, and swallowed a cup of strong coffee.

"Would you like anything more, *yaa Sidi?"* asked Kmuzu.

"No, thank you." I was staring at the far wall, thinking about freedom. I wondered if there was some way I could buy my way out of the police-liaison job. Not with money, anyway, I was sure of that. I don't think it's possible to bribe Papa with money. Still, if I paid very close attention, I just might find some other means of leverage. *Inshallah.*

"Then shall I go downstairs and bring the car around?" Kmuzu asked. I blinked and realized that I had to get going. I didn't have Friedlander Bey's long black limousine at my disposal, but he'd given me a comfortable new electric automobile to use. After all, I was his official representative among the guardians of justice.

Kmuzu, of course, would be my driver now. It occurred to me that I'd have to be very clever to go anywhere without him. "Yes, I'll be down in a minute," I said.

I ran a hand through my hair, which was getting long again. Before I left the house, I put a rack of moddies and daddies in my briefcase. It was impossible to predict what sort of personality I'd need to have when I got to work, or which particular talents and abilities. It was best just to take everything I had and be prepared.

I stood on the marble stairs and waited for Kmuzu. It was the month of Rabi al-Awwal, and a warm drizzle was falling from a gray sky. Although Papa's estate was carved out of a crowded neighborhood in the heart of the city, I could almost pretend that I was in some quiet garden oasis, far from urban grime and noise. I was surrounded by a green lushness that had been coaxed into existence solely to soothe the spirit of one weary old man. I heard the quiet, peaceful trickling of cool fountains, and some energetic birds warbled nearby from the carefully tended fruit trees. On the still air drifted a heavy, sweet perfume of exotic flowers. I pretended that none of this could seduce me.

Then I got into the cream-colored Westphalian sedan

and rode out through the guarded gate. Beyond the wall I
was thrown suddenly into the bustle and clamor of the
city, and with a shock I realized how sorry I was to leave
the serenity of Papa's house. It occurred to me that in
time I could come to be like him.

Kmuzu let me out of the car on Walid al-Akbar Street,
at the station house that oversaw the affairs of the
Budayeen. He told me that he'd be back to drive me
home promptly at four-thirty. I had a feeling that he was
one of those people who was never late. I stood on the
sidewalk and watched as he drove away.

There was always a crowd of young children outside
the station house. I don't know if they were hoping to see
some shackled criminal dragged in, or waiting for their
own parents to be released from custody, or just loitering
in the hopes of begging loose change. I'd been one of
them myself not so very long ago in Algiers, and it didn't
hurt me any to throw a few kiam into the air and watch
them scramble for it. I reached into my pocket and
grabbed a clutch of coins. The older, bigger kids caught
the easy money, and the smaller ones clung to my legs and
wailed *"Baksheesh!"* Every day it was a challenge to shake
my young passengers loose before I got to the revolving
door.

I had a desk in a small cubicle on the third floor of the
station house. My cubicle was separated from its neighbors by pale green plasterboard walls only a little taller
than I was. There was always a sour smell in the air, a
mixture of stale sweat, tobacco smoke, and disinfectant.
Above my desk was a shelf that held plastic boxes filled
with dated files on cobalt-alloy cell-memories. On the
floor was a big cardboard box crammed with bound print-
outs. I had a grimy Annamese data deck on my desk that
gave me trouble-free operation on two out of every three
jobs. Of course, my work wasn't very important, not according to Lieutenant Hajjar. We both knew I was there
just to keep an eye on things for Friedlander Bey. It
amounted to Papa having his own private police precinct
devoted to protecting his interests in the Budayeen.

Hajjar came into my cubicle and dropped another
heavy box on my desk. He was a Jordanian who'd had a
lengthy arrest record of his own before he came to the
city. I suppose he'd been an athlete ten years ago, but he

hadn't stayed in shape. He had thinning brown hair and lately he'd tried to grow a beard. It looked terrible, like the skin of a kiwi fruit. He looked like a mother's bad dream of a drug dealer, which is what he was when he wasn't administering the affairs of the nearby walled quarter.

"How you doin', Audran?" he said.

"Okay," I said. "What's all this?"

"Found something useful for you to do." Hajjar was about two years younger than me, and it gave him a kick to boss me around.

I looked in the box. There were a couple of hundred blue cobalt-alloy plates. It looked like another really tedious job. "You want me to sort these?"

"I want you to log 'em all into the daily record."

I swore under my breath. Every cop carries an electronic log book to make notes on the day's tour: where he went, what he saw, what he said, what he did. At the end of the day, he turns in the book's cell-memory plate to his sergeant. Now Hajjar wanted me to collate all the plates from the station's roster. "This isn't the kind of work Papa had in mind for me," I said.

"What the hell. You got any complaints, take 'em to Friedlander Bey. In the meantime, do what I tell you."

"Yeah, you right," I said. I glared at Hajjar's back as he walked out.

"By the way," he said, turning toward me again, "I got someone for you to meet later. It may be a nice surprise."

I doubted that. "Uh huh," I said.

"Yeah, well, get movin' on those plates. I want 'em finished by lunchtime."

I turned back to my desk, shaking my head. Hajjar annoyed the hell out of me. What was worse, he knew it. I didn't like giving him the satisfaction of seeing me irked.

The funny thing was that Hajjar was in Friedlander Bey's pocket too, but he liked to pretend he was still his own man. Since he'd been promoted and given command, though, Hajjar had gone through some startling changes. He'd begun to take his work seriously, and he'd cut back on his intrigues and profiteering schemes. It wasn't that he'd suddenly discovered a sense of honor; he just realized he'd have to work his tail off to keep from getting fired as a crook and an incompetent.

I selected a productivity moddy from my rack and chipped it onto my posterior plug. The rear implant functions the same as everybody else's. It lets me chip in a moddy and six daddies. The anterior plug, however, is my own little claim to fame. This is the one that taps into my hypothalamus and lets me chip in my special daddies. As far as I know, no one else has ever been given a second implant. I'm glad I hadn't known that Friedlander Bey told my doctors to try something experimental and insanely dangerous. I guess he didn't want me to worry. Now that the frightening part is over, though, I'm glad I went through it. It's made me a more productive member of society and all that.

When I had boring police work to do, which was almost every day, I chipped in an orange moddy that Hajjar had given me. It had a label that said it was manufactured in Helvetia. The Swiss, I suppose, have a high regard for efficiency. Their moddy could take the most energetic, inspired person in the world and transform him instantly into a drudge. Not into a stupid drudge, like what the Half-Hajj's dumbing-down hardware did to me, but into a mindless worker who isn't aware enough to be distracted before the whole assignment is in the Out box. It's the greatest gift to the office menial since conjugal coffee breaks.

I sighed and took the moddy, then reached up and chipped it in.

The immediate sensation was as if the whole world had lurched and then caught its balance. There was an odd, metallic taste in Audran's mouth and a high-pitched ringing in his ears. He felt a touch of nausea, but he tried to ignore it because it wouldn't go away until he popped the moddy out. The moddy had trimmed down his personality like the wick of a lamp, until there was only a vague and ineffectual vestige of his true self left.

Audran wasn't conscious enough even to be resentful. He remembered only that he had work to do, and he pulled a double handful of cobalt-alloy plates out of the box. He slotted six of them into the adit ports beneath the battered data deck's comp screen. Audran touched the

control pad and said, "Copy ports one, two, three, four,
five, six." Then he stared blankly while the deck recorded
the contents of the plates. When the run was finished, he
removed the plates, stacked them on one side of the desk,
and loaded in six more. He barely noticed the morning
pass as he logged in the records.

"Audran." Someone was saying his name.

He stopped what he was doing and glanced over his
shoulder. Lieutenant Hajjar and a uniformed patrolman
were standing in the entrance to his cubicle. Audran
turned slowly back to the data deck. He reached into the
box, but it was empty.

"Unplug that goddamn thing."

Audran faced Hajjar again and nodded. It was time
to pop the moddy.

There was a dizzy swirl of disorientation, and then I
was sitting at my desk, staring stupidly at the Helvetian
moddy in my hand. "Jeez," I murmured. It was a relief to
be fully conscious again.

"Tell you a secret about Audran," Hajjar said to the
cop. "We didn't hire him because of his wonderful quali-
ties. He really don't have any. But he makes a great spin-
dle for hardware. Audran's just a moddy's way of gettin' its
daily workout." The cop smiled.

"Hey, you gave me this goddamn moddy in the first
place," I said.

Hajjar shrugged. "Audran, this is Officer Shaknahyi."

"Where you at?" I said.

"All right," said the cop.

"You got to watch out for Audran," Hajjar said. "He's
got one of those addictives personalities. He used to make
a big deal out of not havin' his brain wired. Now you never
see him without some kind of moddy stuck in his head."

That shocked me. I hadn't realized I'd been using my
moddies so much. I was surprised anyone else had noticed.

"Try to overlook his frailties, Jirji, 'cause you and him
are gonna be workin' together."

Shaknahyi gave him a sharp look. I did the same.
"What do you mean, 'working together'?" said the cop.

"I mean what I said. I got a little assignment for you
two. You're gonna be workin' very closely for a while."

"You taking me off the street?" asked Shaknahyi.

Hajjar shook his head. "I never said that. I'm pairin' Audran with you on patrol."

Shaknahyi was so outraged, I thought he was going to split down the middle. "Shaitan take my kids first!" he said. "You think you're teaming me up with a guy with no training and no experience, you're goddamn crazy!"

I didn't like the idea of going out on the street. I didn't want to make myself a target for every loon in the Budayeen who owned a cheap needle gun. "I'm supposed to stay here in the station house," I said. "Friedlander Bey never said anything about real cop work."

"Be good for you, Audran," said Hajjar. "You can ride around and see all your old buddies again. They'll be impressed when you flash your badge at them."

"They'll hate my guts," I said.

"You're both overlooking one small detail," said Shaknahyi. "As my partner, he's supposed to guard my back every time we walk into some dangerous situation. To be honest, I don't have a lick of faith in him. You can't expect me to work with a partner I don't trust."

"I don't blame you," said Hajjar. He looked amused by the cop's opinion of me. My first impression of Shaknahyi wasn't so good, either. He didn't have his brain wired, and that meant he was one of two kinds of cop: Either he was a strict Muslim, or else he was one of those guys who thought his own naked, unaugmented brain was more than a match for the evildoers. That's the way I used to be, but I learned better. Either way, I wouldn't get along with him.

"And I don't want the responsibility of watching his back," I said. "I don't need that kind of pressure."

Hajjar patted the air in a kind of soothing motion. "Well, forget about that. You're not gonna be chasin' down bad guys on the street. You're gonna be conductin' an unofficial investigation."

"What kind of investigation?" asked Shaknahyi suspiciously.

Hajjar waved a dark green cobalt-alloy plate. "Got a big file here on Reda Abu Adil. I want you two to learn it backwards and forwards. Then you're gonna meet the man and stick to him like shadows."

"His name's come up a couple of times at Papa's house," I said. "Who is he?"

"He's Friedlander Bey's oldest rival." Hajjar leaned against the pale green wall. "They got a competition goes back a hundred years."

"I know about him," said the cop gruffly.

"Audran only knows about small-time thugs in the Budayeen. Abu Adil don't come near the Budayeen. Keeps his interests far away from Papa's. Carved out a little kingdom for himself on the north and west sides of town. Even so, I got a request from Friedlander Bey to put him under surveillance."

"You're doing this just because Friedlander Bey asked you to?" asked Shaknahyi.

"You bet your ass. He's got a suspicion that Abu Adil is thinkin' about breakin' their truce. Papa wants to be ready."

Well, until I found my leverage with Friedlander Bey, I was his puppet. I had to do whatever he and Hajjar told me to do.

Shaknahyi, however, didn't want any part of it. "I wanted to be a cop because I thought I could help people," he said. "I don't make a lot of money, I don't get enough sleep, and every day I mix into one goddamn crisis after another. I never know when somebody's gonna pull a gun on me and use it. I do it because I believe I can make a difference. I didn't sign on to be some rich bastard's personal spy. How long has this outfit been for sale, anyway?" He glowered at Hajjar until the lieutenant had to look away.

"Listen," I said to Shaknahyi, "what's your problem with me?"

"You're not a cop, for one thing," he said. "You're worse than a rookie. You'll hang back and let some creep nail me, or else you'll get itchy and shoot a little old lady. I don't want to be teamed with somebody unless I think I can count on him."

I nodded. "Yeah, you right, but I can wear a moddy. I've seen plenty of rookies wearing police officer moddies to help them through the routines."

Shaknahyi threw up his hands. "He just makes it worse," he muttered.

"I said not to worry about a rough time on the street,"

said Hajjar. "This is just an investigation. Mostly desk-job stuff. I don't know what's got you so spooked, Jirji."

Shaknahyi rubbed his forehead and sighed. "All right, all right. I just wanted to have my objection on the record."

"Okay," said Hajjar, "it's been noted. I want to hear regular reports from both of you, 'cause I got to keep Friedlander Bey happy. That's not as easy as it sounds, either." He tossed the cell-memory plate to me.

"Want us to start on this right away?" I asked.

Hajjar gave me a wry look. "If you can fit it into your busy social calendar."

"Make a copy for me," said Shaknahyi. "I'll study the file today, and tomorrow we'll take a ride by Abu Adil's place."

"Fine," I said. I slipped the green plate into my data deck and copied it onto a blank.

"Right," said Shaknahyi, taking the copy and walking out of my cubicle.

"You two didn't hit it off real well," said Hajjar.

"We just have to get the job done," I said. "We don't have to go dancing together."

"Yeah, you right. Why don't you take the rest of the afternoon off? Go home and look through the report. I'm sure you got any questions, Papa can answer them for you."

He left me alone too, and I called Friedlander Bey's house through the data deck. I spoke to one of the Stones That Speak. "Yeah?" he said bluntly.

"This is Audran. Tell Kmuzu to pick me up at the police station in about twenty minutes."

"Yeah," said the Stone. Then I was listening to a dial tone. The Stones make up in curtness what they lack in eloquence.

Twenty minutes later on the dot, Kmuzu swung the electric sedan in toward the curb. I got into the backseat, and he began driving home.

"Kmuzu," I said, "you know anything about a businessman named Reda Abu Adil?"

"A little, *yaa Sidi*," he said. "What do you wish to know?" He never looked away from the road.

"Everything, but not right now." I closed my eyes and let my head fall back against the seat. If only Fried-

lander Bey would tell me as much as he told Kmuzu and
Lieutenant Hajjar. I hated to think that Papa still didn't
entirely trust me.

"When we get back to the estate," said Kmuzu,
"you'll want to talk with Friedlander Bey."

"That's right," I said.

"I warn you that the woman has put him in a surly
mood."

Wonderful, I thought. I'd forgotten about the woman.
Papa was going to want to know why I hadn't murdered
her yet. I spent the rest of that ride thinking up a plausible
excuse.

If I'd known just how difficult things were going to be, I might have had Kmuzu drive me straight out of the city and on to some distant, peaceful place. When I got home—by this time I was used to thinking of Friedlander Bey's palace as home—it was about four o'clock in the afternoon. I decided that I could use a nap. After that, I planned to have a brief meeting with Papa and then go out and spend some time in Chiriga's club. Unfortunately, my slave Kmuzu had other ideas.

"I will be quite comfortable in the small room," he announced.

"I'm sorry?" I said. I didn't know what the hell he was talking about.

"The small room that you use for storage. It will be sufficient for my needs. I will bring a cot."

I looked at him for a moment. "I assumed you'd be sleeping in the servants' wing."

"Yes, I have quarters there, *yaa Sidi*, but I will be better able to look after you if I have a room here also."

"I'm not really interested in having you look after me every minute of the day, Kmuzu. I put a certain value on my privacy."

Kmuzu nodded. "I understand that, but the master of the house directed me—"

I'd heard enough of that. "I don't care *what* the master of the house directed you," I shouted. "Whose slave *are* you, mine or his?"

Kmuzu didn't answer me. He just stared at me with his big, solemn eyes.

"Yeah, well, never mind," I said. "Go ahead and make yourself at home in the storage room. Stack up all my stuff

42

and drag in a mattress if you want." I turned away, deeply
irritated.

"Friedlander Bey has invited you to dine with him
after he speaks to you," said Kmuzu.

"I suppose it doesn't mean anything that I have other
plans," I said. All I got was the same silent stare. Kmuzu
was awful good at that.

I went into my bedroom and undressed. Then I took a
quick shower and thought about what I wanted to say to
Friedlander Bey. First, I was going to tell him that this
slave-spy thing with Kmuzu was going to have to end
pretty goddamn quick. Second, I wanted to let him know
that I wasn't happy about being teamed with Officer
Shaknahyi. And third, well, that's when I realized that I
probably didn't have the nerve to mention anything at all
about items one and two.

I got out of the shower and toweled myself dry. Standing under the warm water had made me feel a lot better
and I decided that I didn't need a nap after all. Instead, I
stared into a closet deciding what to wear. Papa liked it
when I wore Arab dress. I figured what the hell and
picked a simple maroon *gallebeya.* I decided that the
knitted skullcap of my homeland wasn't appropriate, and
I'm not the turban type. I settled on a plain white *keffiya*
and fixed it in place with a simple black rope *akal.* I tied a
corded belt around my waist, supporting a ceremonial
dagger Papa'd given me. Also on the belt, pulled around
behind my back, was a holster with my seizure gun. I hid
that by wearing an expensive tan-colored cloak over the
gallebeya. I felt I was ready for anything: a feast, a debate,
or an attempted assassination.

"Why don't you stay here and get yourself settled
in?" I said to Kmuzu, but instead he followed me downstairs. I just knew he'd do that. Papa's offices were on the
ground floor in the main part of the house connecting the
two wings. When we got there, one of the Stones That
Speak was in the corridor, guarding the door. He glanced
at me and nodded; but when he looked at Kmuzu, his
expression changed. His lip curled just a little. That was
the most emotion I'd ever seen from one of the Stones.

"Wait," he said.

"I will go in with my master," said Kmuzu.

The Stone struck him in the chest and shoved him back a step. "Wait," he said.

"It's all right, Kmuzu," I said. I didn't want the two of them wrestling on the floor here outside Friedlander Bey's office. They could settle their little dominance dispute on their own time.

Kmuzu gave me a cool glance, but said nothing. The Stone bowed his head slightly as I went past him into Papa's waiting room, and then he closed the door behind me. If he and Kmuzu went at it out in the hall, I'd be at a loss to know what to do. What's the proper etiquette when your slave is getting beaten up by your boss's slave? Of course, that wasn't giving Kmuzu the benefit of the doubt. Maybe he had a trick or two of his own. Who knows, he might have been able to handle the Stone That Speaks.

Anyway, Friedlander Bey was in his inner office. He was sitting behind his gigantic desk. He didn't look well. His elbows were on the desktop, and his head was in his hands. He was massaging his forehead. He stood up when I came in. "I am pleased," he said. He didn't sound pleased. He sounded exhausted.

"It's my honor to wish you good evening, O Shaykh," I said. He was wearing an open-necked white shirt with the sleeves rolled up and a pair of baggy gray trousers. He probably wouldn't even notice the trouble I'd taken to dress conservatively. You can't win, right?

"We will dine soon, my son. In the meantime, sit with me. There are matters that need our attention."

I sat in a comfortable chair beside his desk. Papa took his seat again and fiddled with some papers, frowning. I wondered if he was going to talk about the woman, or why he'd decided to saddle me with Kmuzu. It wasn't my place to question him. He'd begin when he was ready.

He shut his eyes for a moment and then opened them, sighing. His sparse white hair was rumpled, and he hadn't shaved that morning. I guessed he had a lot on his mind. I was a little afraid of what he was going to order me to do this time.

"We must speak," he said. "There is the matter of alms-giving."

Okay, I'll admit it: Of all the possible problems he could have chosen, alms-giving was pretty low on my list of what I expected to hear. How foolish of me to think he wanted to discuss something more to the point. Like murder.

"I'm afraid I've had more important things on my mind, O Shaykh," I said.

Friedlander Bey nodded wearily. "No doubt, my son, you truly believe these other things are more important, but you are wrong. You and I share an existence of luxury and comfort, and that gives us a responsibility to our brothers."

Jacques, my infidel friend, would've had trouble grasping his precise point. Sure, other religions are all in favor of charity too. It's just good sense to take care of the poor and needy, because you never know when you're going to end up poor and needy yourself. The Muslim attitude goes further, though. Alms-giving is one of the five pillars of the religion, as fundamental an obligation as the profession of faith, the daily prayer, the fast of Ramadan, and the pilgrimage to Mecca.

I gave the same attention to alms-giving that I gave the other duties. That is, I had profound respect for them in an intellectual sort of way, and I told myself that I'd begin practicing in earnest real soon now.

"Evidently you've been considering this for some time," I said.

"We have been neglecting our duty to the poor and the wayfarers, and the widows and orphans among our neighbors."

Some of my friends—my old friends, my former friends—think Papa is nothing but a murderous monster, but that's not true. He's a shrewd businessman who also maintains strong ties to the faith that created our culture. I'm sorry if that seems like a contradiction. He could be harsh, even cruel, at times; but I knew no one else as sincere in his beliefs or as glad to meet the many obligations of the noble Qur'ân.

"What do you wish me to do, O my uncle?"

Friedlander Bey shrugged. "Do I not reward you well for your services?"

"You are unfailingly gracious, O Shaykh," I said.

"Then it would not be a hardship for you to set aside a fifth part of your substance, as is suggested in the Straight Path. Indeed, I desire to make a gift to you that will swell your purse and, at the same time, give you a source of income independent of this house."

That caught my attention. Freedom was what I hungered for every night as I drifted off to sleep. It was what I thought of first when I woke in the morning. And the first step toward freedom was financial independence.

"You are the father of generosity, O Shaykh," I said, "but I am unworthy." Believe me, I was panting to hear what he was going to say. Proper form, however, required me to pretend that I couldn't possibly accept his gift.

He raised one thin, trembling hand. "I prefer that my associates have outside sources of income, sources that they manage themselves and whose profits they need not share with me."

"That is a wise policy," I said. I've known a lot of Papa's "associates," and I know what kind of sources they had. I was sure he was about to cut me into some shady vice deal. Not that I had scruples, you understand. I wouldn't mind getting my drugs wholesale. I've just never had much of a mind for commerce.

"Until recently the Budayeen was your whole world. You know it well, my son, and you understand its people. I have a great deal of influence there, and I thought it best to acquire for you some small commercial concern in that quarter." He extended to me a document laminated in plastic.

I reached forward and took it from him. "What is this, O Shaykh?" I asked.

"It is a title deed. You are now the owner of the property described upon it. From this day forward it is your business to operate. It is a profitable enterprise, my nephew. Manage it well and it will reward you, *inshallah*."

I looked at the deed. "You're—" My voice choked. Papa had bought Chiriga's club and was giving it to me. I looked up at him. "But—"

He waved his hand at me. "No thanks are necessary," he said. "You are my dutiful son."

"But this is Chiri's place. I can't take her club. What will she do?"

Friedlander Bey shrugged. "Business is business," he said simply.

I just stared at him. He had a remarkable habit of

giving me things I would have been happier without: Kmuzu and a career as a cop, for instance. It wouldn't do any good at all to refuse. "I'm quite unable to express my thanks," I said in a dull voice. I had only two good friends left, Saied the Half-Hajj and Chiri. She was really going to hate this. I was already dreading her reaction.

"Come," said Friedlander Bey, "let us go in to dinner." He stood up behind his desk and held out his hand to me. I followed him, still astonished. It wasn't until later that I realized I hadn't spoken to him about my job with Hajjar or my new assignment to investigate Reda Abu Adil. When you're in Papa's presence, you go where he wants to go, you do what he wants to do, and you talk about what he wants to talk about.

We went to the smaller of the two dining rooms, in the back of the west wing on the ground floor. This is where Papa and I usually ate when we dined together. Kmuzu fell into step behind me in the corridor, and the Stone That Speaks followed Friedlander Bey. If this were a sentimental American holoshow, eventually they'd get into a fight and afterward they'd become the best of friends. Fat chance.

I stopped at the threshold of the dining room and stared. Umm Saad and her son were waiting for us inside. She was the first woman I'd ever seen in Friedlander Bey's house, but even so she'd never been permitted to join us at the table. The boy looked about fifteen years old, which in the eyes of the faith is the age of maturity. He was old enough to meet the obligations of prayer and ritual fasting, so under other circumstances he might have been welcome to share our meal. "Kmuzu," I said, "escort the woman back to her apartment."

Friedlander Bey put a hand on my arm. "I thank you, my son, but I've invited her to meet with us."

I looked at him, my mouth open, but no intelligent reply occurred to me. If Papa wanted to initiate major revolutions in attitude and behavior at this late date, that was his right. I closed my mouth and nodded.

"Umm Saad will have her dinner in her apartment after our discussion," Friedlander Bey said, giving her a stern look. "Her son may then retire with her or remain with the men, as he wishes."

Umm Saad looked impatient. "I suppose I must be grateful for whatever time you can spare me," she said.

Papa went to his chair, and the Stone assisted him. Kmuzu showed me to my seat across the table from Friedlander Bey. Umm Saad sat on his left, and her son sat on Papa's right. "Marîd," said Papa, "have you met the young man?"

"No," I said. I hadn't even seen him before. He and his mother were keeping a very low profile in that house. The boy was tall for his age, but slender and melancholy. His skin had an unnatural yellowish tint, and the whites of his eyes were discolored. He looked unhealthy. He was dressed in a dark blue *gallebeya* with a geometric print, and he wore the turban of a young shaykh—not a tribal leader, but the honorary turban of a youth who has committed the entire Qur'ân to memory.

"Yaa Sidi," said the woman, "may I present to you my handsome son, Saad ben Salah?"

"May your honor be increased, sir," said the boy.

I raised my eyebrows. At least the kid had manners. "Allah be gracious to you," I said.

"Umm Saad," said Friedlander Bey in a gruff voice, "you have come into my house and made extravagant claims. My patience is at an end. Out of respect for the way of hospitality I have suffered your presence, but now my conscience is clear. I demand that you trouble me no more. You must be out of my house by the call to prayer tomorrow morning. I will instruct my servants to give you any assistance you require."

Umm Saad gave him a little smile, as if she found his anger amusing. "I don't believe you've given sufficient thought to our problem. And you've made no provision for the future of your grandson." She covered Saad's hand with her own.

That was like a slap across the face. She was claiming to be Friedlander Bey's daughter or daughter-in-law. It explained why he wanted *me* to get rid of her, instead of doing it himself.

He looked at me. "My nephew," he said, "this woman is not my daughter, and the boy is no kin of mine. This is not the first time a stranger has come to my door claiming blood ties, in the hope of stealing some of my hard-won fortune."

Jeez, I should have taken care of her when he first asked me, before he dragged me into all this intrigue. Someday I'm going to learn to deal with things before they get too complicated. I don't mean that I really would have murdered her, but I might have had a chance to cajole or threaten or bribe her to leave us in peace. I could tell that it was too late now. She wasn't going to accept a settlement; she wanted the ball of wax whole, without any little chunks missing.

"You are certain, O Shaykh?" I said. "That she's not your daughter, I mean?"

For a moment I thought he was going to hit me. Then in a tightly controlled voice he said, "I swear it to you upon the life of the Messenger of God, may blessings be upon him and peace."

That was good enough for me. Friedlander Bey isn't above a little manipulation if it furthers his purposes, but he doesn't swear false oaths. We get along so well partly because he doesn't lie and I don't lie. I looked at Umm Saad. "What proof do you have of your claim?" I said.

Her eyes grew wider. "Proof?" she cried. "Do I need proof to embrace my own father? What proof do *you* have of your father's identity?"

She couldn't have known what a touchy subject that was. I ignored the remark. "Papa—" I stopped myself. "The master of the house has shown you courtesy and kindness. Now he properly requests that you bring your visit to an end. As he said, you may have the help of any of the servants of the house in your departure." I turned to the Stone That Speaks, and his head nodded once. He'd make sure that Umm Saad and her son would be out on the doorstep by the last syllable of the muezzin's morning call.

"Then we have preparations to make," she said, standing. "Come, Saad." And the two of them left the small dining room with as much dignity as if it were their own palace and they the aggrieved party.

Friedlander Bey's hands were pressed flat on the table in front of him. His knuckles were white. He took two or three deep, deliberate breaths. "What do you propose to do, to end this annoyance?" he said.

I looked up, from Kmuzu to the Stone That Speaks. Neither slave seemed to show the least interest in the matter. "Let me understand something first, O Shaykh," I said. "You want to be rid of her and her son. Is it essential that she die? What if I take another, less violent way to discourage her?"

"You saw her and heard her words. Nothing short of violence will bring her scheme to an end. And further— only her death will discourage other leeches from trying the same strategy. Why do you hesitate, my son? The answer is simple and effective. You've killed before. Killing again should not be so difficult. You need not even make it seem accidental. Sergeant Hajjar will understand. He will not proceed with an investigation."

"Hajjar is a lieutenant now," I said.

Papa waved impatiently. "Yes, of course."

"You think Hajjar will overlook a homicide?" Hajjar was bought off, but that didn't mean he'd sit still while I made him look like a fool. I could get away with a lot now, but only if I was careful to preserve Hajjar's public image.

The old man's brow creased. "My son," he said slowly so I wouldn't misunderstand, "if Lieutenant Hajjar balks, he too can be removed. Perhaps you will have better luck with his successor. You can continue this process until the office is filled at last with a police supervisor of sufficient imagination and wit."

"Allah guide you and me," I murmured. Friedlander Bey was pretty damn casual these days about off-bumping as a solution to life's little setbacks. I was struck again by the fact that Papa himself was in no rush to pull any triggers himself. He had learned at an early age to delegate responsibility. And I had become his favorite delegatee.

"Dinner?" he asked.

I'd lost my appetite. "I pray that you'll forgive me," I said. "I have a lot of planning to do. Maybe after your meal, you'll answer some questions. I'd like to hear what you know about Reda Abu Adil."

Friedlander Bey spread his hands. "I don't imagine that I know much more than you," he said.

Now, hadn't Papa twisted Hajjar's arm to start an official investigation? So why was he playing dumb now? Or was this just another test? How many goddamn tests did I have to pass?

Or maybe—and this made it all *real* interesting—

maybe Hajjar's curiosity about Abu Adil didn't come from Papa, after all. Maybe Hajjar had sold himself more than once: to Friedlander Bey, and also to the second-highest bidder, and to the third-highest, and to the fourth . . .

I remembered when I was a hot-blooded fifteen-year-old. I promised my girlfriend, Nafissa, that I wouldn't even look at another girl. And I made the same pledge to Fayza, whose tits were bigger. And to Hanuna, whose father worked in the brewery. Everything was just fine until Nafissa found out about Hanuna, and Fayza's father found out about both of the others. The girls would have cut my balls off and scratched out my eyes. Instead, I slipped out of Algiers while the enemy slept, and so began the odyssey that brought me to this city.

That's a dead, dry story and of little relevance here. I'm just suggesting how much trouble Hajjar was looking at if Friedlander Bey and Reda Abu Adil ever caught on to his two-timing.

"Isn't Abu Adil your chief competitor?" I asked.

"The gentleman may think we compete. I do not think that we are in conflict in any way. Allah grants Abu Adil the right to sell his beaten brass where I am selling my beaten brass. If someone chooses to buy from Abu Adil rather than from me, then both customer and merchant have my blessing. I will get my livelihood from Allah, and nothing Abu Adil can do will help or hinder me."

I thought of the vast sums of money that passed through Friedlander Bey's house, some of it ending up in fat envelopes on my own desk. I was confident that none of it derived from the sale of beaten brass. But it made a pleasant euphemism; I let it go.

"According to Lieutenant Hajjar," I said, "you think Abu Adil is planning to put you out of business altogether."

"Only the Gatherer of Nations shall do that, my son." Papa gave me a fond look. "But I am pleased by your concern. You needn't worry about Abu Adil."

"I can use my position down at the copshop to find out what he's up to."

He stood up and ran a hand through his white hair. "If you wish. If it will ease your mind."

Kmuzu pulled my chair away from the table and I stood up also. "My uncle," I said, "I beg you to excuse me.

May your table be pleasant to you. I wish you a blessed meal."

Friedlander Bey came to me and kissed me on each cheek. "Go in safety, my darling," he said. "I am most pleased with you."

As I left the dining room, I turned to see Papa sitting once again in his chair. There was a grim look on the old man's face, and the Stone That Speaks was bending low to hear something Papa was saying. I wondered just what Friedlander Bey shared with his slave, but not yet with me.

"You've got to finish moving in, don't you?" I said to Kmuzu as we walked back to my apartment.

"I will bring a mattress, *yaa Sidi*. That will be enough for tonight."

"Good. I have some work to do on the data deck."

"The report on Reda Abu Adil?"

I looked at him sharply. "Yes," I said, "that's right."

"Perhaps I can help you get a clearer picture of the man and his motives."

"How is it that you know so much about him, Kmuzu?" I asked.

"When I was first brought to the city, I was employed as a bodyguard for one of Abu Adil's wives."

I thought that information was remarkable. Consider: I begin an investigation of a total stranger, and my brand-new slave turns out to have once worked for that same man. This wasn't a coincidence, I could feel it. I had faith that it'd all fit together eventually. I just hoped I'd still be alive and healthy when it did.

I paused outside the door to my suite. "Go get your bedding and your belongings," I told Kmuzu. "I'll be going through the file on Abu Adil. Don't worry about disturbing me, though. When I'm working, it takes a bomb blast to distract me."

"Thank you, *yaa Sidi*. I will be as quiet as I can."

I began to turn the color lock on the door. Kmuzu gave a little bow and headed toward the servants' quarters. When he'd turned the corner, I hurried away in the opposite direction. I went down to the garage and found my car. It felt strange, sneaking away from my own servant, but I just didn't feel like having him tagging along with me tonight.

I drove through the Christian quarter and then through the upper-class shopping district east of the Budayeen. I parked the car on the Boulevard il-Jameel, not far from where Bill usually sat in his taxi. Before I left the car, I took out my pillcase. It seemed like it had been a long time since I'd treated myself to some friendly drugs. I was well supplied, thanks to my higher income and the many new contacts I'd met through Papa. I selected a couple of blue tri-phets; I was in such a hurry that I swallowed them right there, without water. In a little while I'd be ramping with energy and feeling indomitable. I was going to need the help, because I had an ugly scene ahead of me.

I also thought about chipping in a moddy, but at the last moment I decided against it. I needed to talk with Chiri, and I had enough respect for her to show up in my own head. Afterward, though, things might be different. I might feel like going home as someone else entirely.

Chiri's club was crowded that night. The air was still and warm inside, sweet with a dozen different perfumes, sour with sweat and spilled beer. The sexchanges and pre-op debs chatted with the customers with false cheerfulness, and their laughter broke through the shrill music as they called for more champagne cocktails. Bright bolts of red and blue neon slashed down slantwise behind the bar, and brilliant points of light from spinning mirror balls sparkled on the walls and ceiling. In one corner there was a hologram of Honey Pílar, writhing alone upon a blond mink coat spread on the white sands of some romantic beach. It was an ad for her new sex moddy, *Slow, Slow Burn.* I stared at it for a moment, almost hypnotized.

"Audran," came Chiriga's hoarse voice. She didn't sound happy to see me. "Mr. Boss."

"Listen, Chiri," I said. "Let me—"

"Lily," she called to one of the changes, "get the new owner a drink. Gin and bingara with a hit of Rose's." She looked at me fiercely. "The *tende* is mine, Audran. Private stock. It doesn't go with the club, and I'm taking it with me."

She was making it hard for me. I could only imagine how she felt. "Wait a minute, Chiri. I had nothing to do with—"

"These are the keys. This one's for the register. The

money in there's all yours. The girls are yours, the hassles are yours from now on too. You got any problems you can go to Papa with 'em." She snatched her bottle of *tende* from under the bar. *"Kwa heri*, motherfucker," she snarled at me. Then she stormed out of the club.

Everything got real quiet then. Whatever song had been playing came to an end and nobody put on another one. A deb named Kandy was on stage, and she just stood there and stared at me like I might start slavering and shrieking at any moment. People got up from their stools near me and edged away. I looked into their faces and I saw hostility and contempt.

Friedlander Bey wanted to divorce me from all my connections to the Budayeen. Making me a cop had been a great start, but even so I still had a few loyal friends. Forcing Chiri to sell her club had been another brilliant stroke. Soon I'd be just as lonely and friendless as Papa himself, except I wouldn't have the consolation of his wealth and power.

"Look," I said, "this is all a mistake. I got to settle this with Chiri. Indihar, take charge, okay? I'll be right back."

Indihar just gave me a disdainful look. She didn't say anything. I couldn't stand to be in there another minute. I grabbed the keys Chiri'd dropped on the bar and I went outside. She wasn't anywhere in sight on the Street. She might have gone straight home, but she'd probably gone to another club.

I went to the Fée Blanche, old man Gargotier's café on Ninth Street. Saied, Mahmoud, Jacques, and I hung out there a lot. We liked to sit on the patio and play cards early in the evening. It was a good place to catch the action.

They were all there, all right. Jacques was the token Christian in our crowd. He liked to tell people that he was three-quarters European. Jacques was strictly heterosexual and smug about it. Nobody liked him much. Mahmoud was a sexchange, formerly a slim-hipped, doe-eyed dancing girl in the clubs on the Street. Now he was short, broad, and mean, like one of those evil *djinn* you had to sneak past to rescue the enchanted princess. I heard that he was running the organized prostitution in the Budayeen for Friedlander Bey these days. Saied the Half-Hajj glared at me over the rim of a glass of Johnny Walker, his usual drink. He was wearing his tough-guy moddy, and he was just looking for me to give him an excuse to break my bones.

"Where y'at?" I said.

"You're scum, Audran," said Jacques softly. "Filth."

"Thanks," I said, "but I can't stay long." I sat in the empty chair. Monsieur Gargotier came over to see if I was spending any money tonight. His expression was so carefully neutral, I could tell he hated my guts now too.

"Seen Chiri pass by here in the last few minutes?" I asked. Monsieur Gargotier cleared his throat. I ignored him and he went away.

"Want to shake her down some more?" asked Mahmoud. "Think maybe she walked out with some paper clips that belong to you? Leave her alone, Audran."

I'd had enough. I stood up, and Saied stood up across the table from me. He took two quick steps toward me, grabbed my cloak with one hand, and pulled his other fist straight back. Before he could slug me, I chopped quickly at his nose. A little blood came out of his nostril. He was startled, but then his mouth began to twist in pure rage. I grabbed the moddy on his corymbic implant and ripped it loose. I could see his eyes unfocus. He must have been completely disoriented for a moment. "Leave me the hell alone," I said, pushing him back down in his chair. "All of you." I tossed the moddy into the Half-Hajj's lap.

I headed back down the Street, seething. I didn't know what to do next. Chiri's club—my club, now—was packed with people and I couldn't count on Indihar to keep order. I decided to go back there and try to sort things out. Before I'd walked very far, Saied came up behind me and put his hand on my shoulder. "You're making yourself real unpopular, Maghrebi," he said.

"It's not all my doing."

He shook his head. "You're letting it happen. You're responsible."

"Thanks," I said. I kept walking.

He took my right hand and slapped his badass moddy into it. "You take this," he said. "I think you're gonna need it."

I frowned. "The kind of problems I got call for a clear head, Saied. I got all these moral questions to think about. Not just Chiri and her club. Other things."

The Half-Hajj grunted. "Never understand you,

Marîd," he said. "You sound like a tired old relic. You're as bad as Jacques. If you just choose your moddies carefully, you never have to worry about moral questions. God knows I never do."

That's all I needed to hear. "See you around, Saied," I said.

"Yeah, you right." He turned and headed back to the Fée Blanche.

I went on to Chiri's where I shooed everybody out, closed up the place, and drove back to Friedlander Bey's. I climbed the stairs wearily to my apartment, glad that the long, surprise-filled day was finally over. As I was getting ready for bed, Kmuzu appeared quietly in the doorway. "You shouldn't deceive me, *yaa Sidi.*"

"Your feelings hurt, Kmuzu?"

"I am here to help you. I'm sorry you refused my protection. A time may come when you will be glad to call on me."

"That's quite possibly true," I said, "but in the meantime, how about leaving me alone?"

He shrugged. "Someone is waiting to see you, *yaa Sidi.*"

I blinked at him. "Who?"

"A woman."

I didn't have the energy to deal with Umm Saad now. Then again, it might be Chiri—

"Shall I show her in?" asked Kmuzu.

"Yeah, what the hell." I was still dressed, but I was getting very tired. I promised myself that this was going to be a very short conversation.

"Marîd?"

I looked around. Framed in the door, wearing a ragged brown cloth coat, holding a battered plastic suitcase, was Angel Monroe. Mom.

"Thought I'd come spend a few days with you in the city," she said. She grinned drunkenly. "Hey, ain't you glad to see me?"

When my admirable add-on woke me on Monday morning, I lay in bed for a few moments, thinking. I was willing to admit that maybe I'd made a few mistakes the night before. I wasn't sure how I might have repaired the situation with Chiri, but I should have tried. I owed that much to her and our friendship. I wasn't happy about seeing my mother at the door later, either. I'd solved that problem by digging out fifty kiam and packing her off into the night. I sent Kmuzu with her to find a hotel room. At breakfast, Friedlander Bey offered me some constructive criticism on that decision.

He was furious. There was a husky, hoarse quality to his voice that let me know he was trying like hell not to shout at me. He put his hands on my shoulders, and I could feel him tremble with emotion. His breath was perfumed with mint as he quoted the noble Qur'ân. " 'If one of your parents or both of them attain old age with thee, say not fie unto them nor repulse them, but speak unto them a gracious word. And lower unto them the wing of submission through mercy, and say: My Lord! Have mercy on them both as they did care for me when I was little.' "

I felt shaken. Being inundated by Friedlander Bey's wrath was kind of like practicing for The Day of Judgment. He'd think that comparison was sacrilegious, of course, but he's never been the target of his own fury.

I couldn't keep from stammering. "You mean Angel Monroe." Jeez, that was a lame thing to say, but Papa'd surprised me with this tirade. I still wasn't thinking clearly.

"I'm talking about your mother," he said. "She came to you in need, and you turned her away from your door."

"I provided for her the best way I knew how." I

57

wondered how Papa had heard about the incident in the first place.

"You do not cast your mother out to abide with strangers! Now you must seek the forgiveness of Allah."

That made me feel a little better. This was one of those times when he said "Allah" but he meant "Friedlander Bey." I had sinned against his personal code; but if I could find the right things to say and do, it would be all right again. "O Shaykh," I said slowly, choosing my words carefully, "I know how you feel about women in your house. I hesitated to invite her to stay the night under your roof, and it was too late to consult with you. I balanced my mother's need against your custom, and I did what I thought best." Well, hell, that was almost true.

He glared at me, but I could see that he'd lost the edge of his anger. "Your action was a worse affront to me than having your mother as a guest in my home," he said.

"I understand, O Shaykh, and I beg you to forgive me. I did not mean to offend you or disregard the teaching of the Prophet."

"May the blessing of Allah be upon him and peace," Papa murmured automatically. He shook his head ruefully, but with each passing second his grim expression lightened. "You are still young, my son. This is not the last error of judgment you will make. If you are to become a righteous man and a compassionate leader, you must learn from my example. When you are in doubt, never be afraid to seek my counsel, whatever the time or place."

"Yes, O Shaykh," I said quietly. The storm had passed.

"Now you must find your mother, return her here, and make her welcome in a suitable apartment. We have many unused rooms, and this house is yours as well as mine."

I could tell by his tone that this conversation was over, and I was pretty damn glad. It had been like crossing between the minarets of the Shimaal Mosque on a tightrope. "You are the father of kindness, O Shaykh," I said.

"Go in safety, my nephew."

I went back up to my suite, my breakfast forgotten. Kmuzu, as usual, went with me. "Say," I said, as if the thought had just occurred to me, *"you* didn't happen to let Friedlander Bey know about last night, did you?"

"Yaa Sidi," he said with a blank expression, "it is the

will of the master of the house that I tell him of these things."

I chewed my lip thoughtfully. Talking to Kmuzu was like addressing a mythical oracle: I had to be sure to phrase my questions with absolute precision, or I'd get nonsense for an answer. I began simply. "Kmuzu, you are my slave, aren't you?"

"Yes," he said.

"You obey me?"

"I obey you and the master of the house, *yaa Sidi.*"

"Not necessarily in that order, though."

"Not necessarily," he admitted.

"Well, I'm gonna give you a plain, unambiguous command. You won't have to clear it with Papa because he suggested it to me in the first place. I want you to find a vacant apartment somewhere in the house, preferably far away from this one, and install my mother comfortably. I want you to spend the entire day seeing to her needs. When I get home from work, I'll need to talk to her about her plans for the future, so that means she gets no drugs and no alcohol."

Kmuzu nodded. "She could not get those things in this house, *yaa Sidi.*"

I'd had no problem smuggling my pharmaceuticals in, and I was sure Angel Monroe had her own emergency supply hidden somewhere too. "Help her unpack her things," I said, "and take the opportunity to make sure she's checked all her intoxicants at the door."

Kmuzu gave me a thoughtful look. "You hold her to a stricter standard than you observe yourself," he said quietly.

"Yeah, maybe," I said, annoyed. "Anyway, it's not your place to mention it."

"Forgive me, *yaa Sidi.*"

"Forget it. I'll drive myself to work today."

Kmuzu didn't like that, either. "If you take the car," he said, "how can I bring your mother from the hotel?"

I smiled slowly. "Sedan chair, oxcart, hired camel caravan, I don't care. You're the slave, you figure it out. See you tonight." On my desk was yet another thick envelope stuffed with paper bills. One of Friedlander Bey's little helpers had let himself into my apartment while I'd been downstairs. I took the envelope and my briefcase and left before Kmuzu could come up with another objection.

My briefcase still held the cell-memory file on Abu Adil. I was supposed to have read through it last night, but I never got around to it. Hajjar and Shaknahyi were probably going to be griped, but I didn't care. What could they do, fire me?

I drove first to the Budayeen, leaving my car on the boulevard and walking from there to Laila's modshop on Fourth Street. Laila's was small, but it had character, crammed between a dark, grim gambling den and a noisy bar that catered to teenage sexchanges. The moddies and daddies in Laila's bins were covered with dust and fine grit, and generations of small insects had met their Maker among her wares. It wasn't pretty, but what you got from her most of the time was good old honest value. The rest of the time you got damaged, worthless, even dangerous merchandise. You always felt a little rush of adrenalin before you chipped one of Laila's ancient and shopworn moddies directly into your brain.

She was always—*always*—chipped in, and she never stopped whining. She whined hello, she whined goodbye, she whined in pleasure and in pain. When she prayed, she whined to Allah. She had dry black skin as wrinkled as a raisin, and straggly white hair. Laila was not someone I liked to spend a lot of time with. She was wearing a moddy this morning, of course, but I couldn't tell yet which one. Sometimes she was a famous Eur-Am film or holo star, or a character from a forgotten novel, or Honey Pílar herself. Whoever she was, she'd yammer. That was all I could count on.

"How you doing, Laila?" I said. There was the acrid bite of ammonia in her shop that morning. She was squirting some ugly pink liquid from a plastic bottle up into the corners of the room. Don't ask me why.

She glanced at me and gave me a slow, rapturous smile. It was the look you get only from complete sexual satisfaction or from a large dose of Sonneine. "Marîd," she said serenely. She still whined, but now it was a serene whine.

"Got to go out on patrol today, and I thought you might have—"

"Marîd, a young girl came to me this morning and

said, 'Mother, the eyes of the narcissus are open, and the cheeks of the roses are red with blushing! Why don't you come outside and see how beautifully Nature has adorned the world!' "

"Laila, if you'll just give me a minute—"

"And I said to her, 'Daughter, that which delights you will fade in an hour, and what profit will you then have in it? Instead, come inside and find with me the far greater beauty of Allah, who created the spring.' " Laila finished her little homily and looked at me expectantly, as if she were waiting for me either to applaud or collapse from enlightenment.

I'd forgotten religious ecstasy. Sex, drugs, and religious ecstasy. Those were the big sellers in Laila's shop, and she tested them all out personally. You had her personal Seal of Approval on every moddy.

"Can I talk now? Laila?"

She stared at me, swaying unsteadily. Slowly she reached one scrawny arm up and popped the moddy out. She blinked a couple of times, and her gentle smile disappeared. "Get you something, Marîd?" she said in her shrill voice.

Laila had been around so long, there was a rumor that as a child she'd watched the imams lay the foundation of the Budayeen's walls. But she knew her moddies. She knew more about old, out-of-print moddies than anyone else I've ever met. I think Laila must have had one of the world's first experimental implants, because her brain had never worked quite right afterward. And the way she still abused the technology, she should have burnt out her last gray cells years ago. She'd withstood cerebral torture that would have turned anyone else into a drooling zombie. Laila probably had a tough protective callus on her brain that prevented anything from penetrating. Anything at all.

I started over from the beginning. "I'm going out on patrol today, and I was wondering if you had a basic cop moddy."

"Sure, I got everything." She hobbled to a bin near the back of the store and dug around in it for a moment. The bin was marked "Prussia/Poland/Breulandy." That didn't have anything to do with which moddies were actually in there; Laila'd bought the battered dividers and

scuffed labels from some other kind of shop that was going
out of business.

She straightened up after a few seconds, holding two
shrinkwrapped moddies in her hand. "This is what you
want," she said.

One was the pale blue Complete Guardian moddy I'd
seen other rookie cops wearing. It was a good, basic piece
of procedural programming that covered almost every
conceivable situation. I figured that between the Half-
Hajj's mean-mother moddy and the Guardian, I was covered. "What's this other one?" I asked.

"A gift to you at half price. Dark Lightning. Only this
version's called Wise Counselor. It's what I was wearing
when you came in."

I found that interesting. Dark Lightning was a Nipponese idea that had been very popular fifty or sixty years
ago. You sat down in a comfortable padded chair, and
Dark Lightning put you instantly into a receptive trance.
Then it presented you with a lucid, therapeutic dream.
Depending on Dark Lightning's analysis of your current
emotional state, it could be a warning, some advice, or a
mystical puzzle for your conscious mind to work on.

The high price of the contraption kept it a curiosity
among the wealthy. Its Far Eastern fictions—Dark Lightning usually cast you as a contemptuous Nipponese emperor in need of wisdom, or an aged Zen monk begging
sublimely in the snow—limited its appeal still further.
Lately, however, the Dark Lightning idea had been re-
vived by the growth of the personality module market.
And now apparently there was an Arabic version, called
Wise Counselor.

I bought both moddies, thinking that I wasn't in a
position to turn down any kind of help, friend or fantasy.
For someone who once hated the idea of having his skull
amped, I was sure building up a good collection of other
people's psyches.

Laila had chipped in Wise Counselor again. She gave
me that tranquil smile. It was toothless, of course, and it
made me shiver. "Go in safety," she said in her nasal wail.

"Peace be upon you." I hurried out of her shop,
walked back down the Street, and passed through the
gate to where the car was parked. It wasn't far from there
to the station house. Back at my desk on the third floor, I

opened my briefcase. I put my two purchases, the Complete Guardian and Wise Counselor, in the rack with the others. I grabbed the green cobalt-alloy plate and slotted it into the data deck, but then I hesitated. I really didn't feel like reading about Abu Adil yet. Instead I took Wise Counselor, unwrapped it, then reached up and chipped it in.

After a moment of dizziness, Audran saw that he was reclining on a couch, drinking a glass of lemon sherbet. Facing him on another couch was a handsome man of middle years. With a shock, he recognized the man as the Apostle of God. Quickly, Audran popped the moddy out.

I sat there at my desk, holding Wise Counselor and trembling. It wasn't what I'd expected at all. I found the experience deeply disturbing. The quality of the vision was absolutely realistic—it wasn't like a dream or a hallucination. It didn't feel as if I'd only imagined it; it felt as if I'd truly been in the same room with Prophet Muhammad, blessings and peace be on him.

It should be clear that I'm not a terribly religious person. I've studied the faith and I have tremendous respect for its precepts and traditions, but I guess I just don't find it convenient to practice them. That probably damns my soul for eternity, and I'll have plenty of time in Hell to regret my laziness. Even so, I was shocked by the pure arrogance of the moddy's manufacturer, to presume to depict the Prophet in such a way. Even illustrations in religious texts are considered idolatrous; what would a court of Islamic law make of the experience I'd just had?

Another reason I was shaken, I think, was because in the brief moment before I'd popped the moddy, I'd gotten the distinct impression that the Prophet had something intensely meaningful to tell me.

I started to toss the moddy back into my briefcase, when I had a flash of insight: The manufacturer hadn't depicted the Prophet, after all. The visions of Wise Counselor or Dark Lightning weren't preprogrammed vignettes written by some cynical software scribbler. The moddy was psychoactive. It evaluated my own mental and emotional states, and enabled *me* to create the illusion.

In that sense, I decided, it wasn't a profane mockery of the religious experience. It was only a means of accessing my own hidden feelings. I realized I'd just made a world-class rationalization, but it made me feel a lot better. I chipped the moddy in again.

After a moment of dizziness, Audran saw that he was reclining on a couch, drinking a glass of lemon sherbet. Facing him on another couch was a handsome man of middle years. With a shock, he recognized the man as the Apostle of God.

"As-salaam alaykum," *said the Prophet.*

"Wa alaykum as-salaam, yaa Hazrat," *replied Audran. He thought it was odd that he felt so comfortable in the Messenger's presence.*

"You know," *said the Prophet,* "there is a source of joy that leads you to forget death, that guides you to an accord with the will of Allah."

"I don't know exactly what you mean," *Audran said.*

Prophet Muhammad smiled. "You have heard that in my life there were many troubles, many dangers."

"Men repeatedly conspired to kill you because of your teachings, O Apostle of Allah. You fought many battles."

"Yes. But do you know the greatest danger I ever faced?"

Audran thought for a moment, perplexed. "You lost your father before you were born."

"Even as you lost yours," *said the Prophet.*

"You lost your mother as a child."

"Even as you were without a mother."

"You went into the world with no inheritance."

The Prophet nodded. "A condition forced upon you, as well. No, none of those things were the worst, nor were the efforts of my enemies to starve me, to crush me with boulders, to burn me in my tent, or to poison my food."

"Then, yaa Hazrat," *asked Audran,* "what was the greatest danger?"

"Early in my season of preaching, the Meccans would not listen to my word. I turned to the Sardar of Tayef and asked his permission to preach there. The Sardar gave permission, but I did not know that secretly he plotted to have me attacked by his hired villains. I was badly hurt, and I fell unconscious to the ground. A friend carried me* *out of Tayef and lay me beneath a shady tree. Then he went into the village again to beg for water, but no one in Tayef would give him any."*

"You were in danger of dying?"

Prophet Muhammad raised a hand. *"Perhaps, but is a man not always in danger of dying? When I was again conscious, I lifted my face to Heaven and prayed, 'O Merciful, You have instructed me to carry Your message to the people, but they will not listen to me. Perhaps it is my imperfection that prevents them from receiving Your blessing. O Lord, give me the courage to try again!'*

"Then I noticed that Gabriel the Archangel lay upon the sky over Tayef, waiting for my gesture to turn the village into a blasted wasteland. I cried out in horror: 'No, that is not the way! Allah has chosen me among men to be a blessing to Mankind, and I do not seek to chastise them. Let them live. If they do not accept my message, then perhaps their sons or their sons' sons will.'

"That awful moment of power, when with a lifted finger I might have destroyed all of Tayef and the people who lived there, that was the greatest danger of my life."

Audran was humbled. *"Allah is indeed Most Great,"* he said. He reached up and popped the moddy out.

Yipe. Wise Counselor had sifted through my subskull-ular impulses, then tailored a vision that both interpreted my current turmoil and suggested solutions. But what was Wise Counselor trying to tell me? I was just too dull and literal-minded to understand what it all meant. I thought it might be advising me to go up to Friedlander Bey and say, "I've got the power to destroy you, but I'm staying my hand out of charity." Then Papa would be overcome with guilt, and free me of all obligations to him.

Then I realized that it couldn't be that simple. In the first place, I didn't have any such power to destroy him. Friedlander Bey was protected from lesser creatures like me by *baraka*, the almost magical presence possessed by certain great men. It would take a better person than I to lift a finger against him, even to sneak in and pour poison in his ear while he slept.

Okay, that meant I'd misunderstood the lesson, but it wasn't something I was going to worry about. The next time I met an imam or a saint on the street, I'd have to ask him to explain the vision to me. In the meantime I had more important things to do. I put the moddy back in my briefcase.

Then I loaded the file on Abu Adil and spent about ten minutes glancing through it. It was every bit as boring as I was afraid it would be. Abu Adil had been brought to the city at an early age, more than a century and a half ago. His parents had wandered for many months after the disaster of the Saturday War. As a boy, Abu Adil helped his father, who sold lemonade and sherbets in the Souk of the Tanners. He played in the narrow, twisting alleys of the *medînah,* the old part of town. When his father died, Abu Adil became a beggar to support himself and his mother. Somehow, through strength of will and inner resources, he rejected his poverty and miserable station and became a man of respect and influence in the *medînah.* The report gave no details of this remarkable transformation, but if Abu Adil was a serious rival to Friedlander Bey, I had no trouble believing it had happened. He still lived in a house at the western edge of the city, not far from the Sunset Gate. By all reports it was a mansion as grand as Papa's, surrounded by ghastly slums. Abu Adil had an army of friends and associates in the hovels of the *medînah,* just as Friedlander Bey had his own in the Budayeen.

That was about as much as I'd learned when Officer Shaknahyi ducked his head into my cubicle. "Time to roll," he said.

It didn't bother me in the least to tell my data deck to quit. I wondered why Lieutenant Hajjar was so worked up about Reda Abu Adil. I hadn't run across anything in the file that suggested he was anything but another Friedlander Bey: just a rich, powerful man whose business took on a gray, even black character now and then. If he was like Papa—and the evidence I'd seen indicated that's just what he was—he had little interest in disturbing innocent people. Friedlander Bey was no criminal mastermind, and I doubted that Abu Adil was, either. You could rouse men like him only by trespassing on their territory or by threatening their friends and family.

I followed Shaknahyi downstairs to the garage. "That's mine," he said, pointing to a patrol car coming in from the previous shift. He greeted the two tired-looking cops who got out, then slid behind the steering wheel. "Well?" he said, looking up at me.

I wasn't in a hurry to start this. In the first place, I'd be stuck in the narrow confines of the copcar with Shaknahyi for the duration of the shift, and that prospect didn't excite me at all. Second, I'd really rather sit upstairs and read boring files in perfect safety than follow this battle-hardened veteran out into the mean streets. Finally, though, I climbed into the front seat. Sometimes there's only so much stalling you can do.

"What you carrying?" he said, looking straight out the windshield while he drove. He had a big wad of gum crammed into his right cheek.

"You mean this?" I held up the Complete Guardian moddy, which I hadn't chipped in yet.

He glanced at me and muttered something under his breath. "I'm talking about what you're gonna use to save me from the bad guys," he said. Then he looked my way again.

Under my sport coat I was wearing my seizure gun. I took it out of the holster and showed him. "Got this last year from Lieutenant Okking," I said.

Shaknahyi chewed his gum for a few seconds. "The lieutenant was always all right to me," he said. His eyes slid sideways again.

"Yeah, well," I said. I couldn't think of anything terribly meaningful to add. I'd been responsible for Okking's death, and I knew that Shaknahyi knew it. That was something else I'd have to overcome if we were going to accomplish anything together. There was silence in the car for a little while after that.

"Look, that weapon of yours ain't much good except for maybe stunning mice and birds up close. Take a look on the floor."

I reached under my seat and pulled out a small arsenal. There was a large seizure cannon, a static pistol, and a needle gun that looked like its flechettes could strip the meat from the bones of an adult rhinoceros. "What do you suggest?" I asked.

"How do you feel about splashing blood all over everything?"

"Had enough of that last year," I said.

"Then forget the needle gun, though it's a dandy side

arm. It alternates three sedative barbs, three iced with nerve toxin, and three explosive darts. The seizure cannon may be too hefty for you too. It's got four times the power of your little sizzlegun. It'll stop anybody you aim at up to a quarter of a mile away, but it'll kill a mark inside a hundred yards. Maybe you ought to go with the static gun."

I stuffed the needle gun and the seizure cannon back under the seat and looked at the static gun. "What kind of damage will this do?"

Shaknahyi shrugged. "Hit 'em in the head with that two or three times and you've crippled 'em for life. The head's a small target, though. Get 'em in the chest and it's Heart Attack City. Anywhere else, they can't control their muscles. They're helpless for half an hour. That's what you want."

I nodded and tucked the static gun into my coat pocket. "You don't think I'll—" My telephone began warbling, and I unclipped it from my belt. I figured it was one of my other problems checking in. "Hello?" I said.

"Marîd? This is Indihar."

It seemed like they just weren't making good news anymore. I closed my eyes. "Yeah, how you doing? What's up?"

"You know what *time* it is? You own a club now, Maghrebi. You got a responsibility to the girls on the day shift. You want to get down here and open up?"

I hadn't given the club a goddamn thought. It was something I really didn't want to worry about, but Indihar was right about my responsibility. "I'll get there as soon as I can. Everybody show up today?"

"I'm here, Pualani's here, Janelle quit, I don't know where Kandy is, and Yasmin's here looking for a job."

Now Yasmin too. Jeez. "See you in a few minutes."

"*Inshallah*, Marîd."

"Yeah." I clipped the phone back on my belt.

"Where you got to go now? We don't have time for no personal errands."

I tried to explain. "Friedlander Bey thought he was doing me this big favor, and he bought me my own club in the Budayeen. I don't know a damn thing about running a club. Forgot all about it until now. I got to pass by there and open the place."

Shaknahyi laughed. "Beware of two-hundred-year-old kingpins bearing gifts," he said. "Where's this club?"

"On the Street," I said. "Chiriga's place. You know which one I mean?"

He turned and studied me for a moment without saying anything. Then he said, "Yeah, I know which one you mean." He swung the patrol car around and headed for the Budayeen.

You might think it'd be a kick to zip through the eastern gate in an official car, and drive up the Street when other vehicular traffic is forbidden. My reaction was just the opposite. I scrunched myself down in the seat, hoping no one I knew would see me. I'd hated cops all my life and now I was one; already my former friends were giving me the same treatment I used to give Hajjar and the other police around the Budayeen. I was grateful that Shaknahyi had the sense not to turn on the siren.

Shaknahyi dropped the car right in front of Chiriga's club, and I saw Indihar standing on the sidewalk with Pualani and Yasmin. I was unhappy to see that Yasmin had cut her long, beautiful black hair, which I'd always loved. Maybe since we'd broken up, she felt she had to change things. I took a deep breath, opened the door, and got out. "How y'all doing?" I said.

Indihar glowered at me. "We lost about an hour's tips already," she said.

"You gonna run this club or not, Marîd?" said Pualani. "I can go work by Jo-Mama's real easy."

"Frenchy'd take me back in a Marrakesh minute," said Yasmin. Her expression was cold and distant. Riding around in copcars wasn't improving my status with her at all.

"Don't worry," I said, "I just had a lot on my mind this morning. Indihar, could I hire you to manage the place for me? You know more about running the club than I do."

She stared at me for a few seconds. "Only if you give me a regular schedule," she said. "I don't want to have to come in early after staying late on night shift. Chiri made us do that all the time."

"All right, fine. You got any other ideas, let me know."

"You're gonna have to pay me what other managers make too. And I'm only gonna get up and dance if I feel like it."

I frowned, but she had me in a corner. "That's okay too. Now, who do you suggest to manage at night?"

Indihar shrugged. "I don't trust none of those sluts. Talk to Chiri. Hire her back."

"Hire *Chiri?* To work in her own club?"

"It's not her own club anymore," Yasmin pointed out.

"Yeah, right," I said. "You think she'd do it?"

Indihar laughed. "She'll make you pay her three times what any other manager on the Street gets. She'll give you hell about it too, and she'll steal you blind out of the register if you give her half a chance. But she'll still be worth it. Nobody can make money like Chiri. Without her, you'll be renting this property to some rug merchant inside of six months."

"You hurt her feelings real bad, Marîd," said Pualani.

"I know, but it wasn't my fault. Friedlander Bey organized the whole thing without talking to me about it first. He just dropped the club on me as a surprise."

"Chiri doesn't know that," said Yasmin.

I heard a car door slam behind me. I turned and saw Shaknahyi walking toward me, a big grin on his face. All I needed now was to have him join in. He was really enjoying this.

Indihar and the others hated my guts for turning cop, and the cops felt the same way because to them I was still a hustler. The Arabs say, "You take off your clothes, you get cold." That's advice against cutting yourself off from your support group. It doesn't offer any help if your friends show up in a mob and strip you naked against your will.

Shaknahyi didn't say a word to me. He went up to Indihar, bent, and whispered something in her ear. Well, a lot of the girls on the Street have this fascination with cops. I never understood it, myself. And some of the cops don't mind taking advantage of the situation. It just surprised me to find out that Indihar was one of those girls, and that Shaknahyi was one of those cops.

It didn't occur to me to add this to the list of recent unnatural coincidences: My new partner just happened to have a thing going with the new manager of the club Friedlander Bey had just given me.

"Got everything settled here, Audran?" Shaknahyi asked.

"Yeah," I said. "I got to talk to Chiriga sometime today."

"Indihar's right," said Yasmin. "Chiri's gonna give you a hard time."

I nodded. "She's entitled, I guess, but I'm still not looking forward to it."

"Let's mount up," said Shaknahyi.

"If I got time later," I said, "I'll drop in and see how y'all are doing."

"We'll be fine," said Pualani. "We know how to do *our* jobs. You just watch your ass around Chiri."

"Protect your middle," said Indihar. "If you know what I mean."

I waved and headed back to the patrol car. Shaknahyi gave Indihar a little kiss on the cheek, then followed me. He got behind the wheel. "Ready to work now?" he asked. We were still sitting at the curb.

"How long you known Indihar? I never seen you come into Chiri's club."

He gave me this wide-eyed innocent look. "I been knowing her for a long time," he said.

"Right," I said. I just left it there. It didn't sound like he wanted to talk about her.

A shrill alarm went off, and the synthesized voice of the patrol car's comp deck crackled. "Badge number 374, respond immediately to bomb threat and hostage situation, Café de la Fée Blanche, Ninth Street North."

"Gargotier's place," said Shaknahyi. "We'll take care of it." The comp deck fell silent.

And Hajjar had promised me I wouldn't have to worry about anything like this. *"Bismillah ar-Rahman ar-Raheem,"* I murmured. In the name of Allah, the Compassionate, the Merciful.

This time as we rode up the Street, Shaknahyi let the siren scream.

There was a crowd gathered outside the low railing of the Café de la Fée Blanche's patio. An old man sat at one of the white-painted iron tables, drinking something from a plastic tumbler. He seemed oblivious to the crisis that was occurring inside the bar. "Get him out of here," Shaknahyi growled at me. "Get these other people out of here too. I don't know what's happening in there, but we got to treat it like the guy has a real bomb. And when you got everybody moved back, go sit in the car."

"But—"

"I don't want to have to worry about you too." He ran around the corner of the café to the north, heading for the café's rear entrance.

I hesitated. I knew backup units would be getting here soon, and I decided to let them handle the crowd control. At the moment, there were more important things to worry about. I still had Complete Guardian, and I tore open the shrinkwrap with my teeth. Then I chipped the moddy in.

Audran was sitting at a table in the dimly lighted San Saberio salon in Florence, listening to a group of musicians playing a demure Schubert quartet. Across from him sat a beautiful blond woman named Costanzia. She raised a cup to her lips, and her china-blue eyes looked at him over the rim. She was wearing a subtle, fascinating fragrance that made Audran think of romantic evenings and soft-spoken promises.

"This must be the best coffee in Tuscany," she murmured. Her voice was sweet and gentle. She gave him a warm smile.

"We didn't come here to drink coffee, my darling," he said. "We came here to see the season's new styles."

She waved a hand. "There is time enough for that. For now, let's just relax."

Audran smiled fondly at her and picked up his delicate cup. The coffee was the beautiful color of polished mahogany, and the wisps of steam that rose from it carried a heavenly, enticing aroma. The first taste overwhelmed Audran with its richness. As the coffee, hot and wonderfully delicious, went down his throat, he realized that Costanzia had been perfectly correct. He had never before been so satisfied by a cup of coffee.

"I'll always remember this coffee," he said.

"Let's come back here again next year, darling," said Costanzia.

Audran laughed indulgently. "For San Saberio's new fashions?"

Costanzia lifted her cup and smiled. "For the coffee," she said.

After the advertisement, there was a blackout during which Audran couldn't see a thing. He wondered briefly who Costanzia was, but he put her out of his mind. Just as he began to panic, his vision cleared. He felt a ripple of dizziness, and then it was as if he'd awakened from a dream. He was rational and cool and he had a job to do. He had become the Complete Guardian.

He couldn't see or hear anything that was happening inside. He assumed that Shaknahyi was making his way quietly through the café's back room. It was up to Audran to give his partner as much support as possible. He jumped the iron railing into the patio.

The old man at the table looked up at him. "No doubt you are eager to read my manuscripts," he said.

Audran recognized the man as Ernst Weinraub, an expatriate from some Central European country. Weinraub fancied himself a writer, but Audran had never seen him finish anything but quantities of anisette or bourbon whiskey. "Sir," he said, "you're in danger here. I'm going to have to ask you to go out into the street. For your own safety, please move away from the café."

"It's not even midnight yet," Weinraub complained. "Just let me finish my drink."

Audran didn't have time to humor the old drunk. He

left the patio and walked decisively into the interior of the bar.

The scene inside didn't look very threatening. Monsieur Gargotier was standing behind the bar, beneath the huge, cracked mirror. His daughter, Maddie, was sitting at a table near the back wall. A young man sat at a table against the west wall, under Gargotier's collection of faded prints of the Mars colony. The young man's hands rested on a small box. His head swung to look at Audran. "Get the fuck out," he shouted, "or this whole place goes up in a big bright bang!"

"I'm sure he means it, monsieur," said Gargotier. He sounded terrified.

"Bet your ass I mean it!" said the young man.

Being a police officer meant sizing up dangerous situations and being able to make quick, sure judgments. Complete Guardian suggested that in dealing with a mentally disturbed individual, Audran should try to find out why he was upset and then try to calm him. Complete Guardian recommended that Audran not make fun of the individual, show anger, or dare him to carry out his threat. Audran raised his hands and spoke calmly. "I'm not going to threaten you," Audran said.

The young man just laughed. He had dirty long hair and a patchy growth of beard, and he was wearing a faded pair of blue jeans and a plaid cotton shirt with its sleeves torn off. He looked a little like Audran had, before Friedlander Bey had raised his standard of living.

"Mind if I sit and talk with you?" asked Audran.

"I can set this off any time I want," said the young man. "You got the guts, sit down. But keep your hands flat on the table."

"Sure." Audran pulled out a chair and sat down. He had his back to the barkeep, but out of the corner of his eye he could see Maddie Gargotier. She was quietly weeping.

"You ain't gonna talk me out of this," said the young man.

Audran shrugged. "I just want to find out what this is all about. What's your name?"

"The hell's that got to do with anything?"

"My name is Marîd. I was born in Mauretania."

"You can call me Al-Muntaqim." The kid with the

bomb had appropriated one of the Ninety-Nine Beautiful Names of God. It meant "The Avenger."

"You always lived in the city?" Audran asked him.

"Hell no. Misr."

"That's the local name for Cairo, isn't it?" asked Audran.

Al-Muntaqim jumped to his feet, furious. He jabbed a finger toward Gargotier behind the bar and screamed, "See? See what I mean? That's just what I'm talkin' about! Well, I'm gonna stop it once and for all!" He grabbed the box and ripped open the lid.

Audran felt a horrible pain all through his body. It was as if all his joints had been yanked and twisted until his bones pulled apart. Every muscle in his body felt torn, and the surface of his skin stung as if it had been sandpapered. The agony went on for a few seconds, and then Audran lost consciousness.

"You all right?"

No, I didn't feel all right. On the outside I felt red-hot and glowing, as if I'd been staked out under the desert sun for a couple of days. Inside, my muscles felt quivery. I had lots of uncontrollable little spasms in my arms, legs, trunk, and face. I had a splitting headache and there was a horrible, sour taste in my mouth. I was having a lot of trouble focusing my eyes, as if someone had spread thick translucent gunk over them.

I strained to make out who was talking to me. I could barely make out the voice because my ears were ringing so loud. It turned out to be Shaknahyi, and that indicated that I was still alive. For an awful moment after I came to, I thought I might be in Allah's green room or somewhere. Not that being alive was any big thrill just then. "What—" I croaked. My throat was so dry I could barely speak.

"Here." Shaknahyi handed a glass of cold water down to me. I realized that I was lying flat on my back on the floor, and Shaknahyi and Monsieur Gargotier were standing over me, frowning and shaking their heads.

I took the water and drank it gratefully. When I finished, I tried talking again. "What happened?" I said.

"You fucked up," Shaknahyi said.

"Right," I said.

A narrow smile creased Shaknahyi's face. He reached down and offered me a hand. "Get up off the floor."

I stood up wobbly and made my way to the nearest chair. "Gin and bingara," I said to Gargotier. "Put a hit of Rose's lime in it." The barkeep grimaced, but he turned away to get my drink. I took out my pillcase and dug out maybe eight or nine Sonneine.

"I heard about you and your drugs," said Shaknahyi.

"It's all true," I said. When Gargotier brought my drink, I swallowed the opiates. I couldn't wait for them to start fixing me up. Everything would be just fine in a couple of minutes.

"You could've gotten everybody killed, trying to talk that guy down," Shaknahyi said. I was feeling bad enough already, I didn't want to listen to his little lecture right then. He went ahead with it anyway. "What the hell were you trying to do? Establish rapport or something? We don't work that way when people's lives are in danger."

"Yeah?" I said. "What *do* you do?"

He spread his hands like the answer should have been perfectly obvious. "You get around where he can't see you, and you ice the motherfucker."

"Did you ice me before or after you iced Al-Muntaqim?"

"That what he was calling himself? Hell, Audran, you got to expect a little beam diffusion with these static pistols. I'm real sorry I had to drop you too, but there's no permanent damage, *inshallah.* He jumped up with that box, and I wasn't gonna wait around for you to give me a clear shot. I had to take what I could get."

"It's all right," I said. "Where's The Avenger now?"

"The meat wagon came while you were napping. Took him off to the lock ward at the hospital."

That made me a little angry. "The mad bomber gets shipped to a nice bed in the hospital, but I got to lie around on the filthy floor of this goddamn saloon?"

Shaknahyi shrugged. "He's in a lot worse shape than you are. You only got hit by the fuzzy edge of the charge. He took it full."

It sounded like Al-Muntaqim was going to feel pretty rotten for a while. Didn't bother me none.

"No percentage in debating morality with a loon," said Shaknahyi. "You go in looking for the first opportunity

o stabilize the sucker." He made a trigger-pulling motion
with his right index finger.

"That's not what Complete Guardian was telling
me," I said. "By the way, did you pop the moddy for me?
What did you do with it?"

"Yeah," said Shaknahyi, "here it is." He took the
moddy out of a shirt pocket and tossed it down on the floor
beside me. Then he raised his heavy black boot and
stamped the plastic module into jagged pieces. Brightly
colored fragments of the webwork circuitry skittered
across the floor. "Wear another one of those, I do the same
to your face and then I kick the remnants out of my patrol
car."

So much for Marîd Audran, Ideal Law Enforcement
Officer.

I stood up feeling a lot better, and followed Shaknahyi
out of the dimly lighted bar. Monsieur Gargotier and his
daughter, Maddie, went with us. The bartender tried to
thank us, but Shaknahyi just raised a hand and looked
modest. "No thanks are necessary for performing a duty,"
he said.

"Come in for free drinks anytime," Gargotier said
gratefully.

"Maybe we will." Shaknahyi turned to me. "Let's
ride," he said. We went out through the patio gate. Old
Weinraub was still sitting beneath his Cinzano umbrella,
apparently oblivious to everything that had gone on.

On the way back to the car I said, "It makes me feel
kind of good to be welcome somewhere again."

Shaknahyi looked at me. "Accepting free drinks is a
major infraction."

"I didn't know they *had* infractions in the
Budayeen," I said. Shaknahyi smiled. It seemed that
things had thawed a little between us.

Before I got into the car, a muezzin from some
mosque beyond the quarter chanted the afternoon call to
prayer. I watched Shaknahyi go into the patrol car's backseat and come out with a rolled prayer rug. He spread the
rug on the sidewalk and prayed for several minutes. For
some reason it made me feel very uncomfortable. When
he finished, he rolled the prayer rug again and put it back
in the car, giving me an odd look, a kind of silent reproach.

We both got into the patrol car, but neither of us said anything for a while.

Shaknahyi cruised back down the Street and out of the Budayeen. Curiously, I was no longer wary of being spotted in the copcar by any of my old friends. In the first place, the way they'd been treating me, I figured the hell with 'em. In the second place, I felt a little different now that I'd been fried in the line of duty. The experience at the Fée Blanche had changed my thinking. Now I appreciated the risks a cop has to take day after day.

Shaknahyi surprised me. "You want to stop somewhere for lunch?" he asked.

"Sounds good." I was still pretty weak and the sunnies had left me a little lightheaded, so I was glad to agree.

"There's a place near the station house we sometimes go to." He punched the siren and made some fast time through the traffic. About a block from the beanery, he turned off the horn and glided into an illegal parking place. "Police perks," he said, grinning at me. "There ain't many others."

When we got inside, I was pleasantly surprised. The cookshop was owned by a young Mauretanian named Meloul, and the food was pure Maghrebi. By bringing me here, Shaknahyi more than made up for the pain he'd caused me earlier. I looked at him, and suddenly he didn't seem like such a bad guy.

"Let's grab this table," he said, picking one far from the door and against a wall, where he could watch the other customers and keep an eye on what was happening outside too.

"Thanks," I said. "I don't get food from home very often."

"Meloul," he called, "I got one of your cousins here."

The proprietor came over, carrying a stainless steel pitcher and basin. Shaknahyi washed his hands carefully and dried them on a clean white towel. Then I washed my hands and dried them on a second towel. Meloul looked at me and smiled. He was about my age, but taller and darker. "I am Berber," he said. "You are Berber too, yes? You are from Oran?"

"I've got a little Berber blood in me," I said. "I was born in Sidi-bel-Abbès, but I grew up in Algiers."

He came toward me, and I stood up. We exchanged

kisses on the cheek. "I live all my life in Oran," he said. "Now I live in this fine city. Sit down, be comfortable, I bring good food to you and Jirji."

"The two of you got a lot in common," said Shaknahyi.

I nodded. "Listen, Officer Shaknahyi," I said, "I want to—"

"Call me Jirji. You slapped on that goddamn moddy and followed me into Gargotier's. It was stupid, but you had guts. You been initiated, sort of."

That made me feel good. "Yeah, well, Jirji, I want to ask you something. Would you say you were very religious?"

He frowned. "I perform the duties, but I'm not gonna go out on the street and kill infidel tourists if they don't convert to Islam."

"Okay, then maybe you could tell me what this dream means."

He laughed. "What kind of dream? You and Brigitte Stahlhelm in the Tunnel of Love?"

I shook my head. "No, nothing like that at all. I dreamed I met the Holy Prophet. He had something to tell me, but I couldn't understand it." I related the rest of the vision Wise Counselor had created for me.

Shaknahyi raised his eyebrows, but he said nothing for a few moments. He played with the ends of his mustache as he thought. "Seems to me," he said finally, "it's about simple virtues. You're supposed to remember humility, as Prophet Muhammad, blessings and peace be upon him, remembered it. Now's not the time for you to make great plans. Later maybe, Allah willing. That make any sense to you?"

I kind of shivered, because as soon as he said it, I knew he was right. It was a suggestion from my backbrain that I shouldn't worry about handling my mother, Umm Saad, and Abu Adil all by myself. I should take things slowly, one thing at a time. They would all come together eventually. "Thanks, Jirji," I said.

He shrugged. "No thanks are necessary."

"I bring you good food," said Meloul cheerfully, setting a platter between Shaknahyi and me. The mounded-up couscous was fragrant with cinnamon and saffron, and it made me realize just how hungry I was. In a well in the

middle of the ring of couscous, Meloul had piled bite-sized
pieces of chicken and onions browned in butter and fla-
vored with honey. He also brought a plate of bread and
cups of strong black coffee. I could hardly keep myself
from diving right in.

"It looks great, Meloul," said Shaknahyi.

"May it be pleasant to you." Meloul wiped his hands
on a clean towel, bowed to us, and left us to our meal.

"In the name of Allah, the Compassionate, the
Merciful," Shaknahyi murmured.

I offered the same brief grace, and then allowed myself to scoop up a chunk of chicken and some of the couscous. It tasted even better than it smelled.

When we'd finished, Shaknahyi called for our bill.
Meloul came to the table, still smiling. "No charge. My
countrymen eat for free. Policemen eat for free."

"That's kind of you, Meloul," I said, "but we're not
allowed to accept—"

Shaknahyi drank the last of his coffee and put down
his cup. "It's all right, Marîd," he said, "this is different.
Meloul, may your table last forever."

Meloul put his hand on Shaknahyi's shoulder. "May
God lengthen your life," he said. He hadn't turned a copper fiq on our patronage, but he looked pleased.

Shaknahyi and I left the cookshop well fed and comfortable. It seemed a shame to spoil the rest of the afternoon with police work.

An old woman sat begging on the sidewalk a few
yards from Meloul's. She was dressed in a long black coat
and black kerchief. Her sun-darkened face was deeply
scored with wrinkles, and one of her sunken eyes was the
color of milk. There was a large black tumor just in front of
her right ear. I went up to her. "Peace be upon you, O
Lady," I said.

"And upon you be peace, O Shaykh," she said. Her
voice was a gritty whisper.

I remembered that I still had the envelope of money
in my pocket. I took it out and opened it, then counted out
a hundred kiam. It hardly made a dent in my roll. "O
Lady," I said, "accept this gift with my respect."

She took the money, astonished by the number of
bills. Her mouth opened, then shut. Finally she said, "By
the life of my children, you are more generous than Haaj

tim, O Shaykh! May Allah open His ways to you." Haatim is the personification of hospitality among the nomad tribesmen.

She made me feel a little self-conscious. "We thank God every hour," I said quietly, and turned away.

Shaknahyi didn't say anything to me until we were sitting in the patrol car again. "Do that a lot?" he asked.

"Do what?"

"Drop a hundred kiam on strangers."

I shrugged. "Isn't alms-giving one of the Five Pillars?"

"Yeah, but you don't pay much attention to the other four. That's odd too, because for most people, parting with cash is the toughest duty."

In fact, I was wondering myself why I'd done it. Maybe because I was feeling uncomfortable about the way I'd been treating my mother. "I just felt sorry for that old woman," I said.

"Everybody in this part of the city does. They all take care of her. That was Safiyya the Lamb Lady. She's a crazy old woman. You never see her without a pet lamb. She takes it everywhere. She lets it drink from the fountain at the Shimaal Mosque."

"I didn't see any lamb."

He laughed. "No, her latest lamb got run over by a shish kebab cart a couple of weeks ago. Right now she has an imaginary lamb. It was standing there right beside her, but only Safiyya can see it."

"Uh yeah," I said. I'd given her enough to buy herself a couple of new lambs. My little bit to alleviate the suffering of the world.

We had to skirt the Budayeen. Although the Street runs in the right direction, it comes to a dead end at the entrance to a cemetery. I knew a lot of people in there—friends and acquaintances who'd died and been dumped in the cemetery, and the still breathing who were so desperately poor that they'd taken up residence in the tombs.

Shaknahyi passed to the south of the quarter, and we drove through a neighborhood that was entirely foreign to me. At first the houses were of moderate size and not too terribly rundown; but after a couple of miles, I noticed that everything around me was getting progressively shabbier. The flat-roofed white stucco homes gave way to

blocks of ugly tenements and then to burned-out, vacant
lots dotted with horrible little shacks made of scrap plywood and rusting sheets of corrugated iron.

We drove on, and I saw groups of idle men leaning
against walls or squatting on the bare earth sharing bowls
of liquor, probably *laqbi,* a wine made from the date
palm. Women screamed to each other from the windows.
The air was foul with the smells of wood smoke and human excrement. Children dressed in long tattered shirts
played among the garbage strewn in the gutters. Years
ago in Algiers I had been like these hungry urchins, and
maybe that's why the sight of them affected me so much.

Shaknahyi must have seen the expression on my face.
"There are worse parts of town than Hâmidiyya," he said.
"And a cop's got to be ready to go into any kind of place
and deal with any kind of person."

"I was just thinking," I said slowly. "This is Abu Adil's
territory. It doesn't look he does all that much for these
people, so why do they stay loyal to him?"

Shaknahyi answered me with another question.
"Why do you stay loyal to Friedlander Bey?"

One good reason was that Papa'd had the punishment center of my brain wired when the rest of the work
was done, and that he could stimulate it any time he
wanted. Instead, I said, "It's not a bad life. And I guess I'm
just afraid of him."

"Same goes for these poor *fellahîn.* They live in terror of Abu Adil, and he tosses just enough their way to
keep them from starving to death. I just wonder how
people like Friedlander Bey and Abu Adil get that kind of
power in the first place."

I watched the slums pass by beyond the windshield.
"How do you think Papa makes his money?" I asked.

Shaknahyi shrugged. "He's got a thousand cheap hus-
tlers out there, all turning over big chunks of their earn-
ings for the right to live in peace."

I shook my head. "That's only what you see going on
in the Budayeen. Probably seems like vice and corruption
are Friedlander Bey's main business in life. I've lived in
his house for months now, and I've learned better. The
money that comes from vice is just pocket change to Papa.
Counts for maybe five percent of his annual income. He's

got a much bigger concern, and Reda Abu Adil is in the same business. They sell order."

"They sell *what?*"

"Order. Continuity. Government."

"How?"

"Look, half the countries in the world have split up and recombined again until it's almost impossible to know who owns what and who lives where and who owes taxes to whom."

"Like what's happening right now in Anatolia," said Shaknahyi.

"Right," I said. "The people in Anatolia, when their ancestors lived there it was called Turkey. Before that it was the Ottoman Empire, and before that it was Anatolia again. Right now it looks like Anatolia is breaking up into Galatia, Lydia, Cappadocia, Nicaea, and Asian Byzantium. One democracy, one emirate, one people's republic, one fascist dictatorship, and one constitutional monarchy. There's got to be somebody who's staying on top of it all, keeping the records straight."

"Maybe, but it sounds like a tough job."

"Yeah, but whoever does it ends up the real ruler of the place. He'll have the real power, because all the little states will need his help to keep from collapsing."

"It makes a weird kind of sense. And you're telling me that's what Friedlander Bey's racket is?"

"It's a service," I said. "An important service. And there are lots of ways for him to exploit the situation."

"Yeah, you right," he said admiringly. We turned a corner, and there was a long, high wall made of dark brown bricks. This was Reda Abu Adil's estate. It looked like it was every bit as huge as Papa's. As we stopped at the guarded gate, the luxuriousness of the main house seemed even grander contrasted to the ghastly neighborhood that surrounded it.

Shaknahyi presented our credentials to the guard. "We're here to see Shaykh Reda," he said. The guard picked up a phone and spoke to someone. After a moment, he let us continue.

"A century or more ago," Shaknahyi said thoughtfully, "crime bosses had these big illicit schemes to make money. Sometimes they also operated small legal businesses for practical reasons, like laundering their money."

"Yeah? So?" I said.

"Look at it: You say Reda Abu Adil and Friedlander Bey are two of the most powerful men in the world, as 'consultants' to foreign states. That's entirely legitimate. Their criminal connections are much less important. They just provide livelihoods for the old men's dependents and associates. Things have gotten turned around ass-backwards."

"That's progress," I said. Shaknahyi just shook his head.

We got out of the patrol car, into the warm afternoon sunshine. The grounds in front of Abu Adil's house had been carefully landscaped. The fragrance of roses was in the air, and the strong, pleasant scent of lemons. There were cages of songbirds on either side of an ancient stone fountain, and the warbling music filled the afternoon with a languorous peace. We went up the ceramic-tiled path to the mansion's geometrically carved front door. A servant had already opened it and was waiting for us to explain our business.

"I'm Officer Shaknahyi and this is Marîd Audran. We've come to see Shaykh Reda."

The servant nodded but said nothing. We followed him into the house, and he closed the heavy wooden door behind us. Sunlight streamed in from latticed windows high over our heads. From far away I heard the sound of someone playing a piano. I could smell lamb roasting and coffee brewing. The squalor only a stone's throw away had been completely shut out. The house was a self-contained little world, and I'm sure that's just as Abu Adil intended it.

We were led directly into Abu Adil's presence. I couldn't even get in to see Friedlander Bey that quickly.

Reda Abu Adil was a large, plump old man. He was like Papa in that it was impossible to guess just how old he might be. I knew for a fact that he was at least a hundred twenty-five. It wouldn't surprise me to learn that he was just as old as Friedlander Bey. He was wearing a loose white robe and no jewelry. He had a carefully trimmed white beard and mustache and thick white hair, out of which poked a dove-gray moddy with two daddies snapped in. I was expert enough to notice that Abu Adil did not have a protruding plug, as I had; his hardware chipped into a corymbic socket.

Abu Adil reclined on a hospital bed that had been elevated so that he could see us comfortably as we spoke. He was covered by an expensive hand-embroidered blanket. His gnarled hands lay outside the cover, flat on either side of his body. His eyes were heavy-lidded, as if he were drugged or desperately sleepy. He grimaced and groaned frequently while we stood there. We waited for him to say something.

He did not. Instead, a younger man standing beside the hospital bed spoke up. "Shaykh Reda welcomes you to his home. My name is Umar Abdul-Qawy. You may address Shaykh Reda through me."

This Umar person was about fifty years old. He had bright, mistrustful eyes and a sour expression that looked like it never changed. He too looked well fed, and he was dressed in an impressive gold-colored robe and metallic blue caftan. He wore nothing on his head and, like his master, a moddy divided his thinning hair. I disliked him from the getgo.

It was clear to me that I was facing my opposite number. Umar Abdul-Qawy did for Abu Adil what I did for Friedlander Bey, although I'm sure he'd been at it longer and was more intimate with the inner workings of his master's empire. "If this is a bad time," I said, "we can come back again."

"This is a bad time," said Umar. "Shaykh Reda suffers the torments of terminal cancer. You see, then, that another time would not necessarily be better."

"We pray for his well-being," I said.

A tiny smile quirked the edge of Abu Adil's lips. *"Al-lah yisallimak,"* said Umar. "God bless you. Now, what has brought you to us this afternoon?"

This was inexcusably blunt. In the Muslim world, you don't inquire after a visitor's business. Custom further requires that the laws of hospitality be observed, if only minimally. I'd expected to be served coffee, if not offered a meal as well. I looked at Shaknahyi.

It didn't seem to bother him. "What dealings does Shaykh Reda have with Friedlander Bey?"

That seemed to startle Umar. "Why, none at all," he said, spreading his hands. Abu Adil gave a long, pain-filled moan and closed his eyes tightly. Umar didn't even turn in his direction.

"Then Shaykh Reda does not communicate at all with him?" Shaknahyi asked.

"Not at all. Friedlander Bey is a great and influential man, but his interests lie in a distant part of the city. The two shaykhs have never discussed anything of a business nature. Their concerns do not meet at any point."

"And so Friedlander Bey is no hindrance or obstacle to Shaykh Reda's plans?"

"Look at my master," said Umar. "What sort of plans do you think he has?" Indeed, Abu Adil looked entirely helpless in his agony. I wondered what had made Lieutenant Hajjar set us on this fool's errand.

"We received some information, and we had to check it out," said Shaknahyi. "We're sorry for the intrusion."

"That's quite all right. Kamal will see you to the door." Umar stared at us with a stony expression. Abu Adil, however, made an attempt to raise his hand in farewell or blessing, but it fell back limply to the blanket.

We followed the servant back to the front door. When we were alone again outside, Shaknahyi began to laugh. "That was some performance," he said.

"What performance? Did I miss something?"

"If you'd read the file all the way through, you'd know that Abu Adil doesn't have cancer. He's never had cancer."

"Then—"

Shaknahyi's mouth twisted in contempt. "You ever hear of Proxy Hell? It's a bunch of lunatics who wear bootleg, underground moddies turned out in somebody's back room. They're recordings taken from real people in horrible situations."

I was dismayed. "Is that what Abu Adil's doing? Wearing the personality module of a terminal cancer patient?"

Shaknahyi nodded as he opened the car door and got in. "He's chipped into vicarious pain and suffering. You can buy any kind of disease or condition you want on the black market. There are plenty of deranged masochists like him out there."

I joined him in the patrol car. "And I thought the girls and debs on the Street were misusing the moddies. This adds a whole new meaning to the word *perversion*."

Shaknahyi started up the car and drove around the fountain toward the gate. "They introduce some new technology and no matter how much good it does for most people, there's always a crazy son of a bitch who'll find something twisted to do with it."

I thought about that, and about my own bodmods, as we drove back to the station house through the wretched district that was home to Reda Abu Adil's faithful followers.

7

During the next week, I spent as much time in the patrol car as I did at my computer on the third floor of the station house. I felt good after my first experiences as a cop on patrol, although it was clear that I still had a lot to learn from Shaknahyi. We intervened in domestic squabbles and investigated robberies, but there were no more dramatic crises like Al-Muntaqim's clumsy bomb threat.

Shaknahyi had let several days pass, and now he wanted to follow up on our visit to Reda Abu Adil. He guessed that Friedlander Bey had told Lieutenant Hajjar to assign this investigation to us, but Papa was still pretending he wasn't interested in whatever it was about. Our delicate probing would be a lot more successful if someone would just tell us what we wêre trying to uncover.

Yet there were other concerns on my mind. One morning, after I'd dressed and Kmuzu had served me breakfast, I sat back and thought about what I wanted to accomplish that day.

"Kmuzu," I said, "would you wake my mother and see if she'll speak to me? I need to ask her something before I go to the station house."

"Of course, *yaa Sidi.*" He looked at me warily, as if I were trying to pull another fast one. "You wish to see her immediately?"

"Soon as she can make herself decent. *If* she can make herself decent." I caught Kmuzu's disapproving expression and shut up.

I drank some more coffee until he returned. "Umm Marîd will be glad to see you now," Kmuzu said.

I was surprised. "She never liked getting up much before noon."

"She was already awake and dressed when I knocked on her door."

Maybe she'd turned over a new leaf, but I hadn't been listening close enough to hear it. I grabbed my brief-case and sport coat. "I'll just drop in on her for a couple of minutes," I said. "No need for you to come with me." I should have known better by then; Kmuzu didn't say a word, but he followed me out of the apartment and into the other wing, where Angel Monroe had been given her own suite of rooms.

"This is a personal matter," I told Kmuzu when we got to her door. "Stay out here in the hall if you want." I rapped on the door and went in.

She was reclining on a divan, dressed very modestly in a shapeless black dress with long sleeves, a version of the outfit conservative Muslim women wear. She also had on a large scarf hiding her hair, although the veil over her face had been loosened on one side and hung down over her shoulder. She puffed on the mouthpiece of a *narjilah*. There was strong tobacco in the water pipe now, but that didn't mean there hadn't been hashish there recently, or that it wouldn't be there again soon.

"Morning of well-being, O my mother," I said.

I think she was caught off guard by my courteous greeting. "Morning of light, O Shaykh," she replied. Her brow furrowed as she studied me from across the room. She waited for me to explain why I was there.

"Are you comfortable here?" I asked.

"It's all right." She took a long pull on the mouthpiece and the *narjilah* burbled. "You done pretty well for yourself. How'd you happen to land in this lap of luxury? Performing personal services for Papa?" She gave me a crooked leer.

"Not the services you're thinking of, O Mother. I'm Friedlander Bey's administrative assistant. He makes the business decisions and I carry them out. That's as far as it goes."

"And one of his business decisions was to make you a cop?"

"That's exactly the way it was."

She shrugged. "Uh yeah, if you say so. So why'd you

decide to put me up here? Suddenly worried about your old mom's welfare?"

"It was Papa's idea."

She laughed. "You never was an attentive child, O Shaykh."

"As I recall, you weren't the doting mother, either. That's why I'm wondering why you showed up here all of a sudden."

She inhaled again on the *narjîlah.* "Algiers is boring. I lived there most of my life. After you came to see me, I knew I had to get out. I wanted to come here, see the city again."

"And see me again?"

She gave me another shrug. "Yeah, that too."

"And Abu Adil? You drop by his palace first, or haven't you been over there yet?" That's what we in the cop trade call a shot in the dark. Sometimes they pay off, sometimes they don't.

"I ain't having nothing more to do with that son of a bitch," she said. She almost snarled.

Shaknahyi would have been proud of me. I kept my emotions under control and my expression neutral. "What's Abu Adil ever done to you?"

"That sick bastard. Never mind, it's none of your business." She concentrated on her water pipe for a few moments.

"All right," I said. "I'll respect your wishes, O my mother. Anything I can do for you before I leave?"

"Everything's great. You run along and play Protector of the Innocent. Go roust some poor working girl and think of me."

I opened my mouth to make some sharp reply, but I caught myself in time. "You get hungry, or you need anything, just ask Youssef or Kmuzu. May your day be happy."

"Your day be prosperous, O Shaykh." Whenever she called me that, there was heavy irony in her voice.

I nodded to her and left the room, closing the door quietly behind me. Kmuzu was in the corridor, right where I'd left him. He was so goddamn loyal, I almost felt like scratching him behind the ears. I didn't buy that act for a minute.

"It would be well for you to greet the master of the house before we leave for the police station," he said.

"I don't need you to rehearse me on my manners, Kmuzu." He had this way of annoying me. "Are you implying that I don't know my duties?"

"I imply nothing, *yaa Sidi.* You are inferring."

"Sure." You just can't argue with a slave.

Friedlander Bey was already in his office. He sat behind his great desk, massaging his temples with one hand. Today he was wearing a pale yellow silk robe with a starched white shirt over it, buttoned to the neck and with no tie. Over the shirt he had on an expensive-looking herringbone-tweed suit jacket. It was a costume only an old and revered shaykh could get away with wearing. I thought it looked just fine. "Habib," he said. "Labib."

Habib and Labib are the Stones That Speak. The only way you can tell them apart is to call one of the names. There's an even chance one of 'em will blink. If not, it doesn't really make any difference. In fact, I couldn't swear that they blink in response to their own names. They may be doing it just for fun.

Both of the Stones That Speak were in the office, standing on either side of a straight-backed chair. In the chair, I was surprised to see, was Umm Saad's young son. The Stones each had one hand on Saad's shoulders, and the hands were kneading and crushing the boy's bones. He was being put to the question. I've had that treatment, and I can testify that it isn't a lick of fun.

Papa smiled briefly when I came into the room. He did not greet me, but looked back at Saad. "Before you came to the city," he said in a low voice, "where did you and your mother dwell?"

"Many places," Saad answered. There was fear in his voice.

Papa returned to rubbing his forehead. He stared down at his desktop, but waved a few fingers at the Stones That Speak. The two huge men tightened their grip on the boy's shoulders. The blood drained from Saad's face, and he gasped.

"Before you came to the city," Friedlander Bey repeated calmly, "where did you live?"

"Most recently in Paris, O Shaykh." Saad's voice was thin and strained.

The answer startled Papa. "Did your mother like living among the Franj?"

"I guess so."

Friedlander Bey was doing an admirable impersonation of a bored person. He picked up a silver letter opener and toyed with it. "Did you live well in Paris?"

"I guess so." Habib and Labib began to crush Saad's collarbones. He was encouraged to give more details. "We had a big apartment in the Rue de Paradis, O Shaykh. My mother likes to eat well and she likes giving parties. The months in Paris were pleasant. It surprised me when she told me we were coming here."

"And did you labor to earn money, so your mother could eat Franji food and wear Franji clothing?"

"I did no labor, O Shaykh."

Papa's eyes narrowed. "Where do you think the money came from to pay for these things?"

Saad hesitated. I could hear him moan as the Stones applied still more pressure. "She told me it came from her father," he cried.

"Her father?" said Friedlander Bey, dropping the letter opener and looking at Saad directly.

"She said from you, O Shaykh."

Papa grimaced and made a quick gesture with both hands. The Stones moved back, away from the youth. Saad slumped forward, his eyes tightly closed. His face was shiny with sweat.

"Let me tell you one thing, O clever one," said Papa. "And remember that I do not lie. I am *not* your mother's father, and I am *not* your grandfather. We share no blood. Now go."

Saad tried to stand, but collapsed back into the chair. His expression was grim and determined, and he glared at Friedlander Bey as if he were trying to memorize every detail of the old man's face. Papa had just called Umm Saad a liar, and I'm sure that at that moment the boy was entertaining some pitiful fantasy of revenge. At last he managed to stand up again, and he made his way shakily to the door. I intercepted him.

"Here," I said. I took out my pillcase and gave him two tabs of Sonneine. "You'll feel a lot better in a few minutes."

He took the tabs, looked me fiercely in the eye, and dropped the sunnies to the floor. Then he turned his back on me and left Friedlander Bey's office. I bent down and reclaimed the Sonneine. To paraphrase a local proverb: a white tablet for a black day.

After the formal greetings, Papa invited me to be comfortable. I sat in the same chair from which Saad had just escaped. I have to admit that I suppressed a little shudder. "Why was the boy here, O Shaykh?" I asked.

"He was here at my invitation. He and his mother are once again my guests."

I must have missed something. "Your graciousness is legendary, O my uncle; but whey do you permit Umm Saad to intrude on your peace? I know she upsets you."

Papa leaned back in his chair and sighed. At that moment, he showed every year of his long life. "She came to me humbly. She begged my forgiveness. She brought me a gift." He gestured to a platter of dates stuffed with nutmeats and rolled in sugar. He smiled ruefully. "I don't know where she got her information, but someone told her that these are my favorite treat. Her tone was respectful, and she made a claim upon my hospitality that I could not dismiss." He spread his hands, as if that explained it all.

Friedlander Bey observed traditions of honor and generosity that have all but disappeared in this day and age. If he wanted to welcome a viper back into his home, I had nothing to say about it. "Then your instructions concerning her have changed, O Shaykh?" I asked.

His expression did not alter. He didn't even blink. "Oh no, that's not what I mean. Please kill her as soon as it's convenient for you, but there's no hurry, my son. I find I'm getting curious about what Umm Saad hopes to accomplish."

"I will conclude the matter soon," I said. He frowned. *"Inshallah,"* I added quickly. "Do you think she's working for someone else? An enemy?"

"Reda Abu Adil, of course," said Papa. He was very matter-of-fact about it, as if there wasn't the slightest cause for concern.

"Then it was you, after all, who ordered the investigation of Abu Adil."

He raised a plump hand in denial. "No," he insisted, "I had nothing to do with that. Speak to your Lieutenant Hajjar about it."

Lot of good that would do. "O Shaykh, may I ask you

another question? There's something I don't understand about your relationship to Abu Adil."

Suddenly he looked bored again. That put me on my guard. I gave a reflexive glance over my shoulders, half expecting to see the Stones That Speak moving in close behind me. "Your wealth comes from selling updated data files to governments and heads of state, doesn't it?"

"That is greatly oversimplified, my nephew."

"And Abu Adil pursues the same business. Yet you told me you do not compete."

"Many years before you were born, before even your mother was born, Abu Adil and I came to an agreement." Papa opened a plain clothbound copy of the holy Qur'ân and glanced at the page. "We avoided competition because someday it could result in violence and harm to ourselves or those we love. On that long-ago day we divided the world, from Morocco far in the west to Indonesia far in the east, wherever the beautiful call of the muezzin awakens the faithful from sleep."

"Like Pope Alexander drawing the Line of Demarcation for Spain and Portugal," I said.

Papa looked displeased. "Since that time, Reda Abu Adil and I have had few dealings of any sort, although we live in the same city. He and I are at peace."

Yeah, you right. For some reason, he wasn't going to give me any direct help. "O Shaykh," I said, "it's time for me to go. I pray to Allah for your health and prosperity." I came forward and kissed him on the cheek.

"You will make me lonely for your presence," he replied. "Go in safety."

I left Friedlander Bey's office. In the hallway, Kmuzu tried to take my briefcase from me. "It is unseemly for you to carry this, when I am here to serve you," he said.

"You want to go through it and look for drugs," I said with some irritation. "Well, there aren't any in there. I got them in my pocket, and you'll have to wrestle me to the ground first."

"You are being absurd, *yaa Sidi,*" he said.

"I don't think so. Anyway, I'm not ready to leave for the office yet."

"It is already late."

"Goddamn it, I know that! I just want to have a few

words with Umm Saad, now that she's living under this roof again. Is she in the same suite?"

"Yes. This way, *yāa Sidi.*"

Umm Saad, like my mother, stayed in the other wing of the mansion. While I followed Kmuzu through the carpeted halls, I opened my briefcase and took out Saied's moddy, the tough, ruthless personality. I chipped it in. The effect was remarkable. It was the opposite of the Half-Hajj's dumbing-down module, which had narrowed and blurred my senses. This one, which Saied always called Rex, seemed to focus my attention. I was filled with purpose; but more than that, I was determined to drive straight toward my goal, and I'd crush anything that tried to obstruct me.

Kmuzu knocked lightly on Umm Saad's door. There was a long pause, and I heard no one stirring inside. "Get out of the way," I said to Kmuzu. My voice was a mean growl. I stepped up to the door and rapped on it sharply. "You want to let me in?" I called. "Or you want me to let myself in?"

That got a response. The boy swung the door open and stared at me. "My mother isn't—"

"Out of the way, kid," I said. I pushed him aside.

Umm Saad was sitting at a table, watching the news on a small holoset. She looked up at me. "Welcome, O Shaykh," she said. She wasn't happy.

"Yeah, right," I said. I sat in a chair across the table from her. I reached across and tapped the holoset off. "How long you known my mother?" I asked. Another shot in the dark.

Umm Saad looked perplexed. "Your mother?"

"Goes by Angel Monroe sometimes. She's staying down the hall from you."

Umm Saad shook her head slowly. "I've only seen her once or twice. I've never spoken to her."

"You must've known her before you came to this house." I just wanted to see how big this conspiracy was.

"Sorry," she said. She gave me a wide-eyed, innocent smile that looked as out of place on her as it would have on a desert scorpion.

Okay, sometimes a shot in the dark doesn't get you anywhere. "And Abu Adil?"

"Who's that?" Her expression was all angelic and virtuous.

I started to get angry. "I just want some straight answers, lady. What I got to do, bust up your kid?"

Her face got very serious. She was doing "sincere" now. "I'm sorry, I really don't know any of those people. Am I supposed to? Did Friedlander Bey tell you that?"

I assumed she was lying about Abu Adil. I didn't know if she'd been lying about my mother. At least I could check that out later. If I could believe my mother.

I felt a heavy hand on my shoulder. "*Yaa Sidi?*" said Kmuzu. He sounded afraid that I might rip Umm Saad's head off and hand it to her.

"All right," I said, still feeling wonderfully malignant. I stood up and glared down at the woman. "You want to stay in this house, you're gonna have to learn to be more cooperative. I'm gonna talk to you again later. Think up some better answers."

"I'll be looking forward to it," said Umm Saad. She batted her heavy fake eyelashes at me. It made me want to punch her face in.

Instead, I turned and stalked out of the apartment. Kmuzu hurried behind me. "You can take the personality module out now, *yaa Sidi*," he said nervously.

"Hell, I like it. Think I'll leave it in." Actually I *did* enjoy the feeling it gave me. There seemed to be a constant flood of angry hormones in my blood. I could see why Saied wore it all the time. Still, it wasn't the right one to wear around the station house, and Shaknahyi'd promised to annihilate any moddy I wore in his presence. I reached up reluctantly and popped it out.

I could feel the difference immediately. My body was still quivering from the leftover adrenalin, but I calmed down pretty quick. I returned the moddy to my briefcase, then grinned at Kmuzu. "I was pretty tough, huh?" I said.

Kmuzu didn't say a word, but his look let me know just how low his opinion was.

We went outside, and I waited while Kmuzu brought the car around. When Kmuzu let me out at the station house, I told him to go back home and keep Angel Monroe out of trouble. "And pay attention around Umm Saad and the boy too," I said. "Friedlander Bey is sure she's somehow connected to Reda Abu Adil, but she's playing it very cagey. Maybe you can learn something."

"I will be your eyes and ears, *yaa Sidi*," he said.

As usual, the crowd of hungry young boys was loitering outside the copshop. They'd all begun waving and screaming when they saw my Westphalian sedan pull up to the curb. "O Master!" they cried. "O Compassionate!"

I reached for a handful of coins as I usually did, but then I remembered the Lamb Lady I'd helped the week before. I took out my wallet and dropped a five-kiam bill on each of the kids. "God open upon you," I said. I was a little embarrassed to see that Kmuzu was watching me closely.

The boys were astonished. One of the older kids took my arm and steered me away from the rest. He was about fifteen years old, and already there was a dark shadow of beard on his narrow face. "My sister would be interested to meet such a generous man," he said.

"I'm just not interested in meeting your sister."

He grinned at me. Three of his yellow teeth had been broken off in some fight or accident. "I have a brother as well," he said. I winced and went past him into the building. Behind me, the boys were yelling my praises. I was real popular with them, at least until tomorrow, when I'd have to buy their respect all over again.

Shaknahyi was waiting for me by the elevator. "Where you at?" he said. It seemed that no matter how early I got to work, Shaknahyi got there earlier.

"Aw right," I said. Actually, I was still tired and I felt mildly nauseated. I could chip in a couple of daddies that would take care of all that, but Shaknahyi had me intimidated. Around him I functioned with just my natural talents and hoped they were still enough.

It wasn't that long ago that I prided myself on having an unwired brain as smart and quick as any moddy in the city. Now I was putting all my confidence in the electronics. I'd become afraid of what might happen if I had to face a crisis without them.

"One of these days, we're gonna have to catch Abu Adil when he's not chipped in," said Shaknahyi. "We don't want to make him suspicious, but he's got some tough questions to answer."

"What questions?"

Shaknahyi shrugged. "You'll hear 'em next time we pass by there." For some reason, he wasn't confiding in me any more than Papa had.

Sergeant Catavina found us in the corridor. I didn't know much about him except he was Hajjar's right-hand man, and that meant he had to be bent one way or another. He was a short man who lugged around too much weight by about seventy pounds. He had wavy black hair parted by a moddy plug, always with at least one daddy chipped in because he didn't understand five words in Arabic. It was a total mystery to me why Catavina had come to the city. "Been lookin' for you two," he said. His voice was shrill, even filtered through the Arabic-language daddy.

"What is it?" I asked.

Catavina's predatory brown eyes flicked between me and Shaknahyi. "Just got a tip on a possible homicide." He handed Shaknahyi a slip of paper with an address on it. "Go take a look."

"In the Budayeen," said Shaknahyi.

"Yeah," said the sergeant.

"Whoever called this in, anybody recognize the voice?"

"Why should anybody recognize the voice?" asked Catavina.

Shaknahyi shrugged. "We got two or three leads like this in the last couple of months, that's all."

Catavina looked at me. "He's one of these conspiracy guys. Sees 'em everywhere." The sergeant walked away, shaking his head.

Shaknahyi glanced at the address again and jammed the slip of paper into a shirt pocket. "Back of the Budayeen, spitting distance from the graveyard," he said.

"If it isn't just a crank call," I said. "If there *is* a body in the first place."

"There will be."

I followed him down to the garage. We got into our patrol car and cut across the Boulevard il-Jameel and under the big gate. There was a lot of pedestrian traffic on the Street that morning, so Shaknahyi angled south on First Street and then west along one of the narrow, garbage-strewn alleys that wind between the flat-roofed, stucco-fronted houses and the ancient brick tenements.

Shaknahyi drove the car up onto the sidewalk. We got out and took a good look at the building. It was a pale green two-story house in terrible disrepair. The entryway and front parlor stank of urine and vomit. The wooden lattices covering the windows had all been smashed some time ago, from the look of things. Everywhere we walked, we crunched broken brick and shards of glass. The place had probably been abandoned for many months, maybe years.

It was very still, the dead hush of a house where the power is off and even the faint whir of motors is missing. As we made our way up from the ground floor to the family's rooms above, I thought I heard something small and quick scurrying through the trash ahead of us. I felt my heart pounding in my chest, and I missed the sense of calm competence I'd gotten from Complete Guardian.

Shaknahyi and I checked a large bedroom that had once belonged to the owner and his wife, and another room that had been a child's. We found nothing except more sad destruction. A corner of the house had entirely collapsed, leaving it open to the outside; weather, vermin, and vagrants had completed the ruin of the child's bedroom. At least here the fresh air had scoured out the sour, musty smell that choked the rest of the house.

We found the corpse in the next room down the hall. It was a young woman's body, a sexchange named Blanca who used to dance in Frenchy Benoit's club. I'd known her well enough to say hello, but not much better. She lay on her back, her legs bent and turned to one side, her arms thrown up above her head. Her deep blue eyes were open, staring obliquely at the water-stained ceiling above my shoulder. She was grimacing, as if there'd been something horrible with her in the room that had first terrified her and then killed her.

"This ain't bothering you, is it?" asked Shaknahyi.

"What you talking about?"

He tapped Blanca's hand with the toe of his boot. "You're not gonna throw up or nothing, are you?"

"I seen worse," I said.

"Just didn't want you throwing up or nothing." He bent down beside Blanca. "Blood from her nose and ears. Lips drawn back, fingers clutching like claws. She was juiced at close range by a good-sized static gun, I'll bet. Look at her. She hasn't been dead half an hour."

"Yeah?"

He lifted her left arm and let it fall. "No stiffness yet. And her flesh is still pink. After you're dead, gravity makes the blood settle. The medical examiner will be able to tell better."

Something struck me as kind of odd. "So the call that came into the station—"

"Bet you kiams to kitty cats the killer made the call himself." He took out his radio and his electronic log.

"Why would a murderer do that?" I asked.

Shaknahyi gazed at me, lost in thought. "The hell should I know?" he said at last. He made a call to Hajjar, asking for a team of detectives. Then he entered a brief report in his log. "Don't touch nothing," he said to me without looking up.

He didn't have to tell me that. "We done here?" I asked.

"Soon as the gold badges show up. In a hurry to travel?"

I didn't answer. I watched him pocket his electronic log. Then he took out a brown vinyl-covered notebook and a pen and made some more notations. "What's that for?" I asked.

"Just keeping some notes for myself. Like I said, there's been a couple of other cases like this lately. Somebody turns up dead and it seems like the bumper himself tips us off."

By the life of my eyes, I thought, if this turns out to be a serial killer, I'm going to pack up and leave the city for good. I glanced down at Shaknahyi, who was still squatting beside Blanca's body. "You don't think it's a serial killer, do you?" I asked.

He stared through me again for a few seconds. "Nah," he said at last, "I think it's something much worse."

8

I remembered how much Hajjar's predecessor, Lieutenant Okking, had liked to harass me. Still, no matter how hard it had been to get along with Okking, he'd always gotten the job done. He'd been a shrewd if not brilliant cop, and he'd had a genuine concern for the victims he saw in a day's work. Hajjar was different. To him it was all a day's work, all right, but nothing more.

It didn't surprise me to learn that Hajjar was next to useless. Shaknahyi and I watched as he went about his investigation. He frowned and looked down at Blanca. "Dead, huh?" he said.

I saw Shaknahyi wince. "We got every reason to think so, Lieutenant," he said in a level voice.

"Any ideas who'd want to shade her?"

Shaknahyi looked at me for help. "Could be anybody," I said. "She was probably wearing the wrong moddy for the wrong customer."

Hajjar seemed interested. "You think so?"

"Look," I said. "Her plug's bare."

The lieutenant's eyes narrowed. "So what?"

"A moddy like Blanca never goes anywhere without *something* chipped in. It's suspicious, that's all."

Hajjar rubbed his scraggly mustache. "I guess you'd know all about that. Not much to go on, though."

"The plainclothes boys can work miracles sometimes," Shaknahyi said, sounding very sincere but winking to let me know just how little regard he had for them.

"Yeah, you right," said Hajjar.

"By the way, Lieutenant," said Shaknahyi, "I was wondering if you wanted us to keep after Abu Adil. We didn't get very far with him last week."

"You want to go out there again? To his house?"

101

"To his majestic palatial estate, you mean," I said.

Hajjar ignored me. "I didn't mean for you to persecute the guy. He throws a lot of weight in this town."

"Uh huh," said Shaknahyi. "Anyway, we're not doing any persecuting."

"Why do you want to bother him again in the first place?" Hajjar looked at me, but I didn't have an answer.

"I got a hunch that Abu Adil has some connection to these unsolved homicides," said Shaknahyi.

"*What* unsolved homicides?" Hajjar demanded.

I could see Shaknahyi grit his teeth. "There've been three unsolved homicides in the last couple of months. Four now, including her." He nodded toward Blanca's body, which the M.E.'s boy had covered with a sheet. "They could be related, and they could be connected to Reda Abu Adil."

"They're not unsolved homicides, for God's sake," said Hajjar angrily. "They're just open files, that's all."

"Open files," said Shaknahyi. I could tell he was really disgusted. "You need us for anything else, Lieutenant?"

"I guess not. You two can get back to work."

We left Hajjar and the detectives going over Blanca's remains and her clothes and the dust and the moldy ruins of the house. Outside on the sidewalk, Shaknahyi pulled my arm and stopped me before I got into the patrol car. "The hell was that about the bitch's missing moddy?" he asked.

I laughed. "Just hot air, but Hajjar won't know the difference. Give him something to think about, though, won't it?"

"It's good for the lieutenant to think about something now and then. His brain needs the exercise." Shaknahyi grinned at me.

We were both ready to call it a day. The sky had clouded over and a brisk, hot wind blew grit and smoke into our faces. Angry, grumbling thunder threatened from far away. Shaknahyi wanted to go back to the station house, but I had something else to take care of first. I unclipped the phone from my belt and spoke Chiri's commcode into it. I heard it ring eight or nine times before she answered it. "Talk to me," she said. She sounded irked.

"Chiri? It's Marîd."

"What do *you* want, motherfucker?"

"Look, you haven't given me any chance to explain. It's not my fault."

"You said that before." She gave a contemptuous laugh. "Famous last words, honey: 'It's not my fault.' That's what my uncle said when he sold my mama to some goddamn Arab slaver."

"I never knew—"

"Forget it, it ain't even true. You wanted a chance to explain, so explain."

Well, it was show time, but suddenly I didn't have any idea what to say to her. "I'm real sorry, Chiri," I said.

She just laughed again. It wasn't a friendly sound.

I plunged ahead. "One morning I woke up and Papa said, 'Here, now you own Chiriga's club, isn't that wonderful?' What did you expect me to say to him?"

"I know you, honey. I don't expect you to say *anything* to Papa. He didn't have to cut off your balls. You sold 'em."

I might have mentioned that Friedlander Bey had paid to have the punishment center of my brain wired, and that he could stimulate it whenever he wanted. That's how he kept me in line. But Chiri wouldn't have understood. I might have described the torment Papa could cause me anytime he touched the right keypad. None of that was important to her. All she knew was that I'd betrayed her.

"Chiri, we been friends a long time. Try to understand. Papa got this idea to buy your club and give it to me. I didn't know a thing about it in advance. I didn't want it when he gave it to me. I tried to tell him, but—"

"I'll bet. I'll just bet you told him."

I closed my eyes and took a deep breath. I think she was enjoying this a lot. "I told him about as much as anyone can tell Papa anything."

"Why *my* place, Marîd? The Budayeen's full of crummy bars. Why did he pick mine?"

I knew the answer to that: because Friedlander Bey was prying me loose from the few remaining connections to my old life. Making me a cop had alienated most of my friends. Forcing Chiriga to sell her club had turned her against me. Next, Papa'd find a way to make Saied the Half-Hajj hate my guts too. "Just his sense of humor,

Chiri," I said hopelessly. "Just Papa proving that he's always around, always watching, ready to hit us with his lightning bolts when we least expect it."

There was a long silence from her. "And you're gutless too."

My mouth opened and closed. I didn't know what she was talking about. "Huh?"

"I said you're a gutless *panya.*"

She's always slinging Swahili at me. "What's a *panya,* Chiri?" I asked.

"It's like a big rat, only stupider and uglier. You didn't dare do this in person, did you, motherfucker? You'd rather whine to me over the phone. Well, you're gonna have to face me. That's all there is to it."

I squeezed my eyes shut and grimaced. "Okay, Chiri, whatever you want. Can you come by the club?"

"*The* club, you say? You mean, *my* club? The club I used to own?"

"Yeah," I said. "Your club."

She grunted. "Not on your life, you diseased jackass. I'm not setting foot in there unless things change the way I want 'em. But I'll meet you somewhere else. I'll be in Courane's place in half an hour. That's not in the Budayeen, honey, but I'm sure you can find it. Show up if you think you can handle it." There was a sharp click, and then I was listening to the burr of the dial tone.

"Dragged you through it, didn't she?" said Shaknahyi. He'd enjoyed every moment of my discomfort. I liked the guy, but he was still a bastard sometimes.

I clipped the phone back on my belt. "Ever hear of a bar called Courane's?"

He snorted. "This Christian chump shows up in the city a few years ago." He was wheeling the patrol car through Rasmiyya, a neighborhood east of the Budayeen that I'd never been in before. "Guy named Courane. Called himself a poet, but nobody ever saw much proof of that. Somehow he got to be a big hit with the European community. One day he opens what he calls a salon, see. Just a quiet, dark bar where everything's made out of wicker and glass and stainless steel. Lots of potted plastic plants. Nowadays he ain't the darling of the brunch crowd anymore, but he still pulls this melancholy expatriate routine."

"Like Weinraub on Gargotier's patio," I said.

"Yeah," said Shaknahyi, "except Courane owns his own dive. He stays in there and doesn't bother anybody. Give him that much credit, anyway. That where you're gonna meet Chiri?"

I looked at him and shrugged. "It was her choice."

He grinned at me. "Want to attract a lot of attention when you show up?"

I sighed. "Please no," I muttered. That Jirji, he was some kidder.

Twenty minutes later we were in a middle-class district of two-and three-story houses. The streets were broader than in the Budayeen, and the whitewashed buildings had strips of open land around them, planted with small bushes and flowering shrubs. Tall date palms leaned drunkenly along the verges of the pavement. The neighborhood seemed deserted, if only because there were no shouting children wrestling on the sidewalks or chasing each other around the corners of the houses. It was a very settled, very sedate part of town. It was so peaceful, it made me uncomfortable.

"Courane's is just up here," said Shaknahyi. He turned into a poorer street that was little more than an alley. One side was hemmed in by the back walls of the same flat-roofed houses. There were small balconies on the second floor, and bright lamp-lit windows obscured by lattices made of narrow wooden strips. On the other side of the alley were boarded-up buildings and a few businesses: a leatherworker's shop, a bakery, a restaurant that specialized in bean dishes, a bookstall.

There was also Courane's, out of place in that constricted avenue. The proprietor had set out a few tables, but no one lingered in the white-painted wicker chairs beneath these Cinzano umbrellas. Shaknahyi tapped off the engine, and we got out of the patrol car. I supposed that Chiri hadn't arrived yet, or that she was waiting for me inside. My stomach hurt.

"Officer Shaknahyi!" A middle-aged man came toward us, a welcoming smile on his face. He was about my height, maybe fifteen or twenty pounds heavier, with receding brown hair brushed straight back. He shook hands with Shaknahyi, then turned to me.

"Sandor," said Shaknahyi, "this is my partner, Marîd Audran."

"Glad to meet you," said Courane.

"May Allah increase your honor," I said.

Courane's look was amused. "Right," he said. "Can I get you boys something to drink?"

I glanced at Shaknahyi. "Are we on duty?" I asked.

"Nah," he said. I asked for my usual, and Shaknahyi got a soft drink. We followed Courane into his establishment. It was just as I'd pictured it: shiny chrome and glass tables, white wicker chairs, a beautiful antique bar of polished dark wood, chrome ceiling fans, and, as Shaknahyi had mentioned, lots of dusty artificial plants stuck in corners and hanging in baskets from the ceiling.

Chiriga was sitting at a table near the back. "Where you at, Jirji? Marîd?" she said.

"Aw right," I said. "Can I buy you a drink?"

"Never in my life turned one down." She held up her glass. "Sandy?" Courane nodded and went to make our drinks.

I sat down beside Chiri. "Anyway," I said uncomfortably, "I want to talk to you about coming to work in the club."

"Yasmin mentioned something about that," Chiri said. "Kind of a ballsy thing for you to ask, isn't it?"

"Hey, look, I told you what the situation was. How much longer you gonna keep this up?"

Chiri gave me a little smile. "I don't know," she said. "I'm getting a big kick out of it."

I'd reached my limit. I can only feel so guilty. "Fine," I said. "Go get another job someplace else. I'm sure a big, strong *kaffir* like you won't have any trouble at all finding somebody who's interested."

Chiri looked hurt. "Okay, Marîd," she said softly, "let's stop." She opened her bag and took out a long white envelope, and pushed it across the table toward me.

"What's this?" I asked.

"Yesterday's take from your goddamn club. You're supposed to show up around closing time, you know, to count out the register and pay the girls. Or don't you care?"

"I don't really care," I said, peeking at the cash. There

was a lot of money in the envelope. "That's why I want to hire you."

"To do what?"

I spread my hands. "I want you to keep the girls in line. And I need you to separate the customers from their money. You're famous for that. Just do exactly what you used to."

Her brow furrowed. "I used to go home every night with all of this." She tapped the envelope. "Now I'm just gonna get a few kiam here and there, whatever you decide to spill. I don't like that."

Courane arrived with our drinks and I paid for them. "I was gonna offer you a lot more than what the debs and changes get," I said to Chiri.

"I should hope so." She nodded her head emphatically. "Bet your ass, honey, you want me to run your club for you, you're gonna have to pay up front. Business is business, and action is action. I want 50 percent."

"Making yourself a partner?" I'd expected something like that. Chiri smiled slowly, showing those long, filed canines. She was worth more than 50 percent to me. "All right," I said.

She looked startled, as if she hadn't expected me to give in so easily. "Should've asked for more," she said bitterly. "And I don't want to dance unless I feel like it."

"Fine."

"And the name of the club stays 'Chiriga's.'"

"All right."

"And you let me do my own hiring and firing. I don't want to get stuck with Floor-Show Fanya if she tickles you into giving her a job. Bitch gets so loaded, she throws up on customers."

"You expect a hell of a lot, Chiri."

She gave me a wolfish grin. "Paybacks are a bitch, ain't they?" she said.

Chiri was wringing every last bit of advantage out of this situation. "Okay, you pick your own crew."

She paused to drink again. "By the way," she said, "that's 50 percent of the *gross* I'm getting, isn't it?"

Chiri was terrific. "Uh yeah," I said, laughing. "Why don't you let me give you a ride back to the Budayeen? You can start working this afternoon."

"I already passed by there. I left Indihar in charge."

She noticed that her glass was empty again, and she held it up and waved it at Courane. "Want to play a game, Marîd?" She jerked a thumb toward the back of the bar, where Courane had a Transpex unit.

It's a game that lets two people with corymbic implants sit across from each other and chip into the machine's CPU. The first player imagines a bizarre scenario in detail, and it becomes a wholly realistic environment for the second player, who's scored on how well he adapts —or survives. Then in turn the second player does the same for the first.

It's a great game to bet money on. It scared the hell out of me at first, though, because while you're playing, you forget it's only a game. It seems absolutely real. The players exercise almost godlike power on each other. Courane's model looked old, a version whose safety features could be bypassed by a clever mechanic. There were rumors of people actually having massive strokes and coronaries while they were chipped into a jiggered Transpex.

"Go ahead, Audran," said Shaknahyi, "let's see what you got."

"All right, Chiri," I said, "let's play."

She stood up and walked back to the Transpex booth. I followed her, and both Shaknahyi and Courane came along too. "Want to bet the other 50 percent of my club?" she said. Her eyes glittered over the rim of her cocktail glass.

"Can't do that. Papa wouldn't approve." I felt pretty confident, because I could read the record of the machine's previous high games. A perfect Transpex score was 1,000 points, and I averaged in the upper 800s. The top scores on this machine were in the lower 700s. Maybe the scores were low because Courane's bar didn't attract many borderline nutso types. Like me. "I'll bet what's inside this envelope, though."

That sounded good to her. "I can cover it," she said. I didn't doubt that Chiri could lay her hands on quite a lot of cash when she needed it.

Courane set fresh drinks down for all of us. Shaknahyi dragged a wicker chair near enough to watch the computer-modeled images of the illusions Chiri and I would create. I fed five kiam into the Transpex machine. "You can go first, if you want," I said.

"Yeah," said Chiri. "It's gonna be fun, making you sweat." She took one of the Transpex's moddy links and socketed it on her corymbic plug, then touched Player One on the console. I took the second link, murmured *"Bismillah,"* and chipped in Player Two.

At first there was only a kind of warm, flickering fog, veined with iridescence like shimmery mother of pearl. Audran was lost in a cloud, but he didn't feel anxious about it. It was absolutely silent and still, not even a whisper of breeze. He was aware of a mild scent surrounding him, the fragrance of fresh sea air. Then things began to change.

Now he was floating in the cloud, no longer sitting or standing, but somehow drifting through space easily and peacefully. Audran still wasn't concerned; it was a perfectly comfortable sensation. Only gradually did the fog begin to dissipate. With a shock Audran realized that he wasn't floating, but swimming in a warm, sun-dappled sea.

Below him waved long tendrils of algae that clung to hillocks of brightly colored coral. Anemones of many hues and many shapes reached their grasping tentacles toward him, but he cut smartly through the water well out of their reach.

Audran's eyesight was poor, but his other senses let him know what was happening around him. The smell of the salt air had been replaced by many subtle aromas that he couldn't name but were all achingly familiar. Sounds came to him, sibilant, rushing noises that echoed in hollow tones.

He was a fish. He felt free and strong, and he was hungry. Audran dived down close to the rolling sea bottom, near the stinging anemones where tiny fishes schooled for protection. He flashed among them, gobbling down mouthfuls of the scarlet and yellow creatures. His hunger was appeased, at least for now. The scent of others of his species wafted by him on the current, and he turned toward its source.

He swam for a long while until he realized that he'd lost the trace. Audran couldn't tell how much time had passed. It didn't matter. Nothing mattered here in the sparkling, sunny seas. He browsed over a gorgeous reef, worrying the delicate featherdusters, sending the scarlet-banded shrimps and the porcelain crabs scuttling.

Above him, the ocean darkened. A shadow passed over him, and Audran felt a ripple of alarm. He could not look up, but compression waves told him that something huge was circling nearby. Audran remembered that he was not alone in this ocean: It was now his turn to flee. He darted down over the reef and cut a zigzag path only a few inches above the sandy floor.

The ravenous shadow trailed close behind. Audran looked for somewhere to hide, but there was nothing, no sunken wrecks or rocks or hidden caves. He made a sharp evasive turn and raced back the way he'd come. The thing that stalked him followed lazily, easily.

Suddenly it dived on him, a voracious, mad engine of murder, all dead black eyes and gleaming chrome-steel teeth. Flushed from the sea bottom, Audran knifed up through the green water toward the surface, though he knew there was no shelter there. The great beast raged close behind him. In a froth of boiling seafoam, Audran broke through the waves, into the fearfully thin air, and —flew. He glided over the white-capped water until, at last, he fell back into the welcoming element, exhausted.

And the nightmare creature was there, its ghastly mouth yawning wide to rend him. The daggered jaws closed slowly, victoriously, until for Audran there was only blackness and the knowledge of the agony to come.

"Jeez," I murmured, when the Transpex returned my consciousness.

"Some game," said Shaknahyi.

"How'd I do?" asked Chiri. She sounded exhilarated.

"Pretty good," said Courane. "Six hundred twenty-three. It was a promising scenario, but you never got him to panic."

"I sure as hell tried," she said. "I want another drink." She gave me a quirky grin.

I took out my pillcase and swallowed eight Paxium with a mouthful of gin. Maybe as a fish I hadn't been paralyzed with fear, but I was feeling a strong nervous reaction now. "I want another drink too," I said. "I'll stand a round for everybody."

"Bigshot," said Shaknahyi.

Both Chiri and I waited until our heartbeats slowed down to normal. Courane brought a tray with the fresh drinks, and I watched Chiri throw hers down in two long gulps. She was fortifying herself for whatever evil things I was going to do to her mind. She was going to need it.

Chiri touched Player Two on the game's console, and I saw her eyes slowly close. She looked like she was napping placidly. That was going to end in a hell of a hurry. On the holoscreen was the same opalescent haze I'd wandered through until Chiri'd decided it was the ocean. I reached out and touched the Player One panel.

Audran gazed down upon the ball of mist, like Allah in the highest of the heavens. He concentrated on building a richly detailed illusion, and he was pleased with his progress. Instead of letting it take on form and reality gradually, Audran loosed an explosion of sensory information. The woman far below was stunned by the purity of color in this world, the clarity of sound, the intensity of the tastes and textures and smells. She cried out and her voice pealed in the cool, clean air like a carillon. She fell to her knees, her eyes shut tightly and her hands over her ears.

Audran was patient. He wanted the woman to explore his creation. He wasn't going to hide behind a tree, jump out and frighten her. There was time enough for terror later.

After a while the woman lowered her hands and stood up. She looked around uncertainly. "Marîd?" she called. Once again the sound of her own voice rang with unnatural sharpness. She glanced behind her, toward the misty purple mountains in the west. Then she turned back to the east, toward the shore of a marshy lake that reflected the impossible azure of the sky. Audran didn't care which direction she chose; it would all be the same in the end.

The woman decided to follow the swampy shoreline to the southeast. She walked for hours, listening to the liquid trilling of songbirds and inhaling the poignant perfume of unknown blossoms. After a while the sun rested on the shoulders of the purple hills behind her, and then slipped away, leaving Audran's illusion in darkness. He provided a full moon, huge and gleaming silver like a serving platter. The woman grew weary, and at last she decided to lie down in the sweet-smelling grass and sleep.

Audran woke her in the morning with a gentle rain shower. "Marîd?" she cried again. He would not answer her. "How long you gonna leave me here?" She shivered.

The golden sun mounted higher, and while it warmed the morning, the heat never became stifling. Just after noon, when the woman had walked almost halfway around the lake, she came upon a pavilion made all of crimson and sapphire-blue silk. "What the hell is all this, Marîd?" the woman shouted. "Just get it over with, all right?"

The woman approached the pavilion anxiously. "Hello?" she called.

A moment later a young woman in a white gown came out of the pavilion. Her feet were bare and her pale blond hair was thrown carelessly over one shoulder. She was smiling and carrying a wooden tray. "Hungry?" she asked in a friendly voice.

"Yes," said the woman.

"My name is Maryam. I've been waiting for you. I'm sorry, all I've got is bread and fresh milk." She poured from a silver pitcher into a silver goblet.

"Thanks." The woman ate and drank greedily.

Maryam shaded her eyes with one hand. "Are you going to the fair?"

The woman shook her head. "I don't know about any fair."

Maryam laughed. "Everybody goes to the fair. Come on, I'll take you."

The woman waited while Maryam disappeared into the pavilion again with the breakfast things. She came back out a moment later. "We're all set now," she said gaily. "We can get to know each other while we walk."

They continued around the lake until the woman saw a scattering of large peaked tents of striped canvas, all with colorful pennants snapping in the breeze. She heard many people laughing and shouting, and the sound of axes biting wood, and metal ringing on metal. She could smell bread baking, and cinnamon buns, and lamb roasting on spits turning slowly over glowing coals. Her mouth began to water, and she felt her excitement growing despite herself.

"I don't have any money to spend," she said.

"Money?" Maryam asked, laughing. "What is money?"

The woman spent the afternoon going from tent to tent, seeing the strange exhibits and miraculous entertainments. She sampled exotic foods and drank concoctions of unknown liquors. Now and then she remembered to be afraid. She looked over her shoulder, wondering when the pleasant face of this fantasy would fall away. "Marîd," she called, "what are you doing?"

"Who are you calling?" asked Maryam.

"I'm not sure," said the woman.

Maryam laughed. "Look over here," she said, pulling on the woman's sleeve, showing her a booth where a heavily muscled woman was shaping a disturbing collage from the claws, teeth, and eyes of lizards.

They listened to children playing strange music on instruments made from the carcasses of small animals, and then they watched several old women spin their own white hair into thread, and then weave it into napkins and scarves.

One of the toothless hags leered at Maryam and the woman. "Take," she said in a gravelly voice.

"Thank you, Grandmother," said Maryam. She selected a pair of human-hair handkerchiefs.

The hours wore on, and at last the sun began to set. The moon rose as full as yestereve. "Is this going to go on all night?" the woman asked.

"All night and all day tomorrow," said Maryam. "Forever."

The woman shuddered.

From that moment she couldn't shake a growing dread, a sense that she'd been lured to this place and abandoned. She remembered nothing of who she'd been before she'd awakened beside the lake, but she felt she'd been horribly tricked. She prayed to someone called Marîd. She wondered if that was God.

"Marîd," she murmured fearfully, "I wish you'd just end this already."

But Audran was not ready to end it. He watched as

the woman and Maryam grew sleepy and found a large tent filled with comfortable cushions and sheets of satin and fine linen. They laid themselves down and slept.

In the morning the woman arose, dismayed to be still trapped at the eternal fair. Maryam found them a good breakfast of sausage, fried bread, broiled tomatoes, and hot tea. Maryam's enthusiasm was undiminished, and she led the woman toward still more disquieting entertainments. The woman, however, felt only a crazily mounting dread.

"You've had me here for two days, Marîd," she pleaded. "Please kill me and let me go." Audran gave her no sign, no answer.

They passed the third day examining one dismaying thing after another: teenage girls who seemed to have living roses in place of breasts; a candlemaker whose wares would not provide light in the presence of an infidel; staged combat between a blind man and two maddened dragons; a family hammering together a scale model of the fair out of iron, a project that had occupied them for generations and that might never be completed; a cage of crickets that had been taught to chirp the Shahada, the Islamic testament of faith.

The afternoon passed, and once again night began to fall. All through the fair, men jammed blazing torches into iron sconces on tall poles. Still Maryam led the woman from tent to tent, but the woman no longer enjoyed the spectacles. She was filled with a sense of impending catastrophe. She felt an urgent need to escape, but she knew she couldn't even find her way out of the infinite fairgrounds.

And then a shrill, buzzing alarm sounded. "What's that?" she asked, startled. All around her, people had begun to flee. "Yallah!" cried Maryam, her face stricken with horror. "Run! Run and save your life!"

"What is it?" the woman shouted. "Tell me what it is!"

Maryam had collapsed to the ground, weeping and moaning. "In the name of Allah, the Beneficent, the Merciful," she muttered over and over again. The woman could get nothing more sensible from her.

The woman left her there, and she followed the stream of terrified people as they ran among the tents.

And then the woman saw them: two immense giants, impossibly huge, hundreds of feet tall, crushing the landscape as they came nearer. They waded among the distant mountains, and then the shocks from their jolting footsteps began to churn the water in the lake. The ground heaved as they came nearer. The woman raised a hand to her breast, then staggered backward a few steps.

One of the giants turned his head slowly and looked straight at her. He was horribly ugly, with a great scar across one empty eye socket and a mouthful of rotten, snaggled fangs. He lifted an arm and pointed to her.

"No," she said, her voice hoarse with fear, "not me!" She wanted to run but she couldn't move. The giant stooped toward her, fierce and glowering. He bent to capture her in his enormous hand.

"Marîd!" the woman screamed. "Please!" Nothing happened. The giant's fist began to close around her.

The woman tried to reach up and unplug the moddy link, but her arms were frozen. She wouldn't escape that easily. The woman shrieked as she realized she couldn't even jack out.

The disfigured giant lifted her off the ground and drew her close to his single eye. His horrid grin spread and he laughed at her terror. His stinking breath sickened the woman. She struggled again to lift her hands, to pull the moddy link free. Her arms were held fast. She screamed and screamed, and then at last she fainted.

My eyes were bleary for a moment, and I could hear Chiri panting for breath beside me. I didn't think she'd be so upset. After all, it was only a Transpex game, and it wasn't the first time she'd ever played. She knew what to expect.

"You're a sick motherfucker, Marîd," she said at last.

"Listen, Chiri, I was just—"

She waved a hand at me. "I know, I know. You won the game and the bet. I'm still just a little shook, that's all. I'll have your money for you tonight."

"Forget the money, Chiri, I—"

I shouldn't have said that. "Hey, you son of a bitch, when I lose a bet I pay up. You're gonna take the money or I'm gonna cram it down your throat. But, God, you've got some kind of twisted imagination."

"That last part," said Courane, "where she couldn't raise her hands to pop the moddy link, that was real cold." He said it approvingly.

"Hell of a sadistic thing to do," said Chiri, shivering. "Last time I ever touch a Transpex with *you*."

"A few extra points, that's all, Chiri. I didn't know what my score was. I might have needed a couple more points."

"You finished with 941," said Shaknahyi. He was looking at me oddly, as if he were impressed by my score and repelled at the same time. "We got to go." He stood up and tossed down the last slug of his soft drink.

I stood up too. "You all right now, Chiri?" I put my hand on her shoulder.

"I'm fine. I'm still shaking off the game. It was like a nightmare." She took a deep breath and let it out. "I got to get back to the club so Indihar can go home."

"Give you a ride?" asked Shaknahyi.

"Thanks," said Chiri, "but I got my own transportation."

"See you later then," I said.

"*Kwa heri,* you bastard." At least she was smiling when she called me that. I thought maybe things were okay between us again. I was real glad about that.

Outside, Shaknahyi shook his head and grinned. "She was right, you know. That was a hell of a sadistic thing. Like unnecessary torture. You *are* a sick son of a bitch."

"Maybe."

"And I got to ride around the city with you."

I was tired of talking about it. "Time to check out yet?" I asked.

"Just about. Let's pass by the station house, and then why don't you come home with me for dinner? You got plans already? You think Friedlander Bey can get along without you for one night?"

I'm not a very sociable person, and I always feel uncomfortable in other people's homes. Still, the idea of spending an evening away from Papa and his Circus of Thrills was immensely attractive. "Sure," I said.

"Let me call my wife and find out if tonight's okay."

"I didn't even know you were married, Jirji."

He just raised his eyebrows at me and spoke his commcode into the phone. He had a brief conversation with his wife and then clipped the phone back on his belt. "She says it's okay," he said. "Now she's got to run around cleaning and cooking. She always goes crazy when I bring somebody home."

"She don't have to do that just for me," I said.

Shaknahyi shook his head. "It's not for you, believe me. She comes from this old-fashioned family, and she's all the time got to prove she's the perfect Muslim wife."

We stopped at the station house, turned the patrol car over to the guys on the night shift, and checked in briefly with Hajjar. Finally we logged out and headed back downstairs to the street. "I usually walk home unless it's pouring rain," said Shaknahyi.

"How far is it?" I asked. It was a pleasant evening, but I wasn't looking forward to a long walk.

"Maybe three, three-and-a-half miles."

"Forget it," I said. "I'll spring for a cab." There are always seven or eight taxis waiting for fares on the Boulevard il-Jameel, near the Budayeen's eastern gate. I looked for my friend Bill, but I didn't see him. We got into another cab, and Shaknahyi gave the driver his address.

It was an apartment house in the part of town called Haffe al-Khala, the Edge of the Wilderness. Shaknahyi and his family lived about as far south as you could go in the city, so near the desert that mounds of sand like infant dunes had crept up against the walls of the buildings. There were no trees or flowers on these streets. It was bare and quiet and dead, as cheerless as any place I've ever seen.

Shaknahyi must have guessed what I was thinking. "This is all I can afford," he said sourly. "Come on, though. It's better inside."

I followed him into the foyer of the apartment house, and then upstairs to his flat on the third floor. He unlocked the front door and was immediately tackled by two small children. They clung to his legs as he came into the parlor. Shaknahyi bent down laughing, and rested his hands on the boys' heads. "My sons," he said to me proudly. "This is Little Jirji, he's eight, and Hâkim, he's four. Zahra's six. She's probably getting in her mother's way in the kitchen."

Well, I don't have much patience with kids. I suppose they're fine for other people, but I've never really understood what they're *for*. I can be polite about them when I have to, though. "Your sons are very handsome," I said. "They do you honor."

"It is as Allah pleases," said Shaknahyi. He was beaming like a goddamn searchlight.

He dislodged Little Jirji and Hâkim and, to my dismay, left me alone with them while he went in to see how supper was progressing. I didn't actually bear these children any ill will, but my philosophy of raising kids is kind of extreme. I think you should keep a baby around for a few days after it's born—until the novelty wears off—and then you put it in a big cardboard box with all the best books of Eastern and Western civilization. Then you bury the box and dig it up again when the kid's eighteen.

I watched uneasily as first Little Jirji and then Hâkim realized I was sitting on the couch. Hâkim lurched toward me, a bright red toy figure in his right hand, another in his mouth. "What do I do now?" I muttered.

"How you boys getting along out here?" said Shaknahyi. I was saved. He came back into the parlor and sat beside me in an old, shabby armchair.

"Great," I said. I said a little prayer to Allah. This looked like it could be a long night.

A very pretty, very serious-faced girl came into the room, carrying a china plate of *hummus* and bread. Shaknahyi took the plate from her and kissed her on both cheeks. "This is Zahra, my little princess," he said. "Zahra, this is Uncle Marîd."

Uncle Marîd! I'd never heard anything so grotesque in my entire life.

Zahra looked up at me, blushed furiously, and ran back into the kitchen while her father laughed. I've always had that effect on women.

Shaknahyi indicated the plate of *hummus*. "Please," he said, "refresh yourself."

"May your prosperity increase, Jirji," I said.

"May God lengthen your life. I'm gonna get us some tea." He got up again and went back into the kitchen.

I wished he'd stop fussing. It made me nervous, and it left me outnumbered by the kids. I tore off some bread and dipped it in the *hummus*, keeping a careful eye on Little Jirji and Hâkim. They seemed to be playing together peacefully, apparently paying no attention to me at all; but I wasn't going to be lulled so easily.

Shaknahyi came back in a few minutes. "I think you know my wife," he said. I looked up. He was standing there with Indihar. He was grinning his damnfool grin, but she looked absolutely pissed.

I stood up, bewildered. "Indihar, how you doing?" I said. I felt like a fool. "I didn't even know you were married."

"Nobody's supposed to know," she said. She glared at her husband, then she turned and glared at me.

"It's all right, sweetheart," Shaknahyi said. "Marîd won't tell anybody, right?"

"Marîd is a—" Indihar began, but then she remembered that I was a guest in her home. She lowered her eyes modestly to the floor. "You honor our family with your visit, Marîd," she said.

I didn't know what to say. This was a major shock: Indihar as beautiful Budayeen dancer by day, demure Muslim wife by night. "Please," I said uncomfortably, "don't go to any trouble for me."

Indihar flicked her eyes at me before she led Zahra out of the room. I couldn't read what she was thinking.

"Have some tea," said Shaknahyi. "Have some more *hummus.*" Hâkim had at last found the courage to look me over. He grabbed my leg and drooled on my pants.

This was going to be even worse than I'd feared.

It was Shaknahyi's small brown notebook, the one he'd carried in his hip pocket. The first time I'd seen it was when we'd investigated Blanca's murder. Now I stared at its vinyl cover, smeared with bloody fingerprints, and wondered about Shaknahyi's coded entries. I supposed I was going to have to find out what they all meant.

This was a week after my visit to Jirji and Indihar's apartment. The day had started off on a low note and it never improved. I looked up to see Kmuzu standing beside my bed holding a tray of orange juice, toast, and coffee. I guess he'd been waiting for my wake-up daddy to kick in. He looked so sick that I almost felt sorry for the poor sucker. "Good morning, *yaa Sidi,*" he said softly.

I felt like hell too. "Where are my clothes?"

Kmuzu winced. "I don't know, *yaa Sidi.* I don't remember what you did with them last night."

I didn't remember much either. There was nothing but sick blackness from the time I came in the front door late last night until just a moment ago. I crawled out of bed naked, my head throbbing, my stomach threatening immediate upheaval. "Help me find my jeans," I said. "My pillcase is in my jeans."

"This is why the Lord forbids drinking," said Kmuzu. I glanced at him; his eyes were closed and he was still holding the tray, but it was tilting dangerously. There was going to be coffee and orange juice all over my bed in a few seconds. That wasn't important to me right then.

My clothes weren't under the bed, which was the logical place to look. They weren't in the closet, and they weren't in the dressing room or the bathroom. I looked on the table in the dining area and in my small kitchen. No luck. I finally found my shoes and shirt rolled up in a ball in

120

the bookcase, crammed between some paperback novels by Lutfy Gad, a Palestinian detective writer of the middle twenty-first century. My jeans had been folded neatly and hidden on my desk beneath several thick sheaves of computer printout.

I didn't even put the pants on. I just grabbed the pillcase and hurried back into the bedroom. My plan was to swallow some opiates, maybe a dozen Sonneine, with the orange juice.

Too late. Kmuzu was staring down in horror at the sticky, sweet-smelling puddle on my bedclothes. He looked up at me. "I'll clean this up," he said, gulping down a wave of nausea, "immediately." His expression said that he expected to lose his comfortable job in the Big House, and be sent out to the dusty fields with the other unskilled brutes.

"Don't worry about it right now, Kmuzu. Just hand me that cup of—"

There was a gentle scraping sound as the coffee cup and saucer slid southward and tumbled over the edge of the tray. I looked at the ruined sheets. At least you couldn't see the orange juice stain anymore.

"*Yaa Sidi*—"

"I want a glass of water, Kmuzu. Right now."

It had been a hell of a night. I'd had the bright idea to go to the Budayeen after work. "I haven't had a night out in a long time," I said to Kmuzu when he arrived to pick me up at the station house.

"The master of the house is pleased that you're concentrating on your work."

"Yeah, you right, but that don't mean I can't see my friends now and then." I gave him directions to Jo-Mama's Greek club.

"If you do this, you will not get home until late, *yaa Sidi.*"

"I know it'll be late. Would you rather I went out drinking in the morning?"

"You must be at the station house in the morning."

"That's a long time from now," I pointed out.

"The master of the house—"

"Turn left here, Kmuzu. *Now!*" I wasn't going to listen to any more argument. I guided him northwest through the twisting streets of the city. We left the car on the boulevard and walked through the gate into the Budayeen.

Jo-Mama's club was on Third Street, jammed tight against the high northern wall of the quarter. Rocky, the relief barmaid, frowned at me when I took a stool at the front bar. She was short and hefty with brushy black hair, and she didn't look glad to see me. "Ya want to see my manager's license, cop?" she said in a sour voice.

"Get a grip, Rocky. I just want a gin and bingara." I turned to Kmuzu, who was still standing behind me. "Grab a seat," I told him.

"Who's this?" said Rocky. "Your slave or something?"

I nodded. "Give him the same."

Kmuzu raised a hand. "Just some club soda, please," he said. Rocky glanced at me, and I shook my head slightly.

Jo-Mama came out of her office and grinned at me. "Marîd, where y'at? You ain't been comin' around no more."

"Been busy," I said. Rocky set a drink in front of me and an identical one in front of Kmuzu.

Jo-Mama smacked his shoulder. "You know your boss here got some guts," she said admiringly.

"I've heard the stories," said Kmuzu.

"Yeah, ain't we all?" said Rocky. Her lip curled just a little.

Kmuzu sipped his gin and bingara and grimaced. "This club soda tastes strange," he said.

"It's the lime juice," I said hastily.

"Yeah, I put some lime in it for ya," said Rocky.

"Oh," said Kmuzu. He took another taste.

Jo-Mama snorted. She's the largest woman I've ever met—big, strong, and often friendly. She has a loud, gruff voice and a remarkable memory for who owes her money and who's done her dirt. When she laughs, you see beer splash out of glasses all around the bar; and when she gets angry, you don't hang around long enough to see anything. "Your friends are at a table in the back," she said.

"Who?"

"Mahmoud and the Half-Hajj and that snotty Christian."

"*Used* to be my friends," I said. Jo-Mama shrugged. I

picked up my drink and went deeper into the dark cavern of the club. Kmuzu followed me.

Mahmoud, Jacques, Saied, and Saied's adolescent American lover, Abdul-Hassan, were sitting at a table near the edge of the stage. They didn't see me at first because they were appraising the dancer, a stranger to me but clearly a real girl. I moved a couple of chairs up to their table, and Kmuzu and I sat down.

"How ya doin', Marîd?" said the Half-Hajj.

"Look who it is," said Mahmoud. "Come in to inspect the permits?"

"That's a bum line I heard already from Rocky," I said.

It didn't bother Mahmoud. Although as a girl he'd been lithe and pretty enough to dance here in Jo-Mama's club, he'd put on weight and muscle after the sexchange. I wouldn't want to fight him to see which of us was tougher.

"Why are we watching this bint?" asked Saied. Abdul-Hassan was glaring spitefully at the girl on stage. The Half-Hajj was teaching him well.

"She's not so bad," said Jacques, giving us the benefit of his militantly conventional viewpoint. "She's very pretty, don't you think?"

Saied spat on the floor. "The debs on the Street are prettier."

"The debs on the Street are constructs," said Jacques. "This girl's natural."

"Shellfish toxin is natural, if that's what you care about," said Mahmoud. "I'd rather watch somebody who's spent some time and effort making herself look good."

"Someone who's spent a fortune on bodmods, you mean," said Jacques.

"What's her name?" I asked.

They ignored my question. "You hear that Blanca's dead?" Jacques said to Mahmoud.

"Probably beaten to death in a police riot," Mahmoud replied. His eyes flicked at me.

I wasn't going to put up with any more of this. I got out of my chair. "Finish your . . . club soda," I said to Kmuzu.

Saied stood up and came closer to me. "Hey, Marîd," he whispered, "don't pay any attention to 'em. They're just trying to bubble your bile."

"It's working," I said.

"They'll get tired of it soon. Everything'll go back the way it used to be."

I downed the rest of my drink. "Sure," I said, surprised by Saied's naïveté. Abdul-Hassan gave me a flirtatious look, batting his thick eyelashes. I wondered what sex he'd be when he grew up.

Jo-Mama had disappeared into her office again, and Rocky didn't bother saying goodbye. Kmuzu trailed me out of the bar. "Well," I said to him, "enjoying yourself?"

He gave me a blank stare. He didn't look pleased.

"We'll pass by Chiri's," I told him. "If anybody even looks at me cross-eyed in there, I can throw him out. It's my club." I liked the way that sounded.

I led Kmuzu south, and then turned up the Street. He came along with a solemn and disapproving look on his face. He wasn't the perfect drinking companion, but he was loyal. I knew he wouldn't abandon me if he met some hot girl somewhere.

"Why don't you loosen up?" I asked him.

"It's not my job to be loose," he said.

"You're a slave. It's your job to be what I tell you to be. Gear down a little."

I got a nice welcome when I went into the club. "Here he comes, ladies," called Chiri, "the boss man." This time she didn't sound bitter when she called me that. There were three sexchanges and two debs working with her. The real girls were all on the day shift with Indihar.

It felt great to feel at home somewhere. "How's it going, Chiri?" I asked.

She looked disgusted. "Slow night," she said. "No money."

"You always say that." I went down and took my usual seat at the far end of the bar, where it curved around toward the stage. I could sit there and look down the whole length of the bar, and see anybody coming into the club. Kmuzu sat beside me.

Chiri flipped a cork coaster toward me. I tapped the place in front of Kmuzu, and Chiri nodded. "Who is this handsome devil?" she asked.

"His name's Kmuzu," I said. "He's uncommunicative."

Chiri grinned. "I can fix that. Where you from, honey?" she asked.

He spoke to Chiri in some African language, but neither she nor I understood a word of it. "I'm Sîdi Marîd's slave," he said.

Chiri was dismayed. She was almost speechless. "Slave? Forgive me for saying it, sweetie, but being a slave's nothing to brag about. You can't really make it sound like an *achievement*, you know?"

Kmuzu shook his head. "There is a long story behind it."

"I guess so," said Chiri, looking at me for an explanation.

"If there's a story, nobody's told me," I said.

"Papa just gave him to you, right? Like he gave you the club." I nodded. Chiri put a gin and bingara on my coaster and another in front of Kmuzu. "If I was you," she said, "I'd be careful what I unwrapped under his Christmas tree from now on."

Yasmin watched me for half an hour before she came up to say hello, and then only because the other two changes were kissing on me and rubbing themselves up against me, trying to get in good with the new owner. It was working, too. "You come a long way, Marîd," Yasmin said.

I shrugged. "I feel like I'm still the same simple *noraf* I've always been."

"You know that's not true."

"Well, I owe it all to you. You're the one who bullied me into getting my skull amped, doing what Papa wanted."

Yasmin looked away. "Yeah, I guess so." She turned toward me again. "Listen, Marîd, I'm sorry if—"

I put my hand on hers. "Don't ever say you're sorry, Yasmin. We got past all that a long time ago."

She looked grateful. "Thanks, Marîd." She leaned over and kissed me on the cheek. Then she hurried back down the bar where two dark-skinned merchant seamen had taken seats.

The rest of the night passed quickly. I downed one drink after another, and I made sure that Kmuzu did the same. He still thought he was drinking club soda with some strange lime juice in it.

Somewhere along the line I began to get drunk, and Kmuzu must have been nearly helpless. I recall Chiri closing the bar about three in the morning. She counted out the register and gave me the money. I gave half the receipts back to her as per our agreement, then paid Yasmin and the other four their wages. I still ended up with another thick wad of bills for myself.

I got a very enthusiastic goodnight kiss from a change named Lily, and a slip of paper with a commcode from someone named Rani. I think Rani gave a slip of paper to Kmuzu too, just to cover her bets.

That's when I really blacked out. I don't know how Kmuzu and I got home, but we didn't bring the car with us. I guess Chiri called us a cab. The next thing I knew, I was waking up in bed and Kmuzu was about to spill orange juice and hot coffee all over me.

"Where's that water?" I called. I stumbled around my suite, holding the sunnies in one hand and my shoes in the other.

"Here, *yaa Sidi*."

I took the glass from him and swallowed the tabs. "There's a couple left for you," I said.

He looked appalled. "I can't—"

"It's not recreational. It's medicine." Kmuzu overcame his aversion to drugs long enough to take a single Sonneine.

I was still far from sober, and the sunnies I'd taken didn't help steady me. I didn't hurt anymore, but I was only vaguely conscious. I dressed quickly without paying much attention to what I put on. Kmuzu offered me breakfast, but the whole idea turned my stomach; for once, Kmuzu didn't badger me into eating. I think he was glad not to have to cook.

We stumbled blearily downstairs. I called a taxi to take me to work, and Kmuzu came with me to pick up the sedan. In the cab, I let my head fall back against the seat, and I closed my eyes and listened to peculiar noises inside my head. My ears were thrumming like the engine room of an ancient tugboat.

"May your day be blessed," said Kmuzu, when we got to the station house.

"May I live to see lunch, you mean," I said. I got out of

the cab and pushed my way through my crowd of young fans, throwing them a little money.

Sergeant Catavina gave me a jaundiced look when I got to my cubicle. "You don't look well," he said.

"I don't feel well."

Catavina clucked his tongue. "I'll tell you what I do when I get a little hung over."

"You don't show up for work," I said, dropping into my molded plastic chair. I didn't feel like conversing with him.

"That always works too," he said. He turned and left my cubicle. He didn't seem to like me, and I didn't seem to care.

Shaknahyi came by fifteen minutes later. I was still staring at my data deck, unable to dig into the mound of paperwork that waited on my desk. "Where you at?" he said. He didn't wait for an answer. "Hajjar wants to see us both right now."

"I'm not available," I said glumly.

"I'll tell him that. Come on, move your ass."

I followed him reluctantly down the corridor to Hajjar's little glass-walled office. We stood in front of his desk while he toyed with a small pile of paper clips. After a few seconds he looked up and studied us. It was a careful act. He had something difficult to tell us, and he wanted us to know that It Would Hurt Him More Than It Hurt Us. "I don't like havin' to do this," he said. He looked real sad.

"Just skip it then, Lieutenant," I said. "Come on, Jirji, let's leave him alone."

"Shut up, Audran," said Hajjar. "We got an official complaint from Reda Abu Adil. I thought I told you to lay off him." We hadn't gone out to see Abu Adil again, but we'd been talking to as many of his crummy underlings as we could corner.

"Okay," said Shaknahyi, "we'll lay off."

"The investigation is finished. We compiled all the information we need."

"Okay," said Shaknahyi.

"You both understand? Leave Abu Adil alone from now on. We ain't got a thing on him. He's not under any kind of suspicion."

"Right," said Shaknahyi.

Hajjar looked at me. "Fine," I said.

Hajjar nodded. "Okay. Now I got somethin' else I want you two to check out." He handed Shaknahyi a sheet of pale blue paper.

Shaknahyi glanced at it. "This address is right nearby," he said.

"Uh huh," said Hajjar. "There been some complaints from people in the neighborhood. Looks like another baby peddler, but this guy's got an ugly wrinkle. If this On Cheung's there, cuff him and bring him in. Don't worry about evidence; we'll make some up later if you don't find nothin'. If he ain't there, go through what you find and bring the good stuff back here."

"What do we charge him with?" I asked.

Hajjar shrugged. "Don't need to charge him with nothing. He'll hear all about it soon enough at his trial."

I looked at Shaknahyi; he shrugged. This was how the police department used to operate in the city a few years ago. Lieutenant Hajjar must have gotten nostalgic for the good old days before due process.

Shaknahyi and I left Hajjar's office and headed toward the elevator. He jammed the blue paper in his shirt pocket. "This won't take long," he said. "Then we can get something to eat." The idea of food nauseated me; I realized that I was still half-loaded. I prayed to Allah that my condition wouldn't get us into trouble on the street.

We drove about six blocks to an area of crumbling red brick tenements. Children played in the street, kicking a soccer ball back and forth and leaping on each other with loud shrieks. *"Yaa Sidi! Yaa Sidi!"* they cried when I got out of the copcar. I realized that some of them were the kids I distributed cash to every morning.

"You're becoming a celebrity in this neighborhood," Shaknahyi said with some amusement.

Groups of men were sitting in front of the tenements on battered kitchen chairs, drinking tea and arguing and watching traffic go by. Their conversation died as soon as we appeared. They watched us walk by with narrowed, hate-filled eyes. I could hear them muttering about us as we passed.

Shaknahyi consulted the blue sheet and checked the address of one of the tenements. "This is it," he said. There was a dark storefront on the ground floor, its display window obscured by flattened cardboard boxes taped in place on the inside.

"Looks abandoned," I said.

Shaknahyi nodded and walked back to where some of the men were watching us closely. "Anybody know anything about this On Cheung?" he asked.

The men looked at each other, but none of them said anything.

"Bastard's been buying kids. You seen him?"

I didn't think any of the unshaven, hungry-looking men would help us, but finally one of them stood up. "I'll talk to you," he said. The others mocked him and spat at his heels as he followed Shaknahyi and me down the sidewalk.

"What you know about it?" Shaknahyi asked.

"This On Cheung shows up a few months ago," said the man. He looked over his shoulder nervously. "Every day, women come here to his shop. They bring children, they go inside. A little while later they come out again, but they don't come out with the children."

"What does he do with the kids?" I asked.

"He breaks their legs," said the man. "He cuts off their hands or pulls out their tongues so people will feel sorry for them and give them money. Then he sells them to slavemasters who put them on the street to beg. Sometimes he sells the older girls to pimps."

"On Cheung would be dead by sundown if Friedlander Bey knew about this," I said.

Shaknahyi looked at me like I was a fool. He turned back to our informant. "How much does he pay for a kid?"

"I don't know," said the man. "Three, maybe five hundred kiam. Boys are worth more than girls. Sometimes pregnant women come to him from other parts of the city. They stay a week, a month. Then they go home and tell their family that the baby died." He shrugged.

Shaknahyi went to the storefront and tried the door. It rattled but wouldn't open. He took out his needle gun and smashed a glass panel over the lock, then reached in and opened the door. I followed him into the dark, musty storefront.

There was trash strewn everywhere, broken bottles and Styrofoam food containers, shredded newspaper and bubblewrap packing material. A strong odor of pine-

scented disinfectant hung in the still air. There was
single battered table against one wall, a light fixture hang
ing from the ceiling, a stained porcelain sink in a bac
corner with one dripping faucet. There was no other fu
niture. Evidently On Cheung had had some warning o
the police interest in his industry. We walked around th
room, crunching glass and plastic underfoot. There wa
nothing more we could do there.

"When you're a cop," said Shaknahyi, "you spend
lot of time being frustrated."

We went outside again. The men on the kitche
chairs were shouting at our informant; none of them ha
any use for On Cheung, but their friend had broken som
goddamn unwritten code by talking to us. He'd have t
suffer for it.

We left them going at it. I was disgusted by the whol
thing, and glad I hadn't seen evidence of what On Cheun
had been up to. "What happens now?" I asked.

"To On Cheung? We file a report. Maybe he's move
to another part of the city, maybe he's left the city alto
gether. Maybe someday somebody'll catch him and cu
his arms and legs off. Then he can sit on a street corne
and beg, see how *he* likes it."

A woman in a long black coat and gray kerchie
crossed the street. She was carrying a small baby wrappe
in a red-and-white-checked *keffiya*. "*Yaa Sidi?*" she said t
me. Shaknahyi raised his eyebrows and walked away.

"Can I help you, O my sister?" I said. It was highly
unusual for a woman to speak to a strange man on the
street. Of course, I was just a cop to her.

"The children tell me you are a kind man," she said
"The landlord demands more money because now I have
another child. He says—"

I sighed. "How much do you need?"

"Two hundred fifty kiam, *yaa Sidi.*"

I gave her five hundred. I took it out of last night'
profits from Chiri's. There was still plenty left.

"What they say about you is true, O chosen one!" she
said. There were tears slipping from her eyes.

"You embarrass me," I said. "Give the landlord his
rent, and buy food for yourself and your children."

"May Allah increase your strength, *yaa Sidi!*"

"May He bless you, my sister."

She hurried back across the street and into her building. "Makes you feel all warm inside, don't it?" Shaknahyi
said. I couldn't tell if he was mocking me.

"I'm glad I can help out a little," I said.

"The Robin Hood of the slums."

"There are worse things to be called."

"If Indihar could see this side of you, maybe she
wouldn't hate your guts so much." I stared at him, but he
only laughed.

Back in the patrol car, the comp deck spoke up.
"Badge number 374, respond immediately. Escaped murderer Paul Jawarski has been positively identified in
Meloul's on Nûr ad-Din Street. He is desperate, well
armed, and he will shoot to kill. Other units are on their
way."

"We'll take care of it," said Shaknahyi. The comp
deck's crackle faded away.

"Meloul's is where we ate lunch that time, right?" I
said.

Shaknahyi nodded. "We'll try to ease this bastard
Jawarski out of there before he puts holes in Meloul's
couscous steamer."

"Holes?" I asked.

Shaknahyi turned and gave me a broad grin. "He
likes old-fashioned pistols. He carries a .45 automatic. Put
a dimple in you big enough to throw a leg of lamb
through."

"You heard of this Jawarski?"

Shaknahyi swung into Nûr ad-Din Street. "We street
cops have been seeing his picture for weeks. Claims he's
killed twenty-six men. He's the boss of the Flathead Gang.
There's ten thousand kiam on his head."

Evidently I was supposed to know what he was talking about. "You don't seem too concerned," I said.

Shaknahyi raised a hand. "I don't know whether the
tip's genuine or just another pipe dream. We get as many
fake calls as good ones in this neighborhood."

We were the first to arrive at Meloul's. Shaknahyi
opened his door and got out. I did the same. "What do you
want me to do?" I asked.

"Just keep the citizens out of the way," he said. "In
case there's some—"

There was a volley of shots from inside the restaurant.

Those projectile weapons make a respectable noise. They sure catch your attention when they go off, not like the spitting and hissing of static and seizure guns. I dropped to the sidewalk and tried to wrestle my static gun free of my pocket. There were more shots and I heard glass shattering nearby. The windshield, I guessed.

Shaknahyi had fallen back alongside the building, out of the line of fire. He was drawing his own weapon.

"Jirji," I called.

He waved to me to cut off the back of the restaurant. I got up and moved a few yards, and then I heard Jawarski run out the front door. I turned and saw Shaknahyi chasing after him, firing his needle gun down Nûr ad-Dîn Street. Shaknahyi shot four times, and then Jawarski turned. I was looking straight at them, and all I could think about was how big and black the mouth of Jawarski's gun looked. It seemed like it was pointed straight at my heart. He fired a few times and my blood froze until I realized I hadn't been hit.

Jawarski ran into a yard a few doors from Meloul's, and Shaknahyi went in after him. The fugitive must have realized that he couldn't cut through to the next street, because he doubled back toward Shaknahyi. I got there just as the two men stood facing each other, shooting it out. Jawarski's gun emptied and he turned and ran to the back of a two-story house.

We chased him through the yard. Shaknahyi ran up a flight of steps in the back, pushed open a door, and went inside the house. I didn't want to, but I had to follow him. As soon as I opened the back door, I saw Shaknahyi. He was leaning against a wall, shoving a fresh clip into his needle gun. He didn't seem to be aware of the large, dark stain that was spreading across his chest.

"Jirji, you're shot," I said, my mouth dry and my heart hammering.

"Yeah." He took a deep breath and let it out. "Come on."

He walked slowly through the house to the front door. He went outside and stopped a civilian in a small electric car. "Too far to get the patrol car," he said to me, panting for breath. He looked at the driver. "I'm shot," he said, getting into the car.

I got in beside him. "Take us to the hospital," I ordered the mousy little man behind the wheel.

Shaknahyi swore. "Forget that. Follow him." He pointed to Jawarski, who was crossing the open space between the house he'd hidden in and the next.

Jawarski saw us and fired as he ran. The bullet went through the window of the car, but the bald-headed driver kept on going. We could see Jawarski dodging from one house to another. Between houses, he'd turn and take a few shots at us. Five more bullets spanged into the car.

Finally Jawarski got to the last house on the block, and he ran up the porch. Shaknahyi steadied his needle gun and fired. Jawarski staggered inside. "Come on," said Shaknahyi, wheezing. "I think I got him." He opened the car door and fell to the pavement. I jumped out and helped him to his feet. "Where are they?" he murmured.

I looked over my shoulder. A handful of uniformed cops were swarming up the stairs of Jawarski's hiding place, and three more patrol cars were racing up the street. "They're right here, Jirji," I said. His skin was starting to turn an awful gray color.

He leaned against the shot-up car and caught his breath. "Hurts like hell," he said quietly.

"Take it easy, Jirji. We'll get you to the hospital."

"Wasn't no accident, the call about On Cheung, then the tip on Jawarski."

"What you talking about?" I asked.

He was in a lot of pain, but he wouldn't get in the car. "The Phoenix File," he said. He looked deeply into my eyes, as if he could burn this information directly into my brain. "Hajjar let it slip about the Phoenix File. I been keeping notes ever since. They don't like it. Pay attention to who gets my parts, Audran. But play dumb or they'll take *your* bones too."

"The hell is a Phoenix File, Jirji?" I was frantic with worry.

"Take this." He gave me the vinyl-covered notebook from his hip pocket. Then his eyes closed and he slumped backward across the hood of the car. I looked at the driver. "Now you want to take him to the hospital?"

The shrimpy bald-headed man stared at me. Then he looked at Jirji. "You think you can keep that blood off my upholstery?" he asked.

I grabbed the little motherfucker by the front of his shirt and threw him out of his own car. Then I gently eased Shaknahyi into the passenger seat and drove to the hospital as fast as I've ever driven.

It didn't make any difference. I was too late.

One of Khayyám's rubâiyyat kept going through my mind. Something about regret:

Again, again, Repentance oft before
I vowed—but was I sober when I swore?
Again, again I failed, for younger thoughts
my frail Repentance into tatters tore.

"Chiri, please," I said, holding up my empty glass. The club was almost empty. It was late and I was very tired. I closed my eyes and listened to the music, the same shrill, thumping hispo music Kandy played every time she got up to dance. I was getting tired of hearing the same songs over and over again.

"Why don't you go home?" Chiri asked me. "I can take care of the place by myself. What's the matter, don't you trust me with the cash?"

I opened my eyes. She'd put a fresh vodka gimlet in front of me. I was in a bottomless melancholy, the kind that doesn't get any help at all from liquor. You can drink all night and you never get loaded. You end up with a bad stomach and a pounding headache, but the relief you expect from your troubles never comes. " 'S all right," I said. "I got to stay. You go ahead and close up, though. Nobody's come in for an hour at least."

"What you say, boss," said Chiri, giving me a worried look. I hadn't told her about Shaknahyi. I hadn't told anybody about him.

"Chiri, you know somebody I can trust to do a little dirty work?"

She didn't look shocked. That was one of the reasons I liked her so much. "You can't find somebody with your

135

cop connections? You don't have enough thugs working for you at Papa's?"

I shook my head. "Somebody who knows what he's doing, somebody I can count on to keep a low profile."

Chiri grinned. "Somebody like what you used to be before your lucky number came up. What about Morgan? He's dependable and he probably won't sell you out."

"I don't know," I said. Morgan was a big blond guy, an American from Federated New England. He and I didn't travel in the same circles, but if Chiri recommended him, he was probably all right.

"What you need done?" she asked.

I rubbed my cheek. Reflected in the back mirror, my red beard was beginning to show a lot of gray. "I want him to track somebody down for me. Another American."

"See there? Morgan's a natural."

"Uh huh," I said sourly. "If they blow each other away, nobody'll miss 'em. Can you get hold of him tonight?"

She looked doubtful. "It's two o'clock in the morning."

"Tell him there's a hundred kiam in it for him. Just for showing up and talking to me."

"He'll be here," said Chiri. She dug an address book out of her bag and grabbed the bar's phone.

I gulped down half the vodka gimlet and stared at the front door. Now I was waiting for two people.

"You want to pay us?" Chiri said some time later.

I'd been staring at the door, unaware that the music had been turned off and the five dancers had gotten dressed. I shook my head to clear the fog out of it, but it didn't do much good. "How'd we do tonight?" I asked.

"Same as always," said Chiri. "Lousy."

I split the receipts with her and began counting out the dancers' money. Chiri had a list of how many drinks each girl had gotten from the customers. I figured out the commissions and added them to the wages. "Nobody better come in late tomorrow," I said.

"Yeah, right," said Kandy, snatching up her money and hurrying for the door. Lily, Rani, and Jamila were close behind her.

"You all right, Marîd?" asked Yasmin.

I looked up at her, grateful for her concern. "I'm fine," I said. "Tell you all about it later."

"Want to go out for some breakfast?"

That would have been wonderful. I hadn't gone out with Yasmin in months. I realized that it had been a very long time since I'd gone out with *anybody*. I had something else to do tonight, though. "Let me postpone that," I said. "Tomorrow, maybe."

"Sure, Marîd," she said. She turned and went out.

"There *is* something wrong, huh?" said Chiri.

I just nodded and folded up the rest of the night's cash. No matter how fast I gave it away, it just kept accumulating.

"And you don't want to talk about it."

I shook my head. "Go on home, Chiri."

"Just gonna sit here in the dark by yourself?"

I made a shooing motion with my hand. Chiri shrugged and left me alone. I finished the vodka gimlet, then went behind the bar and made myself another one. About twenty minutes later, the blond American came into the club. He nodded to me and said something in English.

I just shook my head. I opened my briefcase on the bar, took out an English-language daddy, and chipped it in. There was just a moment while my mind worked to translate what he'd said, and then the daddy kicked in and it was as if I'd always known how to speak English. "Sorry to make you come out so late, Morgan," I said.

He ran a large hand through his long blond hair. "Hey, man, what's happenin'?"

"Want a drink?"

"You can draw me a beer if it's free."

"Help yourself," I said.

He leaned across the bar and held a clean glass under one of the taps. "Chiri said something about a hundred kiam, man."

I took out my money. The size of the roll dismayed me. I was going to have to get to the bank more often, or else I'd have to let Kmuzu play bodyguard full-time. I dealt out five twenty-kiam bills and slid them down toward Morgan.

He wiped his mouth with the back of his hand and

scooped up the money. He looked down at the bills, then back at me. "Now I can go, right?" he said.

"Sure," I said, "unless you want to hear how you can make a thousand more."

He adjusted his steel-rimmed spectacles and grinned again. I didn't know if the glasses were functional or just an affectation. If his eyes were bad, he could have had them reconstructed cheaply enough. "This is a lot more interesting than what I was doin', anyway," he said.

"Fine. I just want you to find somebody." I told him all about Paul Jawarski.

When I mentioned the Flathead Gang, Morgan nodded. "He's the guy that killed the cop today?" he asked.

"He got away."

"Well, hey, man, the law will bring him in sooner or later, you can bet on that."

I didn't let my expression change. "I don't want to hear about sooner or later, okay? I want to know where he's at, and I want to ask him a couple of questions before the cops get to him. He's holed up somewhere, probably been stung with a needle gun."

"You're payin' a thousand kiam just to put the finger on this guy?"

I squeezed the wedge of lime into my gimlet and drank some. "Uh huh."

"You don't want me to rough him up a little for you?"

"Just find him before Hajjar does."

"Aha," said Morgan, "I get you, man. After the lieutenant gets his hooks into him, Jawarski won't be available to talk to nobody."

"Right. And we don't want that to happen."

"I guess we don't, man. How much you gonna pay me up front?"

"Five now, five later." I cut him another five hundred kiam. "I get results tomorrow, right?"

His big hand closed on the money and he gave me his predatory grin. "Go get some sleep, man. I'll be wakin' you up with Jawarski's address and commcode."

I stood up. "Finish your beer and let's get out of here. This place is starting to break my heart."

Morgan looked around at the dark bar. "Ain't the same without the girls and the mirror balls goin', is it?" He gulped down the rest of his beer and set the glass gently on the bar.

I followed him toward the front door. "Find Jawarski," I said.

"You got it, man." He raised a hand and ambled away up the Street. I went back inside and sat in my place. My night wasn't over yet.

I drank a couple more gimlets before Indihar showed up. I knew she was going to come. I'd been waiting for her.

She'd thrown on a bulky blue coat and tied a maroon and gold scarf over her hair. Her face was pale and drawn, her lips pressed tightly together. She came to where I was sitting and looked down at me. Her eyes weren't red, though; she hadn't been crying. I couldn't imagine Indihar crying. "I want to talk to you," she said. Her voice was cold and calm.

"That's why I been sitting here," I said.

She turned away and stared at herself in the wall of mirrors behind the stage. "Sergeant Catavina said you weren't in very good shape this morning. That true?" She looked at me again. Her expression was perfectly empty.

"Is what true?" I said. "That I wasn't feeling well?"

"That you were high or hung over today when you went out with my husband."

I sighed. "I showed up at the station house with a hangover. It wasn't crippling, though."

Her hands began clenching and unclenching. I could see her jaw muscles twitch. "You think it might have slowed you down any?"

"No, Indihar," I said, "I don't think it affected me at all. You want to blame me for what happened? Is that what this is about?"

Her head turned very slowly. She stared directly into my eyes. "Yes, I want to blame you. You didn't back him up fast enough. You didn't cover him. If you'd been there for him, he wouldn't be dead."

"You can't say that, Indihar." I had a sick, hollow feeling in my belly because I'd been thinking the same thing all day. The guilt had been growing in me since I'd left Shaknahyi lying on a cot at the hospital with a bloody sheet over his face.

"My husband would be alive and my children would

still have a father. They don't now, you know. I haven't told them yet. I don't know *how* to tell them. I don't know how to tell myself, if you want to know the truth. Maybe tomorrow I'll realize that Jirji's dead. Then I'll have to find a way to get through the day without him, through the week, through the rest of my life."

I felt a sudden nausea and closed my eyes. It was as if I weren't really there, as if I were just dreaming this nightmare. When I opened my eyes, though, Indihar was still looking at me. It had all happened, and she and I were going to have to play out this terrible scene. "I—"

"Don't tell me you're sorry, you son of a bitch," she said. Even then she didn't raise her voice. "I don't want to hear anybody tell me he's sorry."

I just sat there and let her say whatever she needed to say. She couldn't accuse me of anything that I hadn't already confessed to in my own mind. Maybe if I hadn't gotten so drunk last night, maybe if I hadn't taken all those sunnies this morning—

Finally she just stared at me, a look of despair on her face. She was condemning me with her presence and her silence. She knew and I knew, and that was enough. Then she turned and walked out of the club, her gait steady, her posture perfect.

I felt absolutely destroyed. I found the phone where Chiri'd left it and spoke my home commcode into it. It rang three times and then Kmuzu answered. "You want to come get me?" I said. I was slurring my words.

"Are you at Chiriga's?" he asked.

"Yeah. Come quick before I kill myself." I slapped the phone down on the bar and made myself another drink while I waited.

When he arrived, I had a little present for him. "Hold out your hand," I said.

"What is it, *yaa Sidi?*"

I emptied my pillcase into his upturned palm, then clicked the pillcase closed and put it back in my pocket. "Get rid of 'em," I said.

His expression didn't change as he closed his fist. "This is wise," he said.

"I'm way overdue." I got up from my stool and followed him back into the cool night air. I locked the front door of Chiri's and then let Kmuzu drive me home.

I took a long shower and let the hot needle spray blast my skin until I felt myself begin to relax. I dried off and went into my bedroom. Kmuzu had brought me a mug of strong hot chocolate. I sipped it gratefully.

"Will you be needing anything else tonight, *yaa Sidi?*" he asked.

"Listen," I said, "I'm not going into the station house in the morning. Let me sleep, all right? I don't want to be bothered. I don't want to answer any phone calls or deal with anybody's problems."

"Unless the master of the house requires you," said Kmuzu.

I sighed. "That goes without saying. Otherwise—"

"I will see that you're not disturbed."

I didn't chip in the wake-up daddy before I went to bed, and I got a restless night's sleep. Bad dreams woke me again and again until I fell into deep, exhausted sleep at dawn. It was close to noon when I finally got out of bed. I dressed in my old jeans and work shirt, a costume I didn't wear very often around Friedlander Bey's mansion.

"Would you like some breakfast, *yaa Sidi?*" asked Kmuzu.

"No, I'm taking a vacation from all that today."

He frowned. "There is a business matter for your attention later."

"Later," I agreed. I went to the desk where I'd thrown my briefcase the night before, and took Wise Counselor from the rack of moddies. I thought my troubled mind could use some instant therapy. I seated myself in a comfortable black leather chair and chipped the moddy in.

Once upon a time in Mauretania there was or maybe there wasn't a famous fool, trickster, and rascal named Marîd Audran. One day Audran was driving his cream-colored Westphalian sedan on his way to take care of some important business, when another car collided with his. The second car was old and broken down, and although the accident was clearly the fault of the other driver, the man jumped out of the wrecked heap and began scream-ing at Audran. "Look what you've done to my magnificent vehicle!" shouted the driver, who was Police Lieutenant Hajjar. Reda Abu Adil, Hassan the Shiite, and Paul Jawar-

*ski also got out of the car. All four threatened and abused
Audran, although he protested that he had done nothing
wrong.*

*Jawarski kicked the creased fender of Hajjar's auto-
mobile. "It's useless now," he said, "and so the only fair
thing is for you to give us your car."*

*Audran was outnumbered four to one and it was clear
that they were not in a mood to be reasonable, so he
agreed.*

*"And will you not reward us for showing you the
path of honor?" asked Hajjar.*

*"If we hadn't insisted," said Hassan, "your actions
would have put your soul in jeopardy with Allah."*

*"Perhaps," said Audran. "What do you wish me to
pay you for this service?"*

*Reda Abu Adil spread his hands as if it mattered
little. "It is but a token, a symbol between Muslim brothers," he said. "You may give us each a hundred kiam." So
Audran handed the keys to his cream-colored Westphalian sedan to Lieutenant Hajjar, and paid each of the four
a hundred kiam.*

*All afternoon, Audran pushed Hajjar's wrecked car
back to town in the hot sun. He parked it in the middle of
the souk and went to find his friend, Saied the Half-Hajj.
"You must help me get even with Hajjar, Abu Adil, Hassan, and Jawarski," he said, and Saied was agreeable.
Audran cut a hole in the floor of the derelict automobile,
and Saied lay by the opening covered with a blanket so
that none could see him, with a small bag of gold coins.
Then Audran started the engine of the car and waited.*

*Not long after, the four villains happened by. They
saw Audran sitting in the shade of the ruined automobile
and laughed. "It won't drive an inch!" mocked Jawarski.
"What are you warming the engine for?"*

*Audran glanced up. "I have my reasons," he said, and
he smiled as if he had a wonderful secret.*

*"What reasons?" demanded Abu Adil. "Has the sum-
mer sun at last broiled your brains?"*

*Audran stood and stretched. "I guess I can tell you,"
he said lightly. "After all, I owe my good fortune to you."*

"Good fortune?" asked Hajjar suspiciously.

"Come," said Audran. "Look." He led the four vil-

lains to the back of the car where the battery cap had been left open. "Piss in the battery," *he said.*

"You've surely gone crazy," *said Jawarski.*

"Then I will do it myself," *said Audran, and he did, relieving himself into the wreck's battery.* "Now we must wait a moment. There! Did you hear that?"

"I heard nothing," *said Hassan.*

"Listen," *said Audran. And there came a gentle chink! chink! sound from beneath the car.* "Take a look," *he commanded.*

Reda Abu Adil got down on hands and knees, ignoring the dust and the indignity, and peered under the car. "May his faith be cursed!" *he cried.* "Gold!" *He stretched out on the ground and reached under the car; when he straightened up again, he held a handful of gold coins. He showed them to his companions in amazement.*

"Listen," *said Audran. And they all heard the chink! chink! of more gold coins falling to the ground.*

"He pisses yellow into the car," *murmured Hassan,* "and yellow gold falls from it."

"May Allah let you prosper if you let me have my car back!" *cried Lieutenant Hajjar.*

"I'm afraid not," *said Audran.*

"Take your goddamn cream-colored Westphalian sedan and we'll call it a fair trade," *said Jawarski.*

"I'm afraid not," *said Audran.*

"We'll each give you a hundred kiam as well," *said Abu Adil.*

"I'm afraid not," *said Audran.*

They begged and begged, and Audran refused. Finally they offered to give him back his sedan plus five hundred kiam from each of them, and he accepted. "But come back in an hour," *he said.* "That's still my piss in the battery." *And they agreed. Then Audran and Saied went off and divided their profit.*

I yawned as I popped Wise Counselor out. I'd enjoyed the vision, except for seeing Hassan the Shiite, who was dead and who could stay dead for all I cared. I thought about what the little story might mean. It might mean that my unconscious mind was hard at work coming up with clever ways to outsmart my enemies. I was glad to

learn this. I already knew that I wasn't going to get anywhere by force. I didn't have any.

I felt subtly different after that session with Wise
Counselor: more determined, maybe, but also wonderfully clear and free. I had a grim set to my jaw now and the
sense that no one at all could impose restrictions on me.
I'd been changed by Shaknahyi's death, kicked up to a
higher energy level. I felt as if I were living in pure oxy-
gen, bright and clean and dangerously explosive.

"*Yaa Sidi,*" said Kmuzu softly.

"What is it?"

"The master of the house is ill today and wishes you to
attend to a small business matter."

I yawned again. "Yeah, you right. What kind of business?"

"I do not know."

This liberated feeling let me forget about what Friedlander Bey might think of my clothes. That just wasn't
important anymore. Papa had me under his thumb and
maybe I couldn't do anything about it, but I wasn't going
to be passive any longer. I intended to let him know that;
but when I saw him, he looked so ill that I filed it away for
later.

He lay propped up in bed with a small mountain of
pillows around him and behind his back. A tray table
straddled his legs, and it was stacked high with file folders,
reports, multicolored memory plates, and a tiny
microcomputer. He held a cup of hot aromatic tea in one
hand and one of Umm Saad's stuffed dates in the other.
Umm Saad must have thought she could bribe Papa with
them, or that he would forget his last words to her. To be
honest, Friedlander Bey's problem with Umm Saad
seemed almost trivial to me now, but I did not mention
her.

"I pray for your well-being," I said.

Papa raised his eyes toward me and grimaced. "It is
nothing, my nephew. I feel dizzy and sick to my stomach."

I leaned forward and kissed Papa's cheek, and he
muttered something I could not hear clearly.

I waited for him to explain the business matter he
wanted me to take care of. "Youssef tells me there is a
large, angry woman in the waiting room downstairs," he

said, a frown pulling down his mouth. "Her name is Tema Akwete. She's trying to be patient because she's come a long distance to beg a favor."

"What kind of favor?" I asked.

Papa shrugged. "She represents the new government of the Songhay Republic."

"Never heard of it."

"Last month the country was called the Glorified Segu Kingdom. Before that it was the Magistracy of Timbuktu, and before that Mali, and before that it was part of French West Africa."

"And the Akwete woman is an emissary from the new regime?"

Friedlander Bey nodded. He started to say something, but his eyes closed and his head fell back against the pillows. He passed a hand across his forehead. "Forgive me, my nephew," he said, "I'm not feeling well."

"Then don't concern yourself about the woman. What is her problem?"

"Her problem is that the Segu king was very upset to find out he'd lost his job. Before he fled the palace he sacked the royal treasury, of course—that goes without saying. His gang also destroyed all the vital computer records in the capital. The Songhay Republic opened up shop without the slightest idea of how many people they rule or even where the country's boundaries are. There is no fair basis for taxation, no lists of government employees or descriptions of their duties, and no accurate information concerning the armed forces. Songhay faces immediate catastrophe."

I understood. "So they sent someone here. They want you to restore order."

"Without tax revenue, the new government cannot pay its employees or continue normal services. It's likely that Songhay will soon be paralyzed by general strikes. The army may desert, and then the country will be at the mercy of neighboring nations, if they are any better organized."

"Why is the woman angry with *you*, then?"

Papa spread his hands. "Songhay's problems are not my concern," he said. "I explained to you that Reda Abu Adil and I divided the Muslim world. This country is in his jurisdiction. I have nothing to do with the Sub-Saharan states."

"Akwete should have gone to Abu Adil in the first place."

"Exactly. Youssef gave that message to her, but she screamed and struck the poor man. She thinks we're trying to extort a higher payment from her and her government." Papa set down his teacup and searched through the disordered piles of papers on his blankets, selecting a thick envelope and passing it to me with a trembling hand. "This is the background material and the contract she offered me. Tell her to take it to Abu Adil."

I took a deep breath and let it out. It didn't sound like dealing with Akwete was going to be much fun. "I'll talk to her," I said.

Papa nodded absently. He'd disposed of one minor annoyance, and he was already turning his attention to something else. After a while I murmured a few words and left the room. He didn't even notice that I'd gone.

Kmuzu was waiting for me in the corridor leading from Papa's private apartment. I told him what Friedlander Bey and I had talked about. "I'm gonna see this woman," I said, "and then you and I are gonna take a ride out to Abu Adil's house."

"Yes, *yaa Sidi,* but it may be best if I waited for you in the car. Reda Abu Adil no doubt thinks me a traitor."

"Uh huh. Because you were hired as a bodyguard for his wife and now you look out for me?"

"Because he arranged for me to be a spy in the house of Friedlander Bey, and I no longer consider myself to be in his employ."

I had known from the beginning that Kmuzu was a spy. I'd just thought he was Papa's spy, not Abu Adil's. "You're not reporting everything back to him?"

"Back to whom, *yaa Sidi?*"

"Back to Abu Adil."

Kmuzu gave me a brief, earnest smile. "I assure you that I am not. I am, of course, reporting to the master of the house."

"Well, that's all right, then." We'd gone downstairs, and I stopped outside one of the waiting rooms. The two Stones That Speak stood on either side of the door. They glared menacingly at Kmuzu. Kmuzu glared back. I ignored all of them and went inside.

The black woman jumped to her feet as soon as I'd set foot across the threshold. "I demand an explanation!" she cried. "I warn you, as a lawful ambassador of the government of the Songhay Republic—"

I shut her up with a sharp look. "Madame Akwete," I said, "the message you received earlier was quite accurate. You've truly come to the wrong place. However, I can expedite this matter for you. I'll convey the information and the contract in this envelope to Shaykh Reda Abu Adil, who participated in establishing the Segu Kingdom. He'll be able to help you in the same way."

"And what payment will you expect as a middleman?" Akwete asked sourly.

"None whatsoever. It is a gesture of friendship from our house to a new Islamic republic."

"Our country is still young. We mistrust such friendship."

"That is your privilege," I said, shrugging. "No doubt the Segu king felt the same way." I turned and left the waiting room.

Kmuzu and I walked briskly along the hall toward the great wooden front doors. I could hear Akwete's shoes echoing behind us on the tiled floor. "Wait," she called. I thought I heard a hint of apology in her voice.

I stopped and faced her. "Yes, madame?" I said.

"This shaykh . . . can he do as you say? Or is this some elaborate swindle?"

I gave her a cold smile. "I don't see that you or your country are in any position to doubt. Your situation is hopeless now, and Abu Adil can't make it any worse. You have nothing to lose and everything to gain."

"We are not rich," said Akwete. "Not after the way King Olujimi bled our people and squandered our meager wealth. We have little gold—"

Kmuzu raised a hand. It was very unusual for him to interrupt. "Shaykh Reda is less interested in your gold than in power," he said.

"Power?" asked Akwete. "What kind of power does he want?"

"He will study your situation," said Kmuzu, "and then he will reserve certain information for himself."

I thought I saw the black woman falter. "I insist on going with you to see this man. It is my right."

Kmuzu and I looked at each other. We both knew how naive she was to think she had any rights at all in this situation. "All right," I said, "but you'll let me speak to Abu Adil first."

She looked suspicious. "Why is that?"

"Because I say so." I went outside with Kmuzu, where I waited in the warm sunlight while he went for the car. Madame Akwete followed me a moment later. She looked furious, but she said nothing more.

In the backseat of the sedan, I opened my briefcase and took Saied's tough-guy moddy from the rack and chipped it in. It filled me with the confident illusion that nobody could get in my way from now on, not Abu Adil, Hajjar, Kmuzu, or Friedlander Bey.

Akwete sat as far from me as she could, her hands clasped tightly in her lap, her head turned away from me. I wasn't concerned with her opinion of me. I looked at Shaknahyi's brown vinyl-covered notebook again. On the first page he had written *Phoenix File* in large letters. Beneath that there were several entries:

Ishaq Abdul-Hadi Bouhatta—Elwau Chami (Heart, lungs)
Andreja Svobik—Fatima Hamdan (Stomach, bowel, liver)
Abbas Karami—Nabil Abu Khalifeh (Kidneys, liver)
Blanca Mataro—

Shaknahyi had been sure that the four names on the left were somehow connected; but in Hajjar's words, they were only "open files." Under the names, Shaknahyi had written three Arabic letters: Alif, Lâm, Mîm, corresponding to the Roman letters A, L, M.

What could they mean? Were they an acronym? I could probably find a hundred organizations whose initials were A.L.M. The A and L might form the definite article, and the M might be the first letter in a name: someone called al-Mansour or al-Maghrebi. Or were the letters Shaknahyi's shorthand, an abbreviation referring to a German *(almâni)* or a diamond *(almâs)* or something else? I wondered if I could ever discover what the three letters meant, without Shaknahyi to explain his code.

I slipped an audio chip into the car's holosystem, then put the notebook and Tema Akwete's envelope in the briefcase and locked it. While Umm Khalthoum, The Lady of the twentieth century, sang her laments, I pretended she was mourning Jirji Shaknahyi, crying for Indihar and their children. Akwete still stared out her window, ignoring me. Meanwhile, Kmuzu steered the car through the narrow, twisting streets of Hâmidiyya, the slums that guarded the approach to Reda Abu Adil's mansion.

After a ride of nearly half an hour, we turned into the estate. Kmuzu remained in the car, pretending to doze. Akwete and I got out and went up the ceramic-tiled path to the house. When Shaknahyi and I had been here before, I'd been impressed by the luxurious gardens and the beautiful house. I noticed none of that today. I rapped on the carved wooden door and a servant answered my summons immediately, giving me an insolent look but saying nothing.

"We have business with Shaykh Reda," I said, pushing by him. "I come from Friedlander Bey."

Thanks to Saied's moddy, my manner was rude and brusque, but the servant didn't seem to be upset. He shut the door after Tema Akwete and hurried ahead of me, going down a high-ceilinged corridor, expecting us to follow. We followed. He stopped before a closed door at the end of a long, cool passage. The fragrance of roses was in the air, the smell I'd come to identify with Abu Adil's mansion. The servant hadn't said another word. He paused to give me another insolent look, then walked away.

"You wait here," I said, turning to Akwete.

She started to argue, then thought better of it. "I don't like this at all," she said.

"Too bad." I didn't know what was on the other side of the door, but I wasn't going to get anywhere standing in the hallway with her, so I grabbed the doorknob and went through.

Neither Reda Abu Adil nor his secretary, Umar Abdul-Qawy, heard me come into the office. Abu Adil was in his hospital bed, as he was the previous time I'd seen him. Umar was leaning over him. I couldn't tell what he was doing.

"Allah grant you health," I said gruffly.

Umar jerked upright and faced me. "How did you get in here?" he demanded.

"Your servant brought me to the door."

Umar nodded. "Kamal. I will have to speak to him." He looked at me more closely. "I'm sorry," he said, "I don't recall your name."

"Marîd Audran. I work for Friedlander Bey."

"Ah yes," said Umar. His expression softened just a little. "The last time, you came as a policeman."

"I'm not actually a cop. I look after Friedlander Bey's interests with the police."

A little smile curled Umar's lips. "As you wish. Are you looking after them today?"

"His interests and yours also."

Abu Adil raised a feeble hand and touched Umar's sleeve. Umar bent to hear the old man's whispered words, then straightened up again. "Shaykh Reda invites you to make yourself comfortable," said Umar. "We would have prepared suitable refreshments if you'd let us know you were coming."

I looked around for a chair and seated myself. "A very upset woman came to Friedlander Bey's house today," I said. "She represents a revolutionary government that's just socialized the Glorified Segu Kingdom." I opened my briefcase, took out the envelope from the Songhay Republic, and tossed it to Umar.

Umar looked amused. "Already? I really thought Olujimi would last longer. I suppose once you've transferred all the wealth there is in a country to a foreign bank, there's really no point in being king anymore."

"I didn't come here to talk about that." The Half-Hajj's moddy was making it difficult for me to be civil to Umar. "By the terms of your agreement with Friedlander Bey, this country is under your authority. You'll find all the relevant information in that packet. I left the woman fuming outside in the hallway. She seems like a cutthroat bitch. I'm glad you have to deal with her, and not me."

Umar shook his head. "They always try to order and reorganize our lives for us. They forget how much we can do for their cause if we're in the right mood."

I watched him play with the envelope, turning it around and around on the desk. A weak, drawn-out groan came from Abu Adil, but I'd seen too much real pain in the world to pity the suffering of a Proxy Hell maggot. I looked back at Umar. "If you can do something to make your master more alert," I said, "Madame Akwete needs to speak with him. She seems to think the fate of the Islamic world rests on her shoulders alone."

Umar gave me an ironic smile. "The Songhay Republic," he said, shaking his head in disbelief. "Tomorrow it will be a kingdom again or a conquered province or a fascist dictatorship. And no one will care."

"Madame Akwete will care."

That amused him even more. "Madame Akwete will be one of the first to go in the new wave of purges. But we've talked enough about her. Now we must discuss the matter of your compensation."

I looked at him closely. "I didn't have any thought of payment," I said.

"Of course not. You were fulfilling the agreement, the compact between your employer and mine. Nevertheless, it's always wise to express gratitude to our friends. After all, someone who has helped you in the past is more likely to help you again. Perhaps there is some small service I may do for you in return."

This was the whole purpose behind my little jaunt into Abu Adil's part of town. I spread my hands and tried to look casual. "No, I can't think of anything," I said. "Unless . . ."

"Unless what, my friend?"

I pretended to examine my boot's rundown heel. "Unless you're willing to tell me why you've installed Umm Saad in our household."

Umar pretended to be just as casual. "You must know by now that Umm Saad is a very intelligent woman, but she is by no means as clever as she believes. We wished her only to keep us apprised of Friedlander Bey's plans. We said nothing to her about confronting him directly or abusing his hospitality. She's antagonized your master, and that has made her worthless to us. You may dispose of her as you wish."

"It's only as I suspected," I said. "Friedlander Bey doesn't hold you or Shaykh Reda responsible for her actions."

Umar raised one hand in a rueful gesture. "Allah

gives us tools to use as best we can," he said. "Sometimes a tool breaks and we must discard it."

"Allah be praised," I murmured.

"Praise Allah," said Umar. We seemed to be getting along just fine now.

"One other thing," I said. "The policeman who was with me the last time, Officer Shaknahyi, was shot and killed yesterday."

Umar didn't stop smiling, but his brow furrowed. "We heard the news. Our hearts go out to his widow and children. May Allah grant them peace."

"Yeah. In any event, I greatly desire to have the man who killed him. His name is Paul Jawarski."

I looked at Abu Adil, who writhed restlessly on his hospital bed. The plump old man made a few low, unintelligible sounds, but Umar wasn't paying any attention to him. "Certainly," he said. "We'll be glad to put our resources at your disposal. If any of our associates know anything about this Jawarski, you'll be informed immediately."

I didn't like the way Umar said that. It was too glib and he looked too unhappy. I just thanked him and stood up to go.

"A moment, Shaykh Marîd," he said in a quiet voice. He stood up and took my arm, guiding me to another exit. "I'd like to have a private word with you. Would you mind stepping into the library?"

I felt a peculiar chill. I knew this invitation was coming from Umar Abdul-Qawy, acting independently, not Umar Abdul-Qawy, the secretary of Shaykh Reda Abu Adil. "Fine," I said.

He reached up and popped the moddy he was wearing. He hadn't spared so much as a glance at Abu Adil.

Umar held the door for me, and I went through into the library. I seated myself at a large oblong table of glossy dark wood. Umar didn't sit, however. He paced in front of a high wall lined with bookshelves, idly tossing the moddy in one hand. "I think I understand your position," he said at last.

"Which position is that?"

He waved irritably. "You know what I mean. How much longer will you be content to be Friedlander Bey's trained dog, running and fetching for a madman who doesn't have the wit to realize he's already dead?"

"You mean Papa, or Shaykh Reda?" I asked.

Umar stopped pacing and frowned at me. "I'm speaking of both of them, and I'm sure you goddamn well know it."

I watched Umar for a moment, listening to the trilling of some of the songbirds that were caged all through Abu Adil's house and grounds. It gave the afternoon a false sense of peace and hopefulness. The air in the library was musty and stale. I began to feel caged myself. Maybe it had been a mistake coming here today. "What are you suggesting, Umar?" I asked.

"I'm suggesting that we begin thinking of the future. Someday, not long from now, the old men's empires will be in our hands. Hell, I run Shaykh Reda's business for him right now. He spends the whole day chipped in to . . . to—"

"I know what he's got chipped in," I said.

Umar nodded. "All right, then. This moddy that I use is a recent recording of his mind. He gave it to me because his only sexual kick is jamming himself, or an accurate facsimile of himself. Does that disgust you?"

"You're kidding." I'd heard much worse in my time.

"Forget that, then. He doesn't realize that with his moddy, I'm his equal as far as tending to business is concerned. I *am* Abu Adil, but I have the added advantage of my own native skills. He is Shaykh Reda, a great man; but with this moddy, I am Shaykh Reda and Umar Abdul-Qawy together. Why do I need him?"

I found this all terrifically amusing. "Are you proposing the elimination of Abu Adil and Friedlander Bey?"

Umar looked around himself nervously. "I propose no such thing," he said in a quiet voice. "There are too many other people depending on their judgment and vision. Yet there may come a day when the old men themselves are a hindrance to their own enterprises."

"When the time comes to push them aside," I said, "the right people will know it. And Friedlander Bey, at least, will not begrudge them."

"What if the time is now?" Umar asked hoarsely.

"You may be ready, but I'm not prepared to take over Papa's affairs."

"Even that problem could be solved," insisted Umar.

"Possibly," I said. I didn't let any expression cross my face. I had no idea if we were being watched and recorded, and yet I didn't want to antagonize Umar. I knew now that he was a very dangerous man.

"You will learn that I am right," he said. He tossed the moddy in his hand some more, his brow furrowed again in thought. "Go back to Friedlander Bey now and think about what I've said. We'll talk again soon. If you do not share my enthusiasm, I may need to push you aside along with both our masters." I started to rise from my chair. He raised a hand to stop me. "That is not a threat, my friend," he said calmly. "It is only how I see the future."

"Allah alone sees the future."

He laughed cynically. "If you think that pious talk has any real meaning, I may end up with more power than Shaykh Reda ever dreamed of." He indicated another door on the south side of the library. "You may go out that way. Follow the corridor to the left, and it will lead you to the front entrance. I must go back and discuss this Songhay Republic business with the woman. You needn't worry about her. I'll send her back to her hotel with my driver."

"Thank you for your kindness," I said.

"May you go in peace and safety," he said.

I left the library and followed Umar's directions. Kamal, the servant, met me along the way and showed me out. Again he kept silent as we walked. I went down the steps toward the car, and then I turned to look back. Kamal stood in the doorway, staring after me as if I might be concealing stolen silverware in my clothing.

I got into the sedan. Kmuzu started the engine and swung the car around and out through the main gate. I thought about what Umar had said, what he'd offered me. Abu Adil had exercised his power for almost two centuries. Surely in all that time there had been many young men who'd filled the position Umar now held. Surely some of them had had the same ambitious ideas. Abu Adil still remained, but what had happened to those young men? Maybe Umar had never considered that question. Maybe Umar was nowhere near as smart as he thought he was.

Jirji Shaknahyi had been killed on Tuesday, and it wasn't until Friday that I was able to go into the station house again. It was, of course, the Sabbath, and I toyed with the idea of passing by a mosque on the way, but I felt hypocritical about that. I figured I was such a crummy person that no amount of worshiping could make me acceptable to Allah. I know that's all hollow rationalization—it's the sinners, after all, who need the benefits of prayer most, and not the saints—but I just felt too soiled and guilty to enter the House of God. Besides, Shaknahyi had set an example of true faith, and I'd failed him. I had to redeem myself in my own eyes first, before I could expect to do the same in the eyes of Allah.

My life has been like a rolling ocean, with waves of comfort and ease followed by waves of adversity. No matter how peaceful things get, I know more trouble will soon sweep over me. I've always told everyone how much I preferred being on my own, a solitary agent answerable only to myself. I wished I meant it half as much as I pretended.

I needed every bit of the inner strength and confidence I'd achieved to deal with the obstinate forces around me. I was getting no help at all from Lieutenant Hajjar, Friedlander Bey, or anyone else. No one at the station house seemed particularly interested in talking with me on Friday morning. There were a lot of part-time office workers there, Christians who filled in for the religious Muslims on the Sabbath. Lieutenant Hajjar was there, of course, because on his list of favorite pastimes, religion finished down somewhere between oral surgery and paying taxes. I went immediately to his square, glass-walled office.

Eventually he looked up to see who was looming beside his desk. "What now, Audran?" he snapped. He hadn't seen me in three days, but he made it sound as if I'd been badgering him nonstop all that time.

"Just wanted to know what your plans for me were."

Hajjar looked up from his data deck. He stared at me for a long moment, his mouth twisted as if he'd just chewed a rotten date. "You're flatterin' yourself," he said in a quiet voice. "You don't enter into my plans at all."

"I was just volunteering to help in the investigation of Jirji Shaknahyi's death."

Hajjar raised his eyebrows. He leaned back in his chair. "What investigation?" he asked incredulously. "He was shot by Paul Jawarski. That's all we need to know."

I waited until I could speak without shouting at him. "We have Jawarski in custody?"

"*We?*" demanded Hajjar. "Who's *we?* You mean, does the police department have Jawarski? Not yet. But don't worry, Audran, he won't slip away. We're closin' in on him."

"How do you expect to find him? This is a big city. You think he's just sitting in a room somewhere, waiting for you to show up with a warrant? He's probably back in America by now."

"Good police work's how we'll find him, Audran. You never have much faith in good police work. I know he ain't left town. He's here somewhere, and we're tightenin' the net around him. Just a matter of time."

I didn't like the sound of that. "Tell that to his widow," I said. "She'll be heartened by your confidence."

Hajjar stood up. I'd made him angry. "You accusin' me of somethin', Audran?" he asked, jabbing a stiff forefinger into my chest. "You hintin' that maybe I'm not pushin' this investigation hard enough?"

"I never said nothing, Hajjar. I just wanted to find out what your plans are."

He gave me an evil grin. "What, you think I got nothin' better to do than sit around and worry about how to utilize your special talents? Hell, Audran, we were gettin' along fine without you the last few days. But I suppose now you're here, there must be somethin' for you to do." He sat down again at his desk and riffled through a stack of papers. "Uh yeah, here we go. I want you to go on with that investigation you and Shaknahyi started."

I wasn't happy about that. I wanted to be directly involved in tracking down Jawarski. "I thought you said we were supposed to lay off Abu Adil."

Hajjar's eyes narrowed. "I didn't say anything about Abu Adil, did I? You'd *better* lay off him. I'm talkin' about this dink, On Cheung. The baby seller. Can't afford to let his trail get cold."

I felt a cold chill pass through me. "Anybody can follow up on On Cheung," I said. "I got a special interest in finding Paul Jawarski."

"Marîd Audran, Man on a Mission, huh? Well, forget it. We don't need you roarin' around the city workin' off your grudge. Anyway, you ain't shown me yet that you know what you're doin'. So I'm assignin' you a new partner, somebody with a lot of experience. This ain't some ladies' volunteer club, Audran. You do what I tell you. Or don't you think puttin' On Cheung out of commission is worth your time?"

I gritted my teeth. I didn't like the assignment, but Hajjar was right about it being just as important as collaring Jawarski. "Whatever you say, Lieutenant."

He gave me that same grin. I wanted to whack it off his face. "You'll be ridin' around with Sergeant Catavina from now on. He ought to teach you plenty."

My heart sank. Of all the cops in that station house, Catavina was the man I least wanted to spend time with. He was a bully and a lazy son of a bitch. I knew that if we ever did catch up to On Cheung, it wouldn't be because of Catavina's contributions.

The lieutenant must have read my reaction from my expression. "Any problem with that, Audran?" he asked.

"If I had a problem, is there any chance it would change your mind?"

"None whatsoever," said Hajjar.

"Didn't think so."

Hajjar looked back at the screen of his data deck. "Report to Catavina. I want to hear some good news real soon. You cut the legs out from under this dink, there may be commendations for the two of you."

"I'll get right on it, Lieutenant," I said. I was impressed with Hajjar's cleverness. He'd skillfully maneuvered me away from both Abu Adil and Jawarski by throwing me into a time-consuming but perfectly valid investigation. I was going to have to find a way to accomplish both my official assignment and my own personal goals.

Hajjar paid no further attention to me, so I left his office. I went to find Sergeant Catavina. I'd rather proceed without him, but that wasn't going to be possible.

Catavina wasn't that excited about being paired with me, either. "I already got the word from Hajjar," he told me. We were walking down to the garage, to pick up Catavina's patrol car. Catavina was trying to give me the benefit of all his years' experience in one disjointed lecture. "You ain't a good cop, Audran," he said in a grim voice. "You may never be a good cop. I don't want you fucking up with me like you fucked up Shaknahyi."

"What's that mean, Catavina?" I asked.

He turned and looked at me, his eyes wide. "Figure it out. If you'd known what you was doing, Shaknahyi'd still be alive and I wouldn't have to be holding your hand. Just stay out of my way and do what I tell you."

I was mad as hell, but I didn't say anything. I planned to stay out of his way, all right. I figured I'd have to lose Catavina if I wanted to make any progress.

We got into the patrol car, and he had nothing more to say to me for a long while. That was okay with me. I thought he might drive back to the neighborhood where On Cheung was last known to have operated. Maybe we could learn something useful by interviewing those people again, even though they'd been so uncooperative before.

That wasn't his plan, however. He headed west, in the opposite direction. We drove about a mile and half through an area of narrow, twisting streets and alleys. At last, Catavina pulled up in front of a crumbling apartment building, the tallest building on the block. The windows on the ground floor had been covered over with plywood, and the front door into the foyer had been taken off its hinges. The walls inside and out were covered with spray-painted names and slogans. The lobby reeked; it had been used as a toilet for a long time. As we crossed to the elevator, we crunched broken glass beneath our boots. There was a thick layer of dust and grit over everything.

"What are we doing here?" I asked.

"You'll see," said Catavina. He punched the button for the elevator. When it arrived, I was hesitant about getting in. The condition of the building didn't give me any confidence that the cables would hold our weight. When the elevator asked what floor we wanted, Catavina muttered "Eight." We looked away from each other as the door slid closed. We rode in silence, the only noise coming from the elevator as it creaked its way upward.

We got out on the eighth floor, and Catavina led the way down the dark hallway to room 814. He took a key out of his pocket and unlocked the front door.

"What's this?" I asked, following him into the seedy apartment.

"Police officers' lounge," said Catavina.

There was a large living room, a small kitchen, and a bathroom. There wasn't much furniture—a cheap card table and six chairs in the living room, along with a torn black vinyl couch, a small holoset, and four folding cots. There were uniformed cops asleep on two of the cots. I recognized them but didn't know their names. Catavina dropped heavily onto the couch and stared at me across the bare floor. "Want a drink?" he asked.

"No," I said.

"Bring me some whiskey then. There's ice in the kitchen."

I went into the kitchen and found a good collection of liquor bottles. I tossed a few ice cubes into a glass and poured in three fingers of raw Japanese liquor. "So what are we doing here," I called, thinking of the department's motto, "protecting or serving?" I carried the drink back into the living room and handed it to Catavina.

"You're serving," he said, grunting. "I'm protecting."

I sat down in one of the folding chairs and stared at him, watching him down half the Japanese whiskey in one long gulp. "Protecting what?" I asked.

Catavina smiled contemptuously. "Protecting my ass, that's what. It ain't gonna get shot up while I'm here, that's for damn sure."

I glanced at the two sleeping cops. "Gonna stay here long?"

"Till the shift's over," he said.

"Mind if I take the car and get some work done in the meantime?"

The sergeant looked at me over the rim of his whiskey glass. "Why the hell you want to do that?" he asked.

I shrugged. "Shaknahyi never let me drive."

Catavina looked at me like I was crazy. "Sure, just don't smash it up." He dug in his pocket and fished out the car keys, then tossed them to me. "You better come back and pick me up by five o'clock."

"Right, Sergeant," I said. I left him staring at the holoset, which wasn't even turned on. I rode the elevator back down to the filthy lobby, wondering what I was going to do next. I felt an obligation to find something that might lead me to On Cheung, but instead it was Jirji Shaknahyi who occupied my mind.

His funeral had been the day before, and for a while I thought I'd just stay home. For one thing, I didn't know if I was emotionally settled enough to handle it; for another, I still felt partly responsible for his death, and it didn't seem right for me to attend. I didn't want to face Indihar and the children under those circumstances. Nevertheless, on Thursday morning I went to the small mosque near the station house where the memorial was being held.

Only men were permitted to participate in the worship service. I removed my shoes and performed the ritual ablutions, then entered the mosque and took a place near the back. A lot of the other cops in the congregation seemed to be looking at me with vengeful expressions. I was still an outsider to them, and in their eyes I might as well have pulled the trigger that killed Shaknahyi.

We prayed, and then an elderly, gray-bearded imam delivered a sermon and a eulogy, going through some weary truisms about duty and service and bravery. None of it made me feel any better. I was truly sorry that I'd talked myself into attending the service.

Then we all got up and filed out of the mosque. Except for some birds singing and a dog barking, it was almost supernaturally quiet. The sun burned down from a high, cloudless sky. A faint, tremulous breeze rippled the dusty leaves in the trees, but the air was almost too hot to breathe. The odor of spoiled milk hung like a sour mist over the cobblestone alleys. The day was just too oppressive to draw the business out much longer. I'm sure

Shaknahyi'd had many friends, but right now they all just wanted to get to the graveyard and get him planted.

Indihar led the procession from the mosque to the cemetery. She was dressed in a black dress with her face veiled and her hair covered with a black kerchief. She must have been stifling. Her three children walked beside her, their expressions bewildered and frightened. Chiri had told me that Indihar hadn't had enough money to pay for a tomb in the cemetery in Haffe al-Khala where Shaknahyi's parents were buried, and she wouldn't accept a loan from us. Instead, Shaknahyi was laid to rest in what amounted to a pauper's grave in the cemetery on the western edge of the Budayeen. I followed far behind her as Indihar crossed the Boulevard il-Jameel and passed through the eastern gate. People who lived in the quarter as well as foreign tourists came out and stood on the sidewalks as the funeral party made its way up the Street. I could see many people weeping and murmuring prayers. There was no way to tell if those people even knew who the deceased was. It probably didn't make any difference to them.

All of Shaknahyi's former comrades wanted to help carry the particleboard coffin through the streets, so instead of six pallbearers there was a pushing, shoving mob of uniformed men all straining to reach the flimsy box. The ones who couldn't get near enough to touch it marched alongside and in a long parade to the rear, beating their chests with their fists and shouting testaments of their faith. There was a lot of chanting and fingering of Muslim rosaries. I found myself moving my lips along with the others, reciting ancient prayers that had been inscribed in my memory as a young child. After a while, I too was caught up in the odd mixture of despair and celebration. I found myself praising Allah for visiting so much injustice and horror on our helpless souls.

In the cemetery, I kept my distance again as the unadorned coffin was lowered into the ground. Several of Shaknahyi's closest friends on the police force took turns shoveling in dirt. The mourners offered more prayers in unison, although the imam had declined to accompany the funeral to its conclusion. Indihar stood bravely by, clutching the hands of Hâkim and Zahra, and eight-year-old Little Jirji held tightly to Hâkim's other hand. Some representative of the city went up to Indihar and murmured something, and she nodded gravely. Then all of the uniformed police officers filed past and offered her their individual condolences. That's when I saw Indihar's shoulders begin to slump; I could tell that she had begun to weep. Meanwhile, Little Jirji looked out over the crumbling tombs and overgrown grave markers, his expression perfectly blank.

When the funeral was over, everyone left but me. The police department had provided a small spread of food at the station house, because Indihar didn't have the money for that, either. I saw how humiliating the whole situation was for her. Besides grieving for her husband, Indihar also suffered the pain of having her poverty revealed to all her friends and acquaintances. To many Muslims, an unworthy funeral is as much a calamity for the survivors as the death of the loved one itself.

I chose not to attend the reception at the station house. I stayed behind, staring down at Jirji's unmarked grave, my mind confused and troubled. I said a few prayers alone and recited some passages from the Qur'ân. "I promise you, Jirji," I murmured, "Jawarski won't get away with this." I didn't have any illusions that making Jawarski pay would let Shaknahyi rest any easier, or make Indihar's grief any less, or ease the hardships for Little Jirji, Hâkim, and Zahra. I just didn't know what else to say. Finally I turned away from the grave. I blamed myself for my hesitancy, and prayed that it wouldn't lead to anyone else getting hurt ever again.

The funeral was on my mind as I drove from Catavina's secret coop back to the station house. I heard the rolling rumble of thunder, and it surprised me because we don't get many thunderstorms in the city. I glanced through the windshield up at the sky, but there were no clouds at all in sight. I felt an odd chill, thinking that maybe the thunder had been a humbling sign from God, underscoring my memories of Shaknahyi's burial. For the first time since his death, I felt a deep emotional loss.

I also began to think that my idea of vengeance would not be adequate. Finding Paul Jawarski and bringing him to justice would neither restore Shaknahyi nor free me from the intrigue in which Jawarski, Reda Abu Adil, Friedlander Bey, and Lieutenant Hajjar were somehow involved. In a sudden realization, I knew that it was time to stop thinking of the puzzle as one large problem with one simple solution. None of the individual players knew the entire story, I was certain of that. I'd have to pursue them separately and assemble what clues I could find, hoping that in the end it would all add up to something indictable. If Shaknahyi's hunches were wrong and I was heading off on a fool's errand, I would end up worse than disgraced. I would surely end up dead.

I parked the copcar in the garage and went up to my cubicle on the third floor of the station house. Hajjar rarely left his glass booth, so I didn't think there'd be much chance that he'd catch me. Catch me! Hell, all I was doing was getting some work done.

It had been a couple of weeks since I'd done any serious work at my data deck. I sat down at my desk and put a new cobalt-alloy cell-memory plate in one of the computer's adit ports. "Create file," I said.

"File name," prompted the data deck's indifferent voice.

"Phoenix File," I said. I didn't have a lot of actual information to enter. First I read in the names from Shaknahyi's notebook. Then I stared at the monitor screen. Maybe it was time to follow up on Shaknahyi's research.

All of the satellite decks in the station house were connected to the central police database. The problem was that Lieutenant Hajjar had never entirely trusted me, and so I'd been given only the lowest security clearance. With my password, I could only obtain information that was also available to any civilian who came in the front door of the station house and inquired at the information desk. However, in the months I'd worked at the copshop, I'd casually nosed out all the codes from other paper-pushers with higher ratings. There was a great and active underground involved with circulating classified information among the nonuniformed staff. This was technically highly illegal, of course, but in actual fact it was the only way any of us could get our jobs done.

"Search," I said.

"Enter string to be searched," muttered the Annamese deck in its peculiar American accent.

"Bouhatta." Ishaq Abdul-Hadi Bouhatta was the first

entry in Shaknahyi's notebook, a murder victim whose killer had not yet been caught.

"Enter password," said the computer.

I had the list of security codes scribbled on a torn sheet of paper that I'd hidden in a tech manual. I'd memorized the top-level password long ago, however. It was a twenty-four-character mix of alphanumerics and Arabic Standard Code for Information Interchange symbols. I had to key those in manually.

"Accepted," said the data deck. "Searching."

In about thirty seconds, Bouhatta's complete file appeared on my monitor. I skipped through the personal biography and the details of his death—except to note that he'd been killed at close range by a charge from a static pistol, the same as Blanca. What I wanted to know was where his body had been taken. I found that information in the medical examiner's report, which formed the last page of the file. There'd been no autopsy; instead, Bouhatta's corpse had been delivered to Abu Emir Hospital in Al-Islam Square.

"Search again?" asked the deck.

"No," I said. "Import data."

"Database?"

"Abu Emir Hospital," I said.

The computer thought about that for a moment. "Current security code is sufficient," it decided. There was a long pause while it accessed the computer records of the hospital.

When I saw the hospital's main menu on my screen, I ordered a search of Bouhatta's records. It didn't take long, and I found what I needed. Just as Shaknahyi's notes suggested, Bouhatta's heart and lungs had been removed almost immediately after his death and transplanted into the body of Elwau Chami. I supposed then that Shaknahyi's other information was correct, concerning the victims of the other unsolved murders.

Now I wanted to take his research one important step further. "Search again?" the hospital's database inquired.

"Yes," I said.

"Enter string to be searched."

"Chami." A few seconds later, I saw a list of five names, from Chami, Ali Masoud to Chami, Zayd.

"Select entry," said the deck.

"Chami, Elwau." When the file came up on the screen, I read through it carefully. Chami was a faceless man, not as poor as some, not as rich as others. He was married and had seven children, five sons and two daughters. He lived in a middle-class neighborhood northeast of the Budayeen. The medical records said nothing about any run-ins with the law, of course, but there was one important fact buried in the redundant forms and reports: Elwau Chami operated a small shop in the Budayeen, on Eleventh Street north of the Street. It was a shop I knew well enough. Chami sold cheap Oriental rugs in the front, and he leased the rear of the establishment to an old Pakistani married couple who sold brass ornaments to tourists. The interesting fact was that I knew Friedlander Bey owned the building; Chami probably also worked as gatekeeper for the high-stakes gambling parlor upstairs.

Next I researched Blanca Mataro, the sexchange whose corpse I'd discovered with Jirji Shaknahyi. Her body had been taken to another hospital, and it had provided urgently needed kidneys and liver to a seriously ill young woman she'd never met. This in itself wasn't unusual; many people signed up to donate organs in case of sudden or accidental death. I just found it rather coincidental that the recipient happened to be the niece of Umar Abdul-Qawy.

I spent an hour and a half tracking down files on all the other names in Shaknahyi's notebook. Besides Chami, two of the murder victims—Blanca and Andreja Svobik— had ties to Papa. I was able to prove to my satisfaction that of the other four names, two had rather obvious connections to Reda Abu Adil. I was willing to bet a large sum of money that the rest did too, but I didn't need to pursue the matter any further. None of this was ever going to have to stand up in court. Neither Abu Adil nor Friedlander Bey would ever be dragged in front of a judge.

So what had I learned, after all? One: There had been at least four unsolved murders in the city in the last several weeks. Two: All four victims had been killed in the same way, with a shot at close range from a static pistol. Three: Healthy organs were taken from all four victims after death, because all four were listed in the city's charity file of voluntary donors. Four: All four victims and all four recipients had direct ties to either Abu Adil or Papa.

I had proved Shaknahyi's suspicion beyond the possibility of coincidence, but I knew that Hajjar would still deny that the murders were related. I could point out that the killers had used a static pistol so that none of the internal organs would be damaged, but Hajjar'd shrug that off too. I was pretty damn certain that Hajjar knew about all this already, which was why I'd been put to pasture investigating On Cheung, instead of looking into Shaknahyi's death. There were a lot of powerful men allied against me. It was a good thing I had God on my side.

"Search again?" asked my data deck.

I hesitated. I did have one more name to check, but I really didn't want to know the details. After he'd been shot, Shaknahyi had told me to find out where his parts went. I thought I already knew, although I didn't have an exact name. I was sure that some of Jirji Shaknahyi still lived on in the body of some low-level employee of Abu Adil or Friedlander Bey, or one of their friends or relatives. I was completely disgusted, so I just said "Quit." I looked at the monitor's dark screen and thought about what I needed to do next.

I was just fighting down the urge to find somebody in the station house who might sell me a few sunnies when the phone on my belt rang. I unclipped it and leaned back in my padded chair. "Hello," I said.

"Marhaba," said Morgan's gruff voice.

That was about all the Arabic that he knew. I leaned over and grabbed my English-language daddy from the rack, then reached up and chipped it in.

"Where y'at, man?" he said.

"All right, praise be to God. What's up?"

"Remember how I promised to let you know Wednesday where this Jawarski guy's hidin' out?"

"Yeah, I was wondering when you'd check in."

"Well, turns out I was maybe a little optimistic." He sounded rueful.

"Had a feeling Jawarski'd cover his tracks pretty well."

"Got a feelin' he's had help, man."

I sat up straight. "What do you mean?"

There was a pause before Morgan spoke again. "There's a lot of talk on the street about Shaknahyi's shooting. Most people couldn't care less that a cop got dusted, but I can't find nobody with a personal grudge against Shaknahyi himself. And Jawarski's crazy as a bedbug, so nobody I know would lift a finger to help him get clear."

I closed my eyes and massaged my forehead. "Then why haven't you or I located him yet?" I asked.

"I'm comin' to that. What it comes down to is it looks like the cops are hidin' the son of a bitch."

"Where? Why?" Chiri vouched for Morgan's dependability, but this story of his was a little too incredible.

"Ask your Lieutenant Hajjar. He and Jawarski had some drinks together in the Silver Palm a couple weeks ago."

In the words of the great Christian humorist, Mark Twain, this was too various for me. "Why would Hajjar, a high-ranking police official, set up one of his own officers for a lunatic escaped killer?"

I could almost hear Morgan shrug. "You think maybe Hajjar's involved with somethin' crooked, man?"

I laughed sourly, and Morgan laughed too. "It's not funny, though," I said. "I guessed all along that Hajjar was mixed up with something, but I didn't see him passing orders to Jawarski. Still, it answers some of my own questions."

"What's it all about, then?"

"It's about something called the Phoenix File. I don't know yet what the hell that means. Just keep trying to pin down Jawarski, okay? You learn anything useful about him yet?"

"Some," said Morgan. "He was waitin' around in a jail cell in Khartoum, supposed to be executed. Some guy smuggled a gun in to him. One afternoon Jawarski walks down a corridor and meets two unarmed guards. He shoots the guys, then walks into the jail office and starts firin' all around like a maniac till somebody hands over the keys. Then he unlocks the big main doors and walks out calmly into the street. There's a crowd of people out there 'cause of the gunshots, and he pushes his way through 'em and goes half a block to a waitin' car. Jawarski drives away and there's no sign of him again till he shows up here in the city."

"When was that?" I asked.

"Been here a month, maybe six weeks. Pulled a couple of robberies, killed another couple of people. Then the other day somebody recognized Jawarski in Meloul's and called the cops. Hajjar sent Shaknahyi and you. You know the rest."

"I wonder," I said. "I wonder if somebody really recognized him in the cookshop. Shaknahyi thought that Hajjar had fingered us, putting Jawarski in Meloul's and sending Jirji and me over there to get taken down."

"Could be, man. We'll have to ask Jawarski when we collar him."

"Yeah, you right," I said grimly. "Thanks, Morgan. You keep nosing around."

"You got it, man. I want to earn the rest of that money. Take care of yourself."

"You bet," I said, clipping the phone to my belt again.

It helped that I knew more than my enemies did. I had the advantage of having my eyes open. I still couldn't see where it all was leading me, but at least I understood the extent of the conspiracy I was trying to uncover. I wouldn't be so foolish as to trust anyone entirely. Anyone at all.

When the shift was over, I drove the patrol car back to the "police officers' lounge" and picked up Sergeant Catavina, who had gotten very drunk. I dropped him off at the station house, turned the car over to the night shift, and waited for Kmuzu to arrive. The workday was done, but I still had plenty of investigating to do before I could go to sleep.

Fuad il-manhous was not the brightest person I knew. One look at Fuad and you said to yourself, "This guy is a *fool.*" He looked like the character in a fairy tale who would get three wishes from a *djinn* and blow the first on a plate of beans, the second on a spoon, and the third on cleaning the dish and spoon when he was done eating.

He was tall, but so thin and starved-looking he might have been a refugee from the Benghazi death camps. I once saw my friend Jacques circle Fuad's arm above the elbow with his thumb and forefinger. And Fuad's joints were huge, swollen as if from some horrible bone disease or vitamin deficiency. He had long, dirty brown hair that he combed into a high pompadour, and he wore thick eyeglasses in heavy plastic frames. I don't suppose Fuad had ever had enough cash to afford new eyes, not even the cheap Guatemalan ones with the counterfeit Nikon lenses. His expression was permanently bewildered and hurt, because Fuad was always a beat and a half behind the rest of the band.

Il manhous means something like "the permanently hapless," yet Fuad didn't seem to mind the nickname. In fact, he seemed happy to be recognized at all. And he played the part of fool better than anyone I'd ever known. He had a certain genius for it, as a matter of fact.

I was sitting at a table in Chiriga's with Kmuzu, near the back. We were talking about what my mother had been up to lately. Fuad il-manhous came and stood beside me, holding a cardboard box. "Indihar lets me come in here in the daytime, Marîd," he said in his raspy, twangy voice.

"I got no problem with that," I said. He'd made me

forget what I'd been about to say. I looked up at him, and
he grinned down and shook the cardboard box. Something inside made a rattling sound. "What's in the box?" I
asked.

Fuad took that as an invitation to sit down. He
dragged a chair over from another table, making the legs
shriek on the flooring. "Indihar said as long as nobody
complained, it was all right with her."

"*What's* all right?" I demanded impatiently. I hate
having to pry information out of people. "The hell you got
in there?"

Fuad ran a gnarled hand through his greasy hair and
shot Kmuzu a mistrustful look. Then he hunched forward
over the table, set the box down, and lifted the lid. There
were maybe a dozen cheap gold-filled chains inside. Fuad
reached in with a long forefinger and poked them around.
"See?" he said.

"Uh huh," I said. I looked up and caught Kmuzu's
eye. He was finishing a glass of iced tea—I felt bad about
tricking him into drinking so much liquor that time, and
since then I'd respected his feelings. He set his glass down
carefully on the cocktail napkin. He was keeping his face
free of any expression, but I could tell that he didn't approve of Fuad at all. Kmuzu didn't approve of anything he
saw in Chiri's.

"Where'd you get them, Fuad?" I said.

"Take a look." He grinned. His teeth were bad too.

I fished one of the chains out of the box and tried to
examine it closely, but the light was too dim in the club. I
turned the price tag around. It said two hundred and fifty
kiam. "Sure, Fuad," I said dubiously. "The tourists and
locals we get in here complain about paying eight kiam
for a drink. I think you're gonna have some sales resis-
tance."

"Well, I'm not selling them for that much."

"How much *are* you selling them for?"

Il-Manhous closed his eyes, pretending to concen-
trate. Then he looked at me as if he were begging a favor.
"Fifty kiam?"

I looked back into the box and pushed the chains
around myself. Then I shook my head.

"Okay," said Fuad, "ten kiam, but *yaa lateef!* I won't
make any profit that way."

"Maybe you could sell them for ten," I admitted. "The price tags are from some of the best shops in town."

Fuad grabbed the box away from me. "So they're worth more than ten, huh?"

I laughed. "See," I said to Kmuzu, "the chains are cheap plated metal. Probably not worth fifty fiqs. Fuad here goes into some exclusive boutique and steals some tags with the shop's classy name on them and a price in three figures. Then he ties the tags to his junk jewelry and hawks it to drunken tourists. He figures they might not notice what they're buying, especially out of the bright sunlight."

"That's why I wanted to ask you if it'd be okay to come in during the night shift," said Fuad. "It's even darker in here at night. I'd probably do a whole lot better."

"Nah," I said. "If Indihar wants to let you hustle tourists during the day, that's up to her. I'd rather not have you doing it at night when I might be here."

"Beyond the Budayeen, *yaa Sidi*," Kmuzu pronounced ominously, "they'd cut his hands off if they caught him doing that."

Fuad looked horrified. "You wouldn't let them do anything like that to me, would you, Marîd?"

I shrugged. " 'As for the thief, both male and female, cut off their hands. It is the reward of their own deeds, an exemplary punishment from Allah. Allah is Mighty, Wise.' That's right from the blessed Qur'ân. You could look it up."

Fuad clutched the box to his sunken chest. "You wait till you need something from me, Marîd!" he cried. Then he stumbled toward the door, knocking over a chair and bumping into Pualani on the way.

"He'll get over it," I said to Kmuzu. "He'll be back in here tomorrow. Won't even remember what you told him."

"That's too bad," said Kmuzu gravely. "Someday he'll try to sell one of those chains to the wrong person. He may regret it for the rest of his life."

"Yeah, but that's what makes him Fuad. Anyway, I need to talk to Indihar before the shift changes. You mind if I leave you alone for a couple of minutes?"

"Not at all, *yaa Sidi.*" He stared at me blankly for a moment. It always unsettled me when he did that.

"I'll have somebody bring you another iced tea," I said. Then I got up and went to the bar.

Indihar was rinsing glasses. I'd told her that she didn't have to come into work until she felt better, but she said she'd rather work than sit home with her kids and feel bad. She needed to make money to pay the babysitter, and she still had a lot of expenses from the funeral. All the girls were tiptoeing around her, not knowing what to say to her or how to act. It made for a pretty glum ambience in the club.

"Need something, Marîd?" she said. Her eyes were red and sunken. She looked away from me, back at the glasses in the sink.

"Another iced tea for Kmuzu, that's all," I said.

"All right." She bent to the refrigerator under the bar and brought up a pitcher of iced tea. She poured a glassful and continued to pay no attention to me.

I looked down the bar. There were three new girls working the day shift. I could only remember one of their names. "Brandi," I said, "take this to that tall guy in the back."

"You mean that *kaffir?*" she said. She was short, with fat arms and plump thighs, with large breast implants and brushy hair whose blondness had been artificially encouraged. She had tattoos on both arms, above her right breast, on her left shoulder blade, peeking out of her G-string, on both ankles, and on her ass. I think she was embarrassed by them, because she always wore a fringy black shawl when she sat with customers at the bar, and when she danced she wore bright red platform shoes and high white socks. "Want me to collect from him?"

I shook my head. "He's my driver. He drinks for free."

Brandi nodded and carried the iced tea away. I stayed at the bar, idly spinning one of the round cork coasters. "Indihar," I said at last.

She gave me a weary look. "I said I didn't want to hear you say you were sorry."

I raised a hand. "I'm not gonna say that. I just think you should accept some help now. For your kids' sake, if not your own. I would've been happy to pay for a tomb in

our in-laws' cemetery. Chiri'd be glad to lend you all the
money—"

Indihar let out an exasperated breath and wiped her
hands on a bar towel. "That's something else I don't want
to hear. Jirji and I never borrowed money. I'm not gonna
start now."

"Sure, okay, but the situation is different. How much
pension are you getting from the police department?"

She threw the towel down disgustedly. "A third of
Jirji's salary. That's all. And they're giving me some kind of
song and dance about a delay. They don't think I can start
collecting the pension for at least six months. We were
barely keeping our noses above water before. I don't
know how I'll make it now. I guess I'll have to look for
someplace cheaper to live."

My first thought was that any place cheaper than the
apartment in Haffe al-Khala wouldn't be fit to raise children in. "Maybe," I said. "Look, Indihar, I think you've
earned a paid vacation. Why don't you just let me pay you
for two or three weeks in advance, and you can stay home
with Zahra and Hâkim and Little Jirji. Or you could use
the time to make some extra money, maybe—"

Brandi came back to the bar and plopped down beside me with a contemptuous look on her face. "Motherfucker didn't give me a tip," she said.

I looked at her. She probably wasn't any smarter than
Fuad. "I told you, Kmuzu drinks for free. I don't want you
hustling him."

"Who is he, your special friend?" Brandi asked with a
crooked smile.

I looked at Indihar. "How badly you want this bitch to
keep working here?" I said.

Brandi hopped off the stool and headed toward the
dressing room. "All right, all right," she said, "forget I said
anything."

"Marîd," said Indihar in a low, carefully controlled
voice, "leave me alone. No loans, no deals, no presents.
Okay? Just have enough respect for me to let me work
everything out my own way."

I couldn't argue with her anymore. "Whatever you
want," I said. I turned away and went back to Kmuzu's
table. I truly wished Indihar had let me help her somehow. I'd gained a tremendous amount of admiration for

her. She was a fine, intelligent woman, and kind of on the beautiful side too.

I had a couple of drinks and killed some time, and then it was eight o'clock. Chiri and the night crew came in, and I watched Indihar count out the register, pay the day shift girls, and leave without saying another word to anyone. I went to the bar to say hello to Chiri. "I think Indihar's trying too hard to be brave," I told her.

She sat on her stool behind the bar and surveyed the seven or eight customers. "Yesterday she was telling me about her twelfth birthday," Chiri said in a distant voice. "She said she'd known Jirji all her life. They both grew up in the same little village. She always liked Jirji, and when her parents told her that they'd arranged with the Shaknahyis for the two kids to be married, Indihar was happy."

Chiri leaned down and brought out her private bottle of *tende*. She poured herself half a glassful and tasted it. "Indihar had a traditional childhood," she said. "Her folks were very old-fashioned and superstitious. She grew up in Egypt, where there's this old wives' tale that girls who drink the water of the Nile grow up too passionate. They exhaust their poor husbands. So it's the custom for the girls to be circumcised before their weddings."

"Lots of country Muslims still do that," I said.

Chiri nodded. "The village midwife cut Indihar and put onions and salt on the wound. Indihar stayed in bed for seven days afterward, and her mother fed her lots of chicken and pomegranates. When she finally got up again, her mother gave her a new dress she'd just finished making. Indihar's clitoris was sewn up in the lining. Together the two of them took the dress and threw it into the river."

I shuddered. "Why you telling me all this?"

Chiri swallowed some more *tende*. "So you'll understand how much Jirji meant to Indihar. She told me the circumcision was very painful, but she was glad to have it done. It meant she was finally a grown woman, and she could marry Jirji with the blessings of her family and friends."

"I suppose it's none of my business," I said.

"I'll tell you what's none of your business: badgering her about her financial situation. Leave her alone, Marîd

our intentions are good, and it was right to offer help
after Jirji was killed. But Indihar's said she doesn't want
our money, and you're making her feel worse by bringing
it up all the time."

I let my shoulders sag. "I guess I didn't realize it," I
said. "All right, thanks for letting me know."

"She'll be fine. And if she runs into trouble, she'll let
us know. Now, I want you to put in a good word with
Kmuzu. I like the way that honey looks."

I raised my eyebrows at her. "You just trying to make
me jealous? Kmuzu? He's not a party kind of guy, you
know. You'd eat him alive."

"I'd sure like to give it a shot," she said with her best
file-toothed grin.

Time for another shot in the dark. "Chiri," I said,
"What do the letters A.L.M. mean to you?"

She thought about that for a little while. "The Association of Lesbian Mothers," she said. "This girl Hanina,
used to dance by Frenchy's. She used to get their newslet-
ter. Why?"

I chewed my lip. "That can't be right. If you think of
something else A.L.M. might mean, let me know."

"Okay, honey. What is it, some kind of puzzle?"

"Yeah, a puzzle."

"Well, I'll think about it." She drank a little *tende* and
stared over my head at the mirrored wall behind me. "So
what's this I hear about you flushing all your recreational
drugs? Never thought I'd see the day. We gonna have to
find a new chemical champion?"

"I guess so. I emptied my pillcase right after Jirji
died."

Chiri's expression became serious. "Uh yeah."

There was an uncomfortable silence for a few seconds. "I'll tell you, though," I said at last, "I've had these
strong cravings. It's been pretty hard on me, but I'm keeping away from the drugs."

"Cutting back is one thing, but quitting altogether
seems kind of extreme. I suppose it's for the best, but I've
always believed in moderation in all things, and that goes
for abstinence too."

I smiled. "I appreciate your concern," I said, "but I
know what I'm doing."

Chiri shook her head sadly. "I hope so. I hope you're

not just kidding yourself. You don't have much experienc
handling yourself sober. You could get hurt."

"I'll be fine, Chiri."

"Maybe you should pass by Laila's shop in the morn
ing. She's got these moddies that make you feel lik
you've taken a handful of pills. She's got the whole line
sunnies, beauties, tri-phets, RPM, whatever you want. Yo
chip the moddy in and if you need to use your brain fo
something later, you pop it out and you're straight again.

"I don't know. Sounds dumb to me."

Chiri spread her hands. "It's up to you."

"Make me a gin and bingara?" I didn't want to tal
about drugs anymore. I was beginning to feel the cravin
again.

I watched Yasmin dance on stage while Chiri built m
drink. Yasmin was still the prettiest collection of XY chro
mosomes I've ever known. Since we'd gotten friendl
again, she told me she was sorry she'd cut her long blac
hair. She was letting it grow back. As she moved sensu
ously to the music, she kept glancing down at me. Ever
time she caught my eye, she smiled. I smiled back.

"Here you go, boss," said Chiri, setting the drink on
coaster in front of me.

"Thanks," I said. I picked it up, threw a sizzling loo
toward Yasmin, and went back to sit with Kmuzu. "Say,"
said, "you've got a secret admirer. You know that?"

Kmuzu looked perplexed. "What do you mean, ya
Sidi?"

I grinned at him. "I think Chiriga would like to el
vate your pulse rate."

"That is not possible," he said. He looked very di
turbed.

"Don't you like her? She's really a very nice perso
Don't be scared off by that headhunter routine of hers

"It's not that, yaa Sidi. I do not plan to marry until
am no longer a slave."

I laughed. "That fits in fine with Chiri's plans. I don
think she wants to get married, either."

"I told you when we first met that I am a Christian

Chiri came over to the table and joined us before
could say anything more. "Kmuzu, how you doin'?" sh
said.

"I am well, Miss Chiriga," he said. His tone was almost icy.

"Well, I was wondering if you'd ever made it with anybody who was wearing Honey Pílar's latest. *Slow, Slow Burn*. It's my favorite of all of hers. Leaves me so weak I can barely get up out of bed."

"Miss Chiriga—"

"You can call me Chiri, honey."

"—I wish you'd stop making sexual advances to me."

Chiri looked at me and raised her eyebrows. "Am I making sexual advances? I was just asking if he'd ever made it—"

"Did I hear that Honey Pílar's getting divorced again?" said Rani, one of the night-shift debs who'd wandered over to our table. Evidently none of the customers were tipping or buying anybody cocktails. I knew it was a slow night when Kmuzu and I were the most interesting thing happening in the club.

Chiri looked aggravated. "Somebody get up on the goddamn stage and dance!" she shouted. Then she stood up and went back behind the bar. Lily, the pretty Belgian sexchange, took off her blouse and went to play her music.

"I think I've had about enough of all this excitement," I said, yawning. "Kmuzu, come on. Let's go home."

Yasmin came up and put her hand on my arm. "Will you come in tomorrow?" she asked. "I need to talk to you about something personal."

"You want to talk right now?"

She looked away, embarrassed. "No," she said. "Some other time. But I wanted to give you this." She held out her pocket *I Ching* calculator. She swore by the *I Ching*, and she still believed that it had accurately foretold all the terrible events of several months ago. "Maybe you need it again."

"I don't think so," I said. "Why don't you keep it?"

She put it in my hand and closed my fingers over it. Then she kissed me. It was a gentle, unhurried kiss on the lips. I was surprised to find that it left me trembling.

I said goodnight to Chiri and the debs and changes, and Kmuzu followed me out into the warm, raucous night on the Street. We walked back down to the gate and found the car. All the way home, Kmuzu explained to me that he found Chiri too brazen and shameless.

"But you think she's sexy?" I asked him.

"That's beside the point, *yaa Sidi*," he said. From then on, he just concentrated on his driving.

After we got back to Friedlander Bey's estate, I went to my suite and tried to relax. I took a notebook and stretched out on my bed, trying to order my thoughts. I looked at Yasmin's electronic *I Ching* and laughed softly. For no particular reason, I pressed the white button marked H. The little device played its tinkling tune, and a synthesized woman's voice spoke up. "Hexagram Six. Sung. Conflict. Changes in the first, second, and sixth lines."

I listened to the judgment and the commentary, and then I pressed L for the lines. What it all amounted to was a warning that I was in a difficult period, and that if I tried to force my way toward my goal, I'd encounter a lot of conflict. I didn't need a pocket computer to tell me that.

The image was "Heaven above the waters," and I was advised to stay close to home. The problem was that it was just a little too late for that. "If you determine to confront the difficulties," the mechanical woman cautioned, "you'll make minor progress that will soon be reversed, leaving you in a worse situation than before. Sidestep this trouble by tending your garden and ignoring your powerful adversaries."

Well, hell, I would have loved to do just that. I could have forgotten all about Abu Adil and all about Jawarski, just written Shaknahyi off as a painful tragedy, and let Papa deal with Umm Saad by ordering the Stones That Speak to twist her devious head off. I could have left my mother a fat envelope of cash, kissed Chiriga's club goodbye, and caught the next bus out of the city.

Unfortunately, none of that was possible. I stared at the toy *I Ching* ruefully, then remembered that the changing lines gave me a second hexagram that might indicate where events were leading. I pressed CH.

"Hexagram Seventeen. Sui. Following. Thunder in the lake." Whatever that meant. I was told that I was coming into very positive circumstances. All I had to do was attune my actions into harmony with the personalities of the people I had to deal with. I just had to adapt my own desires to the needs of the times.

"Okay," I said, "that's just what I'll do. I just need someone to tell me what 'the needs of the times' are."

"Such fortune telling is blasphemous," said Kmuzu. "Every orthodox religion in the world forbids it." I hadn't heard him come into my room.

"The idea of synchronicity makes a certain logical sense," I said. Actually, I felt pretty much about the *I Ching* as he did, but I felt it was my job to bait him as much as possible. Maybe something would get him to loosen up a little.

"You are dealing with dangerous people, *yaa Sidi*," he said. "Surely your actions must be governed by reason, not by this child's plaything."

I tossed Yasmin's gimmick to him. "You're right, Kmuzu. Something like that could be dangerous, in the hands of a gullible fool."

"I'll return it to Miss Yasmin tomorrow."

"Fine," I said.

"Will you need anything more tonight?"

"No, Kmuzu, I'm just gonna make some notes to myself, and then I'll get some sleep."

"Then goodnight, *yaa Sidi*."

"Goodnight, Kmuzu." He closed the door to my bedroom behind him.

I got up and undressed, then pulled back the covers on my bed and laid down again. I began listing names in my notebook: Friedlander Bey, Reda Abu Adil and Umar Abdul-Qawy, Paul Jawarski, Umm Saad, Lieutenant Hajjar. The bad guys. Then I made a list of the good guys: me.

I remembered a proverb I'd heard as a child in Algiers. "Fleeing when it is not necessary is better than not fleeing when it *is* necessary." A quick trip to Shanghai or Venice seemed like the only reasonable response to this situation.

I suppose I fell asleep thinking about stuffing a bag full of clothes and money and running off into the honey-suckle-scented night. I was having a bizarre dream about Chiriga's. Lieutenant Hajjar seemed to be running the place, and I went in looking for somebody who might have been Yasmin or possibly Fayza, one of my adolescent loves. There was some kind of argument with my mother about whether or not I'd brought in a case of bottled sherbet, and then I was in school without any clothes on, and I hadn't studied for some important exam.

Someone was shaking me and shouting. "Wake up, *yaa Sidi!*"

"What is it, Kmuzu?" I said blearily. "What's the matter?"

"The house is on fire!" he said. He pulled on my arm until I got out of bed.

"I don't see any fire." I could smell the smoke, though.

"This whole floor is burning. We don't have much time. We've got to get out."

I was completely awake now. I could see a heavy layer of smoke hanging in the bright moonlight that slanted in through the lattice-covered windows. "I'm all right, Kmuzu," I said. "I'll wake Friedlander Bey. Do you think the whole house is on fire, or just this wing?"

"I'm not sure, *yaa Sidi.*"

"Then run over to the east wing and wake my mother. Make sure she gets out all right."

"And Umm Saad as well."

"Yeah, you right." He hurried out of my room. Before I went out into the hall, I stopped to find the telephone on my desk. I punched the city's emergency number, but the line was busy. I muttered a curse and tried again. Still the line was busy. I kept calling and calling; it seemed like hours went by before a woman's voice answered. "Fire," I cried. I was frantic by that time. "The Friedlander Bey estate near the Christian Quarter."

"Thank you, sir," said the woman. "The fire brigade is on its way."

The air had gotten very bad, and the acrid smoke burned my nose and throat as I bent lower trying to breathe. I paused at the entrance to the suite, and then ran back to find my jeans. I know you're supposed to get out of a burning building as quickly as possible, but I still hadn't seen any actual flames and I didn't feel as if I were in any immediate danger. It turned out that I was wrong; while I stopped to pull on my jeans, I was already being burned by the hot ash in the air. I didn't feel it at the time, but I was getting second-degree burns on my head, neck, and shoulders, which were bare. My hair was badly singed, but my beard protected my face. I've since promised myself that I'm never going to shave it off again.

I first saw flames in the corridor. The heat was intense. I ran with my arms around my head, trying to shield my face and eyes. The soles of my feet were badly scorched within ten feet of my apartment. I pounded on Papa's door, sure that I was going to die right there, bravely but foolishly attempting to rescue an old man who was likely already dead. A stray thought lodged in my consciousness, the memory of Friedlander Bey asking me if I had the courage to fill my lungs again with fire.

There was no response. I knocked louder. The fire was blistering the skin on my back and arms, and I'd begun to choke. I took a step back, raised my right leg, and kicked the door as hard as I could. Nothing happened. It was locked, and the bolt had probably expanded in the heat. I kicked again, and this time the wooden frame around the lock splintered. One more kick and the door sprang back, slamming in against the wall of Papa's parlor.

"O Shaykh!" I shouted. The smoke billowed even more densely here. There was the sharp smell of burning plastic in the air, and I knew that I had to get Papa out quickly, before he and I were overcome by poisonous fumes. That made me even less hopeful of finding Friedlander Bey alive. His bedroom was back and to the left, and that door was closed and locked too. I kicked it in, paying no attention to the stabbing pain that shot through my ankle and shin. I'd have time to nurse my injuries later —if I lived.

Papa was awake, lying on his back in bed, his hands clutching the sheet that covered him. I ran to him, and his eyes followed my every movement. He opened his mouth to speak, but no sound came out. He raised one hand feebly. I didn't have time for whatever he was trying to communicate. I just threw back the covers and scooped him up as if he'd been a child. He was not a tall man, but he'd put on a moderate amount of weight since the days of his athletic prime. It didn't matter; I carried him out of the bedroom with a maniac strength that I knew wouldn't last very long. "Fire!" I shouted as I crossed the parlor again. "Fire! Fire!" The Stones That Speak had their rooms adjoining Papa's. I didn't dare set him down to rouse the Stones. I had to keep fighting my way through the flames toward safety.

Just as I reached the far end of the corridor, the two huge men came up behind me. Neither said a word. They were both as naked as the day they'd been born, but that didn't seem to bother them. One of them took Friedlander Bey from me. The other picked me up and carried me the rest of the way, down the stairs and out into the clean, fresh air.

The Stone must have realized how badly I was hurt, how exhausted I was, and how close to collapse I'd come. I was terrifically grateful to him, but I didn't have the strength to thank him. I promised myself that I'd do something for the Stones as soon as I was able—maybe buy them a few infidels to torture. I mean, what do you get the Gog and Magog who have everything?

The firemen were already setting up their equipment when Kmuzu came to see how I was. "Your mother is safe," he said. "There was no fire in the east wing."

"Thank you, Kmuzu," I said. The inside of my nose was raw and painful, and my throat hurt.

One of the firemen rinsed me with sterile water, then wrapped me in a sheet and rinsed me again. "Here," he said, handing me a glass of water. "This'll make your mouth and throat feel better. You're gonna have to go to the hospital."

"Why?" I asked. I hadn't yet realized how badly I was burned.

"I will go with you, *yaa Sidi*," said Kmuzu.

"Papa?" I said.

"He also needs immediate medical attention," said Kmuzu.

"We'll go together then," I said.

The firemen led me to an ambulance. Friedlander Bey had already been put on a stretcher and lifted inside. Kmuzu helped me up into the vehicle. He beckoned toward me, and I leaned down toward him. "While you're recuperating in the hospital," he said softly, "I will see if I can learn who set this fire."

I looked at him for a moment, trying to collect my thoughts. I blinked and realized that all my eyelashes had been burned off. "You think it's arson?" I said.

The ambulance driver closed one of the rear doors. "I

have proof," said Kmuzu. Then the driver closed the second door. A moment later, Papa and I were speeding through the constricted streets, siren screaming. Papa didn't move on his stretcher. He looked pitifully frail. I didn't feel so well myself. I suppose it was my punishment for laughing at Hexagram Six.

My mother had brought me pistachio nuts and fresh figs, but I was still having some trouble swallowing. "Then have some of this," she said. "I even brought a spoon." She took the lid from a plastic bowl and set it on the hospital tray table. She was very self-conscious about this visit.

I was sedated, but not as sedated as I could have been. Still, a mild dose of Sonneine from a perfusor is better than a poke in the eye with a sharp stick. Of course, I own an experimental daddy that blocks pain, and I could have chipped it in and stayed completely clearheaded and lucid. I just didn't want to use it. I hadn't told my doctors and nurses about it, because I'd rather have the drug. Hospitals are too tedious to endure sober.

I lifted my head from the pillow. "What is it?" I asked in a hoarse voice. I leaned forward and took the plastic bowl.

"Curdled camel's milk," said my mother. "You used to love that when you were sick. When you were little." I thought I detected an uncharacteristic softness in her voice.

Curdled camel's milk doesn't sound like something that could get you to jump out of bed with glee. It isn't, and I didn't. I picked up the spoon, however, and made a show of enjoying it just to please her. Maybe if I ate some of the stuff, she'd be satisfied and leave. Then I could call for another shot of Sonneine and take a nice nap. That's what was worst about being in the hospital: reassuring all the visitors and listening to the histories of their own illnesses and accidents, which were always of far more traumatic proportions than yours.

"You were really worried about me, Marîd?" she asked.

"Course I was," I said, letting my head fall back to the pillow. "That's why I sent Kmuzu to make sure you were safe."

She smiled sadly and shook her head. "Maybe you'd be happier if I'd burned up in the fire. Then you wouldn't be embarrassed about me no more."

"Don't worry about it, Mom."

"Okay, honey," she said. She looked at me in silence for a long moment. "How are your burns?"

I shrugged, and that made me wince. "They still hurt. The nurses come in and slather this white gunk on me a couple of times a day."

"Well, I suppose it's good for you. You just let 'em do what they want."

"Right, Mom."

There was another awkward silence. "I suppose there's things I ought to tell you," she said at last. "I ain't been completely honest with you."

"Oh?" This wasn't any surprise, but I thought I'd swallow the sarcastic comments that came to mind, and let her tell her story her own way.

She stared down at her hands, which were twisting a frayed linen handkerchief in her lap. "I know a lot more about Friedlander Bey and Reda Abu Adil than I told you."

"Ah," I said.

She glanced up at me. "I known both of 'em from before. From even before you was born, when I was a young girl. I was a lot better looking in those days. I wanted to get out of Sidi-bel-Abbès, maybe go someplace like Cairo or Jerusalem, be a holoshow star. Maybe get wired and make some moddies, not sex moddies like Honey Pílar, but something classy and respectable."

"So did Papa or Abu Adil promise to make you a star?"

She looked back down at her hands. "I came here, to the city. I didn't have no money when I got here, and I went hungry for a while. Then I met somebody who took care of me for a while, and he introduced me to Abu Adil."

"And what did Abu Adil do for you?"

Again she looked up, but now tears were slipping

down her cheeks. "What do you think?" she said in a bitter voice.

"He promise to marry you?"

She just shook her head.

"He get you pregnant?"

"No. In the end, he just laughed at me and handed me this bus ticket back to Sidi-bel-Abbès." Her expression grew fierce. "I hate him, Marîd."

I nodded. I was sorry now that she'd begun this confession. "So you're not telling me that Abu Adil is my father, right? What about Friedlander Bey?"

"Papa was always good to me when I first came to the city. That's why even though I was so mad at you for finding me in Algiers, I was glad to hear that Papa was taking care of you."

"Some people hate him, you know," I said.

She stared at me, then shrugged. "I went back to Sidi-bel-Abbès, after all, and then after a few years I met your father. It was like my life was passing so fast. You were born, and then you got older and left Algiers. Then more years went by. Finally, right after you came to see me, I got a message from Abu Adil. He said he'd been thinking about me and wanted to see me again."

She had gotten agitated, and now she paused until she calmed down a little. "I believed him," she said. "I don't know why. Maybe I thought I could have a second chance to live my life, get back all those years I lost, fix all the mistakes. Anyway, goddamn if I didn't fuck up all over again."

I shut my eyes and rubbed them. Then I looked at my mother's anguished face. "What did you do?"

"I moved in with Abu Adil again. In that big place he's got in the slums. That's how I know all about him, and about Umm Saad. You got to watch out for her, baby. She works for Abu Adil, and she's planning to ruin Papa."

"I know."

My mother looked bewildered. "You know already? How?"

I smiled. "Abu Adil's little fuck-buddy told me. They've pretty much written off Umm Saad. She's not part of their plans anymore."

"Still," said my mother, raising a warning finger, "you

got to watch out for her. She's got her own schemes in the fire."

"Yeah, I guess so."

"You know about Abu Adil's moddy? The one he's made of himself?"

"Uh huh. That son of a bitch Umar told me all about it. I'd like to get my hands on it for a few minutes."

She chewed her lip thoughtfully. "Maybe I could think of a way."

Yipe. That's all I needed. "It's not that important, Mom," I told her.

She began to weep again. "I'm so sorry, Marîd. I'm so sorry for everything I done, for not being the kind of mother you needed."

Jeez, I really wasn't feeling well enough to deal with her attack of conscience. "I'm sorry too, Mom," I said, and I was surprised to realize that I truly meant it. "I never showed you the respect—"

"I never *earned* no respect—"

I raised both hands. "Why don't we stop before we're fighting over who's hurt who the most? Let's call a truce or something."

"Maybe we could start over again?" Her voice had a peculiar shyness to it.

I had a lot of doubt about all of this. I didn't know if it was possible to start over again, especially after all that had happened between us, but I thought I could give her a chance. "That's fine with me," I said. "I got no love for the past."

She smiled crookedly. "I like living in Papa's house with you, baby. It makes me think I won't have to go back to Algiers and . . . you know."

I took a deep breath and let it out. "I promise you, Mom," I said, "you'll never have to go back to that life again. Just let me take care of you from now on."

She got up and came toward my bed, her arms outstretched, but I wasn't quite ready for an exchange of mother-son affection. I have a little trouble expressing my feelings, I guess, and I've never been a very demonstrative person. I let her bend down and kiss my cheek and give me a hug, and she murmured something that I couldn't make out. I kind of patted her on the back. It was the best I could manage. Then she went back to her chair.

She sighed. "You made me very happy, Marîd. Happier than I got a right to be. All I ever wanted was a chance for a normal life."

Well, what the hell, what did it cost me? "What do you want to do, Mom?" I asked.

She frowned. "I don't really know. Something useful. Something real."

I had a ludicrous image of Angel Monroe as a candy-striper in the hospital. I dismissed the notion immediately. "Abu Adil brought you to the city to spy on Papa, right?"

"Yeah, and I was a sucker to think he really wanted me."

"And on what kind of terms did you leave him? Would you be willing to spy on him for us?"

She looked doubtful. "I really let him know I didn't like being used," she said. "If I went back there, I don't know if he'd believe I was sorry. But maybe he would. He's got a big ego, you know. Men like that, they always think their women'd walk through fire for 'em. I suppose I could make him buy it." She gave me a wry grin. "I was always a good actress. Khalid used to tell me I was the best."

Khalid, I remembered, had been her pimp. "Let me think about it, Mom. I wouldn't get you into anything dangerous, but I'd like to have a secret weapon Abu Adil didn't know anything about."

"Well, anyway, I feel like I owe Papa something. For letting Abu Adil use me like that, and for all Papa's done for me since I came to live in his house."

I wasn't crazy about letting my mother get involved any further with the intrigue, but I was aware that she might be a wonderful source of information. "Mom," I said casually, "what do the letters A.L.M. mean to you?"

"A.L.M.? I don't know. Nothing, really. The Alliance of Lingerie Models? That's a hooker's trade union, but I don't even know if they got a local in this city."

"Never mind. How about the Phoenix File? That ring a bell?"

I saw her flinch just a little. "No," she said slowly, "I never heard of that at all." There was something about the way she said it, though, that persuaded me she was lying. I wondered what she was hiding now. It took the optimistic edge off our previous conversation, making me doubt how

much I could trust her. It wasn't the right time to pursue
the matter, but there'd be a moment of truth when I got
out of the hospital again.

"Mom," I said, yawning, "I'm getting kind of sleepy."

"Oh, baby, I'll go then." She got up and fussed with
my covers. "I'll leave the curdled camel's milk with you."

"Great, Mom."

She bent and kissed me again. "I'll be back tomorrow.
I'm gonna see how Papa's doing now."

"Give him my regards and tell him that I pray to
Allah for his well-being." She went to the door, turned,
and waved to me. Then she was gone.

The door had barely shut before a thought struck me:
The only person who knew that I'd gone to visit my
mother in Algiers had been Saied the Half-Hajj. He must
have located Mom for Reda Abu Adil. It must have been
Saied who'd brought her to the city to spy on Papa and
me. Saied had to be working for Abu Adil. He'd sold me
out.

I promised myself still another moment of truth, one
that the Half-Hajj would never forget.

Whatever the goal of the conspiracy, whatever the
significance of the Phoenix File, it must be tremendously
urgent to Abu Adil. In the past few months, he'd set Saied,
Kmuzu, and Umm Saad to pry into our affairs. I wondered
how many others there were that I hadn't identified yet.

Later that afternoon, just before suppertime, Kmuzu
came to visit. He was dressed in a white shirt, no tie, and a
black suit. He looked like an undertaker. His expression
was solemn, as if one of the nurses outside had just told
him that my situation was hopeless. Maybe my burned
hair would never grow back, or I'd have to live with that
awful, cold white gunk on my skin for the rest of my life.

"How are you feeling, *yaa Sidi?*" he asked.

"I'm suffering from Delayed Post-Fire Stress Syndrome," I said. "I'm just realizing how close I came to not
making it. If you hadn't been there to wake me up—"

"You would have been roused by the fire if you hadn't
been using the sleep add-on."

I hadn't thought of that. "I suppose," I said. "Still, I
owe you my life."

"You rescued the master of the house, *yaa Sidi*. He

shelters me and protects me from Reda Abu Adil. You and I are even."

"I still feel I'm in your debt." How much was my life worth to me? Could I give him something of equivalent value? "How would you like your freedom?" I asked.

Kmuzu's brows drew together. "You know that liberty is what I desire most. You also know it's in the hands of the master of the house. It's up to him."

I shrugged. "I have a certain amount of influence with Papa. I'll see what I can do."

"I would be most grateful, *yaa Sidi.*" Kmuzu's expression had become noncommittal, but I knew he wasn't as cool as he was pretending.

We talked for a few minutes more, and then he got up to go. He reassured me that my mother and our servants would be safe enough, *inshallah.* We had two dozen armed guards. Of course, they hadn't prevented someone from entering the grounds and torching the west wing. Collusion, espionage, arson, attempted murder—it had been a long while since Papa's enemies had so noisily expressed their displeasure.

After Kmuzu left, I got bored very quickly. I turned on the holoset fixed to the furniture across from my bed. It wasn't a very good unit and the projection coordinates were off by a considerable margin. The vertical variable needed adjusting; the actors in some contemporary Central European drama struggled along knee-deep in the dresser. The elaborate production was subtitled, but unfortunately the captions were lost, out of sight with the actors' legs in my sock drawer. Whenever there was a close-up, I'd see the person only from the top of his head to the bottom of his nose.

I didn't think I'd care, because at home I don't watch much holo. In the hospital, however, where the order of the day was boredom, I found myself turning it on again and again all day long. I browsed through a hundred channels from around the world, and I never found anything worth watching. That might have been due to my semistoned state and my lack of concentration; or it might have been the fault of the little amputated figures wading around on the dresser, speaking a dozen different languages.

So I bailed out of the Thuringian tragedy and told the

holoset to turn itself off. Then I got out of bed and put on my robe. That was kind of uncomfortable because of my burns and also because of the white gunk; I hated the way it felt, stuck to my hospital gown. I stuck my feet into the green paper slippers the hospital provided, and headed for the door.

An orderly was coming in just as I was going out, carrying a tray with my lunch. I was pretty hungry and my mouth began to water, even before I found out what was on the plates. I decided to stay in the room until after I ate. "What do we have?" I asked.

The orderly set it down on my tray table. "You got tasty fried liver," he said. His tone let me know it wasn't anything to look forward to.

"I'll eat it later." I left my room and walked slowly down the corridor. I spoke my name to the elevator, and in a few seconds the car arrived. I didn't know how much freedom of movement I had.

When the elevator asked me what floor I wanted, I asked for Friedlander Bey's room number. "VIP Suite One," it told me.

"What floor is that on?" I asked.

"Twenty." That was as high as you could go. This hospital was one of only three in the city with VIP suites. It was the same hospital where I'd had my brainwork done, less than a year before. I liked having a private room, but I didn't really need a suite. I didn't really feel like entertaining.

"Do you wish the twentieth floor?" the elevator asked.

"You bet."

"Do you wish the twentieth floor?"

"Yes," I said. It was a stupid elevator. I stood hunched over while it traveled slowly from the fifteenth floor to the twentieth. I was looking for a posture that didn't feel sticky and squishy, and I wasn't having any luck. I was also starting to get very sick of the white gunk's intense peppermint smell.

I got off on Twenty, and the first thing I saw was a beefy, thick-necked woman in a white uniform sitting in the middle of a circular nurse's station. There was a muscular man nearby too, dressed in a Eur-Am style security guard outfit. He had a huge seizure cannon holstered on his hip, and he looked at me as if he were deciding whether or not to let me live.

"You're a patient in this hospital," said the nurse. Well, she was at least as bright as the elevator.

"Room 1540," I said.

"This is the twentieth floor. What are you doing here?"

"I want to visit Friedlander Bey."

"Just a moment." She frowned and consulted her computer terminal. From her tone of voice, it was obvious she didn't think anyone as scruffy as me could possibly be on her list of approved visitors. "Your name?"

"Marîd Audran."

"Well, here you are." She glanced up at me. I thought maybe when she found my name on the list, she'd show a little grudging respect. No such luck. "Zain, show Mr. Audran to Suite One," she told the guard.

Zain nodded. "Right this way, sir," he said. I followed him down a lushly carpeted hallway, turned into a cross corridor, and stopped outside the door to Suite One.

I wasn't surprised to see one of the Stones standing sentry duty. "Habib?" I said. I thought I saw his expression flicker just a bit. I pushed by him, half-expecting him to reach out his brawny arm to stop me, but he let me pass. I think both Stones accepted me now as Friedlander Bey's deputy.

Inside the suite, the lights were turned off and the shades drawn on the windows. There were flowers everywhere, jammed into vases and growing from elaborate pots. The sweet fragrance was almost sickening; if it had been my room, I would have told a nurse to give some of the flowers to other sick people in the hospital.

Papa lay motionless in his bed. He didn't look well. I knew he'd been burned as badly as I'd been, and his face and arms had been smeared with the same white gunk. His hair was neatly combed, but he hadn't been shaved in a few days, probably because his skin was still too painful. He was awake, but his eyelids drooped. The Sonneine was knocking him out; he didn't have my tolerance.

There was a second room adjoining, and I could see Youssef, Papa's butler, and Tariq, his valet, sitting at a table playing cards. They started to get up, but I signaled

hat they should go on with their game. I sat in a chair
eside Papa's bed. "How do you feel, O Shaykh?" I said.

He opened his eyes, but I could see that it was difficult
or him to stay awake. "I am being well cared for, my
nephew," he said.

That wasn't what I'd asked, but I let it pass. "I pray
very hour for your return to health."

He attempted a weak smile. "It is good that you
ray." He paused to take a deep breath. "You risked your
fe to save me."

I spread my hands. "I did what I had to."

"And you suffered pain and injury on my account."

"It is of small consequence. The important thing is
hat you are alive."

"I owe you a great debt," said the old man wearily.

I shook my head. "It was only what Allah decreed. I
vas but His servant."

He frowned. Despite the Sonneine, he was still in
iscomfort. "When I am well, and we are both again at
ome, you must allow me to find a gift equal to your
eed."

Oh no, I thought, not another gift from Papa. "In the
neantime," I said, "how may I serve you?"

"Tell me: How did the fire start?"

"It was clumsily done, O Shaykh," I said. "Immedi-
tely after we escaped, Kmuzu found matches and half-
urnt rags soaked in some flammable fluid."

Papa's expression was grim, almost murderous. "I
eared as much. Do you have any other clues? Whom do
ou suspect, O my nephew?"

"I know nothing more, but I will investigate the mater tirelessly when I leave the hospital."

He seemed satisfied for the moment. "You must
romise me one thing," he said.

"What do you wish, O Shaykh?"

"When you learn the identity of the arsonist, he must
ie. We cannot appear weak to our enemies."

Somehow I just knew he was going to say that. I was
oing to have to get a little pocket notebook just to keep
rack of everybody I was supposed to murder for him.
Yes," I said, "he will die." I didn't promise that I, person-
lly, would kill the son of a bitch. I mean, *everybody* dies. I
hought I might turn the matter over to the Stones That

Speak. They were like pet leopards; you had to take them
off their leashes now and then and let them run around to
catch their own meal.

"Good," said Friedlander Bey. He let his eyes close

"There are two more matters, O Shaykh," I said hesi
tantly.

He looked at me again. His expression was agonized
"I am sorry, my nephew. I do not feel well. Even before
the fire, I was suffering from some illness. The pain in my
head and belly has grown worse."

"Have the doctors here explained it?"

"No, they are fools. They tell me they can find noth
ing wrong. There are always more tests they wish to run.
am plagued by incompetence and tortured with indig
nity."

"You must put yourself in their hands, my uncle,"
said. "I was treated very well in this hospital."

"Yes, but you were not a frail old man, clinging hope
lessly to life. Every one of their barbarous procedures rob
me of another year of life."

I smiled. "It's not as bad as that, O Shaykh. Let them
discover the cause of your ailment and cure it, and then
soon you will be as strong as ever."

Papa waved a hand impatiently, indicating that he
didn't want to talk about it anymore. "What are these
other worries you will inflict on me?"

I had to approach both of them correctly. They were
very sensitive matters. "The first concerns my servant
Kmuzu," I said. "Even as I rescued you from the fire
Kmuzu rescued me. I promised him that I would ask you
to reward him."

"Why, of course, my son. He surely has earned a good
reward."

"I thought you might give him his freedom."

Papa looked at me in silence, his expression empty
"No," he said slowly, "it is not yet time. I will consider the
circumstances, and decide on some other appropriate
compensation."

"But—" He stopped me with a single gesture. Even
weakened as he was, the force of his personality would no
permit me to press him further when he'd already made
up his mind. "Yes, O Shaykh," I said humbly. "The sec
ond matter concerns the widow and children of Jirj

aknahyi, the police officer who was my partner. They
e in desperate financial straits, and I wish to do more
an merely offer them cash. I seek your permission to
ove them into our house, perhaps for only a little while."

Papa's expression told me that he did not want to talk
y longer. "You are my darling," he said weakly. "Your
ecisions are my decisions. It is good."

I bowed to him. "I will leave you to rest now. May
lah grant you peace and well-being."

"I will miss your presence, O my son."

I got up from my chair and glanced into the other
om. Youssef and Tariq appeared to be engrossed in their
rd game, but I was sure they'd noted every word that
d passed between Papa and me. As I headed for the
oor, Friedlander Bey began to snore. I tried to make no
ise as I left the suite.

I went down in the elevator to my room, and climbed
ck into bed. I was glad to see that the liver lunch had
en taken away. I'd just turned on the holoset again
hen Dr. Yeniknani came in to visit me. Dr. Yeniknani
d assisted the neurosurgeon who'd amped my skull. He
as a dark, fierce-looking Turk who was actually a student
Sufi mysticism. I'd gotten to know him pretty well dur-
g my last stay here, and I was glad to see him again. I
oked up at the holoset and said "Off."

"How are you feeling, Mr. Audran?" said Dr.
eniknani. He came up next to my bed and smiled down
me. His strong teeth looked very white against his
varthy skin and his big, black mustache. "May I sit
own?"

"Please, make yourself comfortable," I said. "So, are
u here to tell me that the fire baked my brain, or is this
st a friendly call?"

"Your reputation suggests that you don't have much
ain left to bake," he said. "No, I just wanted to see how
u were feeling, and if there's anything I can do for you."

"I'm grateful. No, I don't think I need anything. I'd
st like to get out of here already."

"Everyone says that. You'd think we tortured people
here."

"I've had nicer holidays."

"I have an offer for you, Mr. Audran," said Dr.
eniknani. "How would you like to hold off some of the

effects of the aging process? Prevent the degeneration
your mind, the slow deterioration of your memory?"

"Uh oh," I said. "There's some kind of horrible cat
coming, I can tell."

"No catch. Dr. Lisân is experimenting with a tec
nique that promises to do everything I just mentione
Imagine never having to worry about your mental facu
ties wearing out as you get older. Your thought process
will be as sharp and quick when you're two hundred
they are today."

"Sounds great, Dr. Yeniknani. But you're not talki
about vitamin supplements here, are you?"

He gave me a rueful grin. "Well, no, not exactly. D
Lisân is working with plexiform cortical augmentatio
He's wrapping the cerebral cortex of the brain in a me
of microscopic wire reticulations. The mesh is made
incredibly fine gold filaments to which are bonded th
same organic nemes that link your corymbic implant
your central nervous system."

"Uh huh." It sounded like mad scientist stuff to m

"The organic strands pass your brain's electrical ir
pulses from your cerebral cortex to the gold mesh, ar
back in the opposite direction. The mesh serves as a
artificial storage mechanism. Our early results show that
can triple or quadruple the number of neuronal conne
tions in your brain."

"Like adding extra memory to a computer," I sai

"That's too easy an analogy," said Dr. Yeniknani.
could tell that he was getting excited, explaining his r
search to me. "The nature of memory is holographic, yc
know, so we're not just offering you a vast number
empty slots in which to file thoughts and recollections.
goes beyond that—we're supplying you with a better r
dundancy system. Your brain already stores each memor
in many locations, but as brain cells wear out and di
some of these memories and learned activities disappea
With cortical augmentation, however, there is a capabili
for multiply storing information on a level many tim
higher than normal. Your mind will be safe, protecte
against gradual failure, except of course in the case
traumatic injury."

"All I have to do," I said dubiously, "is let you and D

isân plop my brain into a string bag, like a cabbage head the market."

"That's all. You'll never feel a thing." Dr. Yeniknani rinned. "And I think I can promise, in addition, that the igmentation will speed up the processing in your brain. ou'll have the reflexes of a superman. You'll—"

"How many people have you done this to, and how do iey feel about it?"

He studied his long, tapered fingers. "We haven't ac- ually performed the operation on a human subject," he iid. "But our work with laboratory rats shows a lot of romise."

I felt relieved. "I really thought you were trying to ll me on this," I said.

"Just keep it in mind, Mr. Audran," he said. "In a ouple of years we'll be looking for some brave volunteers help us push back the frontiers of medicine."

I reached up and tapped my two corymbic implants. Not me. I've already done my part.

Dr. Yeniknani shrugged. He leaned back in his chair id gazed at me thoughtfully. "I understand that you ved the life of your patron," he said. "I once told you iat death is desirable as our passage to paradise, and that u should not fear it. It is also true that life is even more esirable as our means of reconciliation with Allah, if we ioose to follow the Straight Path. You are a courageous ian."

"I don't think I really did anything brave," I said. "I asn't really thinking about that at the time."

"You do not strictly follow the commands of the Mes- nger of God," said Dr. Yeniknani, "but you are a wor- iipful man in your own way. Two hundred years ago, a an said that the religions of the world are like a lantern ith many different colored glass panels, but that God was e single flame within." He shook my hand and stood up. With your permission."

It seemed that every time I spoke with Dr. Yeniknani, e gave me some Sufi wisdom to think about. "Peace be pon you," I said.

"And upon you be peace," he said. Then he turned id left my room.

I ate supper later, a kind of baked lamb, chick-pea, id bean casserole with onions and tomatoes, which

would have been pretty good if only someone would te
the kitchen staff about the existence of salt and maybe
little lemon juice. Then I was bored all over again, and
turned on the holoset, turned it off, stared at the walls, a
turned it on again. Finally, to my great relief, the tel
phone beside my bed warbled. I answered it and sai
"Praise Allah."

I heard Morgan's voice on the other end. I didn't ha
an English-language daddy with me, and Morgan ca
even find the bathroom in Arabic, so the only words
understood were "Jawarski" and "Abu Adil." I told hi
I'd talk to him when I got out of the hospital; I knew I
didn't understand any more of what I said than I'd unde
stood of him, so I hung up.

I lay back on my pillow and stared up at the ceiling
wasn't really surprised to learn there might be a conne
tion between Abu Adil and the crazy American killer. T
way things were starting to shape up, I wouldn't be su
prised to hear that Jawarski was really my own long-lc
brother.

14

spent almost a week in the hospital. I watched the
holoset and got a lot of reading done, and despite my
wishes a few people came to see me—Lily, the
exchange who had a crush on me, Chiri, Yasmin. There
ere two surprises: the first was a basket of fruit from
mar Abdul-Qawy; the second was a visit from six total
rangers, people who lived in the Budayeen and the
eighborhood around the copshop. Among them I recog-
ized the young woman with the baby to whom I'd given
ome money, that day Shaknahyi and I had been sent to
ok for On Cheung.

She seemed just as shy and embarrassed as she had
hen she'd approached me in the street. "O Shaykh," she
id in a trembling voice, setting a cloth-covered basket
1 my tray table, "we all beseech Allah for your recov-
y."

"Must be working," I said, smiling, "because the doc-
r says I'll be out of here today."

"Praise God," said the woman. She turned to the oth-
s who'd come with her. "These people are the parents
children, the children who call to you in the streets and
the police station house. They are grateful for your
enerosity."

These men and women lived in the kind of poverty
d known most of my life. The odd thing was that they
idn't show any petulance toward me. It may seem un-
rateful, but sometimes you resent your benefactors.
hen I was young, I'd learned how humiliating it can be
take charity, especially when you're so desperate that
ou can't afford the luxury of pride.

It all depends on the attitude of the givers. I'll never
rget how much I hated Christmas as a kid in Algiers.

Christians in the neighborhood used to put together ba
kets of food for my mother, my baby brother, and m
Then they'd come by our shabby apartment and stan
around beaming at us, proud of their good deeds. They'
look from my mother to Hussain to me, waiting until we'
acted appropriately grateful. How many times I wishe
that we weren't so hungry, that we could just throw thos
goddamn canned goods back in their faces!

I was afraid these parents might feel the same wa
about me. I wanted them to know that they didn't have
go through any forelock-tugging acts of appreciation fo
my benefit.

"I'm glad to help, my friends," I said. "But, really,
got my own selfish motives. In the noble Qur'ân it say
'That which you spend for good must go to parents an
near kindred and orphans and the needy and the wa
farer. And whatever good ye do, lo! Allah is aware of it.' S
maybe if I kick a few kiam to a worthy cause, it'll make u
for the night I stayed up partying with the blond twi
from Hamburg."

I saw a couple of my visitors smile. That let me relax
little. "Even so," said the young mother, "we thank you

"Less than a year ago, I wasn't doing so well mysel
Sometimes I was eating only every other day. There we
times when I didn't have a home to go to, and I slept
parks and abandoned buildings. I been lucky since, an
I'm just returning a favor. I remember how much kin
ness everyone showed me when I was broke." Actuall
practically none of that was true, but it sure was gracio
as all hell.

"We'll leave you now, O Shaykh," said the woma
"You probably need your rest. We just wanted to let yc
know, if there's anything we can do for you, it would gi
us much happiness."

I studied her closely, wondering if she meant wh
she said. "As it happens, I'm looking for two guys," I sai
"On Cheung the baby seller, and this killer, Paul Jawarsl
If anyone's got any information, I'd be very grateful."

I saw them exchange uneasy glances. No one sa
anything. It was just as I expected. "Allah grant you pea
and well-being, Shaykh Marîd al-Amîn," murmured t
woman, backing toward the door.

I'd earned an epithet! She'd called me Marîd t

Trustworthy. *"Allah yisallimak,"* I replied. I was glad
when they left.

About an hour later, a nurse came in and told me that
my doctor had signed my release from the hospital. That
was fine with me. I called Kmuzu, and he brought me
some clean clothes. My skin was still very tender and it
hurt to get dressed, but I was just glad to be going home.

"The American, Morgan, wishes to see you, *yaa Sidi,"*
said Kmuzu. "He says he has something to tell you."

"Sounds like good news," I said. I got into the electric
sedan, and Kmuzu closed the passenger door. Then he
went around and got in behind the steering wheel.

"You also have some business matters to take care of.
There is a considerable amount of money on your desk."

"Uh yeah, I guess so." There should be two fat pay
envelopes from Friedlander Bey, plus my share of the
take from Chiri's.

Kmuzu let his glance slide over to me. "Do you have
any plans for that money, *yaa Sidi?"* he asked.

I smiled at him. "What, you got a horse you want me
to back?"

Kmuzu frowned. No sense of humor, I recalled. "Your
wealth has grown large. With the money that came while
you were in the hospital, you have more than a hundred
thousand kiam, *yaa Sidi.* Much good could be done with
that great a sum."

"Didn't know you were keeping such close tabs on
my bank balance, Kmuzu." He was such a friend sometimes, I tended to forget that he was really only a spy. "I
had some ideas about putting the money to good use. A
free clinic in the Budayeen, maybe, or a soup kitchen."

I'd really startled him. "That's wonderful and unex-
pected!" he said. "I heartily approve."

"I'm so glad," I said sourly. I really had been thinking
along those lines, but I didn't know how to begin. "How'd
you like to study the feasibility? All my time is taken up
with this Abu Adil-Jawarski thing."

"I would be more than happy. I don't think you have
enough to fund a clinic, *yaa Sidi,* but providing hot meals
to the poor, that is a worthy gesture."

"I hope it's more than just a gesture. Let me know
when you have some plans and figures for me to look at."

The nice part of all this was that it would keep Kmuzu busy and out of my hair for a while.

When I went into the house, Youssef grinned and gave me a bow. "Welcome home, O Shaykh!" he said. He insisted on wrestling my suitcase away from Kmuzu. The two of them followed me down the corridor.

"Your apartment is still being rebuilt, *yaa Sidi,*" said Kmuzu. "I've made us comfortable in a suite in the east wing. On the first floor, away from your mother and Umm Saad."

"Thank you, Kmuzu." I was already thinking about the work I had to do. I couldn't take any more time off to recuperate. "Is Morgan here now, or do I have to call him?"

"He's in the antechamber of the office," said Youssef. "Is that all right?"

"Fine. Youssef, why don't you give that suitcase back to Kmuzu. He can carry it to our temporary apartment. I want you to let me into Friedlander Bey's inner office. You don't think he'd mind if I used it while he's in the hospital, do you?"

Youssef thought about that for a moment. "No," he said slowly, "I don't see any problem."

I smiled. "Good. I'm gonna have to take care of his business until he's healthy again."

"Then I'll leave you, *yaa Sidi,*" said Kmuzu. "May I begin working on our charity project?"

"As soon as possible," I said. "Go in safety."

"God be with you," said Kmuzu. He turned toward the servants' wing. I went on with Youssef to Papa's private office.

Youssef paused at the threshold. "Shall I send the American in?" he asked.

"No," I said, "let him wait a couple of minutes. I need my English-language add-on, or I won't understand a word he says. Would you mind fetching it?" I told him where to find it. "Then when you come back, you can show Morgan in."

"Of course, O Shaykh." Youssef hurried away to do my bidding.

I felt an unpleasant thrill when I sat in Friedlander Bey's chair, as if I'd occupied a place of unholy strength. I didn't like the feeling at all. For one thing, I had no desire to step into the role of Junior Crime Lord, or even the more legitimate office of International Power Broker. I was at Papa's feet now; but if, Allah forbid, something terminal were to happen to him, I wouldn't hang around to be anointed as his successor. I had other plans for my future.

I glanced through the papers on Papa's desk for a few minutes, finding nothing racy or incriminating. I was about to start rummaging through the drawers when Youssef returned. "I've brought the entire rack, *yaa Sidi,*" he said.

"Thank you, Youssef. Please show Morgan in now."

"Yes, O Shaykh." I was getting to like all this subservience, but that was a bad sign.

I chipped in the English daddy just as the big, blond American came in. "Where y'at, man?" he said, grinning. "I never been here before. You got a nice place."

"Friedlander Bey's got a nice place," I said, indicating that Morgan should make himself comfortable. "I'm just his errand boy."

"Whatever you say. Now, you want to hear what I got?"

I leaned back in the chair. "Where's Jawarski?" I said.

Morgan's grin disappeared. "Still don't know, man. I got the word out to everybody, but I haven't heard a clue. I don't think he's left the city. He's here somewhere, but he's done a damn good job of evaporating."

"Yeah, you right. So what's the good news?"

He rubbed his stubbly chin. "I know somebody who knows somebody that works for some business front that's owned by Reda Abu Adil. It's a shady package delivery service. Anyway, this guy my friend knows says he heard somebody else say that this Paul Jawarski wanted his money. Seems like your friend Abu Adil arranged to make it easy for Jawarski to blast his way out of the pokey."

"A couple of guards died on account of it, but I don't suppose that bothers Abu Adil none."

"I suppose not. So Abu Adil hired Jawarski through this delivery company to come to the city. I don't know what Abu Adil wanted, but you know what Jawarski's specialty is. This friend of mine calls it the Jawarski Finishing School."

"And now Abu Adil is making sure Jawarski stays unstumbled on, right?"

"The way I figure it."

I closed my eyes and thought about it. It made perfect sense. I didn't have hard evidence that Abu Adil had hired Jawarski to kill Shaknahyi, but in my heart I knew it was true. I also knew Jawarski had killed Blanca and the others in Shaknahyi's notebook. And because Lieutenant Hajjar was two-timing both Friedlander Bey and the halls of justice, I was pretty confident that the police were never going to dig Jawarski up. Even if they did, Jawarski would never be prosecuted.

I opened my eyes and stared at Morgan. "Just keep looking, buddy," I said, "because I don't think anybody else is."

"Money?"

I blinked at him. "What?"

"You got any money for me?"

I stood up angrily. "No, I ain't got money for you! I told you I'd pay you another five hundred when you found Jawarski. That's the deal."

Morgan stood up. "All right, man, just take it easy, okay?"

I was embarrassed by my outburst. "I'm sorry, Morgan," I said. "I'm not mad at you. This whole business is making me crazy."

"Uh yeah. I know you were good friends with Shaknahyi. All right, I'll keep at it."

"Thanks, Morgan." I followed him out of the office and showed him to the front door. "We're not gonna let them get away with it."

"Crime don't pay, right, man?" Morgan grinned and slapped my burned shoulder. The pain made me wince.

"Yeah, you right." I walked with him down the curving gravel driveway. I wanted to get away from the house, and if I left right now, I could escape without Kmuzu tagging along. "Like a ride to the Budayeen?" I asked.

"No, that's all right. I got some other stuff to do, man. See you later."

I turned back toward the house and got the car out of the garage. I thought I'd drop in on my club and see if it was still in one piece.

The day shift was still on, and there were only five or

six customers. Indihar frowned and looked away when I caught her eye. I decided to sit at a table, rather than at my usual place at the bar. Pualani came up to say hello. "Want a White Death?" she asked.

"White Death? What's that?"

She shrugged her slender shoulders. "Oh, that's what Chiri calls that awful gin and bingara thing you drink." She grimaced.

"Yeah, bring me a White Death." It wasn't a bad name.

Brandi was on stage, dancing to the Sikh propaganda music that had suddenly become wildly popular. I hated it a lot. I didn't want to listen to political rantings, even if it had a great beat and a catchy two-bar figure.

"Here you go, boss," said Pualani, dropping a cocktail napkin in front of me and pinning it in place with a highball glass. "Mind if I sit down?"

"Huh? Oh, sure."

"Want to ask you about something. I'm thinkin' of, you know, havin' my brain wired so I can use moddies?" She cocked her head to the side and peered at me, as if I might not comprehend what she was telling me. She didn't say anything more.

"Yeah," I said at last. You had to respond like that with Pualani or you could spend the rest of your life trapped in the same conversation.

"Well, everybody says you know more'n anybody about it. I was wonderin' if you could, like, recommend somebody?"

"A surgeon?"

"Uh huh."

"Well, there's plenty of doctors around who'll do it for you. Most of 'em are pretty reliable."

Pualani gave me a pretty frown. "Well, I was wonderin' if I could go to your doctor and use your name."

"Dr. Lisân doesn't have a private practice. But his assistant, Dr. Yeniknani, is a good man."

Pualani squinted at me. "Would you write his name down for me?"

"Sure." I scribbled the name and commcode on the cocktail napkin.

"And also," she said, "does he do tits?"

"I don't think so, honey." Now Pualani had already

spent a small fortune modifying her body. She had a cute ass that had been rounded with silicone, and cheekbones accentuated with silicone, and her chin and nose reshaped, and she'd already had breast implants. She had a devastating figure, and I thought it was a mistake to blow up her bust any more; but I'd learned a long time ago that you can't reason with dancers when it comes to breast size.

"Oh, okay," she said, obviously disappointed. I took a sip of my White Death. Pualani showed no sign of going away. I waited for her to continue. "You know Indihar?" she said.

"Sure."

"Well, she's havin' a lot of trouble. She's really broke."

"I tried giving her a loan, but she wouldn't take it."

Pualani shook her head. "No, she won't take a loan. But maybe you could help her out some other way." Then she got up and wandered toward the front of the club, and sat down next to a couple of Oriental men wearing sailor's caps.

Sometimes I just wished real life would leave me alone. I gulped a little more of my drink, then stood up and went to the bar. Indihar noticed me and came over. "Get you something, Marîd?" she asked.

"Jirji's pension ain't gonna help you very much, right?"

She gave me an annoyed look and turned away. She headed for the other end of the bar. "Don't want your money," she said.

I followed her. "I'm not offering money. How would you like a low-hassle job where you can live free and watch your kids all day? You wouldn't have to pay a baby-sitter."

She turned around. "What's this all about?" Her expression was mistrustful.

I smiled. "I mean bringing Little Jirji, Zahra, and Hâkim and moving into one of the empty apartments in Papa's house. Save you a lot of money every month, Indihar."

She considered that. "Maybe. Why would you want me in Papa's house?"

I had to come up with some phony but real-sounding

reason. "It's my mother. I need someone to keep an eye on her. I'd be willing to pay you whatever you wanted."

Indihar patted the bar with one hand. "Already got a job, remember?"

"Hey," I said, "if that's the problem, you're fired."

Her face lost its color. "The hell you talking about?"

"Think about it, Indihar. I'm offering you a nice home, free rent and meals, plus good money every week for a part-time job making sure my mom doesn't do anything crazy. Your kids'll be taken care of and you won't have to come into this bar every day. You won't have to take your clothes off and dance, and you won't have to deal with the drunk jerks and the lazy-ass girls like Brandi."

She raised her eyebrows. "I'll let you know, Marîd," she said. "Soon as I figure out what kind of hustle you're trying to pull. Sounds too good to be straight, sweetheart. I mean, you're not wearing a Santa Claus moddy or nothing."

"Yeah, you think about it. Talk it over with Chiri. You trust her. See what she thinks."

Indihar nodded. She was still watching me uncertainly. "Even if I say yes," she said, "I'm not gonna fuck you."

I sighed. "Yeah, you right." I went back to my table. A minute after I sat down again, Fuad il-Manhous let himself drop into the other chair. "I woke up the other day," he said in his high-pitched, nasal voice, "and my mama says to me, 'Fuad, we don't have no money, go out and take one of the chickens and sell it.'"

He was starting one of his dumb fables. He was so desperate for attention that he'd make himself look like a total fool just to make me laugh. The sad thing was that even his most fantastic stories were based on Fuad's actual fuck-ups.

He looked at me closely, to make sure I understood him so far. "So I did. I went out to my mama's chicken coop and I chased those chickens around and around till I caught one. Then I carried it down the hill and up the hill and over the bridge and through the streets till I came to the Souk of the Poultry Dressers. Well, I never took a chicken to market before, so I didn't know what to do. I stood there in the middle of the square all day, until I saw the merchants locking their money up in boxes and loading their leftover stuff onto their carts. I'd already heard the sunset call to prayer, so I knew I didn't have much time.

"I took my chicken to one of the men and told him I wanted to sell it, and he looked at it and shook his head. 'This chicken has lost all it's teeth,' he says.

"So I looked at it, and by Allah, he was right. That chicken didn't have a tooth in its head. So I says, 'What will you give me for it?' And the man gave me a handful of copper fîqs.

"Then I walked home with one hand in my pocket and my other hand holding the copper fîqs. Just when I was crossing the bridge over the drainage canal, there was this fierce swarm of gnats. I started waving my hands and swatting them, and then I ran the rest of the way across the bridge. When I got to the other side, I looked and I saw that I didn't have the money anymore. I'd dropped all the coins into the canal."

Fuad coughed quietly. "Can I have a glass of beer, Marîd?" he asked. "I'm getting real thirsty."

I signaled to Indihar to draw one. "You paying for this, Fuad?" I said. His long face fell further. He looked like a puppy about to get a beating. "Just kidding," I said. "The beer's on the house. I want to hear how this story comes out."

Indihar set a mug in front of him, then stood around to hear the rest of the story. *"Bismillah,"* murmured Fuad, and he took a long gulp. Then he set the beer down, gave me a quick, thankful grimace, and started again. "Anyway," he said, "when I got home, my mama was real mad. I didn't have no chicken and I didn't have no money. 'Next time,' she says, 'put it in your pocket.'

" 'Ah,' I go, 'I should have thought of that.' So the next morning, my mama wakes me up and tells me to take another chicken to the souk. Well, I got dressed and went out and chased them around some more and caught one and carried it down the hill and up the hill and across the bridge and through the streets to the souk. And this time I didn't stand in the hot sun all morning and all afternoon. I went right up to the merchant and showed him the second chicken.

" 'This one looks as bad as the one you brought yesterlay,' he says. 'And besides, I'll have to provide space for it here in my stall all day. But I'll tell you what I'll do. I'll give you a big jug of honey in trade. It's very fine honey.' "

"Well, it was a good trade because my mama had four other chickens, but she didn't have no honey. So I took the jug of honey from him and started home. I'd just crossed the bridge when I remembered what my mama told me. I opened the jug and poured the honey in my pocket. By the time I climbed the last hill, it was all gone.

"So my mama was real mad again. 'Next time,' she says, 'balance it on your head.'

" 'Ah,' I go, 'I should have thought of that.' On the third morning, I got up and caught another chicken, and carried it to the souk and brought it to the merchant.

" 'Are all your chickens in such bad shape?' he says. 'Well, in the name of Allah, I will give you my supper for his bird.' And the merchant gave me a mess of curds and whey.

"Well, I remembered what my mama told me, and I balanced it on my head. I went through the streets and across the bridge and down the hill and up the hill. When I got home, my mama asked me what I got for the chicken. 'Enough curds and whey for our evening meal,' I go.

" 'Then where is it?' she says.

" 'On my head,' I go. She took one look and dragged me to the washstand. She poured a whole pitcher of cold water over my head and scrubbed my hair with a stiff brush. All the time she was shouting and blaming me for losing the curds and whey.

" 'Next time, carry it carefully in your hands,' she says.

" 'Ah,' I go, 'I should have thought of that.' So the next morning, very early before the sun came up, I went out to the chicken coop and chose the nicest, fattest chicken that was left. I left the house before my mama woke up, and I carried the chicken down the hill and through the streets to the Souk of the Poultry Dressers.

" 'Good morning, my friend,' says the merchant. 'I see you have another aged, toothless chicken.'

" 'This is a very nice chicken,' I go, 'and I want what it's worth and nothing less.'

"The merchant looked at the chicken closely and

mumbled to himself. 'You know,' he says at last, 'these feathers are stuck on very tight.'

" 'Isn't that how they're supposed to be?' I go.

"He pointed to a row of dead chickens with their heads cut off. 'See any feathers on these?'

" 'No,' I go.

" 'Ever eat a roast chicken with feathers?'

" 'No,' I go.

" 'Then I'm sorry. It will cost me much time and labor to unstick all these feathers. I can only offer you this big, fierce tomcat.'

"I thought that was a good trade, because the tomcat would catch the mice and rats that crept into the coop and stole the chicken feed. I remembered what my mama had told me, and I tried to carry the tomcat carefully in my hands. Just after I went down the hill and before I went up the hill, the tomcat snarled and spit and squirmed and scratched until I couldn't hold him any longer. He jumped out of my hands and ran away.

"I knew my mama was gonna be mad again. 'Next time,' she says, 'tie him with a string and pull him behind you.'

" 'Ah,' I go, 'I should have thought of that.' Now there's only two chickens left, so it took me longer to catch one the next morning, even though I didn't even care which one it was. When I got to the souk, the merchant was very glad to see me.

" 'Praise Allah that we are both well this morning,' he says, smiling at me. 'I see you have a chicken.'

" 'Yeah, you right,' I go. I laid the chicken on the warped board he used for a counter.

"The merchant picked up the chicken and weighed it in his hands, and thumped it with his finger like you'd thump a melon. 'This chicken doesn't lay eggs, does it?' he asks.

" 'Sure, it lays eggs! It's the best egg-laying hen my mama ever had.'

"The man shook his head and frowned. 'You see,' he says, 'that's a problem. Every egg this chicken lays, that's less meat on its bones. This might've been a nice heavy chicken if it hadn't laid no eggs. It's a good thing you brought it to me now, before it shrunk away to nothing.'

" 'All the eggs ought to be worth something,' I go.

" 'I don't see no eggs. I'll tell you what I'll do. I'll trade you this killed, cleaned chicken ready to eat for your egg-ying chicken. You won't find a better deal than that from any of these other poultry dressers. Once they hear this chicken is such a good egg-layer, they won't give you two copper fiqs.'

"I was just glad this man had taken a liking to me, because he was telling me things none of the other merchants would've told me. So I traded my worthless egg-layer for his dressed chicken, even though to me it looked a little scrawny and smelled funny and was kind of the wrong color. I remembered what my mama told me, so I tied a string around it and pulled it along behind me as I walked home.

"You should've heard my mama yelling at me when I got home! That poor plucked chicken was completely ruined. 'By the life of my eyes!' she shouted. 'You are the biggest fool in all the lands of Islam! Next time, carry it on your shoulder!'

" 'Ah,' I go, 'I should have thought of that.'

"So there was one chicken left, and I promised myself that I was gonna get the better of the deal the next day. Again I didn't wait for my mama to wake me. I rose early, scrubbed my face and hands, put on my best suit of clothes, and went out to the coop. It took me an hour to catch that last chicken, which had always been my mama's favorite. It's name was Mouna. Finally I got my hands on its thrashing, flapping body. I carried it out of the chicken coop, down the hill, up the hill, across the bridge, through the streets to the souk.

"But this morning the poultry dresser was not in his stall. I stood there for several minutes, wondering where my friend could be. Finally, a girl came up to me. She was dressed as a modest Muslim woman should be dressed, and I couldn't see her face because of the veil; but when she spoke, I knew from her voice that she probably was the most beautiful girl I'd ever met."

"You can get yourself in a lot of trouble that way," I told Fuad. "I've made the mistake of falling in love over the telephone. More than once."

He frowned at the interruption and went on. "She was probably the most beautiful girl I'd ever met. Any-

way, she says, 'Are you the gentleman who has been trad
ing his chickens with my father every morning?'

"I go, 'I'm not sure. I don't know who your father is. I
this his poultry stall?' She says it is. I go, 'Then I'm tha
gentleman, and I have our last chicken right here
Where's your father this morning?'

"Big bright tears collect in the corners of her eye
She looks up at me with a pitiful expression on her face, a
least the part of it I can see. 'My father is desperately ill
she says. 'The doctor doesn't expect him to live throug
the day.'

"Well, I was shocked by the news. 'May Allah hav
mercy on your father, and grant him health. If he dies, I'
have to sell my chicken to someone else today.'

"The girl didn't say anything for a moment. I don
think she really cared what happened to my chicken. A
last she said, 'My father sent me here this morning to fin
you. His conscience is troubling him. He says that h
traded unfairly with you, and he wishes to make up for i
before he is called to the bosom of Allah. He begs that yo
accept his donkey, the very donkey that faithfully pulle
my father's cart for ten years.'

"I was a little suspicious about this offer. After all,
didn't know this girl as well as I knew her father. 'Let m
get this straight,' I go. 'You want to trade your fine donke
for this chicken?'

" 'Yes,' she says.

" 'I'll have to think it over. It's our last chicken, yo
know.' I thought about it and thought about it, but
couldn't see anything that would make my mama mad.
was sure that finally she'd be happy about one of m
trades. 'All right,' I go, and I grabbed the donkey's rop
halter. 'Take the chicken, and tell your father that I wil
pray for his well-being. May he return tomorrow to hi
stall in this souk, *inshallah.*'

" *'Inshallah,'* the girl says, and she lowered her eye
to the ground. She went away with my mama's las
chicken, and I never saw her again. I think about her a lot
though, because she's probably the only woman I'll eve
love."

"Yeah, you right," I said, laughing. Fuad has this thing
for mean hookers, the kind who carry straight razors. Yo
can find him every night over at the Red Light Lounge

Fatima and Nassir's place. Nobody else I know even has
the guts to go in there alone. Fuad spends a lot of time in
here, falling in love and getting ripped off.

"Anyway," he said, "I started leading the donkey
home, when I remembered what my mama told me. So I
trained and pushed and lifted until I got that donkey to
my shoulders. I got to admit, I really didn't know why my
mama wanted me to carry it that way, when it could walk
by itself just as well as I could. Still, I didn't want her mad
at me anymore.

"I staggered toward home with the donkey across my
back, and as I climbed down the hill, I passed the beautiful
walled palace of Shaykh Salman Mubarak. Now, you know
Shaykh Salman lived in that great mansion with his beautiful daughter, who was sixteen years old and had never
laughed from the time she'd been born. She had never
even smiled. She could talk all right, but she just didn't.
Nobody, not even her wealthy father, had ever heard her
say a single word since the shaykh's wife, the girl's
mother, had died when the girl was three years old. The
doctors said that if anyone could make her laugh, she'd be
able to speak again; or if anyone could make her speak,
she'd then laugh as any normal person might. Shaykh
Salman had made the usual offers of riches and his daughter's hand in marriage, but suitor after suitor had tried and
failed. The girl just sat glumly by the window, watching
the world pass by below.

"That's when I happened to walk by carrying the
donkey. It must have looked pretty weird, upside down
on my back with its hooves waving in the air. I was told
later that the shaykh's beautiful daughter stared at me
and the donkey for a few seconds, and then burst out into
a helpless fit of laughter. She recovered her speech then
too, because she called loudly for her father to come look.
The shaykh was so grateful, he ran out into the road to
meet me."

"Did he give you his daughter?" asked Indihar.

"You bet," said Fuad.

"How romantic," she said.

"And when I married her, I became the richest man
in the city after the shaykh himself. And my mother was
quite pleased, and didn't mind that she had no chickens

left at all. She came to live with my wife and me in the shaykh's palace."

I sighed. "How much of that was true, Fuad?" I asked.

"Oh," he said, "I forgot a part. It turns out that the shaykh was really the poultry dresser, who went to the souk every morning. I don't remember the reason why. And so the veiled girl was just as beautiful as I thought she'd be."

Indihar reached over and grabbed Fuad's half-full mug of beer. She raised it to her lips and finished it off. "I thought the poultry dresser was dying," she said.

Fuad frowned in serious thought. "Yeah, well, he was, see, but when he heard his daughter laughing and calling his name, he was miraculously healed."

"All praise to Allah, Fount of blessings," I said.

"I made up that part about Shaykh Salman and his beautiful daughter," said Fuad.

"Uh huh," said Indihar. "You and your mama really raise chickens?"

"Oh sure," he said eagerly, "but we don't got any right at the moment."

"Because you traded them?"

"I told my mama we should start again with younger chickens that still got their teeth."

"Thank God, I have to go mop up the spilled beer," said Indihar. She went back behind the bar.

I drained the last of my White Death. After Fuad's story, I wanted three or four more drinks. "Another beer?" I asked him.

He stood up. "Thanks, Marîd, but I got to make some money. I want to buy a gold chain for this girl."

"Why don't you give her one of the ones you try selling to the tourists?"

He looked horrified. "She'd scratch my eyes out!" he said. It sounded like he'd found another hot-blooded sweetheart. "By the way, the Half-Hajj said I should show you this." He pulled something out of his pocket and dropped it in front of me.

I picked it up. It was heavy, shiny, and made of steel, about six inches long. I'd never held one in my hand before, but I knew what it was: an empty clip from an automatic pistol.

Not many people used the old projectile weapons

nymore, but Paul Jawarski used a .45 caliber gun. That's
hat this came from.

"Where'd you get this, Fuad?" I asked casually, turn-
ng the clip over in my hands.

"Oh, in the alley behind Gay Che's. Sometimes you
an find money there, it falls out of their pockets when
ney go out into the alley. I showed it to Saied first, and he
aid you'd like to see it."

"Uh huh. I never heard of Gay Che's."

"You wouldn't like it. It's a tough place. I don't ever
o in there. I just hang around in the alley."

"Sounds smart. Where is it?"

Fuad closed one eye and looked thoughtful.
Hâmidiyya. On Aknouli Street."

Hâmidiyya. Reda Abu Adil's little kingdom. "Now,
hy did Saied think I'd want to know about this?" I asked.

Fuad shrugged. "He didn't tell me. Did you? Want to
e it, I mean?"

"Yeah, thanks, Fuad. I owe you one."

"Really? Then maybe—"

"Another time, Fuad." I made a distracted, dismissing
notion with my hand. I guess he took the hint, because in
little while I noticed he was gone. I had a lot to think
bout: Was this a clue? Was Paul Jawarski hiding out in one
f Abu Adil's crummier enterprises? Or was it some kind
f a trap baited by Saied the Half-Hajj, who couldn't know
nat I no longer trusted him?

I didn't have any choice. Trap or not, I was going to
ollow it up. But not just yet.

15

I waited until the next morning before I followed up o
Fuad's information. I had the disconcerting feeling tha
I was being set up, but at the same time I felt I might a
well live dangerously. I sure wasn't getting any closer t
finding Jawarski using more conventional method
Maybe sticking my head on the block would tempt th
executioner to make an appearance.

And then maybe the clip didn't belong to Jawarsk
after all, and there wasn't anything at Gay Che's but a l
of guys in exquisitely tailored caftans.

I thought about this as I walked back on the Stree
past Frenchy Benoit's club to the cemetery. I had a sens
that events were moving quickly to their conclusion, a
though I couldn't yet tell if that ending would be tragic o
happy for me. I wished I had Shaknahyi to advise me, an
I wished I had made better use of his experience while h
was still alive. It was his grave I wanted to visit first.

There were several people at the entrance to th
cemetery, sitting or squatting on the uneven, broken slal
of concrete. They all jumped to their feet when they sav
me, the old men selling Coca-Cola and Sharâb from bat
tered coolers on tricycles, the toothless old women grir
ning and shoving bundles of dead, drooping flowers in m
face, the children crying "O Generous! O Compassio
ate!" and blocking my way. Sometimes I don't respon
well to organized, clamorous begging. I lose a lot of m
sympathy. I pushed through the crowd, stopping only t
trade a couple of kiam for a wilted bouquet. Then I passe
beneath the brick arch, into the cemetery.

Shaknahyi's grave was across the way, near the wa
on the western side. The dirt was still bare, although
little grass had begun to poke through. I bent down an

216

placed the meager bouquet at the grave's head, which in accordance with Muslim tradition pointed toward Mecca.

I stood up and looked back toward Sixteenth Street, over the many graves thrown haphazardly together. The Muslim tombs were each marked with a crescent and star, but there were also a few Christian crosses, a few Stars of David, and many unmarked at all. Shaknahyi's final resting place had only an upended flat rock with his name and the date of his death scratched on. Someday soon that rock would topple over, and no doubt it would be stolen by another mourner too poor to afford a proper marker. Shaknahyi's name would be removed with a little sandpaper or steel wool, and the rock would serve as someone else's headstone until it was stolen again. I made a mental note to pay for a permanent grave marker. He deserved that much, at least.

A young boy in a robe and turban tugged on my sleeve. "O Father of sadness," he said in a high-pitched voice, "I can recite."

This was one of the young shaykhs who'd committed the entire Qur'ân to memory. He probably supported his family by reciting verses in the cemetery. "I will give you ten kiam to pray for my friend," I said. He'd caught me in a weak moment.

"Ten kiam, effendi! Do you want me to recite the whole Book?"

I put my hand on his bony shoulder. "No. Just something comforting about God and Heaven."

The boy frowned. "There's much more about Hell and the eternal flames," he said.

"I know. I don't want to hear that."

"All right, effendi." And he began murmuring the ancient phrases in a singsong voice. I left him beside Shaknahyi's grave and wandered back toward the entrance.

My friend and occasional lover, Nikki, had been laid to rest in a low whitewashed tomb that was already falling into disrepair. Nikki's family certainly could have afforded to bring her body home for burial, but they'd preferred to leave her here. Nikki had been a sexchange, and her family probably didn't want to be embarrassed. Anyway, this lonely tomb seemed to be in keeping with Nikki's hard, loveless life. On my desk in the police station, I still kept a small brass scarab that had belonged to her. A week didn't go by when I didn't think of Nikki.

I passed by the graves of Tamiko, Devi, and Selima, the Black Widow Sisters, and of Hassan the Shiite, the son of a bitch who'd almost killed me. I found myself maundering gloomily along the narrow brick paths, and I decided that wasn't how I wanted to spend the rest of the afternoon. I shook off the growing depression and headed back toward the Street. When I glanced over my shoulder, the young shaykh was still standing beside Shaknahyi's grave, reciting the holy words. I felt sure that he'd stay there ten kiams' worth, even after I was gone.

I had to force my way through the mob of beggars again, but this time I threw a handful of coins to them. When they scrambled for the money, it made it easier to escape. I unclipped my phone from my belt and spoke Saied the Half-Hajj's commcode. I waited a few rings, and I was about to give up when he answered. *"Marhaba,"* he said.

"It's Marîd. How you doin'?"

"Aw right. What's happening?"

"Oh, nothing much. I got out of the hospital."

"Ah! Glad to hear it."

"Yeah, I get tired of that place. Anyway, you with Jacques and Mahmoud?"

"Uh yeah. We're all sitting in Courane's getting drunk. Why don't you come on by?"

"I think I will. I need you to do me a favor."

"Yeah?"

"Tell you about it later. See you in maybe half an hour. *Ma' as-salaama."*

"Allah yisallimak."

I clipped the phone back on my belt. I'd walked all the way back to Chiriga's, and suddenly I had a terrific urge to go in and see if Indihar or any of the girls had a few sunnies or tri-phets they could spare. It wasn't withdrawal I was feeling; it was a hunger that had been growing for many days. It took a lot of willpower to fight off the craving. It would have been so much easier to admit my true nature and give in. I might have, except I knew that later I'd need my brains unaddled.

I kept on walking until I got to Fifth Street, when I was stopped by one of the most unusual sights I've ever seen. Laila, the old black hag who owned the modshop, was standing in the middle of the Street, screaming shrill curses at Safiyya the Lamb Lady, who was standing a block away and yelling her head off too. They looked like two gunfighters from an American holoshow, screeching and snarling and threatening each other. I saw some tourists coming up the street; they stopped and watched the old women nervously, then backed away again toward the eastern gate. I felt the same way. I didn't want to get in between those two witches. You could almost see the green rays shooting out of their eyes.

I couldn't actually understand what they were saying. Their voices were strained and hoarse, and they may not have been screaming in Arabic. I didn't know if the Lamb Lady'd had her skull amped, but Laila never went anywhere without a moddy and a handful of daddies. She could have been ranting in ancient Etruscan for all I knew.

After a little while they both got tired of it. Safiyya left first, making an obscene gesture in Laila's direction and heading back down the Street toward the Boulevard il-Jameel. Laila stared after her, throwing a few final unpleasantries her way. Then, muttering to herself, she turned down Fourth Street. I followed her. I thought I might find a useful moddy in her shop.

When I got there, Laila was behind her cash register, humming to herself and sorting a stack of invoices. When I came in, she looked up and smiled. "Marîd," she said sadly, "do you know how *boring* it is to be the wife of a country doctor?"

"To be honest, Laila, no, I don't." Evidently, she'd chipped in another moddy as soon as she got back to her shop, and now it was as if she hadn't seen the Lamb Lady at all.

"Well," she said slyly, giving me a wicked smile, "if you did know, you wouldn't blame me at all if I considered taking a lover."

"Madame Bovary?" I asked.

She just winked. The effect was moderately hideous.

I began browsing in her dusty bins. I didn't exactly know what I was looking for. "Laila," I called over my shoulder, "do the letters A.L.M. mean anything to you?"

"L'Association des Larves Maboules?"

That meant the Association of Crazy Wimps. "Who are they?" I asked.

"You know. People like Fuad."

"Never heard of it," I said.

"I just made it up, *chéri.*"

"Uh huh." I picked up a moddy package that caught my eye. It was an anthology of fictional types, mostly Eur-Am defenders of the meek, although there was an ancient Chinese poet-king, a Bantu demigod, and a Nordic trick-ster. The only name I recognized was Mike Hammer. I still owned a Nero Wolfe moddy, although the companion hardware, Archie Goodwin, had died horribly under the heel of Saied the Half-Hajj.

I decided to get the anthology. I figured it gave me a wide sampling of skills and personalities. I took it over to Laila. "Just this one today," I said.

"There's a special on—"

"Wrap it, Laila." I handed her a ten-kiam bill. She took my money and looked hurt. I thought about what I'd chip in to visit Gay Che's. I still had Rex, Saied's badass moddy. I decided I'd wear that, and carry this new one in reserve.

"Your change, Marîd."

I took my package, but let the old woman keep the change. "Buy yourself something pretty, Laila," I told her.

She smiled again. "And you know, I expect Leon will bring me a romantic surprise this evening."

"Yeah, you right." I left the shop feeling as creepy as I always did around her.

I took three steps toward the Street, and then I heard blaam! blaam! blaam! A flying chip of concrete cut my face just under my right eye. I threw myself into the doorway of the gambling den next to Laila's. Blaam! blaam! blaam! I heard bricks shatter and saw puffs of red dust drift from the edge of the doorway. I pressed myself in as far as I could. Blaam! blaam! Two more: Someone had just taken eight shots at me with a high-powered pistol.

Nobody came running. Nobody was curious enough to see if I was all right, or maybe needed medical atten-tion. I waited, wondering how long before it was safe to stick my head out again. Was Jawarski still hiding some where across the street, a fresh clip in his .45? Or was this only a warning? Surely, if he truly wanted to kill me, he could have done a better job of it.

I got tired of being scared after a few minutes and left the safety of the doorway. I have to admit that I had a peculiar vulnerable feeling between my shoulder blades as I hurried down to the corner. I decided that this had been Jawarski's way of sending me an invitation. I had no intention of declining; I just wanted to be prepared.

Yet even so, I still had other business to finish before I could turn my full attention to the American. I went to my car and threw the new moddy into the backseat, where I'd left my briefcase. I drove slowly and calmly through the Rasmiyya neighborhood to Courane's. When I got there, I parked the car in the narrow street and took Saied's moddy out of the briefcase. I looked at it thoughtfully for a moment and chipped it in, along with the daddies that blocked pain and fatigue. Then I got out of the car and went into Courane's dim bar.

"Monsieur Audran!" said the expatriate, coming toward me with both hands outstretched. "Your friends told me you'd be coming. It's good to see you again."

"Yeah," I said. I could see the Half-Hajj, Mahmoud, and Jacques at a table near the back.

Courane followed me, speaking in a low voice. "Wasn't that just terrible about Officer Shaknahyi?"

I turned to look at him. "That's what it was, Courane. Terrible."

"I was truly upset." He nodded to let me know how sincere he was.

"Vodka gimlet," I said. That made him go away.

I dragged over a chair and sat at the table with the others. I looked at them but didn't say anything. The last time I'd been with this group, I hadn't been very popular. I wondered if anything had changed.

Jacques was the Christian who was always patronizing me about how he had more European blood than I did. This afternoon he just closed one eye and nodded his head. "I hear you pulled Papa out of a burning building."

Courane arrived with my drink. Instead of answering, I lifted the glass and sipped.

"I was in a fire once," said the Half-Hajj. "Well, actually, I was in a building that burned down about an hour after I left. I could've been killed."

Mahmoud, the male sexchange, snorted. "So, Marîd," he said, "I'm impressed."

"Yeah," I said, "I really just wanted to impress you bastards." I squeezed the wedge of lime into the gimlet. Vitamin C, you know.

"No, really," Mahmoud went on, "everybody's talking about it. It was pretty gutsy."

Jacques shrugged. "Especially if you think that you could've ended up with all of Friedlander Bey's lightspeed clout for yourself. Just by letting the old fucker fry."

"Did you think about that?" asked Mahmoud. "While it was all happening, I mean?"

It was time to take a long swallow of vodka, because I was getting really mad. When I set my glass down again, I looked from one to the other. "You know Indihar, right? Well, since Jirji's been dead, she's having a tough time paying her bills. She won't take a loan from me or Chiri, and she can't make enough tending bar in the club."

Mahmoud's eyebrows went up. "She want to come work for me? She's got a nice ass. I could get her good money."

I shook my head. "She's not interested in that," I said. "She wants me to find a new home for one of her kids. She's got two boys and a girl. I told her she could spare one of the boys."

That shut 'em up for a little while. "Maybe," said Jacques at last. "I can ask around, anyway."

"Do it," I said. "Indihar said she might even be willing to part with the girl too. If they both go together, and if the price is right."

"When do you need to know?" said Mahmoud.

"Soon as you can find out. Now, I got to go. Saied, you mind taking a ride with me?"

The Half-Hajj looked first at Mahmoud, then at Jacques, but neither of them had anything to say. "Guess not," he said.

I took twenty kiam out of my pocket and dropped it on the table. "Drinks are on me," I said.

Mahmoud gave me a judicious look. "We been kind of hard on you lately," he said.

"I hadn't noticed."

"Well, we're glad things are straightened out be-
ween us. No reason things can't be like they were be-
ore."

"Sure," I said, "right."

I gave Saied's shoulder a little shove, and we headed
back out into the sunlight. I stopped him before he got
into the car. "I need you to tell me how to find Gay Che's,"
said.

His face went suddenly pale. "Why the hell you want
to go there?"

"I heard about it, that's all."

"Well, I don't want to go. I'm not even sure I can give
you directions."

"Sure you can, pal," I said, my voice grim and threatening. "You know all about it."

Saied didn't like being pushed around. He stood up
straight, trying to give himself a little height advantage.
"Think you can *make* me go with you?"

I just stared at him, my face empty of emotion. Then
very slowly I raised my right hand up to my lips. I opened
my mouth and bit myself savagely. I ripped a small gobbet
of flesh loose from the inside of my wrist and spat it at the
Half-Hajj. My own blood trickled down the corners of my
mouth. "Look, motherfucker," I growled hoarsely, "that's
what I do to *me*. Wait till you see what I do to *you!*"

Saied shuddered and backed away from me on the
sidewalk. "You're crazy, Marîd," he said. "You gone
fuckin' crazy."

"In the car."

He hesitated. "You're wearing Rex, ain't you? You
shouldn't wear that moddy. I don't like what it does to
you."

I threw back my head and laughed. I was only behav-
ing the way *he* acted when *he* wore the same moddy. And
he wore it often. I could understand why—I was beginning to like it a lot.

I waited until he slid into the passenger seat, then I
went around and got behind the wheel. "Which way?" I
asked.

"South." His voice was tired and hopeless.

I drove for a while, letting him worry about how

much I knew. "So," I said finally, "what kind of place is it?"

"Nothing much." The Half-Hajj was sullen. "A hang out for this jackboot gang, the *Jaish.*"

"Yeah?" From the name, I'd pictured the clientele of Gay Che's like that guy I'd seen in Chiri's a few weeks before, the one in the vinyl pants with his hand chained behind his back.

"The Citizen's Army. They wear these gray uniforms and have parades and pass out a lot of leaflets. I think they want to get rid of the foreigners in the city. Down with the heathen Franj. You know that routine."

"Uh huh. I get the idea from il-Manhous that you spend some time there."

Saied didn't like this conversation at all. "Look, Marîd," he began, but then he fell silent. "Anyway, you gonna believe everything you hear from Fuad?"

I laughed. "What you think he told me?"

"I don't know." He slid farther away from me, up against the passenger door. I almost felt sorry for him. He didn't speak again except to give me directions.

When we got there, I reached under my seat where my weapons were hidden. I had the small seizure gun I'd gotten so long ago from Lieutenant Okking, and the static pistol Shaknahyi'd given me. I looked at the guns thoughtfully. "This a setup, Saied? You supposed to bring me here so Abu Adil's thugs could ice me?"

The Half-Hajj looked frightened. "What's this all about, Marîd?"

"Just tell me why the hell you told Fuad to show me that .45 caliber clip."

He sagged unhappily in his seat. "I went to Shaykh Reda because I was confused, Marîd, that's all. Maybe it's too late now, but I'm real sorry. I just didn't like standing around while you got to be the big hero, when you got to be Friedlander Bey's favorite. I felt left out."

My lip curled. "You mean you set me up to be killed because you were fucking *jealous?*"

"I never meant for anything like that."

I took the empty clip from my pocket and held it in front of his eyes. "An hour ago, Jawarski emptied another one of these at me, in broad daylight on Fourth Street."

Saied rubbed his eyes and muttered something. "I
dn't think this would happen," he said softly.

"What *did* you think would happen?"

"I thought Abu Adil would treat me the way Papa's
eating you."

I stared at him in amazement. "You really hired your-
lf out to Abu Adil, didn't you? I thought you just told him
out my mother. But you're one of his tools, right?"

"I told you I was sorry," he said in an anguished voice.
'll make it up to you."

"Goddamn right you will." I handed him the seizure
n. "Take this. We're going in there and we're gonna
d Jawarski."

The Half-Hajj took the weapon hesitantly. "I wish I
d Rex," he said sadly.

"No, I don't trust you with Rex. I'm gonna keep wear-
g it." I got out of the car and waited for Saied. "Put your
n away. Keep it out of sight unless you need it. Now, is
ere any kind of password or anything?"

"No, you just got to remember nobody in there's very
nd of foreigners."

"Uh huh. Come on, then." I led the way into the bar.
was crowded and noisy and all I saw were men, most of
em dressed in what I guessed was the gray uniform of
is right-wing Citizen's Army. It wasn't dimly lighted
d there wasn't music playing: Gay Che's wasn't that
nd of bar. This was a meeting place for the kind of men
ho liked dressing up as brave soldiers and marching
rough the streets and not actually having shots fired at
em. What these jokers reminded me of was Hitler's SS,
hose main attributes had been perversion and pointless
utality.

Saied and I pushed our way through the mob of men
the bar. "Yeah?" said the surly bartender.

I had to shout to make myself heard. "Two beers," I
id. This didn't look like a place to order fancy drinks.

"Right."

"And we're looking for a guy."

The bartender glanced up from his tap. "Won't find
m here."

"Oh yeah?" He set the beers in front of the Half-Hajj
d me, and I paid. "An American, might still be recover-
g—"

The bartender grabbed the ten-kiam bill I'd la[id]
down. He didn't offer any change. "Look, cap, I don['t]
answer questions, I pour beer. And if some Americ[an]
came in here, these guys'd probably tear him apart."

I took a gulp of the cold beer and looked around t[he]
room. Maybe Jawarski hadn't been in this bar. Maybe [he]
was hiding out upstairs in the building, or in a near[by]
building. "Okay," I said, turning back to the bartend[er,]
"he ain't been in here. But you seen any America[n]
around this neighborhood lately?"

"Didn't you hear me? No questions."

Time to bring out the hidden persuader. I took [a]
hundred-kiam bill from my pocket and waved it in t[he]
bartender's face. I didn't need to say a word.

He looked into my eyes. It was clear that he was to[rn]
by indecision. Finally he said, "Let me have the money[."]

I gave him a tight smile. "Look at it a little long[er.]
Maybe improve your memory."

"Well, stop flashing it around, cap. You'll get us bo[th]
roughed up." I put the money on the bar and covere[d]
with my hand. I waited. The bartender went away for [a]
moment. When he came back, he slid a torn piece [of]
cardboard toward me.

I picked it up. There was an address written on it[. I]
showed the cardboard to Saied. "Know where this is?" [I]
asked.

"Yeah," he said in an unhappy voice, "it's about tw[o]
blocks from Abu Adil's place."

"Sounds right." I handed the hundred kiam to t[he]
bartender, who made it disappear. I took out the stat[ic]
pistol and let him see it. "If you've fucked me over," I sa[id,]
"I'm coming back and using this on you. Understand?["]

"He's there," said the bartender. "Just get out of he[re]
and don't come back."

I put the gun away and shoved my way toward t[he]
door. When we were on the sidewalk again, I looked at t[he]
Half-Hajj. "See now?" I said. "That wasn't so bad."

He gave me a hopeless look. "You want me to go wi[th]
you to find Jawarski, right?"

I shrugged. "No," I said, "I already paid someboo[dy]
else to do that. I don't want to have to come near Jawars[ki]
if I can help it."

Saied was furious. "You mean you put me through all at grief and dragged me into that place for nothing?"

I opened the car door. "Hey, it wasn't for nothing," I d, smiling. "Allah probably agrees it was good for your ıl."

16

The westphalian sedan was headed nor[th]
away from Hâmidiyya. I had my English dad[e]
chipped in and I was speaking on the phone to M[o]r-
gan. "I found him," I said.

"Great, man." The American sounded disappointe[d]
"That mean I don't get the rest of the money?"

"Tell you what I'll do. I'll give you the other fi[ve]
hundred if you baby-sit Jawarski for a few hours. You go[t a]
gun?"

"Yeah. You want me to use it?"

The idea was very tempting. "No. I just want you [to]
keep an eye on him." I read off the address on the piece [of]
cardboard. "Don't let him go anywhere. Hold him til[l I]
get there."

"Sure, man," said Morgan, "but don't take all day. I['m]
not crazy about hangin' around all day with a guy wh[o]
killed twenty-some people."

"I got faith in you. Talk to you later." I hung up t[he]
phone.

"What you gonna do?" asked Saied.

I didn't want to tell him, because despite his earne[st]
confession and apology, I still didn't trust him. "I'm taki[ng]
you back to Courane's," I said. "Or you rather I drop y[ou]
off somewhere in the Budayeen?"

"Can't I go with you?"

I laughed coldly. "I'm gonna visit your favorite kin[g]
pin, Abu Adil. You still on good terms with him?"

"I don't know," said the Half-Hajj nervously. "B[ut]
maybe I ought to go back to Courane's. I thought of som[e]-
thing I got to tell Jacques and Mahmoud."

"I'll bet."

"Besides, I don't need to run into that bastard Um[m]

228

ever again." Saied pronounced the name "Himmar," by changing the vowel just a little and aspirating it. It was an Arabic pun. The word *himmar* means donkey, and Arabs consider the donkey one of the filthiest animals on earth. This was a clever way of insulting Umar, and when he was wearing Rex, the Half-Hajj may even have said it to Abdul-Qawy's face. That may be one of the reasons Saied wasn't popular around Hâmidiyya anymore.

He was quiet for a little while. "Marîd," he said at last, "I meant what I said. I made a bad mistake, turning my coat like that. But I never had no contract with Friedlander Bey or nothing. I didn't think I was hurting anybody."

"I almost died twice, pal. First the fire, then Jawarski."

I pulled the car to the curb outside Courane's. Saied was miserable. "What you want me to say?" he pleaded.

"You got nothing to say. I'll see you you later."

He nodded and got out of the car. I watched him walk into Courane's bar, then I popped the tough-guy moddy. I drove west and north, to Papa's house. Before I confronted Abu Adil, I had two or three other things to take care of.

I found Kmuzu in our temporary apartment, working at my Chhindwara data deck. He looked up when he heard me come into the room. "Ah, *yaa Sidi!*" he said, as pleased as I'd ever seen him. "I have good news. It will cost less to organize charity food distribution than I thought. I hope you'll forgive me for examining your financial situation, but I've learned that you have more than twice what we need."

"That a hint, Kmuzu? I'm only going to open one soup kitchen, not two. You got an operating budget worked out?"

"We can run the food center for a full week on the money you get from Chiriga's on a single night."

"Great, glad to hear it. I was just wondering why you're so excited about this project. How come it means so much to you?"

Kmuzu's expression turned solidly neutral. "I just feel responsible for your Christian moral education," he said.

"I don't buy it," I said.

He looked away. "There is a long story, *yaa Sidi*," he said. "I do not wish to tell it now."

"All right, Kmuzu. Another time."

He turned to me again. "I have information about the fire. I told you I'd found proof it was deliberately set. That night in the corridor between your apartment and that of the master of the house, I discovered rags that had been soaked in some flammable fluid." He opened a desk drawer and took out some badly scorched cloth remnants. They'd been burned in the fire, but hadn't been totally destroyed. I could still see a decorative pattern of eight-pointed stars in pale pink and brown.

Kmuzu held up another cloth. "Today I found this. It's obviously the cloth from which those rags were torn."

I examined the larger cloth, part of an old robe or sheet. There wasn't any doubt that it was the same material. "Where'd you find this?" I asked.

Kmuzu put the rags back in the desk drawer. "In the room of young Saad ben Salah," he said.

"What were you doing poking around in there?" I asked with some amusement.

Kmuzu shrugged. "Looking for evidence, *yaa Sidi*. And I believe I've found enough to be certain of the arsonist's identity."

"The kid? Not Umm Saad herself?"

"I'm sure she directed her son to set the fire."

I wouldn't put it past her, but it didn't quite fit. "Why would she do that, though? Her whole scheme has been to get Friedlander Bey to admit that Saad is his grandson. She wants her son to be heir to Papa's estate. Killing the old man off now would leave her out in the cold."

"Who can say what her reasoning was, *yaa Sidi*? Perhaps she gave up her plan, and now she's seeking revenge."

Jeez, in that case, who knew what she'd try next? "You're keeping an eye on her already, aren't you?" I asked.

"Yes, *yaa Sidi*."

"Well, be extra watchful." I turned to go, then faced him once more. "Kmuzu," I said, "do the letters A.L.M. mean anything to you?"

He gave it a moment's thought. "Only the African Liberation Movement," he said.

"Maybe," I said dubiously. "What about the Phoenix File?"

"Oh, yes, *yaa Sidi*, I heard about it when I worked in Shaykh Reda's house."

I'd run into so many dead ends that I'd almost given up hope. I'd begun to think the Phoenix File was something Jirji Shaknahyi had invented, and that the meaning of the words had died with him. "Why did Abu Adil discuss it with you?" I asked.

Kmuzu shook his head. "Abu Adil never discussed anything with me, *yaa Sidi*. I was only a bodyguard. But bodyguards are often overlooked or forgotten. They become like the furniture in a room. Several times I overheard Shaykh Reda and Umar talk about whom they wished to add to the Phoenix File."

"So what is the damn thing?" I demanded.

"A list," said Kmuzu. "A compilation of the names of everyone who works for Shaykh Reda or Friedlander Bey, either directly or indirectly. And of anyone who owes either of them a great favor."

"Like rosters," I said, puzzled. "But why should the file be so important? I'm sure the police could put together the same list anytime they wanted. Why did Jirji Shaknahyi risk his life investigating it?"

"Each person on the list has a coded entry that describes his physical condition, his tissue-matching profile, and his record of organ transplants and other modifications."

"So both Abu Adil and Papa keep up with their people's health. That's great. I didn't think they'd bother with details like that."

Kmuzu frowned. "You don't understand, *yaa Sidi*. The file is not a list of who might need to receive a transplant. It is a list of available donors."

"Available donors? But these people aren't dead, they're still—" My eyes opened wider and I just stared at him.

Kmuzu's expression let me know that my horrified realization was correct. "Everyone on the list is ranked," he said, "from the lowest underling to Umar and yourself. If a person on the list is injured or becomes ill and needs an organ transplant, Abu Adil or Friedlander Bey may choose to sacrifice someone with a lower rating. This is not always done, but the higher one's rating, the more likely it is that a suitable donor will be chosen."

"May their houses be destroyed! The sons of thieves!" I said softly. This explained the notations in Shaknahyi's notebook—the names on the left side were people who'd been prematurely relaxed to provide spare parts for people on the right side. Blanca had been too far down on the list for her own good; she'd been just another expendable slut.

"Perhaps everyone you know is listed in the Phoenix File," said Kmuzu. "You yourself, your friends, your mother. My name is there as well."

I felt fury growing in me. "Where does he keep it, Kmuzu? I'm gonna shove this file down Abu Adil's throat."

Kmuzu raised a hand. "Remember, *yaa Sidi*, that Shaykh Reda is not alone in this terrible enterprise. He cooperates with our master. They share information, and they share the lives of their associates. A heart from one of Shaykh Reda's minions may be put in the chest of Friedlander Bey's lieutenant. The two men are great competitors, but in this they are cordial partners."

"How long has this been going on?" I asked.

"For many years. The two shaykhs began it to make certain they themselves would never die for lack of compatible organs."

I slammed my fist on the desk. "That's how they've both lived to such doddering old age. They're fucking fossils!"

"And they are insane, *yaa Sidi*," said Kmuzu.

"You didn't tell me where to find it. Where is the Phoenix File?"

Kmuzu shook his head. "I don't know. Shaykh Reda keeps it hidden."

Well, I thought, I'd planned to take a ride out to that neighborhood that afternoon anyway. "Thanks, Kmuzu. You've been a lot of help."

"*Yaa Sidi*, you aren't going to confront Shaykh Reda with this, are you?" He looked very troubled.

"No, of course not," I said. "I know better than to take on both of the old men together. You just keep working on our soup kitchen. I think it's time the House of Friedlander Bey began giving back something to the poor people."

"That is good."

I left Kmuzu working at the data deck. I went back out to the car, revising my schedule for the day in light of the blockbuster that had just gone off at my feet. I drove to the Budayeen, parked the car, and started up the Street to Chiri's.

My phone rang. *"Marhaba,"* I said.

"It's me, man. Morgan." I was glad I was still wearing the English daddy. "Jawarski's here, all right. He's holed up in a crummy apartment in a real slum. I'm hangin' out in the stairwell, watchin' the door. You want me to drop in on the man?"

"No," I said, "just make sure he doesn't leave. I want to know that he'll be there when I come by later. If he tries to go somewhere, though, stop him. Use your gun and back him up into the apartment. Do whatever you got to, but keep him under wraps."

"You got it, man. But don't take too long. This isn't as much fun as I thought it'd be."

I clipped the phone back on my belt and went into the club. Chiri's was pretty crowded for late afternoon. A new black girl named Mouna was on stage. I recalled suddenly that Mouna had been the name of the pet chicken in Fuad's long story. That meant he was probably adoring this girl, and that meant she was probably trouble. I'd have to keep my eyes open.

The other girls were sitting with customers, and love was in bloom all along the bar. It was fucking heart-warming.

I went down to my usual place and waited for Indihar to come over. "White Death?" she asked.

"Not right now. You thought any about what we talked about?"

"About me moving into Friedlander Bey's little cottage? If it wasn't for the kids, I wouldn't give it a second thought. I don't want to owe him nothing. I don't want to be one of Papa's little wenches."

I'd felt that way myself, not so long ago. and now that I'd learned the significance of the Phoenix File, I knew she had even more reason to distrust Papa. "You're right

about that, Indihar," I said, "but I promise you that won't
happen. Papa's not doing this for you; *I* am."

"Is there a difference?"

"Yes. A big one. Now, what's your answer?"

She sighed. "Okay, Marîd, but I'm not going to be one
of *your* wenches, either. You know what I mean?"

"You're not going to fuck me. You already made that
clear."

Indihar nodded. "Just so you understand. I'm mourning my husband. I may go on mourning him forever."

"Take as long as you need. You got a lot of life left to
live, honey," I said. "Someday you'll find someone else."

"I don't even want to think about it."

It was past time to change the subject. "You can start
moving in any time you want, but finish out the shift for
me," I said. "This means I got to find a new daytime
barmaid."

Indihar looked left and right, then leaned closer. "If I
was you," she said in a low voice, "I'd hire somebody from
outside. I wouldn't trust any of these girls to run this place.
They'd rob you blind, especially that Brandi. And Pualani's not bright enough to put the napkin down, *then*
the drink."

"What do you think I should do?"

She chewed her lip for a moment. "I'd hire Dalia
away from Frenchy Benoit. That's what I'd do. Or Heidi
from the Silver Palm."

"Maybe," I said. "Call me if you need anything." It
was just something else I had to worry about. Right now,
though, my thoughts were centered mainly on the
blighted neighborhood on the western side of town. I
walked back out into the late afternoon sun. It had begun
to rain, and there was a good, wet smell coming from the
warm sidewalks.

A few minutes later, I was back in the modshop on
Fourth Street. Twice in one day was enough of Laila to last
anybody a year. I overheard her discussing a module with
a customer. The man needed something to let him do
armadontia. That's the science of converting human teeth
into high-tech weapons. Laila was still Emma: Madame
Bovary, Dentist of Tomorrow.

When the customer left—yes, Laila'd found just what
he was looking for—I tried to tell her what I wanted

without getting into a conversation. "Got any Proxy Hell moddies?" I asked.

She'd already opened her mouth to greet me with some secondhand Flaubertian sentiment, but I'd shocked her. "You don't want that, Marîd," she said in her whiny voice.

"Not for me. It's for a friend."

"None of your friends do that, either."

I stopped myself before I grabbed her by the throat. "It's not for a friend, then. It's for a goddamn enemy."

Laila smiled. "Then you want something *really* bad, right?"

"The worst," I said.

She bustled out from behind her counter and went to the locked door in the rear of the shop. "I don't keep merchandise like that out," she explained as she dug in a pocket for her keys. Actually, they were on a long, green plastic necklace around her neck. "I don't sell Proxy Hell moddies to kids."

"Keys are around your neck."

"Oh, thanks, dear." She unlocked the door and turned to look at me. "Be right back." She was gone a minute or two, and she returned with a small brown cardboard box.

There were three moddies in the box, all plain, gray plastic, all without manufacturer's labels. These were bootleg modules, dangerous to wear. Regular commercial moddies were carefully recorded or programmed, and all extraneous signals were removed. You gambled when you wore an underground moddy. Sometimes bootlegs were "rough," and when you popped them out, you found they'd caused major brain damage.

Laila had stuck handwritten labels on the moddies in the box. "How about infectious granuloma?" she asked.

I considered it for a moment, but decided that it was too much like what Abu Adil had been wearing when I'd first met him. "No," I said.

"Okay," said Laila, pushing the moddies around with her long, crooked forefinger. "Cholecystitis?"

"What's that?"

"Don't have any idea."

"What's the third one?"

Laila held it up and read the label. "D Syndrome."

I shivered. I'd heard about that. It's some kind of awful nerve degeneration, a disease caused by slow viruses. The patient first suffers gaps in both long- and short-term memories. The viruses continue to eat away at the nervous system until the patient collapses, staring and stupid, bedridden and in terrible agony. Finally, in the last stages, he dies when his body forgets how to breathe or keep its heart beating. "How much for this?" I asked.

"Fifty kiam," she said. She looked up slowly into my eyes and grinned. The few teeth she still had were black stumps, and the effect was grotesquely ugly. "You pay extra 'cause it's a hard-to-get item."

"All right," I said. I paid her and stuffed the D Syndrome moddy in my pocket. Then I tried to get out of Laila's shop.

"You know," she said, putting her clawlike hand on my arm, "my lover is taking me to the opera tonight. All of Rouen will see us together!"

I pulled myself away and hurried out the door. "In the name of Allah, the Beneficent, the Merciful," I muttered.

During the long drive out to Abu Adil's estate, I thought about recent events. If Kmuzu were right, then the fire had been started by Umm Saad. I didn't think that young Saad had acted on his own. Yet Umar had assured me that neither he nor Abu Adil still employed Umm Saad. He had flatly invited me to dispose of her, if I found her too irritating. Then if Umm Saad wasn't getting her orders direct from Abu Adil, why had she decided suddenly to take things into her own hands?

And Jawarski. Had he taken a few potshots at me because he didn't like my looks, or because Hajjar had let Abu Adil know that I was nosing around after the Phoenix File? Or were there even more sinister connections that I hadn't yet discovered? At this point, I didn't dare trust Saied or even Kmuzu. Morgan was the only other person who had my confidence, and I had to admit that there really wasn't any good reason to trust him, either. He just reminded me of the way I used to be, before I'd gone to work changing a corrupt system from within.

That, by the way, was my current rationalization for what I was doing, the easy life I was leading. I suppose the bitter truth was that I didn't have the guts to face Fried-

ander Bey's wrath, or the heart to turn my back on his
money. I told myself that I was using my position deep in
the pits of dishonor to help the less fortunate. It didn't
really shut up my guilty conscience.

As I drove, the guilt and loneliness amounted almost
to desperation, and are probably to blame for the tactical
error that came next. Maybe I *should* have had more faith
in Saied or Kmuzu. I could at least have brought one of the
Stones That Speak with me. Instead, I was counting on my
own cleverness to see me through a confrontation with
Abu Adil. After all, I did have two separate plans: First, I
thought I might try bribing him with the D Syndrome
moddy; and second, if he didn't take to buttering up, my
fallback position consisted of hitting him between the
eyes with my full knowledge of what he was up to.

Well, hell, it sounded like a great idea at the time.

The guard at Abu Adil's gate recognized me and
passed me through, although Kamal, the butler, demanded to know what I wanted. "I've brought a gift for
Shaykh Reda," I said. "It's urgent that I talk with him."

He wouldn't let me leave the foyer. "Wait here," he
said with a sneer. "I will see if it is permitted."

"The passive voice should be avoided," I said. He
didn't get it.

He went all the way down to Abu Adil's office, and
came all the way back with the same contemptuous look
on his face. "I'm to bring you to my master," he said. It
sounded like it broke his heart to accommodate me.

He led me into one of Abu Adil's offices, not the same
one I'd seen on my first visit with Shaknahyi. A sweet
smell, maybe incense, filled the air. There were framed
prints of European art masterpieces on the walls, and I
heard a recording of Umm Khalthoum playing softly.

The great man himself was sitting in a comfortable
armchair, with a beautifully embroidered blanket over his
legs. His head lolled back against the back of the chair,
and his eyes were closed. His hands were laid flat on his
knees, and they trembled.

Umar Abdul-Qawy was there, of course, and he didn't
look happy to see me. He nodded to me and put one finger
to his lips. I guessed this was a signal not to mention any of
the things he'd discussed with me concerning his plans to
unseat Abu Adil and rule the old shaykh's empire in his

place. That wasn't why I was here. I had more important
things to worry about than Umar's half-assed power strug
gle.

"I have the honor to wish Shaykh Reda good after
noon," I said.

"May Allah make the afternoon prosperous to you,"
said Umar.

We'll see, I thought. "I beg to present the noble
shaykh with this small gift."

Umar made a small gesture, the little flick of the hand
a lordly king uses to command a peasant to approach. I
wanted to stuff the moddy down his fat throat. "What is
it?" he asked.

I said nothing. I just gave it to him. Umar turned it
over in his hand a few times. Then he looked up at me.
"You are more clever than I gave you credit," he said. "My
master will be greatly pleased."

"I hope he doesn't already have this module."

"No, no." He placed it on Abu Adil's lap, but the old
man made no move to examine it. Umar studied me
thoughtfully. "I would offer you something in return, al
though I'm certain you would be courteous enough to
refuse."

"Try me," I said. "I'd like a little information."

Umar frowned. "Your manners—"

"They're terrible, I know, but what can I say? I'm just
an ignorant beaneater from the Maghreb. Now, I seem to
have uncovered all kinds of incriminating information
about you and Shaykh Reda—about Friedlander Bey too
to be honest. I'm talking about this goddamn Phoenix File
of yours." I waited to see Umar's reaction.

It wasn't long in coming. "I'm afraid, Monsieur
Audran, that I don't know what you're talking about. I
suggest that your master may be engaged in highly illegal
activities, and has attempted to shift the blame—"

"Be silent." Umar and I both turned to stare at Reda
Abu Adil, who had popped the Proxy Hell moddy he'd
been wearing. Umar was badly shaken. This was the first
time Abu Adil had seen fit to participate in a conversation.
It seemed he wasn't just a senile, helpless figurehead.
Without the cancer moddy chipped in, his face lost its
slackness, and his eyes gained an intelligent fierceness.

Abu Adil threw off the blanket and stood up from the

hair. "Hasn't Friedlander Bey explained to you about the Phoenix File?" he demanded.

"No, O Shaykh," I said. "It's something I learned of only today. He has kept the thing hidden from me."

"But you delved into matters that don't concern you." I was frightened by Abu Adil's intensity. Umar had never shown such passion or such strength of will. It was as if I were seeing Shaykh Reda's *baraka*, a different kind of personal magic than Papa's. The moddy of Abu Adil that Umar wore did not hint at the depth of the man. I supposed that no electronic device could hope to capture the nature of *baraka*. This answered Umar's claim that with the moddy he was the equal of Abu Adil. That was just self-delusion.

"I think they concern me," I said. "Isn't my name in that file?"

"Yes, I'm sure it is," said Abu Adil. "But you are placed highly enough that you stand only to benefit."

"I'm thinking of my friends, who aren't so lucky."

Umar laughed humorlessly. "You show your weakness again," he said. "Now you bleed for the dirt beneath your feet."

"Every sun has its setting," I told him. "Maybe someday you'll find yourself slipping down in the Phoenix File ratings. Then you'll wish you'd never heard of it."

"O Master," said Umar angrily, "have you not heard enough of this?"

Abu Adil raised a weary hand. "Yes, Umar. I have no great love for Friedlander Bey, and even less for his creatures. Take him into the studio."

Umar came toward me, a needle gun in his hand, and I backed away. I didn't know what he had in mind, but it wasn't going to be pleasant. "This way," he said. Under the circumstances, I did what he wanted.

We left the office and walked down a connecting hallway, then climbed a stairway to the second floor. There was always an air of peace in this house. The light was filtered through wooden lattices over high windows, and sounds were muffled by thick rugs on the floors. I knew this serenity was an illusion. I knew I'd soon see Abu Adil's true nature.

"In here," he said, opening a thick metal door. He

had a strange, expectant expression on his face. I didn
like it at all.

I went past him into a large soundproofed room
There was a bed, a chair, and a cart with some electroni
equipment on it. The far wall was a single sheet of glas
and beyond it was a small control booth with banks of dia
and readouts and switches. I knew what it was. Reda Ab
Adil had a personality module recording studio in h
home. It was like the hobbyist's ultimate dream.

"Give me the gun," said Abu Adil.

Umar passed the needle gun to his master, then le
the soundproofed room. "I suppose you want to add me t
your collection," I said. "I don't see why. My second-de
gree burns won't be all that entertaining." Abu Adil ju
stared at me with that fixed grin on his face. He made m
skin crawl.

A little while later, Umar returned. He had a lon;
thin metal rod, a pair of handcuffs, and a rope with a hoc
at one end. "Oh jeez," I said. I was starting to feel sick t
my stomach. I was truly afraid that they wanted to recor
more than just that.

"Stand up straight," said Umar, walking around an
around me. He reached out and removed the moddy an
daddies I was wearing. "And whatever you do, don't duc
your head. That's for your own good."

"Thanks for your concern," I said. "I appreciate—
Umar raised the metal rod and brought it down across m
right collarbone. I felt a knife-edge of pain shoot throug
me, and I cried out. He hit me on the other side, across th
other collarbone. I heard the abrupt snapping of bon
and I fell to my knees.

"This may hurt a little," said Abu Adil in the voice of
kindly old doctor.

Umar began beating me on the back with the roc
once, twice, three times. I screamed. He struck me a fe
more times. "Try to stand up," he urged.

"You're crazy," I gasped.

"If you don't stand up, I'll use this on your face."

I struggled to my feet again. My left arm hung use
lessly. My back was a bleeding ruin. I realized I wa
breathing in shallow sobs.

Umar paused and walked around me again, evalua
ing me. "His legs," said Abu Adil.

"Yes, O Shaykh." The son of a bitch whipped the rod cross my thighs, and I fell to the floor again. "Up," runted Umar. "Up."

He hit me where I lay, on my thighs and calves until ley were dripping with blood too. "I'll get you," I said in voice hoarse with agony. "I swear by the blessed rophet, I'll get you."

The beatings went on for a long time, until Umar had owly and carefully worked over every part of me—ex- ept my head. Abu Adil had instructed him to spare my ead, because he didn't want anything to interfere with ne quality of the recording. When the old man decided nat I'd had enough, he told Umar to stop. "Connect him," e said.

I lifted my head and watched. It was almost like being someone else, far away. My muscles jumped in an- uished spasms, and my wounds sent sharp signals of tor- nent through every part of me. Yet the pain had become barrier between my mind and body. I knew that I still urt terribly, but I'd taken enough punishment to send ny body into shock. I muttered curses and pleas to my wo captors, threatening and begging them to give me ack the pain-blocking daddy.

Umar only laughed. He went over to the cart and did omething with the equipment there. Then he carried a arge, shiny moddy link over to me. It looked a lot like the ne we used with the Transpex game. Umar knelt beside ne and showed it to me. "I'm going to chip this in for ou," he said. "It will allow us to record exactly what ou're feeling."

I was having a difficult time breathing. "Motherfuck- rs," I said, my voice a shallow wheeze.

Umar snapped the chrome-steel moddy link onto my nterior corymbic plug. "Now, this is a completely pain- ess procedure," he said.

"You're gonna die," I muttered. "You're gonna uckin' die."

Abu Adil was still holding the needle gun on me, but I ouldn't have done anything heroic anyway. Umar knelt own and fastened my hands behind me with the hand- uffs. I felt like I was going to pass out, and I kept shaking ny head to stay conscious. I didn't want to black out and

be completely at their mercy, though that was probabl
already true.

After he got my wrists bound, Umar caught the hand
cuffs with the hook and pulled on the rope until I stag
gered to my feet. Then he threw the end of the rope ove
a bar mounted on the wall high over my head. I saw wha
he was going to do. "*Yallah,*" I cried. He pulled on the
rope until I was hoisted up on tiptoes with my arms raise
behind my back. Then he pulled some more until my fee
no longer touched the floor. I was hanging from the rope
the full weight of my body slowly pulling my arms from
their sockets.

It was so excruciating, I could only take panting little
breaths. I tried to shut out the horrible pain; I prayed firs
for mercy, then for death.

"Put the moddy in now," said Abu Adil. His voice
seemed to come from another world, from high on a
mountaintop or far below the ocean.

"I take refuge with the Lord of the Dawn," I mur
mured. I kept repeating that phrase like a magic charm

Umar stood on the chair with the gray moddy in his
hand, the D Syndrome moddy I'd brought. He chipped it
onto my posterior plug.

*He was hanging from the ceiling, but he couldn't
remember why. He was in terrible agony. "In the name of
Allah, help me!" he cried. He realized that shouting just
made the pain worse. Why was he here? He couldn't remember. Who had done this to him?*

*He couldn't remember. He couldn't remember any-
thing.*

*Time went by, and he might have been unconscious.
He had the same feeling one has on waking from a particularly vivid dream, when the waking world and the
dream are superimposed for a moment, when aspects of
one distort images of the other, and one must make an
effort to sort them and decide which shall have prece-
dence.*

*How could he explain being alone and bound like
this? He wasn't afraid of the hurting, but he was afraid he
wasn't equal to the task of understanding his situation.
There was the low hum of a fan above his head, and a
faint spicy smell in the air. His body twisted a little on the*

* be, and he felt another slash of pain. He was bothered
re by the notion that he appeared to be involved in a
rible drama and had no sense at all of its significance.*

*"Praise be to Allah, Lord of the Worlds," he whis-
red, "the Beneficent, the Merciful. Owner of the Day of
dgment. Thee alone we worship. Thee alone we ask for
lp."*

*Time passed. The suffering grew. Finally, he did not
member enough even to wince or writhe. Sights and
unds played through his numbed senses upon his
owsing mind. He was beyond evaluating or reacting,
t he was not yet quite dead. Someone spoke to him, but
did not respond.*

"How's that?"

Let me tell you, it was horrible. All of a sudden, un-
rstanding poured back into my consciousness. Every bit
pain that had been held at bay suddenly returned with
vengeance. I must have whimpered, because he kept
ving "It's all right, it's all right."

I looked up. It was Saied. "Hey," I said. It was all I
uld manage.

"It's all right," he told me again. I didn't know if I
ould believe him. He looked pretty worried.

I was lying in an alley between some rundown, aban-
ned tenement buildings. I didn't know how I'd gotten
ere. At the moment, I didn't care.

"These yours?" he said. He was folding a small hand-
l of daddies and three moddies.

One of them was Rex and one was the gray D Syn-
ome moddy. I almost wept when I recognized the pain-
ocker daddy. "Gimme," I said. My hands shook as I
ached up and chipped it in. Almost instantly I felt great
ain, although I knew I still had terrible lacerations and
 least a broken collarbone. The daddy worked faster
an even a ton of Sonneine. "You got to tell me what
u're doing here," I said. I sat up, filled with the illusion
 health and well-being.

"I came after you. Wanted to make sure you didn't
t into any trouble or anything. The guard at the gate
ows me, and so does Kamal. I went into the house and
w what they were doing to you, then I waited till they
agged you out. They must've thought you were dead, or

else they don't care if you recover or not. I grabbed up t
hardware and followed. They dumped you in this stink
alley, and I hid around the corner till they left."

I put my hand on his shoulders. "Thanks," I said.

"Hey," said the Half-Hajj with a loopy grin, "
thanks are needed. Muslim brothers and all that, righ

I didn't want to argue with him. I picked up the th
moddy he'd found. "What's this?" I asked.

"You don't know? It's not one of yours?"

I shook my head. Saied took the moddy from m
reached up, and chipped it in. A moment later his expr
sion changed. He looked awed. "May my father's ba
burn in Hell!" he said. "It's Abu Adil."

17

The Half-Hajj insisted on going with me to find the building where Paul Jawarski was hiding out. "You're a wreck," he told me, shaking his head. "You pop that daddy, you'll realize what bad shape you're in. You should go to the hospital."

"I just got out of the hospital," I said.

"Well, obviously it didn't take. You got to go back again."

"Fine, I'll go when this business with Jawarski's all over. I'll keep the daddy in till then. And I'll probably need Rex."

Saied squinted at me. "You need a lot more than Rex. You need half a dozen of your cop buddies."

I laughed bitterly. "I don't think they'd show up. I don't think Hajjar would even send them."

We were making our way slowly along Hâmidiyya's main north-south avenue. "What do you mean?" asked Saied. "You think Hajjar wants to pull off Jawarski's capture himself? Get himself a commendation and a medal?"

We turned down a narrow trash-choked alley and found the rear of the building we were looking for. "Shaknahyi had the idea that he'd been set up," I said. "He thought maybe Jawarski was working for Hajjar."

"I thought Jawarski was working for Shaykh Reda."

I shrugged. Without the pain-blocker, that would have been excruciatingly painful. "Everybody we know moonlights. Why should Jawarski be any different?"

"No reason, I guess," said the Half-Hajj. "Now, you want me to go in with you?"

"No thanks, Saied. I want you to stay down here and guard this back entrance. I'm going upstairs and talk with

245

Morgan. I want to be alone with Jawarski. I'm gonna send Morgan down to watch the front."

Saied looked worried. "I don't think that's smart, Maghrebi. Jawarski's a clever guy, and he don't mind killing people. You're not in any condition to wrestle with him."

"I won't have to." I reached up and chipped in Rex. I took my static pistol out of my pocket.

"Well, what you gonna do? If Hajjar's just gonna let Jawarski go free—"

"I'm going over Hajjar's head," I said. I was determined that Jawarski wasn't going to escape justice. "I'm gonna call the captain and the police superintendent and the news media. They can't all be crooked."

"I don't see why not," said the Half-Hajj. "But you're probably right. Remember, we'll be right down here if you need help. Jawarski won't get away this time."

I grinned at him. "Bet your ass he won't." I moved past him into the tenement building. I was in a cool, dark hallway that led to a flight of stairs. There was the usual dank, musty smell of an abandoned building. My feet scattered bits of rubble as I climbed up to the third floor. "Morgan?" I called. He probably had a gun in his hand, and I didn't want to surprise him.

"Is that you, man? You sure took long enough getting here."

I arrived at the landing where he was sitting. "Sorry," I said, "I ran into a little trouble."

His eyes got big when he saw how torn and hurt I was. "Looks like you already ran into as much as you can handle today, man."

"I'm fine, Morgan." I took five hundred kiam out of my jeans and paid him the rest of his money. "Now, go keep an eye on the street entrance. I'll call if I need help."

The blond American started downstairs. "You need help," he said dubiously, "it'll be too late by the time you shout."

The daddy had me feeling no pain, and Rex made me think I was equal to any challenge Jawarski might present. I checked the charge in my static pistol, then rapped on the apartment door. "Jawarski," I shouted, "this is Marîd Audran. Jirji Shaknahyi was my partner. I'm here to take you in for his murder."

I didn't have to wait long. Jawarski opened the door, laughing. He was holding a black .45 caliber automatic pistol. *"Stupid* son of a bitch, ain't you?" he said. He stood back so I could get by.

I made sure he saw my weapon as I went past him, but he was so sure of himself that he didn't act the least bit concerned. I sat down on a torn couch opposite the door. Jawarski dropped into an armchair covered in blood-stained floral material. I was shocked by how young he was. I was surprised to see that he was at least five years younger than me.

"Ever hear what Islamic law does to murderers?" I asked him. We were holding our guns on each other, but Jawarski seemed almost nonchalant.

"Nah, it don't make much difference," he said. "I don't care if I die." Jawarski had a peculiar way of talking out of one side of his mouth, as if he thought it made him look tough and fierce. He obviously had some serious psychological problems, but he wasn't going to live long enough to clear them up. "So who told you I was here? I always bumped off squealers. Tell me who it was, so I can fog the bastard."

"You won't get the chance, pal. You can't have the whole city bought off."

"Let's make this quick," he said, trying to upset me. "I'm supposed to collect my money and leave town tonight." He didn't seem to be bothered at all by my static pistol.

He was staring to my right. I let my eyes drift in that direction, toward a small wooden table not far from the couch, covered with newspaper. There were three clips of ammunition lying there. "Was it Hajjar who told you to kill Shaknahyi?" I asked. "Or Umar, Abu Adil's punk?"

"I ain't a squawker," he said. He gave me a twisted grin.

"And the others—Blanca Mataro, the rest of them. You didn't use that .45. How come?"

Jawarski shrugged. "They told me not to. They didn't want any of the parts damaged, I guess. They told me who to put away and I done it with a little static gun. I always called in the tip to the cops myself, so the cripple cart'd get there fast. I guess they didn't want the meat to spoil." He gave a grunting chuckle that set my teeth on edge.

I glanced at the table, thinking that Jawarski migh
not have bothered to put a clip into his pistol before he le
me into the room. He looked like he enjoyed bluffin;
"How many have you killed?" I asked.

"You mean altogether?" Jawarski looked up at th
ceiling. "Oh, I've got twenty-six anyway. That's all I eve
kept track of. Pretty near one for every year. And m
birthday's comin' up soon. How'd you like to be numbe
twenty-seven?"

I felt a rush of fury. "You're real close, Jawarski," I sai
through clenched teeth.

"Go ahead, you got a girl's gun, lay me out if you go
the guts." He was enjoying this, mocking me and goadin
me. "Look, here's a clipping," he said. " 'Jawarski Ba
Man, Legendary Figure,' it says. How 'bout that?"

"Ever think about the people you shoot?" I asked.

"I remember that cop. I turned and let him have it i
the chest. He didn't even wobble, but he shot back at me
I wasn't hit, though, and I beat it around behind th
house. When I got to the other side, I peeked around th
corner and saw the cop I shot coming after me. I let fly a
him again, and ran behind another house. When I looke
again he was still following me. There was blood runnin;
all over the front of his coat then, but he was still followin;
me. God, that guy was a real man."

"Ever think about his family? Shaknahyi had a wife
you know. He had three kids."

Jawarski stared at me, and another crazy grin sprea
slowly across his face. "Fuck 'em," he said.

I stood up and took three steps. Jawarski raised hi
eyebrows at me, inviting me to come closer. As he stood,
tossed him the static gun. He fumbled it against his ches
with his left hand, and I pulled my fist back and cracke
him in the corner of his mouth. Then I grabbed his righ
wrist tightly and turned outward, prepared to break the
bones if I had to. He grunted and dropped the automatic
"I'm not Hajjar," I snarled. "I'm not that goddamn Cat
avina. You're not gonna buy me off, and right now I'm ir
no mood to worry about protecting your civil rights. Un
derstand?" I bent and scooped up his gun. I'd been wrong
It *was* loaded.

Jawarski put a hand to his lips. When he pulled i
away, his fingers were bloody. "You been watching those

oloshows again, buddy," he said. He grinned, still not
erribly worried. "You're no better'n Hajjar. You're no
better'n me, you want to know the truth. You'd put a
ound right through me, if you thought you could get
way with it."

"You're right about that," I said.

"But you think there's too many like Hajjar already.
And it ain't even that Hajjar's a rotten cop. He ain't. He's
ust acting the way they all act, the way everybody ex-
ects him to act, the way he's *supposed* to act. It ain't
vrong if everybody knows about it ahead of time. I'll tell
ou a secret: You're gonna end up just like Shaknahyi.
ou're gonna help little old ladies across the street until
ou're old enough to retire, and then some young son of a
itch like me is gonna plant you in the ground." He
eached his little finger into his ear and jiggled it a few
imes. "And then," he said thoughtfully, "after you're
one, the young son of a bitch is gonna jam your wife."

My face felt hard and tense, frozen into a cold stare. I
aised the pistol calmly and held it steadily, pointed be-
ween Jawarski's eyes. "Watch it," he said scornfully.
That ain't a toy."

I grabbed back the static pistol and put it in my
ocket. I motioned for Jawarski to sit down, and I re-
urned to my seat on the couch. We looked at each other
or a few seconds. I was breathing hard; Jawarski looked
ike he was enjoying himself.

"I'll bet you're doing everything you can to comfort
haknahyi's widow," he said. "You jammed her yet?"

I felt rage and frustration growing in me again. I
ated hearing his lies, his justifications for crime and cor-
uption. The worst part was that he was telling me
haknahyi had died stupidly, for no good reason. I wasn't
oing to let him say that. "Shut up," I said in a strained
oice. I found myself waving the automatic pistol at
awarski.

"See? You can't shoot. It'd be smart to shoot. I'll get
way clean otherwise, 'cause no matter who locks me up,
'll be sprung. Shaykh Reda will make sure I get sprung.
'll never be brought to trial in this town."

"No, you wouldn't be," I said, knowing it was proba-
ly true. I fired once. The explosion was tremendous, and
he booming crack rumbled on forever, like thunder.

Jawarski fell backward in slow motion, half of his face blasted away. There was blood everywhere. I dropped the pistol to the floor. I'd never shot anyone with a projectile weapon before. I backed away and fell against the couch, unable to catch my breath.

When I'd come through the door, I hadn't planned to kill this man, but I had done it. It had been a conscious decision. I had taken the responsibility for seeing justice done, because I'd become certain it would be done no other way. I looked at the blood on my hands and arms.

The door crashed loudly into the room. Morgan ran in first, followed by Saied. They stopped just inside the threshold and took in the scene. "Aw right," said the Half-Hajj quietly. "That's one loose end tied up tight."

"Listen, man," said Morgan, "I got to go. You don't need me for anything more, do you?"

I just stared at them. I wondered why they weren't horrified too.

"Let's go, man," said Morgan. "Somebody might've heard that."

"Oh, somebody heard it, all right," Saied said. "But in this neighborhood, nobody's dumb enough to check on it."

I reached up and popped the tough-guy moddy. I'd had enough of Rex for a while. We left the apartment and went down the stairs. Morgan turned one way on the sidewalk, and the Half-Hajj and I turned the other.

"What now?" asked Saied.

"We got to go get the car," I said. I didn't like the idea at all. The sedan was still back at Abu Adil's. I really didn't feel like going back there so soon after the bastard mind-raped me. I *was* going back there; I had that score to settle. But not just yet, not just now.

Saied must have guessed my feelings from the tone of my voice. "Tell you what," he said. "I'll go get the car, you sit here and wait. Won't take long."

"Fine," I said, and I gave him the keys. I was immensely grateful that he'd come looking for me, and that I could count on him for help. I had no trouble trusting him again. That was good, because even with the pain-override daddy chipped in, my body was near collapse. I needed to get to a doctor soon.

I didn't want to sit down on a step, because I thought

d have a hard time standing again. Instead, I leaned
gainst the white stucco front of a small, tottery house.
verhead, I heard the shrill peenting cries of nighthawks
s they swooped over the rooftops hunting for insects. I
ared across the street at another apartment building,
nd I saw wild, healthy ferns growing from horizontal
rfaces up and down the wall, weeds that had found
vorable conditions in the most unlikely place. Cooking
nells drifted from open windows: cabbage boiling, meat
asting, bread baking.

I was immersed in life here, yet I could not forget that
d shed a murderer's blood. I was still holding the auto-
atic pistol. I didn't know how I was going to dispose of it.
ly mind wasn't thinking clearly.

After a while, I saw the cream-colored sedan stop
eside me at the curb. Saied got out and helped me
round to the passenger side. I slid into the seat, and he
losed the door. "Where to?" he asked.

"Goddamn hospital," I said.

"Good idea."

I closed my eyes and felt the car thrumming through
he streets. I dozed a little. Saied woke me when we got
here. I shoved my static pistol and the .45 under the seat,
nd we got out of the car.

"Listen," I said, "I'm just going into the emergency
oom and get patched up. After that, I got a few people to
ee. Why don't you get going?"

The Half-Hajj's brows narrowed. "What's the matter?
till don't trust me?"

I shook my head. "It's not that, Saied. I've gotten over
ll that. It's just sometimes I work better without an audi-
nce, okay?"

"Sure. A busted collarbone ain't enough for you. You
on't be happy till we got to bury you in five separate
ontainers."

"Saied."

He raised both hands. "All right, all right. You want to
torm back in on Shaykh Reda and Himmar, that's your
usiness."

"I'm not gonna face them again," I said. "I mean, not
et."

"Uh yeah, well, let me know when you do."

"You bet," I said. I gave him twenty kiam. "You ca get a cab here, can't you?"

"Uh huh. Give me a call later." He gave me back th keys to my car.

I nodded and went up the curving drive to the eme gency room entrance. Saied had brought me to the sam hospital I'd been in twice before. I was beginning to fe comfortable there.

I filled out their damn forms and waited half an hou until one of the residents could see me. He pumped som thing under the skin of my shoulder with a perfusor, the went about manipulating the broken bones. "This is prol ably gonna hurt," he said.

Well, he didn't know that I had software chipped i that took care of that. I was probably the only person i the world who had that add-on, but I wasn't a well-know celebrity. I made some appropriate grunts and grimace but on the whole I acted brave. He immobilized my le arm with a kind of superstiff shrinkwrap. "You're handlin this real well," he said.

"I've had esoteric training," I said. "The control pain is all in the mind." That was true enough; it wa plugged into the mind on the end of a long, plasti sheathed silver wire.

"Whatever," said the doctor. When he finished wit my collarbone, he treated the cuts and scrapes. Then h scribbled something on a prescription pad. "Still, I' gonna give you this for pain. You may find that you need i If you don't, great." He ripped the page loose and hande it to me.

I glanced at it. He'd written me for twenty Nofeq painkillers so feeble that in the Budayeen you couldn trade ten of them for a single Sonneine. "Thanks," I sai bluntly.

"No sense being a hero and toughing it out whe medical science is there to help." He glanced around an decided that he was finished with me. "You'll be all rigl in about six weeks, Mr. Audran. I advise you to see you own physician in a few days."

"Thanks," I said again. He gave me some papers and took them to a window and paid cash. Then I went ov into the main lobby of the hospital and took the elevato up to the twentieth floor. There was a different nurse o duty, but Zain, the security guard, recognized me. I went down the hall to Suite One.

A doctor and a nurse stood beside Papa's bed. They turned to look at me as I came in, their faces grim. "Is something wrong?" I asked, frightened.

The doctor rubbed his gray beard with one hand. He's in serious trouble," he said.

"What the hell happened?" I demanded.

"He'd been complaining of weakness, headaches, and abdominal pain. For a long while we couldn't find anything to explain it."

"Yes," I said, "he'd been getting ill at home, before the fire. He was too sick to escape by himself."

"We ran more sensitive tests," said the doctor, "and finally something turned up positive. He's been given a rather sophisticated neurotoxin, apparently over a period of weeks."

I felt cold. Someone had been poisoning Friedlander Bey, probably someone in the house. He certainly had enough enemies, and my recent experience with the Half-Hajj proved that I couldn't dismiss anyone as a suspect. Then, suddenly, my eyes fell on something resting on Papa's tray table. It was a round metal tin, its cover lying beside it. In the tin was a layer of dates stuffed with nutmeats and rolled in sugar.

"Umm Saad," I murmured. She'd been feeding those dates to him since she'd come to live in his house. I went to the tray table. "If you analyze these," I told the doctor, "I'll bet you'll find the source."

"But who—"

"Don't worry about who," I said. "Just make him well." This was all because I'd been so caught up in my own vendetta against Jawarski that I hadn't given proper attention to Umm Saad. As I headed for the door I thought, didn't Augustus Caesar's wife poison him with figs from his own tree, to get rid of him so her son could be emperor? I excused myself for overlooking the similarity before; there's so goddamn much history, it just can't help repeating itself.

I went down and bailed my car out of the parking lot, then drove to the station house. I had myself completely under control by the time the elevator brought me up to the third floor. I headed toward Hajjar's office; Sergeant

Catavina tried to stop me, but I just shoved him up against a painted plasterboard wall and kept walking. I flung open Hajjar's door. "Hajjar," I said. All the anger and disgust I felt toward him were in those two syllables.

He glanced up from some paperwork. His expression turned fearful when he saw the look on my face. "Audran," he said. "What is it?"

I lofted the .45 onto his desk in front of him. "Remember that American we were looking for? The guy who killed Jirji? Well, they found him lying on the floor of some rattrap. Somebody shot him with his own gun."

Hajjar stared unhappily at the automatic. "Somebody shot him, huh? Any idea who?"

"Unfortunately, no." I gave him an evil grin. "I don't have a microscope or nothing, but it looks to me like whoever did it also wiped his fingerprints right off the weapon. We may never solve this murder, either."

Hajjar sat back in his reclining chair. "Probably not. Well, at least the citizens will be glad to hear that Jawarski's been neutralized. Good police work, Audran."

"Yeah," I said. "Sure." I turned to leave, and I got as far as the door. Then I faced him again. "That's one down, know what I mean? And two to go."

"The hell you talking about?"

"I mean Umm Saad and Abu Adil are next. And something else: I know who you are and I know what you're doing. Watch your ass. The guy who blew Jawarski away is out there, and he may have you in his sights next." I had the pleasure of seeing Hajjar's superior grin vanish. When I left his office, he was muttering to himself and reaching for his phone.

Catavina was waiting in the corridor by the elevator. "What'd you say?" he asked worriedly. "What'd you tell him?"

"Don't worry, Sarge," I said, "your afternoon nap is safe, at least for a while. But I wouldn't be surprised if suddenly there's a call to reform the police department. You might have to start acting like a real cop for a change." I pushed the button for the elevator. "And lose some weight while you're at it."

My mood was a little better as I rode back down to the ground floor. When I walked back into the early evening sunlight, I felt almost normal.

Almost. I was still a prisoner of my own guilt. I'd
planned to go home and find out more details about
Umuzu's relationship to Abu Adil, but I found myself
heading in the other direction. When I heard the evening
call to prayer, I left the car on Souk el-Khemis Street.
There was a small mosque there, and I paused in the
courtyard to remove my shoes and make the ablution.
Then I went into the mosque and prayed. It was the first
time I'd done that seriously in years.

Joining in worship with the others who came to this
neighborhood mosque didn't cleanse me of my doubts
and bad feelings. I hadn't expected that they would. I did
feel a warmth, however, a sense of belonging that had
been missing from my life since childhood. For the first
time since coming to the city, I could approach Allah in all
humility, and with sincere repentance my prayers might
be accepted.

After the prayer service, I spoke with an elder of the
mosque. We talked for some time, and he told me that I
had been right to come and pray. I was grateful that he
didn't lecture me, that he made me comfortable and welcome.

"There is one more thing, O Respected One," I said.

"Yes?"

"Today I killed a man."

He did not seem terribly shocked. He stroked his long
beard for several seconds. "Tell me why you did this," he
said at last.

I told him everything I knew about Jawarski, about
his record of violent crimes before he'd come to the city,
about his shooting of Shaknahyi. "He was a bad man," I
said, "but, even so, I feel like a criminal myself."

The elder put one hand on my shoulder. "In the Sûrah of The Cow," he said, "it is written that retaliation is
prescribed in the matter of murder. What you did is no
crime in the eyes of Allah, all praise to Him."

I looked deeply into the old man's eyes. He wasn't
merely trying to make me feel better. He wasn't just putting my conscience at ease. He was reciting the law as the
messenger of God had revealed it. I knew the passage of
the Qur'ân he'd mentioned, but I needed to hear it from
someone whose authority I respected. I felt wholly ab-
solved. I almost wept with gratitude.

I left the mosque in a strange mixture of moods: I w.
filled with unrequited rage toward Abu Adil and Um:
Saad, but at the same time I felt a well-being and gladne
I could not describe. I decided to make another stop b.
fore I went home.

Chiri was taking over the night shift when I came in
the club. I sat on my usual stool at the bend of the ba
"White Death?" she asked.

"No," I said, "I can't stay long. Chiri, you got ai
Sonneine?"

She stared at me for a few seconds. "I don't think s
How'd you hurt your arm?"

"Any Paxium then? Or beauties?"

She rested her chin in her hand. "Honey, I thougl
you'd sworn off drugs. I thought you were being cle.
from now on."

"Aw hell, Chiri," I said, "don't give me a hard time

She just reached under the counter and came up wit
her little black pillcase. "Take what you want, Marîd," sl
said. "I guess you know what you're doing."

"I sure do," I said, and I helped myself to half a doze
caps and tabs. I got some water and swallowed them, and
didn't even pay much attention to what they were.

18

I didn't do anything strenuous for a week or so, but my mind raced like a frantic greyhound. I plotted revenge against Abu Adil and Umar a hundred different ways: I scalded their flesh in boiling vats of noxious fluids; I let loose hideous plague organisms that would make their Proxy Hell moddies seem like summer colds; I hired teams of sadistic ninjas to creep into the great house and slaughter them slowly with subtle knife wounds. In the meantime, my body began to recover its strength, although all the superluminal brain augmentation in the world couldn't speed up the knitting of broken bones.

The delay was almost more than I could stand, but I had a wonderful nurse. Yasmin had taken pity on me. Saied had been responsible for distributing the story of my heroics. Now everyone in the Budayeen knew how I'd faced down Jawarski single-handed. They'd also heard that he'd been so shamed by my moral example that he embraced Islam on the spot, and that while we prayed together Abu Adil and Umar tried to tiptoe in and kill me, but Jawarski leaped between us and died saving the life of his new Muslim brother.

Then there was the sequel, in which Umar and Abu Adil captured me and took me back to their evil castle, where they tortured me, mind-raped me, and forced me to sign blank checks and deceptive home repairs contracts until Saied the Half-Hajj burst in to my rescue. What the hell. I didn't see that embellishing the facts a little hurt him or me.

In any event, Yasmin was so attentive and solicitous, I think Kmuzu was a little jealous. I didn't see why. Many of the attentions I received from Yasmin weren't in Kmuzu's job description at all. I awoke one morning to find her straddling me, rubbing my chest. She didn't have a stitch of clothing on.

"Well," I said sleepily, "in the hospital, the nurses rarely take their uniforms off."

"They've had more training," said Yasmin. "I'm a beginner at this, I'm still not entirely sure what I'm doing."

"You know what you're doing, all right," I said. Her massaging moved slowly south. I was waking up fast.

"Now, you're not supposed to do anything too strenuous, so let me do all the work."

"Fine," I said. I looked up at her and remembered how much I loved her. I also remembered how crazy she could make me in bed. Before I got completely carried away, I said, "What if Kmuzu comes in?"

"He's gone to church. Besides," she said wickedly, "even Christians must learn about sex sooner or later. Otherwise, where do new Christians come from?"

"Missionaries convert them from people who are minding their own business," I said.

But Yasmin really didn't intend to get into a religious discussion. She raised up and slid herself down on top of me. She let out a happy sigh. "It's been a long time," she said.

"Yeah," I said. It was all I could think to say; my concentration was elsewhere.

"When my hair gets long again, I'll be able to tickle you with it like I used to."

"You know," I said, beginning to breathe heavily, "I've always had this fantasy—"

Yasmin's eyes opened wide. "Not with my hair, you won't!" she said. Well, we all have our inhibitions. I just didn't think I'd ever suggest anything kinky enough to shock Yasmin.

I'm not going to claim that we jammed all morning until we heard Kmuzu enter the living room. First of all, I hadn't jammed anyone at all in weeks; second, being together again made both of us frantic. It was a short bout, but very intense. Afterward, we held each other and didn't say anything for a while. I could have fallen back to sleep, but Yasmin doesn't like that.

"You ever wish I was a tall, willowy, blond woman?" she asked.

"I've never gotten along very well with real women."

"You like Indihar, I know you do. I've seen you looking at her."

"You're crazy. She's just not as bad as the other girls."

I felt Yasmin shrug. "But do you ever wish I was tall and blond?"

"You could've been. When you were still a boy, you could've asked the surgeons for that."

She buried her face against my neck. "They told me I didn't have the skeleton," she said, her voice muffled.

"I think you're perfect just the way you are." I waited a beat. "Except you've got the biggest feet I've ever seen in my life."

Yasmin sat up quickly. She wasn't amused. "You want your other collarbone broken, *baheem?*"

It took me half an hour and a long hot shower together to restore peace. I got dressed and watched Yasmin get herself ready to go out. For once, she wasn't running late. She didn't have to go to work until eight o'clock that evening. "Coming by the club later?" she asked, looking at my reflection in the mirror over my dresser.

"Sure," I said. "I've got to make my presence felt, or all you employees will get the idea I'm running a resort."

Yasmin grinned. "You ain't running nothing, honey," she said. "Chiri runs that club, like she always has."

"I know." I'd come to enjoy owning the place. I'd originally planned to turn the club back to Chiri as soon as possible, but now I'd decided to hang on to it for a while. It made me feel great to get special treatment from Brandi, Kandy, Pualani and the others. I liked being Mr. Boss.

After Yasmin left, I went to my desk and sat down. My original apartment had been repaired and painted, and I was living again on the second floor of the west wing. Staying just down the hall from my mother had been nerve-wracking, even for only a few days, even after our surprise reconciliation. I felt recovered enough to turn my attention back to the unfinished business of Umm Saad and Abu Adil.

When I finally decided that I couldn't put it off any longer, I picked up the tan-colored moddy, the recording of Abu Adil. *"Bismillah,"* I murmured, and then hesitantly I reached up and chipped it in.

Madness, by the life of the Prophet!

Audran felt as if he were peering through a narrow tunnel, seeing the world with Abu Adil's mean, self-centered outlook. Things were only good for Abu Adil or bad for Abu Adil; if they were neither, they did not exist.

The next thing Audran noticed was that he was in a state of sexual arousal. Of course; Abu Adil's only sexual pleasure came from jamming himself, or a facsimile of himself. That's what Umar was—a frame on which to hang this electronic duplicate. And Umar was too stupid to realize that's all he was, that he had no other qualifications that made him valuable. When he displeased Abu Adil, or began to bore him, Umar would be replaced immediately, as so many others had been disposed of over the years.

What about the Phoenix File? What did A.L.M. mean?

Of course, the memory was right there . . . Alif Lâm. Mîm.

They weren't initials at all. They weren't some unknown acronym. They came from the Qur'ân. Many of the sûrahs in the Qur'ân began with letters of the alphabet. No one knew what they meant. Indications of some mystical phrase, perhaps, or the initials of a scribe. Their significance had been lost through the centuries.

There was more than one sûrah that began with Alif Lâm. Mîm, but Audran knew immediately which one was special. It was Sûrah Thirty, called The Romans; the important line read "Allah is He Who created you and then sustained you, then causeth you to die, then giveth life to you again." It was obvious that, just like Friedlander Bey, Shaykh Reda also pictured his own face when he spoke the name of God.

And suddenly Audran knew that the Phoenix File, with its lists of unsuspecting people who might be murdered for organs, was recorded on a cobalt-alloy memory plate hidden in Abu Adil's private bedroom.

And other things became clear to Audran as well. When he thought of Umm Saad, Abu Adil's memory related that she was not, in fact, any relation to Friedlander Bey, but that she had agreed to spy on him. Umm Saad's reward would be the removal of her name and that of her son from the Phoenix File. She would never have to worr

*at someday someone she did not even know might have
eater need of her heart or her liver or her lungs.*

*Audran learned that it had been Umm Saad who'd
red Paul Jawarski, and Abu Adil had extended his pro-
ction to the American killer. Umm Saad had brought
warski to the city and passed along the assignments
om Shaykh Reda to kill certain people listed on the
oenix File. Umm Saad was partly responsible for those
aths, and for the fire and the poisoning of Friedlander
y.*

*Audran was sickened, and the horrible, floating feel-
g of insanity was threatening to overwhelm him. He
ached up and grabbed the moddy and pulled it free.*

Yipe. That was the first time I'd ever used a moddy
corded from a living person. It had been a disgusting
perience. It had been like being immersed in slime,
cept that you could wash slime away; having your mind
uled was more intimate and more terrible. From now
, I promised myself, I'd stick with fictional characters
d moddy constructs.

Abu Adil was even more brainsick than I'd imagined.
ill, I'd learned a few things—or, at least, my suspicions
d been confirmed. Surprisingly, I could understand
mm Saad's motivations. If I'd known about the Phoenix
le, I'd have done anything to get my name off it too.

I wanted to talk some of this over with Kmuzu, but he
asn't back from his Sabbath service yet. I thought I'd see
my mother had anything more to tell me.

I crossed the courtyard to the east wing. There was a
tle pause when I knocked on her door. "Coming," she
lled. I heard glass clinking, then the sound of a drawer
ening and shutting. "Coming." When she opened the
or to me, I could smell the Irish whiskey. She'd been
ry circumspect during her stay in Papa's house. I'm sure
e drank and took drugs as much as ever, but at least she
d the self-control not to parade herself around when
e was smashed.

"Peace be on you, O Mother," I said.

"And on you be peace," she said. She leaned against
e door a little unsteadily. "Do you want to come in, O
aykh?"

"Yes, I need to talk to you." I waited until she'd

opened the door wider and stepped back. I came in ar
took a seat on the couch. She faced me in a comfortab
armchair.

"I'm sorry," she said, "I got nothin' to offer you."

"Uh yeah, that's okay." She looked well. She ha
abandoned the outlandish makeup and clothing, and no
she rather resembled my former mental image of he
Her hair was brushed, she was suitably dressed, and sł
was modestly seated with her hands folded in her lap
recalled Kmuzu's comment that I judged my moth
more harshly than I judged myself, and forgave her tł
drunkenness. She wasn't hurting anybody.

"O Mother," I said, "you said that when you can
back to the city, you made the mistake of trusting Al
Adil again. I know that it was my friend Saied wł
brought you here."

"You know that?" she said. She seemed wary.

"And I know about the Phoenix File. Now, why we
you willing to spy on Friedlander Bey?"

Her expression was amazed. "Hey," she said, "
somebody offered to cross you off that goddamn lis
wouldn't you do just about anything? I mean, hell, I to
myself I wouldn't give Abu Adil nothin' he could rea
use against Papa. I didn't think I was hurtin' nobody."

That's just what I'd hoped to hear. Abu Adil ha
squeezed Umm Saad and my mother in the same vis
Umm Saad had responded by trying to kill everyone
our house. My mother had reacted differently; she'd fle
to Friedlander Bey's protection.

I pretended that the matter wasn't important enoug
to discuss further. "You also said that you wished to o
something useful with your life. You still feel that way"

"Sure, I suppose," she said suspiciously. She looke
uncomfortable, as if she were waiting for me to conden
her to some horrible fate of civic consciousness.

"I've put away some money," I said, "and I've give
Kmuzu the job of starting up a kind of charity kitchen :
the Budayeen. I was wondering if you'd like to help wit
the project."

"Oh sure," she said, frowning, "whatever you want
She couldn't have been less enthusiastic if I'd asked her t
cut out her own tongue.

"What's wrong?" I asked.

I was startled to see tears slipping down her pale
cheek. "You know, I didn't think I'd come to this. I'm still
good lookin', ain't I? I mean, your father thought I was
beautiful. He used to tell me that all the time, and that
wasn't so long ago. I think if I had some decent clothes—
not that stuff I brought with me from Algiers—I could still
turn a few heads. No reason I got to be lonely the rest of
my life, is there?"

I didn't want to get into that. "You're still attractive,
Mother."

"You bet your ass," she said, smiling again. "I'm gonna
get me a short skirt and some boots. Don't look at me that
way, I mean a *tasteful* short skirt. Fifty-seven years old
ain't so bad these days. Look at Papa."

Yeah, well, Papa was lying helpless in a hospital bed,
too weak to pull his own sheet up under his chin.

"And you know what I want?" she asked with a
dreamy expression.

I was afraid to ask. "No, what?"

"I saw this picture of Umm Khalthoum in the souk.
Made out of thousands of flat-head nails. This guy
pounded 'em all into this big board, then painted each nail
head a different color. You can't see what it is close up, but
then you step back, it's this gorgeous picture of The
Lady."

"Yeah, you right," I said. I could just see it hanging on
the wall over Friedlander Bey's expensive and tasteful
furniture.

"Well, hell, I got some money put away too." I must
have looked surprised, because she said, "I got some
secrets of my own, you know. I been around, I seen things.
Got my own friends and I got my own cash. So don't think
you can order my life for me just 'cause you set me up
here. I can pick up and leave anytime I want."

"Mother," I said, "I really don't want to tell you how
to act or what to do. I just thought you might like helping
out in the Budayeen. There's a lot of people there as poor
as we used to be."

She wasn't listening closely. "We used to be poor,
Marîd," she said, drifting off to a fantasy recollection of
what those times had been like, "but we was always
happy. Those were the *good* days." Then her expression

turned sad, and she looked at me again. "And look at m now."

"Got to go," I said. I stood up and headed for the doo "May your vigor continue, O Mother. By your leave."

"Go in peace," she said, coming with me to the doc "Remember what I told you."

I didn't know what she meant. Even under the be conditions, conversations with my mother were fille with little information and much static. With her, it wa always one step forward and two steps back. I was glad see that she didn't seem to have any thoughts of returnir to Algiers, or going into her old line of work here. At leas that's what I thought she'd meant. She'd said somethir about "turning some heads," but I hoped she mea purely in a noncommercial way. I thought about the things as I went back to my suite in the west wing.

Kmuzu had returned, and was gathering up our dir laundry. "A call came for you, *yaa Sidi*," he said.

"Here?" I wondered why it hadn't come on my pe sonal line, on the phone I wore on my belt.

"Yes. There was no message, but you are supposed call Mahmoud. I left the number on your desk."

This could be good news. I'd planned to tackle th second of my three targets next—Umm Saad; but sh might have to wait. I went to the desk and spok Mahmoud's commcode into the phone. He answered in mediately. *"Allô,"* he said.

"Where y'at, Mahmoud. It's Marîd."

"Good. I have some business to discuss with you."

"Let me get comfortable." I pulled out a chair and s down. I couldn't help a grin from spreading over my fac "Okay, what you got?"

There was a slight pause. "As you know, I was great saddened by the death of Jirji Shaknahyi, may the bles ings of Allah be on him."

I knew nothing of the kind. If I hadn't known Indih was married, I doubted if Mahmoud or Jacques or an body else knew either. Maybe Chiriga. Chiri always kne these things. "It was a tragedy to the entire city," I said. was staying noncommittal.

"It was a tragedy to our Indihar. She must be helple with grief. And to have no money now, that must mak her situation even harder. I'm sorry that I suggested sh

ork for me. That was callous. I spoke quickly before I
nsidered what I was saying."

"Indihar is a devout Muslim," I said coldly. "She's not
out to turn tricks for you or for anyone."

"I know that, Marîd. No need for you to be so defen-
ve on her behalf. But she's realized that she can't sup-
ort all her children. You mentioned that she'd be willing
place one of them in a good foster home, and perhaps
rn enough that way to feed and clothe the others in a
roper manner."

I hated what I was doing. "You may not know it," I
id, "but my own mother was forced to sell my little
rother when we were children."

"Now, now, Maghrebi," said Mahmoud, "don't think
f it as 'selling.' No one's got the right to sell a child. We
n't continue this conversation if you maintain that atti-
de."

"Fine. Whatever you say. It's not selling; call it what-
ver you want. The point is, have you found someone who
ight be interested in adopting?"

Mahmoud paused. "Not exactly," he said at last. "But
know a man who frequently acts as go-between, arrang-
g these matters. I've dealt with him before, and I can
ouch for his honesty and delicacy. You can see that these
ansactions require a great amount of sympathy and
ct."

"Sure," I said. "That's important. Indihar is in enough
ain as it is."

"Exactly. That's why this man is so highly recom-
ended. He's able to place a child in a loving home imme-
iately, and he's able to present the natural parent with a
ash gift in such a way as to prevent any guilt or recrimi-
ations. It's just his way. I think Mr. On is the perfect
olution to Indihar's problem."

"Mr. On?"

"His name is On Cheung. He's a businessman from
ansu China. I've had the privilege of acting as his agent
efore."

"Uh yeah." I squeezed my eyes shut and listened to
e blood roaring in my head. "This is leading us into the
opic of money. How much will this Mr. On pay, and do
ou get a cut of it?"

"For the elder son, five hundred kiam. For the

younger son, three hundred kiam. For the daughter, tw
hundred fifty. There are also bonuses: an extra two hun
dred kiam for two children, and five hundred if Indiha
relinquishes all three. I, of course, take 10 percent. If yo
have arranged with her for a fee, that must come from th
remainder."

"Sounds fair enough. That's better than Indihar ha
hoped, to be truthful."

"I told you that Mr. On was a generous man."

"Now what? Do we meet somewhere or what?"

Mahmoud's voice was growing excited. "Of cours
both Mr. On and I will need to examine the children, to b
sure they're fit and healthy. Can you have them at 7 Ra
ben Garcia Street in half an hour?"

"Sure, Mahmoud. See you then. Tell On Cheung t
bring his money." I hung up the phone. "Kmuzu,"
called, "forget about the laundry. We're going out."

"Yes, *yaa Sidi*. Shall I bring the car around?"

"Uh huh." I got up and threw a *gallebeya* over m
jeans. Then I stuffed my static pistol in the pocket. I didn
trust either Mahmoud or the baby seller.

The address was in the Jewish Quarter, and it turne
out to be another storefront covered with newspape
very much like the place Shaknahyi and I had invest
gated in vain. "Stay here," I told Kmuzu. Then I got out o
the car and went to the front door. I rapped on the glas
and after a little while Mahmoud opened the door an inc
or two.

"Marîd," he said in his husky voice. "Where's Indiha
and the children?"

"I told 'em to stay in the car. I want to check this ou
first. Let me in."

"Sure." He swung the door wider, and I pushed pas
him. "Marîd, this is Mr. On."

The baby seller was a small man with brown skin an
brown teeth. He was sitting on a battered metal foldin
chair at a card table. There was a metal box at his elbow
He looked at me through a pair of wire-rimmed specta
cles. No Nikon eyes for him, either.

I stepped across the filthy floor and held out my han
to him. On Cheung peered up at me and made no move t
shake hands. After a few seconds, feeling like a fool,
dropped my hand.

"Okay?" asked Mahmoud. "Satisfied?"

"Tell him to open the box," I said.

"I don't tell Mr. On to do anything," said Mahmoud. He's a very—"

"Everything okay," said On Cheung. "You look." He pped open the top of the metal box. There was a stack of ndred-kiam bills in there that could have bought every ild in the Budayeen.

"Great," I said. I reached into my pocket and brought t the pistol. "Hands on heads," I said.

"You son of a bitch," shouted Mahmoud. "What's this, robbery? You're not gonna get away with it. Mr. On will ake you sorry. That money's not going to do you a damn t of good. You'll be dead before you spend a fiq of it."

"I'm still a cop, Mahmoud," I said sadly. I closed the etal box and handed it to him. I couldn't carry it with my e good arm and still point the static pistol. "Hajjar's en looking for On Cheung for a long time. Even a ooked cop like him has to bust somebody for real now d then. I guess it's just your turn."

I led them out to the car. I kept the gun on them hile Kmuzu drove to the station house. All four of us ent up to the third floor. Hajjar was startled as our little rade entered his glass-walled office. "Lieutenant," I id, "this is On Cheung, the baby seller. Mahmoud, drop e box of money. It's supposed to be evidence, but I don't pect anybody'll ever see it again after today."

"You never cease to amaze me," said Hajjar. He shed a button on his desk, calling cops from the outer fice.

"This one's for free," I said. Hajjar looked puzzled. "I ld you I still had two to go. That's Umm Saad and Abu dil. These stiffs are kind of a bonus."

"Right, thanks a lot. Mahmoud, you can go." The utenant looked up at me and shrugged his shoulders. You really think Papa'd let me hold him?" he said. I ought about that for a moment and realized he was ght.

Mahmoud looked relieved. "Won't forget this, aghrebi," he muttered as he shoved by me. His threat dn't worry me.

"By the way," I said, "I quit. You want anybody to file affic reports or enter logbook records from now on, you

get somebody else. You need somebody to waste his tim
on wild-goose chases, get somebody else. You need hel
covering up your own crimes or incompetence, chec
with somebody else. I don't work here anymore."

Hajjar smiled cynically. "Yeah, some cops react tha
way when they face real pressure. But I thought you'd la
longer, Audran."

I slapped him twice, quickly and loudly. He ju
stared at me, his own hand coming up slowly to touch h
stinging cheeks. I turned and walked out of the offic
followed by Kmuzu. Cops were coming from all aroun
and they'd seen what I'd done to Hajjar. Everybody wa
grinning. Even me.

Kmuzu," I said as he drove the sedan back to the house, "would you invite Umm Saad to have dinner with us?"

He looked across at me. He probably thought I was a complete fool, but he was great at keeping his opinions to himself. "Of course, *yaa Sidi,*" he said. "In the small dining room?"

"Uh huh." I watched the streets of the Christian Quarter go by, wondering if I knew what I was doing.

"I hope you're not underestimating the woman," said Kmuzu.

"I don't think so. I think I've got a healthy regard for what she's capable of. I also think she's basically sane. When I tell her I know about the Phoenix File, and about her reasons for insinuating herself in our house, she'll realize the game is over."

Kmuzu tapped the steering wheel with his index fingers. "If you need help, *yaa Sidi,* I'll be there. You won't have to face her alone, as you faced Shaykh Reda."

I smiled. "Thanks, Kmuzu, but I don't think Umm Saad is as loony or as powerful as Abu Adil. She and I will just be sitting down to a meal. I intend to stay in control, *inshallah.*"

Kmuzu gave me one more thoughtful glance, then turned his attention back to driving.

When we arrived at Friedlander Bey's mansion, I went upstairs and changed my clothes. I put on a white robe and a white caftan, into which I transferred my static pistol. I also popped the pain-blocking daddy. I didn't really need it all the time anymore, and I was carrying plenty of sunnies just in case. I felt a flood of annoying aches and pains, all of which had been blocked by the

daddy. The worst of all was the throbbing discomfort i
my shoulder. I decided there was no point in sufferin,
bravely, and I went right for my pillcase.

While I waited for Umm Saad's response to my invita
tion, I heard the sunset call to prayer from Papa's muez
zin. Since my talk with the elder of the mosque in Sou.
el-Khemis Street, I'd been worshiping more or less regu
larly. Maybe I didn't manage to hit all five daily prayers
but I was doing decidedly better than ever before. Now
went downstairs to Papa's office. He kept his prayer ru,
there, and he had a special *mihrab* built into one wall. Th
mihrab is the shallow semicircular alcove you find in ev
ery mosque, indicating the precise direction of Mecca
After I washed my face, hands, and feet, I unrolled th
prayer mat, cleared my mind of uncertainty, and ad
dressed myself to Allah.

When I'd finished praying, Kmuzu murmured
"Umm Saad waits for you in the small dining room."

"Thank you." I rolled up Papa's prayer rug and put i
away. I felt determined and strong. I used to believe tha
this was a temporary illusion caused by worship, but now
thought that doubt was the illusion. The assurance wa
real.

"It is good that you've regained your faith, *yaa Sidi,*
said Kmuzu. "Sometime you must let me tell you of th
miracle of Jesus Christ."

"Jesus is no stranger to Muslims," I replied, "and hi
miracles are no secret to the faith."

We went into the dining room, and I saw Umm Saa
and her young son sitting in their places. The boy hadn'
been invited, but his presence wouldn't stop me fron
what I planned to say. "Welcome," I said, "and may Alla
make this meal wholesome to you."

"Thank you, O Shaykh," said Umm Saad. "How i
your health?"

"Fine, all praise be to Allah." I sat down, and Kmuz
stood behind my chair. I noticed that Habib had come int
the room as well—or maybe it was Labib, whichever o
the Stones wasn't guarding Papa in the hospital. Umn
Saad and I exchanged more pleasantries until a servin
woman brought in a platter of *tahini* and salt fish.

"Your cook is excellent," said Umm Saad. "I hav
relished each meal here."

"I am pleased," I said. More appetizers were brought
t: cold stuffed grape leaves, stewed artichoke hearts,
d eggplant slices stuffed with cream cheese. I indicated
at my guests should serve themselves.

Umm Saad piled generous portions of each dish on
r son's plate. She looked back at me. "May I pour coffee
r you, O Shaykh?" she asked.

"In a moment," I said. "I'm sorry that Saad ben Salah
here to hear what I've got to say. It's time to confront
u with what I've learned. I know all about your work for
aykh Reda, and how you've attempted to murder
iedlander Bey. I know that you ordered your son to set
e fire, and I know about the poisoned stuffed dates."

Umm Saad's face went pale with horror. She had just
ken a bite of a stuffed grape leaf, and she spat it out and
opped the remainder on her plate. "What have you
ne?" she said hoarsely.

I picked up another stuffed grape leaf and put it in my
outh. When I finished chewing, I said, "I've done noth-
g as terrible as you're thinking."

Saad ben Salah stood up and moved toward me. His
ung face was twisted in an expression of rage and hate.
3y the beard of the Prophet," he said, "I won't allow you
speak that way to my mother!"

"I only speak the truth," I said. "Isn't that so, Umm
ad?"

The boy glared at me. "My mother had nothing to do
ith the fire. That was my own idea. I hate you, and I hate
iedlander Bey. He's my grandfather, yet he denies me.
e leaves his own daughter to suffer in poverty and mis-
y. He deserves to die."

I sipped some coffee calmly. "I don't believe it," I
id. "It's commendable of you to shoulder the blame,
ad, but it's your mother who's guilty, not you."

"You're a liar!" cried the woman.

The boy leaped toward me, but Kmuzu put himself
tween us. He was more than strong enough to restrain
ad.

I turned again to Umm Saad. "What I don't under-
and," I said, "is why you've tried to kill Papa. I don't see
at his death would benefit you at all."

"Then you don't know as much as you think," she
id. She seemed to relax a little. Her eyes flicked from me

to Kmuzu, who still held her son in an unbreakable gri
"Shaykh Reda promised me that if I discovered Frie
lander Bey's plans, or eliminated him so that Shaykh Re
would have no further obstacle, he would take back my clai
to be mistress of this house. I would take over Friedland
Bey's estate and his business ventures, and I would the
turn over all matters of political influence to Shayk
Reda."

"Sure," I said, "and all you'd have to do is trust Ab
Adil. How long do you think you'd last before he elim
nated you the way you eliminated Papa? Then he cou
unite the two most powerful houses in the city."

"You're just inventing stories!" She got to her fee
turning to look at Kmuzu again. "Let my son go."

Kmuzu looked at me. I shook my head.

Umm Saad took a small needle gun from her bag.
said, let my son go!"

"My lady," I said, holding up both hands to show th
she had nothing to fear from me, "you've failed. Put dow
the gun. If you go on, not even the resources of Shayk
Reda will protect you from the vengeance of Friedland
Bey. I'm sure Abu Adil's interest in your affairs has con
to an end. At this point, you're only deluding yourself

She fired two or three flechettes into the ceiling to l
me know she was willing to use the weapon. "Release n
boy," she said hoarsely. "Let us go."

"I don't know if I can do that," I said. "I'm sure Frie
lander Bey would want to—"

I heard a sound like *thitt! thitt!* and realized th
Umm Saad had fired at me. I sucked in a deep breat
waiting to feel the bite of pain that would tell me whe
I'd been wounded, but it didn't happen. Her agitation ha
spoiled her aim even at this close range.

She swung the needle gun toward Kmuzu, who r
mained motionless, still shielded by Saad's body. Then sh
turned back toward me. In the meantime, however, th
Stone That Speaks had crossed the few feet between u
He raised one hand and chopped down on Umm Saad
wrist, and she dropped the needle gun. Then the Ston
raised his other hand, clenched into a huge fist.

"No," I shouted, but it was too late to stop him. With
powerful backhand clout, he knocked Umm Saad to th
floor. I saw a bright trail of blood on her face below he

plit lip. She lay on her back with her head twisted at a grotesque angle. I knew the Stone had killed her with one blow. "That's two," I whispered. Now I could give my complete attention to Abu Adil. And Umar, the old man's deluded plaything.

"Son of a dog!" screamed the boy. He struggled a moment, and then Kmuzu permitted him to go to her. He bent and cradled his mother's corpse. "O Mother, Mother," he murmured, weeping.

Kmuzu and I let him mourn her for a short while. "Saad, get up," I said finally.

He looked up at me. I don't think I've ever seen so much malignity in a person's face. "I'll kill you," he said. "I promise you that. All of you."

"Get up, Saad," I said. I wished this hadn't happened, but it was too late for regrets.

Kmuzu put his hand on Saad's shoulder, but the boy shrugged it off. "You must listen to my master," said Kmuzu.

"No," said Saad. Then his hand flashed out quickly for his mother's needle gun. The Stone stamped down on the boy's forearm. Saad collapsed beside his mother, holding his arm and whimpering.

Kmuzu knelt and took the needle gun. He stood up again and gave the weapon to me. "What do you wish to do, *yaa Sidi?*" he asked.

"About the boy?" I looked at Saad thoughtfully. I knew that he bore me nothing but malice, but I only pitied him. He had been only a pawn in his mother's bargain with Abu Adil, a dupe in her vicious scheme to usurp Friedlander Bey's power. I didn't expect that Saad could understand that, of course. To him, Umm Saad would always be a martyr and a victim of cruel injustice.

"What is to be done?" Kmuzu said, breaking in on my thoughts.

"Oh, just let him go. He's certainly suffered enough." Kmuzu stood aside, and Saad got to his feet, holding his bruised forearm close to his chest. "I'll make all the proper preparations for your mother's funeral," I said.

Once again, his expression twisted in loathing. "You will not touch her!" he cried. "I will bury my mother." He backed away from me and stumbled toward the door. When he reached the exit, he turned to face me. "If there

are such things as curses in this world," he uttered in a
feverish voice, "I call them all down on you and your
house. I will make you pay a hundred times for what
you've done. I swear this three times, on the life of the
Prophet Muhammad!" Then he fled the dining room.

"You have made a bitter enemy, *yaa Sidi,*" said
Kmuzu.

"I know," I said, "but I can't worry about it." I just
shook my head sadly.

A telephone on the sideboard warbled, and the Stone
answered it. "Yes?" he said. He listened for a moment,
then held it out to me.

I took it from him. "Hello?" I said.

There was just one word from the caller, "Come." It
had been the other Stone.

I felt chilled. "We've got to get to the hospital," I said.
I glanced down at Umm Saad's body, undecided what to
do.

Kmuzu understood my problem. "Youssef can make
the arrangements, *yaa Sidi,* if that's what you wish."

"Yes," I said. "I may need both of you."

Kmuzu nodded, and we left the dining room with
Labib or Habib right behind me. We went outside, and
Kmuzu drove the sedan around to the front of the house. I
got in the back. I thought the Stone would have an easier
time cramming himself into the passenger seat.

Kmuzu raced through the streets almost as wildly as
Bill the taxi driver. We arrived at Suite One just as a male
nurse was leaving Papa's room.

"How is Friedlander Bey?" I asked fearfully.

"He's still alive," said the nurse. "He's conscious, but
you can't stay long. He's going into surgery shortly. The
doctor is with him now."

"Thank you," I said. I turned to Kmuzu and the
Stone. "Wait outside."

"Yes, *yaa Sidi,*" said Kmuzu. The Stone didn't even
grunt. He just cast a quick, hostile glance at Kmuzu.

I went into the suite. I saw another male nurse shaving Papa's skull, evidently prepping it for surgery. Tariq,
his valet, stood by looking very worried. Dr. Yeniknani
and another doctor sat at the card table, discussing something in low voices.

"Praise God you're here," said the valet. "Our master as been asking for you."

"What is it, Tariq?" I asked.

He frowned. He looked almost on the point of tears. don't understand. The doctors can explain. But now ou must let our master know that you're here."

I went to Papa's bedside and looked down at him. He emed to be dozing, his breath light and fluttery. His skin as an unhealthy gray color, and his lips and eyelids were nnaturally dark. The nurse finished shaving his head, d that just accentuated Papa's bizarre, deathlike appearance.

He opened his eyes as I stood there. "You have made lonely, my nephew," he said. His voice was faint, like ords carried on the wind.

"May God never make you lonely, O Shaykh," I said. I ent and kissed him on the cheek.

"You must tell me," he began. His breath wheezed nd he couldn't finish his sentence.

"All goes well, praise Allah," I said. "Umm Saad is no ore. I have yet to instruct Abu Adil on the folly of plotng against you."

The corners of his mouth quirked. "You will be rearded. How did you defeat the woman?"

I wished he would stop thinking in terms of debts and ewards. "I have a personality module of Shaykh Reda," I id. "When I chipped it in, I learned many things that ave been useful."

He caught his breath and looked unhappy. "Then you now—"

"I know of the Phoenix File, O Shaykh. I know that ou protect that evil thing in cooperation with Abu Adil."

"Yes. And you know also that I am your mother's randfather. That you are my great-grandson. But do you nderstand why we kept that knowledge a secret?"

Well, no, I hadn't known that until just that moment, lthough if I'd been wearing Abu Adil's moddy and topped to think about myself or my mother, the informaon might have popped into my consciousness.

So all that stuff about Papa possibly being my father vas just Mom being cute and clever. I guess she'd known he truth all along. And that's why Papa'd been so upset hen I'd kicked her out of the house when she first came

to the city. That's why Umm Saad had caused him s
much grief: Because everybody but me understood tha
she was trying to squeeze out the natural heirs, with Ab
Adil's assistance. And Umm Saad was using the Phoen
File to blackmail Papa. Now I saw why he allowed her t
remain in the house so long, and why he preferred that
dispose of her.

And ever since Friedlander Bey's divine finger fir
descended from the clouds to tap me so long ago, I'd bee
aimed toward lofty ends. Had I been cut out to be mere
Papa's indispensable, reluctant assistant? Or had I bee
groomed all along to inherit the power and the wealt
every bit of it, along with the terrible life-and-death dec
sions Papa made every day?

How naive I'd been, to think that I might find a wa
to escape! I was more than just under Friedlander Bey
thumb; he owned me, and his indelible mark was writte
in my genetic material. My shoulders sagged as I realize
that I would never be free, and that any hope of libert
had always been empty illusion.

"Why did you and my mother keep this secret fron
me?" I asked.

"You are not alone, my . . . son. As a young man,
fathered many children. When my own eldest son died
he was older than you are now, and he has been dea
more than a century. I have dozens of grandchildren, on
of whom is your mother. In your generation, I do no
know how many descendants I can claim. It would no
have been appropriate for you to feel unique, to use you
relationship with me to further selfish ends. I needed to b
sure that you were worthy, before I acknowledged you a
my chosen one."

I wasn't as thrilled by that speech as he probabl
thought I should be. He sounded like a lunatic pretendin
to be God, passing on his blessing like a birthday present
Papa didn't want me to use my connection for selfish ends
Jeez, if that wasn't the height of irony!

"Yes, O Shaykh," I said. It didn't cost me anything t
sound docile. Hell, he was going to have his skull carved ir
a few minutes. Still, I made no promises.

"Remember," he said softly, "there are many other:
who would take away your privileged position. You have
scores of cousins who may someday do you harm."

Great. Something else to look forward to. "Then the computer records I searched—"

"Have been changed and changed again many times over the years." He smiled faintly. "You must learn not to put your faith in truth that has only electronic existence. Is it not our business, after all, to supply versions of that truth to the nations of the world? Have you not learned how supple truth can be?"

More questions occurred to me every second. "Then my father was truly Bernard Audran?"

"The Provençal sailor, yes."

I was relieved that I knew one thing for certain.

"Forgive my, my darling," murmured Papa. "I did not wish to reveal the Phoenix File to you, and that made it more difficult for you to deal with Umm Saad and Abu Adil."

I held his hand; it trembled in my grasp. "Don't worry, O Shaykh. It's almost over."

"Mr. Audran." I felt Dr. Yeniknani's large-knuckled hand on my shoulder. "We'll be taking your patron down to surgery now."

"What's wrong? What are you going to do?"

It was obvious that there wasn't time to go into a long explanation. "You were right about the tainted dates. Someone had been feeding him the poison for some time. It has severely impaired his medulla, the part of the brain that controls respiration, heartbeat, and wakefulness. It's been damaged to such an extent that, unless something is done very soon, he will fall into an irreversible coma."

My mouth was dry, and my heart was racing. "What are you going to do?" I asked.

Dr. Yeniknani looked down at his hands. "Dr. Lisân believes the only hope is a partial medullar transplant. We have been waiting for healthy tissue from a compatible donor."

"And today you've found it?" I wondered who on that goddamn Phoenix File had been sacrificed for this.

"I can't promise success, Mr. Audran. The operation has only been tried three or four times before, and never in this part of the world. But you must know that if any surgeon can offer you hope, it's Dr. Lisân. And of course, I will be attending. Your patron will have all the skill at our disposal, and all the prayers of his faithful friends."

I nodded dumbly. I looked up to see two male nurse lifting Friedlander Bey from his hospital bed onto wheeled cart. I went to grasp his hand once more.

"Two things," he said in a husky whisper. "You hav moved the policeman's widow into our home. When th four months of proper mourning are over, you mu marry her."

"Marry her!" I was so startled, I forgot to be proper respectful.

"And when I recover from this illness—" He yawne almost unable to keep his eyes open against the medic tion the nurses had given him. I lowered my head to catc his words. "When I am again well, we will go to Mecca

That wasn't what I expected, either. I guess groaned. "Mecca," I said.

"The pilgrimage." He opened his eyes. He looke frightened, not of the surgery but of his unfulfilled oblig tion to Allah. "It is past time," he said, and then the wheeled him away.

I decided the wise thing was to wait until my arm was
unwrapped before I faced down Abu Adil. After all, the
great Salah ad-Dîn didn't reconquer Jerusalem and
drive out the Franj Crusaders by riding down into battle
with half his army. Not that I planned to get into a fistfight
with Shaykh Reda or Umar, but I'd taken enough nicks
and scrapes lately to learn a little prudence.

Things had quieted down considerably. For a time,
we worried and prayed to Allah for Friedlander Bey's
recovery. He'd survived the surgery and Dr. Lisân had
pronounced it a success; but Papa slept almost around the
clock, day after day. He roused occasionally and talked
with us, although he was terribly confused about who we
all were and what century it was.

With Umm Saad and her son gone, the atmosphere in
the house was more cheerful. I concerned myself with
Papa's business matters, acting in his place to settle dis-
putes among the city's caterers of the ungodly. I let Mahmoud know that I would be tough but fair as Friedlander
Bey's deputy, and he seemed to accept that. At least, he
dropped his resentment. That may have been just an act.
You can never accurately read Mahmoud.

I also had to handle a major foreign crisis, when the
new tyrant of Eritrea came to me demanding to know
what was going on in his own country. I took care of that
mess, thanks to Papa's impeccable record keeping and
Tariq and Youssef's knowledge of where everything was.

My mother continued to alternate between modestly
mature and brazenly foolish. Sometimes when we talked,
we were sorry for the way we'd punished each other in
the past. Other times, we wanted to slit each other's
throats. Kmuzu told me that this kind of relationship is not

279

unusual between parent and child, particularly after bot
have reached a certain age. I accepted that, and I didn
worry about it anymore.

Chiriga's continued to make lots of money, and bot
Chiri and I were satisfied. I guess she would've been mor
satisfied if I'd sold the club back to her, but I enjoye
owning it too much. I decided to hang on to it a little whi
longer, the way I decided to hang on to Kmuzu.

When the muezzin's call to prayer came, I answere
it a large percentage of the time, and went to the mosqu
on a Friday or two. I was becoming known as a kind an
generous man, not just in the Budayeen but all throug
the city. Wherever I went, people called me Shayk
Marîd al-Amîn. I didn't completely stop taking drug
however, because I was still injured and I saw no reason t
take the chance of enduring unnecessary agony.

All in all, the month after I'd kissed off the polic
department was a welcome experiment with peace an
quiet. It all came to an end one Tuesday, just before lunc
when I answered the phone. *"Marhaba,"* I said.

"Praise be to God. This is Umar Abdul-Qawy."

I didn't say anything for a few seconds. "The hell d
you want?" I said.

"My master is concerned for the health of Fried
lander Bey. I'm calling to inquire as to his condition."

I was coming to a quick boil. I didn't really know wha
to say to Umar. "He's fine. He's resting."

"Then he's able to take care of his duties?" There wa
a smugness in his voice that I hated a lot.

"I said he's fine, all right? Now, I got work to do."

"Just a second, Monsieur Audran." And then his voic
got positively sanctimonious. "We believe you may hav
something that properly belongs to Shaykh Reda."

I knew what he was talking about, and it made m
smile. I liked being the screwer rather than the screwee
"I don't know what you mean, Himmar." I don't know
something made me say it. I knew it would pluck hi
beard.

"The moddy," he said. "The goddman moddy."

I paused to savor what I heard in his voice. "Wel
hell," I said, "you got it all wrong. As I recall, *you* have th
goddamn moddy. Remember? *Himmar?* You cuffed m
hands behind my back, and then you beat me bloody, an

en you jacked me into a moddy link and read off my
ain. You guys done with it yet?"

There was silence. I think Umar hoped I wouldn't
member that moddy. That's not what he wanted to talk
out. I didn't care, I had the floor. "How's it work, you
n of a bitch?" I said. "You wear my brain while that sick
astard jams you? Or the other way around? How am I,
mar? Any competition for Honey Pílar?"

I heard him trying to get himself under control. "Per-
aps we could arrange an exchange," he said at last.
haykh Reda truly wishes to make amends. He wants his
ersonality module returned. I'm sure he would agree to
ve you the recording we made of you plus a suitable cash
ttlement."

"Cash," I said. "How much?"

"I can't say for certain, but I'm sure Shaykh Reda
ould be very generous. He realizes that he's put you
rough a great deal of discomfort."

"Yeah, you right. But business is business, and action
action. How much?"

"Ten thousand kiam," said Umar.

I knew that if I balked, he'd name a higher figure; but
vasn't interested in their money. "Ten thousand?" I said,
ying to sound impressed.

"Yes." Umar's voice got smug again. He was going to
ay for that. "Shall we meet here, in an hour? Shaykh
eda instructed me to say that our staff is preparing a
ecial midday meal in your honor. We hope you'll let our
ast differences go, Shaykh Marîd. Shaykh Reda and
iedlander Bey must join together now. You and I must
e partners in harmony. Don't you agree?"

"I do testify that there is no god but Allah," I declared
lemnly.

"By the Lord of the Kaaba," swore Umar, "this will be
memorable day for both our houses."

I hung up the phone. "Damn straight about that," I
id. I sat back in my chair. I didn't know who would have
e upper hand when the afternoon was over, but the
ys of the false peace had come to an end.

I'm not a total fool, so I didn't go to Abu Adil's palace
one. I took one of the Stones That Speak with me, as well
Kmuzu and Saied. Now, the latter two had been ex-
oited by Shaykh Reda, and they both felt they had scores

to settle with him. When I asked if they'd like to join me i
my devious charade, they eagerly agreed.

"I want a chance to make up for selling you out t
Shaykh Reda," said the Half-Hajj.

I was checking my two weapons, and I looked u
"But you've already done that. When you pulled me out
that alley."

"Nah," he said, "I still feel like I owe you at least on
more."

"You have an Arabic proverb," said Kmuzu though
fully. " 'When he promised, he fulfilled his promise. Whe
he threatened, he did not fulfill his threat, but he forgave
It is equivalent to the Christian idea of turning the oth
cheek."

"That's right," I said. "But people who live their liv
by proverbs waste their time doing lots of stupid thing
'Getting even is the best revenge' is my motto."

"I wasn't counseling retreat, *yaa Sidi*. I was only ma
ing a philological observation."

Saied gave Kmuzu an irritated look. "And this b
bald guy is something else you got to pay back Abu Ac
for," he said.

The ride out to Abu Adil's palace in Hâmidiyya w
strangely pleasant. We laughed and talked as if we we
on some enjoyable picnic or outing. I didn't feel afrai
even though I wasn't wearing a moddy or any daddie
Saied talked almost nonstop in the scatterbrained wa
that had given him his nickname. Kmuzu kept his ey
straight ahead as he drove, but even he put in a ligh
hearted comment now and then. Habib or Labib—whic
ever he was—sat beside Saied in the backseat and did h
silent sandstone giant routine.

Abu Adil's guard passed us immediately through th
gate, and we drove up through the beautifully landscap
grounds. "Let's wait a minute," I said, as Kamal, the bu
ler, opened the house's massive, carved front door.
checked my static pistol again and passed the sm
seizure gun to the Half-Hajj; Kmuzu had the needle gu
that had formerly belonged to Umm Saad. The Stor
didn't need any weapon beyond his own bare hands.

I clucked my tongue impatiently. "What is it, y
Sidi?" asked Kmuzu.

"I'm deciding what to wear." I browsed through n

k of moddies and daddies. I finally decided that I'd
ar Rex and carry the Abu Adil moddy. I also chipped in
daddies that blocked pain and fear.

"When this is over," Saied said wistfully, "can I have
k back? I really miss wearing him."

"Sure," I said, even though I enjoyed wearing the
lass moddy myself. Saied just wasn't the same without
For now, I let him have the anthology. I was hoping to
Mike Hammer put his fist in Abu Adil's face.

"We must be careful," said Kmuzu. "We cannot be
ed, because treachery runs in Shaykh Reda's blood like
bilharzia worm."

"Thanks," I said, "but I'm not likely to forget it."

Then the four of us got out of the car and walked up
ceramic-tiled path to the door. It was a warm, pleasant
, and the sun felt good on my face. I was dressed in a
ite *gallebeya* and my head was covered with a knitted
erian skullcap. It was a simple costume, and it made
look humble.

We followed Kamal to a meeting room on the second
r. I felt myself tense as we passed Abu Adil's recording
dio. I took a few deep breaths, and by the time the
ler bowed us into his master's presence, I was relaxed
in.

Abu Adil and Umar were sitting on large pillows
ead in a semicircle in the center of the room. There
s a raised platform in the midst of the arrangement,
already several large bowls of food had been set there,
ng with pots of coffee and tea.

Our hosts rose to greet us. I noticed immediately that
ther of them had any hardware chipped in. Abu Adil
ne to me, smiling broadly. He embraced me and said,
hlan wa sahlan!" in a cheerful voice. "Welcome, and be
reshed!"

"I am glad to see you again, O Shaykh. May Allah
en His ways to you."

Abu Adil was happy to see how subdued I was behav-
. He wasn't happy, however, that I'd brought Kmuzu,
ed, and the Stone. "Come, rinse the dust from your
ds," he said. "Let me pour water for you. Of course,
ir slaves are welcome too."

"Watch it, chum," growled Saied, wearing the Mike
mmer moddy. "I'm no slave."

"Exactly, of course," said Abu Adil, never losing good humor.

We made ourselves comfortable on the cushions a exchanged still more of the obligatory complimen Umar poured me a cup of coffee, and I said, "May y table last forever."

"May God lengthen your life," said Umar. He was nearly so happy as his boss.

We sampled the food and chatted amiably for a wh The only sour note was struck by the Half-Hajj, who s out an olive pit and said, "This all you got?" Shaykh Re face froze. I had a hard time not laughing out loud.

"Now," said Abu Adil after a proper amount of ti had passed, "will you object if I bring up the matter business?"

"No, O Shaykh," I said, "I am eager to conclude t matter."

"Then give me the personality module you took fr this house." Umar handed him a small vinyl satchel, wh Abu Adil opened. There were banded stacks of fresh t kiam bills in it.

"I ask something more in trade," I said.

Umar's face darkened. "You are a fool if you think y can change our bargain now. The agreement was thousand kiam."

I ignored him. I turned to Abu Adil. "I want you destroy the Phoenix File."

Abu Adil laughed delightedly. "Ah, you are a rema able man. But I know that from wearing this." He held the moddy he'd made the day he'd mind-raped me. "T Phoenix File is life to me. Because of it, I have lived to t advanced age. I will no doubt need it again. With the fil may live another hundred years."

"I'm sorry, Shaykh Reda," I said, taking out my sta pistol, "but I'm very determined." I glanced at friends. They too held their weapons on Abu Adil a Umar.

"No more of this foolishness," said Umar. "You ca here to exchange moddies. Let's complete the trans tion, and then whatever happens in the future is in hands of Allah."

I kept my gun pointed at Abu Adil, but I took a from my cup of coffee. "The refreshments are most exc

nt, O Shaykh," I said. I set my cup down again. "I want
ou to destroy the Phoenix File. I've worn your moddy, I
now where it is. Kmuzu and Saied can hold you here
hile I go get it."

Abu Adil didn't seem the least bit upset. "You're bluff-
g," he said, spreading his hands. "If you've worn my
oddy, then you know that I have copies. The moddy will
ll you where one or two duplicate files are, but Umar has
ill others, and you won't learn where they are."

"Hell," said the Half-Hajj, "I bet I can make him
lk."

"Never mind, Saied," I said. I realized that Abu Adil
as right; we were at an impasse. Destroying a bubble
ate here and a printout there would accomplish noth-
g. I couldn't destroy the *concept* of the Phoenix File, and
this point Abu Adil would never agree to abandon it.

Kmuzu leaned nearer. "You must persuade him to
ve it up, *yaa Sidi*."

"Any ideas?"

"Unfortunately, no."

I had one last trump to play, but I hated to use it. If it
iled, Abu Adil would win, and I'd never be able to pro-
ct myself or Friedlander Bey's interests against him.
ill, there was no other choice. "Shaykh Reda," I said
owly, "there are many other things recorded on your
oddy. I learned astonishing things about what you've
ne and what you plan to do."

Abu Adil's expression grew worried for the first time.
What are you talking about?" he asked.

I tried to look unconcerned. "You know, of course,
at the strict religious leaders disapprove of brain im-
ants. I couldn't find an imam who'd had one, so none of
em could chip in your moddy and experience it di-
ctly. But I did speak with Shaykh Al-Hajj Muhammad
n Abdurrahman, who leads prayers at the Shimaal
osque."

Abu Adil stared at me, his eyes wide. The Shimaal
osque was the largest and most powerful congregation
the city. The pronouncements of its clergy often had
e force of law.

I was bluffing, of course. I'd never set foot inside the
imaal Mosque. And I'd just invented that imam's name.

Shaykh Reda's voice faltered. "What did you discus
with him?"

I grinned. "Why, I gave him a detailed description
all your past sins and your intended crimes. Now, there's
fascinating technical point that hasn't been cleared u
yet. I mean, the religious elders haven't ruled on wheth
or not a personality module recorded from a living perso
is admissible as evidence in a court of Islamic law. Yo
know and I know that such a moddy is wholly reliabl
much more so than any sort of mechanical lie detecto
But the imams, bless their righteous hearts, are debatin
the matter back and forth. It may be a long while befor
they pass a ruling, but then again, you may already be
very serious trouble."

I paused to let what I'd said sink in. I'd just made u
this religious-legal wrangle on the fly, but it was entirel
plausible. It was a question that Islam would have to com
to grips with, just as the faith had had to deal with ever
other technological advance. It was only a matter of judg
ing how the science of neuroaugmentation related to th
teachings of Prophet Muhammad, may the blessings
Allah be on him and peace.

Abu Adil moved restlessly on his cushion. He wa
obviously wrestling with two unpleasant options: destroy
ing the Phoenix File, or being turned over to the notor
ously unforgiving representatives of the Messenger
God. Finally, he gave a great sigh. "Hear my decision," h
said. "I offer you Umar Abdul-Qawy in my place."

I laughed. There was a horrified squeal from Uma
"The hell do we want with *him?*" asked the Half-Hajj.

"I'm sure you learned from the moddy that Uma
originated many of my less honorable business practices
said Abu Adil. "His guilt is nearly as great as my own.
however, have power and influence. Maybe not enough t
hold off the wrath of the city's entire Islamic communit
but certainly enough to deflect it."

I appeared to consider this point. "Yes," I said slowl
"it would be very difficult to convict you."

"But not difficult at all to convict Umar." Shayk
Reda looked at his assistant. "I'm sorry, my boy, bι
you've brought this on yourself. I know all about you
shabby plottings. When I wore Shaykh Marîd's modd
didn't I find out about your conversation with him? Th

in which he turned down your invitation to dispose of
and Friedlander Bey?"

Umar's face had gone deathly pale. "But I never in-
ded—"

Abu Adil did not seem angry, only very sad. "Did you
nk you were the first to have that notion? Where are
ur predecessors, Umar? Where are all the ambitious
ing men who've held your position that last century
a half? Almost every one of them plotted against me,
ner or later. And they are all gone now and forgotten.
t as you will be."

"Face it, Himmar," taunted Saied, "you have to wear
shirt you sewed. Paybacks are a bitch, ain't they?"

Abu Adil shook his head. "I will be sorry to lose you,
har. I couldn't have cared for you more if I'd been your
e father."

I was amused, and glad that events were turning out
I planned. A line of American fiction occurred to me:
you lose a son it's possible to get another—but there's
ly one Maltese falcon."

Umar, though, had other ideas. He jumped up and
eamed at Abu Adil. "I'll see you dead first! All of you!"

Saied fired the seizure gun before Umar even drew
own weapon. Umar collapsed to the floor, writhing in
avulsions, his face twisted in an ugly grimace. At last, he
s still. He'd be unconscious for a few hours but he'd
over, and he'd feel like hell for a long time afterward.

"Well," said the Half-Hajj, "he folds up real nice."

Abu Adil let out a sigh. "This is not how I intended for
s afternoon to go."

"Really?" I said.

"I must admit, I've underestimated you. Do you wish
take him with you?"

I didn't really want to be saddled with Umar because,
er all, I hadn't actually spoken to the imam. "No," I
d, "I think I'll leave him in your hands."

"You can be assured there will be justice," said
aykh Reda. The look he turned on his scheming assis-
it was chilling. I was almost sorry for Umar.

"Justice," I said, using an old Arab saying, "is that you
uld restore things to their places. I would like my
ddy now."

"Yes, of course." He leaned across the still form of

Umar Abdul-Qawy and put the moddy in my hand. "A
take the money," he said.

"No, I don't think so," I said. "But I'll keep the mod
I have of you. To guarantee your cooperation."

"If you must," he said unhappily. "You understa
that I have not agreed to abandon the Phoenix File."

"I understand." Then I was struck by a sudd
thought. "I have one last request, however."

"Yes?" He looked suspicious.

"I wish to have my name removed from the file, a
the names of my friends and relatives."

"Of course," said Abu Adil, glad that my last dema
was so easy to fulfill. "I would be pleased to oblige. Mer
send me a complete list at your convenience."

Later, as we walked back to the car, Kmuzu and Sai
congratulated me. "That was a complete victory," said t
Half-Hajj.

"No," I said, "I wish it were. Abu Adil and Papa s
have that goddamn Phoenix File, even if some of c
names will be taken off. I feel like I'm trading the lives
my friends for the lives of other innocent people. I t
Shaykh Reda, 'Go ahead, kill those other guys, I do
care.' "

"You accomplished as much as was possible, y
Sidi," said Kmuzu. "You should be grateful to God."

"I suppose." I popped Rex and gave the moddy
Saied, who grinned to have it back. We rode back to t
house; Kmuzu and Saied discussed what had happened
great length, but I just rode in silence, wrapped in gloo
thoughts. For some reason, I felt like a failure. I felt as if
made an evil compromise. I also felt uncomfortably s
that it wouldn't be my last.

Late that night, I was awakened by someone openi
the door to my bedroom. I lifted my head and saw
woman enter, dressed in a short, clinging negligee.

The woman lifted the covers and slipped into b
beside me. She put one hand on my cheek and kissed n
It was a great kiss. I woke up completely. "I bribed Kmu
to let me in," she whispered. I was surprised to realiz
was Indihar.

"Yeah? How do you bribe Kmuzu?"

"I told him I'd take your mind off your pain."

"He knows I got pills and software to do that." I roll

er on my side to face her. "Indihar, what are you doing
ere?" I asked. "You said you weren't going to sleep with
e."

"Well, I changed my mind," she said. She didn't
und very enthusiastic. "Here I am. I've been thinking
out how I acted when . . . after Jirji died."

"May the mercy of Allah be on him," I murmured. I
it my arm around her. Despite her attempt to be brave,
could feel warm tears on her face.

"You've done a lot for me, and for the kids."

Yipe. "That's why you're here? Because you're grate-
l?"

"Well," she said, "yes. I'm in your debt."

"You don't love me, do you, Indihar?"

"Marîd," she said, "don't get me wrong. I like you,
it—"

"But that's all there is. Listen, I really don't think
ing here together is a great idea. You told me you
eren't going to sleep with me, and I respected that."

"Papa wants us to be married," she said. Her voice
ok on an angry edge.

"He thinks it shames his house for us to be living
gether otherwise. Even if we aren't, you know, sleeping
gether."

"Even though my children need a father, and they
ke you, I won't marry you, Marîd. I don't care what Papa
ys."

Actually, marriage was something I thought hap-
ened only to other people, like fatal traffic accidents. I
ill felt an obligation to take care of Shaknahyi's widow
id children, and if I had to marry someone, I could do
orse than Indihar. But still . . .

"I think Papa may forget all about it by the time he
ets out of the hospital."

"Just so you understand," said Indihar. She gave me
other kiss—this one chastely on the cheek—and then
e quietly got out of my bed and went back to her own
om.

I felt like such a noble son of a bitch. I'd made her feel
tter, but deep down I had no confidence at all that
iedlander Bey would forget his decree. All I could think
out was Yasmin, and if she'd still go out with me after I
as married to Indihar.

I couldn't get back to sleep. I just turned from one side to the other, twisting the sheets up into a tangled mess. Finally I gave up and got out of bed and went in the study. I sat in the comfortable leather armchair and picked up the Wise Counselor moddy. I looked at it for a few seconds, wondering if it could possibly make sense of of recent events. *"Bismillah,"* I murmured. Then I reached up and chipped it in.

Audran seemed to be in a deserted city. He wandered through narrow, congested alleys—hungry, thirsty, and very tired. After a while he turned a corner and came into a great market square. The booths and stalls were deserted, empty of merchandise. Still, Audran recognized where he was. He was back in Algeria. "Hello?" he shouted. There was no answer. He remembered an old saying: "I came to the place of my birth, and cried, 'The friends of my youth, where are they?' An echo answered, 'Where are they?'

He began to weep with sadness. Then a man spoke and Audran turned. He recognized the man as the Messenger of God. "Shaykh Marîd," said the Prophet, may blessings be on him and peace, "don't you consider me the friend of your youth?"

And Audran smiled. "Yaa Hazrat, does not everyone in the world desire your friendship? But my love for Allah so completely fills my heart that there is no room there for love or hate for anyone."

"If that is true," said Prophet Muhammad, "then you are blessed. Remember, though, that this verse was revealed: 'Thou shalt never reach the broad door of piety until thou givest away what thou lovest best.' What do you love best, O Shaykh?"

I awoke, but this time I didn't have Jirji Shaknahyi to explain the vision. I wondered what the answer to the Prophet's question might be: comfort, pleasure, freedom. I hated the idea of giving up any of those, but I might as well get used to the idea. My life with Friedlander Bey rarely entailed the notions of ease or liberty.

But my life needn't begin again until morning. In the meantime, I had the problem of getting through the night. I went to search for my pillcase.

A SPECIAL PREVIEW
from
The Exile Kiss
the stunning new novel by
GEORGE ALEC
EFFINGER

Thoroughly entrenched as Friedlander Bey's right-hand man, Marîd Audran looks at life from a whole new perspective. But this new life is not without its dangers. In the following scene, Audran discovers what can happen when a onetime street hustler gets too close to the ones who wield the real power.

It never occurred to me that I might be kidnapped. There was no reason why it should. The day had certainly begun innocently enough. I'd snapped wide awake just before dawn, thanks to an experimental add-on I wear on my anterior brain implant. I had been invited with Friedlander Bey to an evening reception at the palace of Shaykh Mahali, the amir of the city.

On the way there, Papa said to me, "There is more to this than joy over your recent marriage. The amir has said that he cannot permit a feud to exist between myself and Shaykh Reda Abu Adil."

"Ah, I see. And tonight's celebration will be the amir's attempt to reconcile you?"

"His *futile* attempt to reconcile us." Friedlander Bey frowned at the apple, then stabbed it fiercely with the knife and put it aside. "There will be no peace between Shaykh Reda and myself. That is quite simply impossible. But I can see that the amir is in a difficult position: When kings do battle, it is the peasants who die."

I smiled. "Are you saying that you and Shaykh Reda are the kings in this case, and the prince of the city is the peasant?"

"He certainly cannot match our power, can he? His influence extends over the city, while we control entire nations."

I sat back in my chair and gazed at him. "Do you expect another attack tonight, my grandfather?"

Friedlander Bey rubbed his upper lip thoughtfully. "No," he said slowly, "not tonight, while we're under the protection of the prince. Shaykh Reda is certainly not that foolish. But soon, my nephew. Very soon."

"I'll be on my guard," I said, standing and taking my leave of the old man. The last thing in the world I wanted to hear was that we were being drawn into another intrigue.

The pleasant edge was taken off the evening by the grand entrance of Reda Abu Adil. He came in noisily, and greeted the other guests as if he and not the amir were the host of the party. He was dressed very much as I was, including a *keffiya* which I knew was hiding his own corymbic implant. Behind Abu Adil trailed a young man, probably his new administrative assistant and lover. The young man had short blond hair, wire-rimmed spectacles, and thin, bloodless lips.

Abu Adil's expression turned to joy when he saw Friedlander Bey and me. "My old friends!" he cried, crossing the ballroom and pulling Papa to his feet. They embraced, although Papa said nothing at all. Then Shaykh Reda turned to me. "And here is the lucky bridegroom!"

I didn't stand up, which was a blatant insult, but Abu Adil pretended not to notice. "I've brought you a fine gift!" he said, looking around to be certain that everyone was paying attention. "Kenneth, give the young man his gift."

The blond kid stared at me for a brief moment, sizing me up, then he reached into his jacket's inner pocket and took out an envelope. He held it out toward me between two fingers, but he wasn't going to come close enough for me to take it. Apparently he thought this was some kind of contest.

Personally, I didn't care. I went to him and grabbed the envelope. He gave me a little quirk of the lips and raised his eyebrows, as if to say "We'll sort out where we stand later."

I remembered where I was and who was watching, so I tore open the envelope and took out a folded sheet of paper. I read Abu Adil's gift, but I couldn't make any sense of it. I read it again, and it wasn't any clearer the second time. "I don't know what to say," I said.

Shaykh Reda laughed. "I knew you'd be pleased!" Then he turned slowly, so that his words would be heard easily by the others. "I have used my influence with the *Jaish* to obtain a commission for Marîd Audran. He's now an officer in the Citizens' Army!"

The *Jaish* was this unofficial right-wing outfit that I'd run into before. They liked to dress up in gray uniforms and parade through the streets. Originally their mission was to rid the city of foreigners. As time passed, and as more of the paramilitary group's funding came from people like Reda Abu Adil—who himself had come to the city at a young age— the aim of the *Jaish* changed. Now it seemed that its mission was to harass Abu Adil's enemies, foreigner and native alike.

"I don't know what to say," I said again. It was a pretty bizarre thing for Shaykh Reda to have done, and for the life of me, I couldn't figure what his motive had been. Knowing him, however, it would all become painfully clear soon enough.

"All our past disagreements have been

settled," said Abu Adil cheerfully. "We'll be friends and allies from now on. We must work together to better the lives of the poor *fella-hîn* who depend on us."

The assembled guests liked that sentiment and applauded. I glanced at Friedlander Bey, who only gave me a slight shrug. It was obvious to us both that Abu Adil had some new scheme unfolding before our eyes.

"Then I toast the bridegroom," said Shaykh Mahali, rising. "And I toast the ending of conflict between Friedlander Bey and Reda Abu Adil. I am known among my people as an honest man, and I have tried to rule this city with wisdom and justice. This peace between our houses will make my own task simpler." He lifted his cup of coffee, and everyone else stood and followed suit. To all but Papa and me, it must have seemed a hopeful time of reconciliation. I felt nothing but a growing knot of dread deep in my belly.

By the time we left the party I was quite full of food and coffee, and I'd had enough conversation with wealthy strangers to last me many days.

I had been given a veritable hillock of gifts by the amir and by many of the other guests. These were still on display in the ballroom, and would be gathered up and delivered to Friedlander Bey's house the next day. As Papa and I emerged into the warm night air, I felt well fed and content. We passed through the gardens again, and I admired the carefully tended flowering trees and their shimmering images in the reflecting pool. Faintly over the water came the sound of laughter, and I heard the liquid trickle of fountains, but otherwise the night was still.

Papa's limousine was sheltered in Shaykh Mahali's garage. We'd begun to cross the grassy courtyard toward it, when its headlights flashed on. The ancient car—one of the few internal-combustion vehicles still operating in the city—rolled slowly toward us. The driver's window slid silently down, and I was surprised to see not Tariq but Hajjar, the crooked police lieutenant who supervised the affairs of the Budayeen.

"Get in the car," he said. "Both of you."

I looked at Friedlander Bey, who only shrugged. We got in the car. Hajjar probably thought he was in control, but Papa didn't seem the least bit worried, even though there was a big guy with a needle gun in his hand facing us on the jump seat.

"The hell's this all about, Hajjar?" I said.

"I'm placing both of you under arrest," said the cop. He pressed a control, and the glass panel slid up between him and the passenger compartment. Papa and I were alone with Hajjar's goon, and the goon didn't seem interested in making conversation.

"Just stay calm," said Papa.

"This is Abu Adil's doing, isn't it?" I said.

"Possibly." He shrugged. "It will all be made clear according to the will of Allah."

I couldn't help fretting. I hate being helpless. I watched Friedlander Bey, a prisoner in his own limousine, in the hands of a cop who'd taken the pay of both Papa and his chief rival, Reda Abu Adil. For a few minutes, my stomach churned and I rehearsed several clever and heroic things I'd do when Hajjar let us out of the car again. Then, as we drove through the twisting, narrow back streets of the city, my mind began searching for some clue as to what was happening to us now.

After what seemed like an hour of driving, the limousine came to a stop. I didn't know where we were. I looked at Hajjar's goon and said, "What's going on?"

"Shut up," the goon informed me.

Hajjar got out of the car and held the door open for Papa. I climbed out after him. We were standing beside some buildings made of corrugated metal, looking at a private suborbital shuttle across a broad concrete apron, its running lights flashing but its three giant thrusters cool and quiet. If this was the main airfield, then we were about thirty miles north of the city. I'd never been here before.

I was getting worried, but Papa still had a calm look on his face. Hajjar pulled me aside. "Got your phone on you, Audran?" he said quietly.

"Yeah," I said. I always wear it on my belt.

"Let me use it a minute, okay?"

I unclipped my phone and handed it to Hajjar. He grinned at me, dropped the phone to the pavement, and stomped it into tiny broken pieces. "Thanks," he said.

"What's going on?" I shouted, grabbing him by the arm.

Hajjar just looked at me, amused. Then his goon grabbed me and pinned both of my arms behind my back. "We're going to get on that shuttle," he said. "There's a qadi who has something to tell the both of you."

We were taken aboard the suborbital and made to take seats in an otherwise empty front cabin. Hajjar sat beside me, and his goon sat beside Friedlander Bey. "We have a right to know where you're taking us," I said.

Hajjar examined his fingernails, pretending indifference. "Tell you the truth," he said, gazing out the window, "I don't actually know where you're going. The qadi may tell you that when he reads you the verdict."

"Verdict?" I cried. "What verdict?"

"Oh," said Hajjar with an evil grin, "haven't you figured it out? You and Papa are on trial. The qadi will decide you're guilty while you're being deported. Doing it this way saves the legal system a lot of time and money. I should've let you kiss the ground good-bye, Audran, because you're never going to see the city again!"

The Exile Kiss, George Alec Effinger's third
el in the gripping odyssey of Marîd Audran,
ran has just begun to enjoy the privileged life
vealth and power when he and Friedlander
 are suddenly accused of murder. They are
tenced to exile and unceremoniously aban-
ed in the desert. The two must somehow sur-
 their enforced pilgrimage long enough to
k their way back to a now hostile Budayeen—
 avenge themselves against their accusers.

ad **THE EXILE KISS,** *on sale in July*
0 wherever Doubleday Foundation
ks are sold.

After years of observing us,
abducting us,
and experimenting upon us,
they have finally made
their first mistake . . .

<u>NIGHTEYES</u>
Garfield Reeves-Stevens

"A highly involving, tremendously entertaining thriller . . . Reeves-Stevens has taken a whole body of what I'd call 'pseudo-knowledge,' that body of testimony surrounding so-called alien abductions, and has fashioned a walloping suspense story from them. . . . [Nighteyes] is a hypnotic, high-voltage novel, and I loved it."

—Stephen King

A Bantam Spectra Book

Astronaut Edward Gibson has traveled 34.5
million miles in space. With his stunning debut
novel he returns to space and takes his readers
along for the ride. . . .

REACH

Edward Gibson

[Reach] fascinates not only with its futuristic space-
adventure plot but with its authoritative, fully enthralling evocation of what space travel is really like. An
aspiring achievement.''

—*Kirkus Reviews*

Edward Gibson brings to his extraordinary novel of outer
space a vision that could only have been created by one who
has experienced space's vast, quiet darkness. It is the story
of *Wayfarer Two*, a space expedition launched in search of
its predecessor, *Wayfarer One*, mysteriously lost beyond the
edge of the solar system. Once they arrive at their destina-
tion, mission head Jake Ryder and his crew encounter a
power that is overwhelming, terrifying in its immensity, a
power beyond anything humanity had ever conceived of
before.

Ed Gibson was an astronaut with the Right Stuff. It's
apparent that as an author he still has the Right Stuff.
In most books I've read the astronauts think and talk
like Hollywood actors. Not so here. It's a pleasure to
find characters who think and act like real astronauts.''

—Alan Bean, *Apollo 12* and *Skylab 2* astronaut

On sale now wherever Bantam Spectra Books are sold

PHILIP JOSÉ FARMER'S
THE DUNGEON

☐ 27346 **BLACK TOWER:**
Dungeon #1 *Richard Lupoff* $3.95

☐ 27640 **THE DARK ABYSS:**
Dungeon #2 *Bruce Coville* $3.95

☐ 27958 **VALLEY OF THUNDER:**
Dungeon #3 *Charles de Lint* $3.95

☐ 28185 **THE LAKE OF FIRE:**
Dungeon #4 *Robin Bailey* $3.95

☐ 28338 **THE HIDDEN CITY:**
Dungeon #5 *Charles de Lint* $3.95

☐ 28542 **THE FINAL BATTLE:**
Dungeon #6 *Richard Lupoff* $3.95

Look for them at your bookstore or use this page to order: